THE TIME OF ASPEN FALLS

MARCIA LYNN McCLURE

Published by Distractions Ink
P.O. Box 15971
Rio Rancho, NM 87174

Published by Distractions Ink
©Copyright 2011 by M. Meyers
A.K.A. Marcia Lynn McClure
Cover Photography by
©Photowitch and ©Iakov Kalinin | Dreamstime.com
Cover Design by
Sheri L. Brady | MightyPhoenixDesignStudio.com

First Printed Edition: February 2009
Second Printed Edition: September 2011

All character names and personalities in this work of fiction
are entirely fictional,
created solely in the imagination of the author.
Any resemblance to any person living or dead is coincidental.

McClure, Marcia Lynn, 1965—
The Time of Aspen Falls: a novel/by Marcia Lynn McClure.

ISBN: 978-0-9838074-7-6

Library of Congress Control Number: 2011937945

Printed in the United States of America

For Groovy Gina—
Autumn Angel,
Jewel of the Pacific Northwest!

Thank you
for wearing orange sweaters,
for loving pumpkins,
for enduring and treasured friendship
always…
and especially
when the time of aspen falls!

CHAPTER ONE

"I thought autumn would never get here!"

Aspen sighed. She smiled and bit into a crisp, tart apple. The early autumn breeze was cool; the sun blushed a soothing orange and gold. The sweet perfume of ripening apples and pears in the orchard caressed the air like some rich, intoxicating delight—respiring harvest fragrances—whispering the serenity of the season.

Gina reached out, plucking an untimely apple from a nearby branch. She rubbed it briskly on the front of her shirt. Biting into her own apple, Gina winced as the sharp taste of fruit harvested too soon soaked her tongue.

"We're gonna get sick eating these too early, you know," she said.

Aspen smiled and shrugged her shoulders. "So? Some things are worth a stomachache. Don't you think?" she asked.

Gina shrugged and grimaced as she bit the apple again. "Like what?"

"Like sitting in the branches of an apple tree, eating apples that aren't quite ripe," Aspen offered.

"Or really, really spicy, warm-from-the-oven pumpkin cookies," Gina added.

Aspen nodded. "Really spicy pumpkin pie too."

The orchard was so peaceful, slathered in the comforting feel of summer's hushed leaving—of autumn's ambrosial arrival.

Gina frowned as she studied the apple in her hand. "You know…it wouldn't be so sour if we had some caramel to drizzle over it."

Aspen giggled, shaking her head. Gina thought everything tasted better with something drizzled over it. Peaches tasted better with a hearty helping of thick, delicious cream drizzled over them—pot roast tasted better drizzled with gravy. Gina Wicksoth drizzled something over nearly everything solid she ate. Still, Aspen agreed. The tart apples they were eating could've used a little sweetening—a little drizzling of caramel. Actually, a generous, mixing bowl full of caramel would've been better. Yet, as they were actually eating their apples while sitting in an apple tree, a mixing bowl full of caramel just wasn't handy.

"I don't know how you stay so skinny," Aspen said. "You drizzle everything over everything and eat like a horse!"

Gina tossed her head as she giggled. Her short, wavy hair seemed to feather a cocoa-colored sigh in the cooler autumn breeze. "I just have a high metabolism."

"You have a good luck streak going," Aspen said.

"That's probably true," Gina admitted. "Still, this apple is making my stomach feel nasty." Gina reached out, plucking another apple from the tree. "Here," she began, briskly rubbing the new apple on her shirt sleeve, "maybe this one is riper."

Aspen smiled, amused by her friend's determination. She relaxed against the tree trunk at her back, gazing up through the lacy lattice of apple tree leaves overhead.

"I cannot *wait* until October," she sighed.

"I know!" Gina said. Aspen watched as Gina took a bite of the new apple in her right hand, then a bite of the first apple now held in her left. Chewing, she looked back and forth between them, her blue-green eyes curious, a puzzled expression furrowing her brow. "I'm gonna get sick, Aspen Falls," she said, taking another bite of the new apple.

Aspen giggled. "Like I said, some things are worth it."

Aspen loved sitting in the old apple tree with Gina. Every autumn they would spend hours and hours perched in the branches of Old Goldie—eating apples, talking, planning, and dreaming. They'd dubbed the tree "Old Goldie" the year they both turned twelve. It seemed fitting that the old tree bearing such beautiful Golden Delicious apples should have a special name. When they were younger, Aspen and Gina had spent days on end laughing, eating apples, and planning out their lives perched up in Old Goldie's branches. Now in their early twenties, neither young woman had "days on end" to spend in such serene contemplation. Yet they managed to climb up into the old apple tree a couple of times a week each autumn. The apple tree times with Gina were some of Aspen's most treasured memories.

"You know what's worse on your stomach than sour apples, don't you?" Gina asked. She tossed the apple in her left hand to the ground and took another bite of the remaining one she held.

"Love!" Aspen answered in unison with Gina.

Both women giggled, and Gina put her hand over her heart. "Join me now in a recitation of our creed."

Aspen giggled again as she placed her hand over her heart and nodded.

Simultaneously, they began to recite a poem they'd written and memorized as silly little girls—written and memorized after Aspen had her heart broken by Mike Archuleta in the fifth grade.

"I'll never throw up again, I say,
The way I did this rotten day
When jerk-faced Mike gave back my note
(the one I shoulda never wrote).
I'll ignore the cute boys, each one, and then...
When I'm grown up—the handsome men!
'Cause it sure ain't worth the stomachache...
Or all the cookies that we bake!
And if I throw up again, I'd like
To barf on guys like stupid Mike!"

Aspen nearly toppled off the tree limb she was sitting on—for, having finished their recitation, she and Gina were nearly rolling with uncontrollable laughter.

"W-we so stink at poetry!" Gina laughed.

"W-w-we so stink at love!" Aspen gasped. Her back hurt; her

stomach hurt. It was the best hurt she knew—the pain of irrepressible laughter!

Still laughing, Gina nodded and gasped, "We do! We totally do!"

Aspen sighed as her laughter began to subside. Naturally, she experienced the little syncopated bursts of giggles that always followed a belly-busting laugh session. Still, it did subside, and Aspen bit into the tart, juicy apple in her hand.

"Of course, it's not our fault we stink at love," she said, wagging an index finger at Gina.

"That's right!" Gina nodded and tossed a juicy apple core to the grassy orchard ground below. "How can we expect to be successful in love when there aren't any real men left in the world?"

It was a subject Aspen and her best friend had plowed through time and again—the sad lack of "real men" in modern society.

"I mean," Gina began, plucking a leaf from the tree and rubbing it between her fingers, "where did they all go? All those guys our grandmas talk about? I remember when I was little I saw an old Marlboro Man ad in some antique magazine my grandma still had in her garage—you know, some handsome, rugged, tough guy out riding the range on his horse. Oh, sure, it was a cigarette ad…but still, those guys were totally masculine!"

"The kind of guy who would sew up his own wound while defending a woman's honor with a bare-fisted, mean right hook," Aspen added.

"Yeah," Gina sighed. "What happened to those kinds of guys?"

Aspen smiled and shrugged. She'd always loved the old Marlboro Man magazine ads too. She brushed a strand of stray nut-brown hair from her cheek and said, "Well, in truth…they probably all succumbed to health complications brought on by smoking during the photo shoots."

Gina nodded. "Probably. What an awful thought…and how sad! Still, you have to admit they were hot! Real men, you know?"

"Oh, I totally know!" Aspen agreed. "I can honestly say that the only real-men types I've ever seen in real life—other than my dad and brothers, of course—are always really old…like, elderly."

"Oh, totally!" Gina agreed. "I was down in Corrales the other day getting a sack of green chili for my grandma, and there was this guy—an old, old, old man...I mean, like, he had to be, like, eighty—and he was wearing these worn-out, tattered old Levi's, banged-up old boots, a long-sleeved button-up white shirt, and a beat-up cowboy hat. He had a big scar down one side of his face and gnarled hands...skin like leather." She paused for a moment, reflecting on seeing the man.

"And?" Aspen prodded.

Gina sighed. "And he walked around to the side of the building—you know, over there at Wagner's Produce where they roast chili. He walked around over there and got on a horse. He rode past me toward the river, tipped his hat, and said, 'Mornin' miss.' I thought, what the heck? Why can't he be twenty-five or thirty instead of a hundred and ninety-three?"

"I think I've seen that guy!" Aspen felt her heart pinch a little in her bosom. She'd seen an elderly man fitting Gina's description riding along the riverbank only days before when she'd been on a picnic with her family. "I thought the same thing! But eighty—that's just a little too old for me."

"And I bet he's a war veteran...World War II, probably. You know, a man with honor, patriotism, and values." Gina sighed. "They're gone... all of them. At least, there aren't any our age."

Aspen bit her lip. Should she tell Gina? Should she tell her what she'd discovered just two weeks before? Part of her was afraid to—afraid that in telling Gina her treasure-find would be lost somehow. Still, Gina was her best friend—her trusted and loyal friend. They'd shared nearly every secret of their entire lives. It was time to share this one.

Aspen lowered her voice and said, "I know where one is."

"One what?"

"A real man. At least...I get the feeling he's one. I've been watching him, and I think—"

"You've been watching him?" Gina interrupted. "You mean, like, from a window with binoculars or something?"

"No, you dingdong!" Aspen giggled, shaking her head at her friend's imagination. "In the park—near the shop during my lunch break. He runs past me every day on my lunch hour."

"Runs past you? You mean like a burglar? Or a UPS guy? I always wanted to go out with a UPS guy."

Aspen shook her head and giggled. "No. He runs past me—like, jogs…for exercise."

"Oh!" Gina exclaimed.

Aspen smiled, knowing full well Gina was still thinking about her imaginary UPS guy.

"Well, who is he?"

Aspen shrugged again. She rolled her deep green eyes and answered, "I don't know. Just some guy! He's, like, totally gorgeous, of course."

"Of course," Gina giggled.

"But there's a lot more to it than that."

"Like what? Like…give me some examples."

Aspen sighed. She frowned for a moment as she tried to think of a way to give details to Gina.

"Well, a lot of it is in the way he moves—the way his shoulders sort of dip back and forth when he slows to a walk. He saunters instead of walks. Do you know what I mean?"

Gina nodded. "Nice start. What else?"

Aspen frowned. "It's hard to explain. I mean, there was the time he picked up this boy who'd fallen off his scooter. A little boy—like, four or five—was riding a scooter thing, and he fell. The guy stopped, picked the boy up, and then bent and inspected the boy's little banged-up knees. I heard him say, 'Let's find your mom, okay, buddy?' and then he took the kid's hand and led him over to his mom."

"Very heroic indeed!" Gina teased.

"No, I'm serious! I can't explain it," Aspen argued. "It's in the way he moves—the fact that he's got a big scar running up the side of one calf."

"Scars are always nice," Gina said. "Like a masculinity bonus or something."

Aspen nodded. "Total bonus."

"Nike or something else?" Gina asked.

Aspen knew exactly what her friend meant. Gina and Aspen had always judged boys and men—always gauged their potential to be perfectly masculine—by the brand of athletic gear they wore. It was the only brand they paid attention to—that and Levi's.

"Nike," Aspen said.

"Good start!" Gina smiled, her eyes twinkling with intrigue. "What kind of Nike stuff?"

"Kind of ratty, worn-out Nike T-shirt…black. And basketball shoes," Aspen answered. "Perfect, huh?"

Gina nodded. "It's a good sign—that he's not all decked out in perfectly matching sweatpants and running shoes. Shows he's not a prima donna."

"And absolutely no jogging shorts," Aspen added. "Nike basketball shorts."

"Nice!" Gina's smile broadened. She rubbed her hands together in mischievous anticipation. "Hair color?"

"Like…dark, dark brown…almost black. Sometimes I can't even tell."

"Perfect! Eye color?"

Aspen shook her head. "I haven't been close enough to see."

"We'll hope for blue or brown. Skin color? Is he pasty or tan?"

"Totally tan…like he works outside a lot."

"Like…farmer's tan or all-over tan?"

Again Aspen shook her head. "Hard to tell with a T-shirt on."

"Hmmm," Gina mumbled, pensive. "Height and weight?"

Aspen giggled. This was a game she and Gina had played for years. In their quest to find a real man now and then, they had a standard of details that must be met.

"Over six foot, for sure. Maybe one ninety?"

"Now," Gina began. Aspen had a hard time keeping a straight face—Gina's was so serious! "Have you had a good look at his hands? I mean…neat, girly, manicured nails? Or a few scrapes, scratches, and calluses?"

"Again, I haven't been close enough."

"Well, it sounds like this one's got potential," Gina said. "When can I get a good look at him?"

"He's mine! Finders keepers, remember," Aspen warned, wagging an index finger at her friend.

"Yeah, yeah, yeah." Gina rolled her eyes with exaggerated exasperation. She waved one hand as if the *finders keepers* rule didn't hold any weight. "Should I meet you for lunch tomorrow?"

"Sure," Aspen answered. "Tomorrow's good. Meet me in that park near the shop. I'll be there at, like…around noon. There's a bench under a little cottonwood tree, right where the sidewalk bends."

"I'll have to take my lunch a little early and drive over there," Gina mused. "Should I bring my camera?"

"Are you crazy?" Sometimes Aspen thought Gina was nuts. Still, what it boiled down to was something to be admired: never being self-conscious. Gina had no inhibitions at all!

"I'll stick it in my purse…just in case," Gina said. She smiled and plucked another apple from the branch before her.

"I thought you were feeling sick," Aspen reminded.

Gina shrugged her shoulders. She rubbed the apple on the front of her shirt and bit into it. "Some things are worth it," she said.

❧

"When will he be here? I haven't got all day!"

"Shhh!" Aspen scolded her friend. "Any minute. He might have had to stop a crime or something."

Gina sighed with impatience, rolled her eyes, crossed her legs, and began shaking her foot.

Aspen smiled, amused as the entire park bench wiggled with Gina's impatient foot-wiggling. She was nervous herself, butterflies fluttering in her stomach the way they did every day at lunch, each time she thought about the handsome real-man stranger jogging past the bench—jogging past her.

"Now try not to stare," Aspen said.

"I never stare," Gina assured her.

"You always stare."

"I do not!"

"You do too! And no ogling."

"I never ogle," Gina argued.

"You always ogle," Aspen said.

"I do not. I visually investigate."

Aspen giggled. She shook her head at Gina's excuse.

"Oh my heck!" she heard Gina exclaim in a whisper. "I think I see him!"

Aspen felt her heart leap in her chest as she looked up to see the handsome real-man stranger rounding a corner some ways away. Yes! It was him. She was amazed—amazed at how he seemed to grow more attractive every day!

"That's him!" Aspen whispered. She swallowed the lump in her throat and began to open the brown bag in her lap, attempting to appear as if she were actually interested in what she'd brought for lunch.

"Have mercy!" Gina breathed.

"Don't stare!" Aspen whispered.

"I'm not," Gina assured her.

Aspen looked up to see Gina staring, mouth agape, in the direction of the approaching man.

"He's getting closer! Quit staring!"

"He's getting more gorgeous the closer he gets…and I'm not!"

"You are!"

"How can I not? Just look at him!"

Aspen couldn't stand it. She had to look—and she did!

As she looked up, her breath caught in her throat, and she felt certain she'd never be able to draw a regular breath again. Time seemed to slow around her; in those moments, she was certain it had. The man was jogging up the sidewalk toward them. He would reach them in a few more moments, but in that very instant, moments turned into minutes—minutes into hours.

Tall, dark, and handsome, the real-man stranger was the epitome of attractive masculinity! Aspen studied him from head to toe, just as she did every day. His hair was short—not military short, long enough to run fingers through, yet short enough he could easily be a business man. His jaw was square, accentuated by just the right amount of five-o'clock shadow. His nose was straight, and his lips—his lips weren't pinchy thin—full, but not Hollywood fake full—just right. His shoulders were broad, the muscles in his upper arms well-defined. He wore a red Nike T-shirt, black basketball shorts, and a pretty beat-up pair of basketball shoes.

As Aspen watched him approach, the soundtrack in her mind began to play Nora Jones's "Come Away with Me." She could actually hear it at that moment, echoing in her mind—soothing, alluring, romantic. In her momentary daydreams, she could almost envision herself walking next to the real-man stranger, holding his hand as he led her down an autumn leaf-littered path near the river. How could he not be wonderful? He was so handsome! Still, experience had taught Aspen a lot about men: mostly that if they looked too good to be true...

Aspen was startled out of her reverie as Gina's elbow met with her ribs. Simultaneously, she saw the real-man stranger smile and slow to a walk.

"Check it out," Gina whispered. "Another one!"

Aspen looked in the direction Gina nodded to see another handsome man approaching. Certainly he wasn't as handsome as Aspen's jogger, but he was attractive enough to warrant a look.

"What's up, man?" the new guy greeted as he approached Aspen's jogger.

Aspen thought she might bolt and run as the real-man stranger stopped only a few feet away.

"Not much," the real-man stranger greeted as the other man took his hand. The two men bumped opposing shoulders and patted each other once on the back.

"Did you see the game?" the new guy asked. There was a tone of mild disgust in his voice.

The real-man stranger shook his head. "Dude...they deserved to lose. They gotta step it up if they want to have a decent season."

"Nice voice," Gina whispered.

"Shut up!" Aspen growled in a whisper—though it was true. She couldn't believe she'd actually heard his voice—his deep, fascinating, mesmerizingly masculine voice. She actually felt goose bumps prickling her arms at its intonation.

"When he starts past us...kick your shoe off or something. Something to get his attention," Gina suggested, still whispering—but barely.

"Absolutely not!" Aspen breathed.

"What? You're just gonna spend every lunch hour for the rest of your life waiting for this guy to jog by so you can*not* let him catch you looking at him?"

"Exactly."

"That's ridiculous!"

"That's life! Do you really think a guy like that would look twice at me?"

Gina shrugged. "All it takes is once. One look can last forever."

Aspen rolled her eyes. "Yeah...if he looked at you."

"Oh my heck!" Gina exclaimed, drawing out each word for dramatic effect.

"What now?" Aspen asked. She looked back to where the real-man stranger stood talking to his friend. "Oh," she breathed as she watched the real-man stranger lift up the front of his shirt to wipe the sweat off his face.

"He works out," Gina mumbled. "Abs like that...you have to work out for those."

"My heck! We're like two teenagers at a Zac Efron movie," Aspen whispered, stifling a giggle.

"Zac Efron's hot," Gina said. "And anyway...this guy..." she began, shaking her head as she studied the real-man stranger with admiration. "This guy puts any movie star to shame! Besides, what woman do you know who isn't truly still seventeen at heart?"

Aspen couldn't stop a heavy sigh escaping her lungs as she studied the real-man stranger. Oh, he was handsome—too handsome to really contemplate too much. Guys like the real-man stranger always dated really gorgeous blond girls—girls that had enough beauty to be their counterpart. Guys like the real-man stranger were just guys to daydream about.

"They're breaking it up," Gina whispered. "Do it! Kick your shoe off. Drop your lunch or something!"

"No!" Aspen whispered.

"Later, man," the real-man stranger said.

"Later," his friend replied.

The real-man stranger resumed his jogging—passed Aspen for the seemingly umpteen millionth time. She watched him go, knowing full well she'd be back at the park for lunch the next day. It was like an obsession—an addiction of sorts. She couldn't imagine a workday without sitting on the park bench, waiting for the real-man stranger to jog by.

"Have mercy!" Gina exclaimed once he'd turned another corner and was out of sight. Gina turned to Aspen. "How long have you been watching him at lunch?"

Aspen shrugged. "A couple of weeks."

"A couple of weeks? Why did you wait so long to tell me?"

Aspen shrugged again. "I think—I think I thought I was dreaming him up." She shook her head and pulled a bag of chips out of her lunch sack. "Besides, you know how guys are…especially eye candy like this one."

"You have got to meet this guy, Aspen!" Gina exclaimed.

Aspen emphatically shook her head as she said, "No. I don't want to ruin it."

"Ruin what?" Gina asked. "You don't even know him! Nothing has happened between you."

"Exactly," Aspen said. "That way the daydream will never be ruined. I can always imagine he would've liked me and—"

"Oh, brother," Gina interrupted. "You are not gonna just sit here and watch life jog by! What if he's the one?"

"He's not the one," Aspen said.

"But what if he is?"

"He's not."

"But what if he is?"

"He's not! He's too good-looking."

Gina sighed. "You are so Elizabeth Bennet from P and P."

"I am not," Aspen defended herself.

Gina had compared her to Elizabeth Bennet, the heroine in Jane Austen's book *Pride and Prejudice*, too many times to count.

"You are so!" Gina argued. "If a man's too good-looking, you automatically think he's a brainless jerk or something."

Aspen shrugged. "Has it ever been proven otherwise to me?" Aspen frowned and turned to look at her friend. "And besides, what about you? You're always looking for some perfect guy to come walking along wearing a UPS uniform. Why are you so fixated on UPS guys in the first place?"

Gina shook her head and said, "I've always loved UPS guys."

"Because they're the ones who bring the presents at Christmas," Aspen giggled.

"Exactly! When did a UPS guy ever bring me something that wasn't wonderful?"

"But you never say anything to them. You just smile, take your package, and watch them drive away." Aspen looked down the path—down the path where the real-man stranger had jogged only moments before.

"What do you expect me say to them?" Gina asked.

Aspen shrugged. "I don't know. How about something like, 'I'm entirely free to go out with you on Friday night.'"

"Oh, of course!" Gina exclaimed with sarcasm. "That's just it! I'll just say that next time one dashes up to the door to deliver something."

"I don't expect you to flirt with every UPS guy. Just one special one."

"I don't receive enough packages to find one special one," Gina said.

"Maybe you need to hang out at the UPS facility downtown," Aspen suggested.

"Okay, this conversation has reached the ridiculous stage." Gina giggled, but Aspen felt her shoulders round to a droop—felt tired and discouraged all of a sudden.

"We're a couple of cowards," she said.

Gina nodded. She reached into her purse and pulled out a banana.

"Yep," she began, "and the vision of us as spinsters at the age of sixty, climbing up into Old Goldie together, is getting clearer and clearer."

Aspen nodded and opened her potato chips. "I'll probably take to drowning my sorrows and regrets in Doritos and be too fat to climb a tree by then."

Gina nodded and sighed. She peeled her banana, took a bite, and studied it while she chewed. "You know…this would taste a whole lot better with some chocolate syrup drizzled over it."

⁓

Aspen blew softly into the mug of warm cider pressed to her lips. The comforting aroma of mulling spices—of cinnamon sticks, allspice, and cloves, simmered with orange rind in apple cider—soothed her senses. Nora Jones's voice crooned "Come Away with Me" from the iPod dock, and Aspen sighed. It had been a long day. It seemed every customer who came into the bookstore had something to complain about. Aspen shook her head, unable to believe a customer would argue and complain with seven different editions of *To Kill a Mockingbird* to choose from. Still, in the next moment, she raised her eyebrows and nodded. She glanced up to her own bookshelf—to the thirty-seven different copies of Jane Austen titles, the fifteen different editions of *Jane Eyre*, and the nearly forty printed versions of Elizabeth Gaskell's works. Who was she to judge? Book collectors were an odd variety; she should know.

Aspen sipped warm cider from her mug. She closed her eyes and let her head rest back against the couch. Instantly a vision of the handsome real-man stranger entered her mind. She was glad she'd shared him with Gina; it proved he was real. There had been times over the past couple of weeks that Aspen had wondered if maybe she had been drifting into some sort of weird hallucinations every day in the park. Yet Gina had seen him now—he was real.

She wondered what it would feel like to make eye contact with him—to feel his hand in a handshake. She wondered if he had fresh breath or not-so-fresh.

"Definitely fresh," she said aloud to herself.

She sighed, opened her eyes, and took another sip of cider. There was always tomorrow. Tomorrow Gina had agreed to meet her for

Martin & Carolyn Johnson are pleased to
announce the marriage of their daughter

Brittany Diane

to

Rogelio Aguirre

son of Rigoberto & Consuelo Aguirre

SATURDAY, FEBRUARY 14, 2015
CARDSTON, ALBERTA, TEMPLE

YOU ARE INVITED TO ATTEND
A CALLING RECEPTION IN
THEIR HONOUR THAT EVENING
DANCE TO FOLLOW

Barnwell LDS Church | 7:00–8:30 PM

Dinner & Dessert served.

WISHING WELL PROVIDED

lunch again. Times were when she and Gina had eaten lunch together every day—until Gina moved over to being the radiographer at the new urgent care. It was farther away, not so convenient. Still, they had agreed to meet in the park again. Aspen would see him again—tomorrow—while she and Gina enjoyed lunch beneath the little cottonwood in the park. Oh, she already knew he was too good to be true—probably a conceited, egotistical jerk. Still, he was gorgeous, and she liked to pretend he was a nice guy.

Aspen released another sigh and picked up the remote. She pointed it at the iPod dock, pausing Nora Jones before clicking on the TV. She smiled as the familiar theme song to *Leave It to Beaver* began and Jerry Mathers's cute little freckled face appeared on the screen.

Her cell rang, and she smiled when she saw "Gina" flash on the screen.

She opened her phone and greeted, "Hey, girl. What's up?"

"Pasta drizzled with butter for dinner on this end," Gina's voice answered. "And you?"

"*Leave It to Beaver* is on."

"Oh my heck! What channel? I love Wally Cleaver!"

Aspen giggled. "Me too!"

"My vision of the perfect man is Wally Cleaver dressed up in a UPS uniform and jogging through the park!" Gina said.

Aspen laughed and nodded. "Did any UPS guys come into the urgent care today?"

"Oh my heck, yes! He was a gorgeous one too."

"Did you tell him you wanted to be bound tightly in his arms… showered with kisses from his delicious lips?" Aspen teased.

"Of course not! I just grabbed him by the collar of his sexy brown shirt and planted one right on his kisser," Gina giggled through her sarcasm.

"Good for you! I'm glad you finally found some guts."

"Me? All you'd have to do is stick your foot out and trip the jogger guy, and he'd be proposing in the next second!"

Aspen laughed and shook her head. "We so stink at love."

"We do!" Gina laughed. "I'll see you tomorrow at lunch. 'Kay?"

"High noon it is," Aspen said. "'Bye."

"'Bye, girl," Gina said a moment before dead air returned.

Aspen tossed her phone onto the cushion beside her. She sipped her cider and smiled as "the Beave" rationalized his current predicament to his mother.

Still, even Wally Cleaver couldn't entirely distract Aspen from her daydreams of the handsome jogger. She wondered what he was doing at that moment, what he was eating for dinner. She wondered where he lived, what his job was. For an instant, she considered tripping him up the next day. She could pretend it was an accident. She shook her head and rolled her eyes at her own stupidity. Chances were the guy already had a girlfriend. Even if he didn't, what would he want with a plain little bookstore clerk? Some things were just better left to daydreaming.

Aspen sipped her cider and watched the goings-on in the Cleaver household. It was a cozy night—somewhat lonesome, perhaps, but cozy all the same. And, after all, what was wrong with just plain cozy? Nothing. Absolutely nothing.

CHAPTER TWO

"I thought you forgot or something," Aspen said as Gina plopped down beside her on the bench.

Gina shook her head and sighed. "I had that creepy Mr. Gonzales today."

"Ew! The one who always flirts the whole time you're taking his X-rays?"

Gina nodded and wrinkled her nose. "He drives me nuts and always throws off my schedule."

Aspen tried to ignore the nervous disappointment rising in her own chest. What if the real-man stranger quit jogging this way? What if she never saw him again? The thought actually made her a little nauseated. She tried to remind herself that gorgeous guys were always jerks—that she was sitting there in the park purely because she appreciated Mother Nature's handiwork.

"Wait! Here he comes," Gina said. She nodded to their left, and Aspen was rendered breathless for a moment when she caught sight of the handsome real-man stranger jogging toward them.

"It's like he stepped out of a dream, isn't it?" Aspen asked. Her heart leapt as he neared them. She wondered how she could be so shallow, daydreaming about a man she'd never even met simply because his appearance attracted her. Yet sometimes she wondered if there were something else—wondered if something much deeper drew her to him. Still, she knew it was just rationalization—an excuse her mind was concocting to try and justify spending her lunch hour in the park every day.

Aspen heard Gina gasp.

"I know, I know. He's way hot," Aspen said.

"U-um…now, Aspen…now don't panic," Gina stammered.

Gina glanced up to the real-man stranger. He would be right in front of them in a matter of moments. Should she wait? Should she wait to tell her arachnophobic friend? Should she wait to tell Aspen that a huge spider had just dropped out of the tree overhead—and landed on her shoulder?

Panic began to envelop Gina as she watched the large, black-and-yellow, bulbous-bodied spider crawl toward Aspen's neck. Aspen was scared to death of spiders! They completely freaked her out. Yet Gina knew if she said something now, well, Aspen would no doubt commence her usual spider dance—leap up and start screaming, *Get it off me! Get it off me!* as she hopped around in a circle. Still, the spider was inching closer and closer to Aspen's neck—just as the real-man stranger jogged closer and closer. Gina was certain the spider would reach Aspen's neck before the real-man stranger did.

"What do you mean?" Aspen asked. Was her shirt unbuttoned or something? The real-man stranger was closing fast. Aspen glanced down to the front of her shirt. She shouldn't have worn it! It seemed this particular shirt was always popping a button open. Still, all the buttons seemed fastened.

"N-now just remain calm," Gina was saying. "He'll be past you in a minute, and then I'll—"

Aspen drew in deep breath. There was only one reason Gina would be telling her to remain calm—telling her to remain calm and staring at her shoulder. Aspen gasped and clamped a hand over her mouth in an effort to remain calm. Yet the fear—the terror—was rising in her faster than she could even attempt to control it. She leapt to her feet, suddenly unaware of anything else.

"Get it off me!" she choked. "Gina! Get it off me!"

"Just hold still a moment longer, Aspen," Gina said. She stood, still staring at the large spider on Aspen's shoulder. Gina hated spiders as much as the average Jane, but Aspen was terrified of them.

Gina glanced past Aspen. The real-man stranger was almost to them. One more moment—if Aspen could just hold on one more…

"Gina!" Aspen screeched. "Get it off me! Get it off me!"

"But Aspen, that guy is almost—"

"Get it off me!" Aspen cried as she began to hop around in a circle—entirely panicked!

Aspen's mind was overtaken—overtaken with fear and panic! Where was it? She didn't know! Her shoulder—Gina had been looking at her shoulder. It would be in her hair next! Aspen screamed and shouted, "Get it off me! Get it off me!"

"What's wrong?" the real-man stranger asked Gina as he jogged to a halt in front of them.

Gina could only point at Aspen, astounded that the real-man stranger had spoken to her. "Spider," she told him. "On her shoulder. They freak her out."

"Apparently," he mumbled. His strong brow puckered into a frown as he turned to Aspen.

Aspen managed to stop her spider dance long enough to see the real-man stranger reach toward her shoulder. She held her breath as she saw him take hold of one of the spider's legs with his bare fingers.

"It's all right, miss," he said. "It's just a big garden spider." He held the spider by its leg—held it up for her to see.

"Don't show it to her like that!" Gina exclaimed. "It freaks her out worse!"

Aspen couldn't breathe—she felt sick, dizzy.

Gina gasped as Aspen swayed.

"Breathe! You'll pass out! You'll pass out right here in the park!"

Gina's eyes widened as the stranger squished the spider between his thumb and forefinger, wiping the guts and goo on the front of his shirt, just in time to catch a fainting Aspen in his arms.

He looked to Gina, an expression of *What do I do now?* on his handsome face.

Gina could only shake her head. Aspen had never fainted all the way before. Usually Gina would just sweep the spider away; Aspen would continue the panicked spider dance for a few more moments and then begin to settle down. Still, the spider's body had been at least the size of a nickel. That, coupled with the fact the real-man stranger had picked it off her shoulder like a piece of lint and then shown it to her—it had been too much.

The real-man stranger shifted Aspen's weight to one arm and began lightly patting her face with his free hand.

"Miss? Hey, lady?" he said.

The thought traveled through Gina's mind she ought to pull the camera out of her purse and take a photo. Aspen would want to see proof that the real-man stranger had held her in his arms—being she was unconscious and would never remember the reality of it.

Slowly Aspen began to become vaguely aware. She could hear Gina's voice—someone else's voice as well. The feel of someone roughly patting her cheek caused her eyes to open to narrow slits. It was then she knew she was dreaming. She had to be—for it was the handsome face of the real-man stranger she thought she saw.

"Hey," he said. "You okay?"

Like a flash of horrible reality, realization and memory flooded her mind. The spider! A quick vision of the stranger holding a giant spider in front of her face flickered through her brain. Instantly, she began to quiver with wild, uncontrollable trembling—the second phase of her spider fear.

"Is she okay?" the real-man stranger asked Gina.

"Yeah," Gina said. "She always shivers for a while after being startled by a you-know-what."

"A sp-spider, Gina," Aspen stammered breathlessly.

"But it's cool now, okay?" the real-man stranger said. "It's gone. You're all good."

Aspen tried to support her own weight, but she couldn't quite stabilize herself, and the man wrapped both arms around her to keep her from falling. She wasn't sure if it was residual weakness from being frightened by the spider or residual delight at being so close to the real-man stranger.

In that one lingering moment, however brief, she saw his eyes were the darkest brown she had ever seen—so brown it was difficult to discern his pupil. Waves of goose bumps raced over her body as she realized he supported her in his arms.

"I-I'm sorry," she stammered. "They freak me out." She tried to push herself from his embrace.

"It's okay," he said. "I kind of hate snakes." He grinned at her, a friendly, reassuring grin.

Aspen couldn't help but smile at him.

"Here," he said. "Sit down until you feel better." He gently deposited her on the bench, hunkering down before her and asking, "You sure you're okay?"

"Yeah," Aspen said. "Just embarrassed and humiliated beyond explanation." She felt the fire of embarrassment's heated blush rising to her cheeks. She thought she felt something crawling in her hair and quickly ran her fingers through it.

"Thank you," Gina said to the real-man stranger as he stood.

"Will she be okay?" Aspen heard him ask. She wouldn't look up at him. She couldn't. She wanted to cry! How could this have happened? How embarrassing! He must think she was a total idiot.

"Yeah," Gina answered. "She gets over it pretty quick…usually."

"Cool," the real-man stranger said. "You girls have a nice day." He meant to leave. Aspen knew she should thank him. Forcing herself to look up at him, she felt her heart flutter when she saw he was looking at her somewhat expectantly.

"Thank you," she said. She frowned and shook her head, adding, "And I'm so sorry. I'm…I'm so sorry."

"For what?" he asked. He smiled a moment before he turned and jogged away, and his smile left Aspen's mouth agape. His smile was utterly gorgeous!

"You should've just kicked a shoe off yesterday like I suggested in the first place," Gina said. She plopped down on the bench beside Aspen.

Aspen was sure she felt something crawling on her neck and wriggled as she brushed at the place. There was nothing there, of course—only residual panic.

"Well, hindsight is everything," Aspen grumbled.

"Still," Gina began, smiling, "at least you met him."

Aspen frowned and wrinkled her nose in disgust. "I didn't meet him! I made a fool of myself in front of him!"

Gina shrugged. "So you're scared of spiders. Well…now he knows one of your most intimate secrets. Look at it that way: you've already been on intimate terms with him."

Aspen rolled her eyes, irritated with Gina and still disgusted with herself.

"And anyway…look at the bright side!"

"The bright side? How can there be a bright side? He thinks I'm an idiot!"

"Maybe. But I bet he says hi tomorrow when he jogs by."

Aspen looked to her friend and frowned. "You think I'm going to be sitting here tomorrow when he comes by? Do you really think I'm going to be sitting here so he can jog by and think, 'Oh, there's that weird girl who freaked out yesterday because of a spider'? No way!"

"Aspen Falls!" Gina scolded. "You cannot give up now! My parents met when my dad was a volunteer firefighter and my mom's roommates got her stuck in the laundry chute of their apartment complex."

"That is not the same thing, Gina, and you know it!"

"Exactly. My mom was naked! And don't try to tell me this was more embarrassing than that."

Aspen shrugged. "You're right. Nothing is more embarrassing than that."

"Exactly! So buck up, show up here tomorrow for lunch, and see if he says hi to you."

"I can't," Aspen sighed.

"Why not?"

"Tomorrow's Saturday, and we're both off." Aspen smiled and giggled as realization rinsed over her friend.

"Okay, Monday then," Gina giggled.

"I'll think about it," Aspen said, still smiling.

Gina studied Aspen for a moment. "It was great, wasn't it? He's got arms like tree trunks, and you were wrapped in them for a moment. It's sinking in now…and it was great, wasn't it?"

Goose bumps rippled over Aspen's arms at the memory. In that moment she could even remember how he smelled—like cologne and cinnamon gum. Like perspiration too—the hot, sunshine kind, not the stinky kind.

"It *was* great!" Aspen admitted.

Gina laughed. "See? It was worth a spider dance and fainting!" She reached into her purse and withdrew a peach. "I wonder what his name is. Probably something like Matt or Michael or something."

"I can't even begin to guess," Aspen sighed. She reached into the brown paper bag next to her and pulled out a bagel, packaged in a sandwich baggy.

"Mmm!" Gina said, nodding at the bagel. "Cream cheese?"

"And green chili," Aspen said.

Gina nodded her approval and took a bite of her peach. "I suppose this will entirely spoil the rodeo for you tomorrow."

Aspen shook her head. "What's gonna entirely spoil the rodeo for me tomorrow is the fact I'm going with Brad Spencer. I can't believe you talked me into going with him."

"But you love the rodeo!" Gina reminded.

"I love the rodeo. But Brad…I don't know, there's something that just weirds me out about him."

"Well, how do you think I feel? I'm not that big on Jimmy Jensen either. But you and I…we need to have some fun. I think we spend too much time—"

"I know, I know," Aspen interrupted. "You're right."

Aspen and Gina had decided months before that they spent too much time looking for the perfect match for each of them. They figured maybe they'd missed the real precious stones for being distracted by the flash of obvious good looks and personality. Thus, they'd agreed on a double-date night to the rodeo with Brad Spencer and his friend Jimmy Jensen.

"Maybe Jimmy will turn out to be a really nice guy. Brad too," Gina suggested.

"Maybe," Aspen said. She was determined to be positive. Still, the feel of the real-man stranger's arms around her—the scent of his cologne and cinnamon gum—it would be a lot to forget.

"Do you have any of those little sugar packets left?" Gina asked.

Aspen glanced up to see Gina staring at the peach in her hand.

"Just one," Aspen said. "Why?"

"This peach is a little lacking in sweetness."

Aspen shook her head, smiling as she dug through her purse for the sugar packet she knew was in there somewhere.

"Ever notice it seems we do nothing but eat when we're together?" she asked, handing the packet to Gina.

Gina shrugged. "Good friends and good food—it's the spice of life!"

Aspen giggled as she watched Gina tear a corner off the sugar packet. As Gina sprinkled the contents onto her peach, Aspen looked up the path—looked to where the real-man stranger had disappeared around the corner. If she never saw him again—if she never found the courage to return to the park at lunchtime—at least they'd touched. He touched her—held her, in fact. It was something, and something was always better than nothing.

※

"Here ya go," Brad said, holding a cup of cold root beer toward Aspen.

"Thank you," Aspen said. She smiled and accepted the drink.

"What did I miss?" he asked.

"The team branding is all," Jimmy answered.

As Brad sat down next to her, Aspen sipped her root beer and smiled. Brad seemed to be a really nice guy. He and Jimmy had been prompt in picking her and Gina up, and they'd been polite too.

"My Aunt Jenny used to barrel race," Gina said. "We have a videotape of her horse taking a fall and rolling right over her."

"Was she hurt?" Jimmy asked.

"Nope. And neither was the horse. But you wouldn't know it by the video."

"A lot of people don't like rodeo anymore," Brad said. "They think it's inhumane."

"That's because nobody farms and ranches anymore. They don't understand the history of it all."

Aspen looked to Gina. They both smiled, and Aspen knew exactly what her friend was thinking. Gina and Aspen both loved rodeo. There was something nostalgic and real about it, for Aspen especially. It seemed to speak to her, the rodeo. All of it spoke to her soul. Sitting there, that very moment, she felt almost more at home than she had anywhere else in months. The smell of the dirt and the horse and cow manure was oddly soothing to her senses. The sound of the announcer, the roar of the crowd—all of it pleased her.

Aspen had been going to the rodeos in Albuquerque ever since she could remember, especially in September. She could still remember her father carrying her in from the car after a late night spent at Tingley Coliseum when she was no more than three or four. She loved it!

"Mutton busting is my favorite!" Gina said as the announcement was made that the mutton busting would begin shortly.

"Totally!" Aspen giggled.

"I just have to say it," Jimmy began, smiling at Gina. "There aren't too many girls I know who enjoy rodeo."

"I love it!" Gina told him. She smiled at him, and Aspen was glad Gina was having fun. They'd both worried so much. After all, Gina had worked with Brad and Jimmy at the urgent care. Neither girl really knew a whole lot about either man. It was kind of a risk, going out with men they weren't comfortably familiar with. Still, Aspen and Gina had figured it would be safe enough, if they went on a double date.

The crowd cheered and then roared with applause and laughter as the first sheep carrying a small, helmeted child was released into the arena.

"He's hanging in there! Look at him," Brad laughed.

Aspen felt her eyes fill with tears—tears of delight—as she watched the five- or six-year-old boy hold onto the sheep for dear life. She knew every bull and bronc rider in the coliseum probably started out with mutton busting, and it was so fun to cheer for the kids whose rodeo dreams were just beginning.

The little boy finally fell off the sheep's back, and the crowd cheered louder, applauding his efforts. Aspen giggled as the little boy got up and kicked the dirt with disappointment.

"Mickey Chavez, ladies and gentlemen!" the announcer called over the loud speaker. "What a ride, Mickey! We'll see you out of the chute on a spinner in a few years."

The crowd applauded, cheered, and whistled. Little Mickey Chavez paused in the center of the arena, flashed a toothless smile, and waved to the audience.

"He is adorable!" Aspen said. She couldn't understand why her emotions were so close to the surface—just sentimental feelings welling up, she guessed.

Gina leaned over and whispered into Aspen's ear, "And so is *he*!"

"Who?" Aspen asked. It wasn't like Gina to be rude and check out other guys when she was on a date.

"Look five rows down…to the left."

Aspen followed Gina's instructions, gasping when she saw the real-man-stranger jogger from the park. The gorgeous park jogger cupped his hands around his mouth and shouted something toward the arena a moment before applauding.

Aspen's eyes widened as she looked to Gina.

"What the heck?" Aspen breathed.

Gina's eyes widened as well as she continued to applaud.

"What are the odds of that?" Gina whispered as the crowd settled down.

Another mutton buster was out of the chute, and Aspen's eyebrows rose as the handsome real-man-stranger jogger fairly leapt to his feet, over the row in front of him, and against the bars that ran the perimeter of the arena.

"And it's Cole Todd, girls and boys. Look at that ride!" the announcer exclaimed.

Aspen watched, awed as the handsome real-man stranger applauded and shouted as the little boy rode the sheep past the middle of the arena. The small boy sauntered back across the arena, and the handsome real-man-stranger shouted something to him.

Aspen and Gina watched as the real-man stranger climbed back into his seat and said something to the guy sitting next to him. His smile was divine—resplendent—dazzling! Aspen was mesmerized by it—by him—by his presence at the rodeo.

"What the heck is he doing here?" Aspen asked Gina in a whisper.

Gina shrugged. "I don't know. But if you weren't obsessed before, I'm sure you will be now. Kind of throws a wrench in your 'all good looking guys are jerks' theory…doesn't it?"

"There goes another one!" Brad chuckled.

Aspen looked to see another child hanging on to the back of a sheep enter the arena. Still, she couldn't keep her gaze from drifting to the handsome real-man stranger sitting just a few rows down. What was he doing at the rodeo? Park joggers didn't like rodeo—did they?

"I'm going for nachos, Gina," Jimmy said. "You want anything?"

"No…but thanks, Jimmy," Gina said.

As Jimmy stood and left, Brad leaned over to Aspen and said, "Look at the program. Wild cow milking next. Man! That's a brutal one."

"Yeah," Aspen said.

She was distracted, however, as a young man suddenly appeared below them in the arena. The young man walked over to the audience and hauled himself over the bars and onto the walkway in front of the crowd. He shouted something, and Aspen and Gina exchanged inquisitive glances as the handsome real-man stranger stood up and hollered something back. The crowd was too loud for either of them to hear what the verbal exchange was. Still, Aspen felt her eyes widen as the young man from the arena reached around behind him and pulled a T-shirt out of the waist of his pants. He tossed it to the real-man stranger. Aspen's mouth fell agape as the real-man stranger proceeded to strip off the T-shirt he'd been wearing and replace it with the one the man from the arena had given him.

Again she and Gina exchanged glances.

Tan all over, Gina mouthed. *And totally buff!*

"I saw that," Aspen said.

"Check it out!" Brad said. "They're recruiting a team member from the audience. They must be short one guy."

"What do you mean?" Aspen asked.

Brad nodded toward the real-man stranger, who followed the other young man in climbing over the bar and jumping down into the arena.

"Read the T-shirt," Brad explained, pointing to the real-man stranger. "Wild cow milking. Team Corrales."

"Surely not!" Gina exclaimed. "You'd have to be crazy to do that!"

Brad chuckled. "Crazy…or have done it many times before."

Aspen felt overheated—almost sick to her stomach. How could the real-man-stranger jogger guy now be on a wild cow milking team? He was a jogger!

"Ladies and gentlemen, boys and girls!" the announcer began. "Are you ready?"

The crowd whooped and hollered, applauded and shouted their assurance.

"Gina!" Aspen said. "You've got to be kidding me!" She watched as someone handed the handsome real-man stranger a cowboy hat. He firmly settled it on his head and nodded to his teammates—an indication he was ready.

"I'm thinking you should've kicked a shoe out in front of this guy a long time ago!" Gina laughed.

"Wild cow milking at the New Mexico State Fair is about to begin!" the announcer called. "Are you ready, boys?"

Aspen watched, entirely disbelieving as the handsome real-man stranger nodded in unison with the other two men poised at a chute at one end of the arena.

"The first team to successfully squirt milk into a longneck bottle and get to the circle wins!" the announcer began. "And hold your breath, folks! It really is as dangerous as it looks."

As Tom Cochrane's version of "Life Is a Highway" began to blast through the arena, Brad shouted, "Man! These guys are crazy!"

Aspen held her breath as a horn sounded and the "wild cows" were let out of the chutes. The crowd cheered and hollered as each team chased down their chosen cow. Aspen shook her head as she watched the handsome real-man stranger catch hold of the rope tied to the bolting cow's neck. The shouting and cheering was deafening, but Aspen could only stare, breathless with disbelief, as the real-man stranger and his teammates wrestled with the enormous cow.

"He's pretty good!" Brad exclaimed. "No wonder they wanted him down there."

"He's got her! He's got her!" Gina squealed, clapping her hands. "Breathe, Aspen!" she laughed.

Aspen watched as the real-man stranger wrapped his arms around the cow's neck. Digging his boots into the arena soil, he struggled as the cow twisted, charged, and turned. Still, as the other teams struggled to even keep hold of their ropes, the real-man stranger's team seemed to be making progress.

"This guy knows what he's doing. See how he's got her by the neck and the nose?" Brad hollered over the roar of the crowd.

Aspen watched as the real-man stranger wrestled with the cow. One of his teammates, a very husky, powerful-looking cowboy, anchored the rope. The cow bucked and fought, kicking the men and knocking them around without mercy. She was doing damage too! Aspen winced as the cow managed to land a hoof to the cowboy holding the milk bottle. The real-man stranger, boot heels dug into the dirt, twisted the cow's head, and she forfeited for a moment, pausing in her wild thrashing. The third team member struggled to milk the cow as the real-man stranger struggled to keep her still enough for him to do it.

"They've got her!" Brad laughed as the husky cowboy anchoring the rope pulled the hat from his head and began waving it in the air.

Seconds later, the cowboy with the bottle was running toward a circle near the chutes. The husky cowboy waved his hat in the air a moment before letting go of the rope. The real-man stranger was the last to let go. The cow easily rose to her feet and lumbered away. The husky cowboy threw an arm around the real-man stranger's shoulders as they headed toward the chutes.

The deafening roar of the crowd caused Aspen's adrenalin to pump even faster. She watched as the real-man stranger waved to the crowd, pulled the hat off his head, and threw it into the air in celebration of victory.

The entire event began and ended in less than two minutes. Aspen stood stunned, unable to believe she'd just witnessed the park jogging guy help win a wild cow milking event.

The announcer hollered out the names of the winners, but the crowd roared too loud for Aspen to discern them.

"What did I miss?" Jimmy asked. He took his seat beside Gina, smiling at her. "Nachos?" he offered.

"No, thanks," Gina said.

"Wild cow milking, dude!" Brad answered. "And you should have seen this guy they pulled out of the audience, man. He was awesome!"

"You should have kicked off a shoe in the park long ago," Gina mumbled under her breath.

"Yeah, yeah, yeah," Aspen said, rolling her eyes.

"Here he comes. Man! He's pretty banged up!" Brad said, pointing to the real-man stranger as he sauntered across the arena toward them.

"That guy? He looks familiar," Jimmy said.

Aspen watched the real-man stranger climb up out of the arena. His T-shirt was torn, and blood trickled down one arm from his elbow and from one corner of his mouth. The people he'd been sitting with stood up, swarming him as he returned to his seat. Stripping off the torn T-shirt, he replaced it with the one he'd been wearing earlier. Wadding up the torn team T-shirt, he wiped the blood from his face and arm. Everyone near him slapped high-fives with him—smiling, laughing, and offering congratulations.

Aspen simply sat still, too stunned to believe it all.

She stared at the back of the real-man stranger's head, wishing he would turn around, wishing she could get one more look at his brilliant smile.

"Hey, man!" Brad called as the crowd simmered down.

Aspen wished then she wouldn't have wished the real-man stranger would turn around—because he did—and looked right at her!

"Hey!" he called, rising to his feet again and turning toward them. "Arachnophobia girl!"

Aspen forced herself not to throw up from being mortified with embarrassment. Likewise, she forced a smile as the real-man stranger climbed the rows of seats advancing toward them.

"Great job, man!" Brad greeted, offering a hand.

The real-man stranger shook Brad's hand and said, "Thanks, man!"

"You look familiar," Jimmy said.

The real-man stranger frowned a puzzled frown for a moment and said, "You too." He looked to Gina and then Aspen. "But I recognize you two lovely ladies from the park yesterday." He smiled and winked at Aspen. "No spiders today, right?"

"Not yet," Aspen managed. She could feel the crimson blush on her cheeks.

"I figured it out! Rake Locker, right?" Jimmy asked then.

"Yeah," the handsome real-man stranger chuckled.

"Jimmy Jensen," Jimmy said, offering a hand.

"Oh, yeah!" the handsome real-man stranger exclaimed, shaking Jimmy's hand. "We worked at Sam's Club together in high school."

"That's it," Jimmy said.

"Rake Locker?" Gina whispered. "Mercy! Even his name is perfect."

"How you been?" Rake asked Jimmy.

"Good, and you?"

"Can't complain."

"Hey, Rake!" someone called from the row below.

"Gotta go," Rake Locker said. "You guys have fun." He looked at Aspen, pointing an index finger at her and adding, "And you keep clear of spiders." He nodded to Gina as he turned around and said, "Nice seeing you girls again." He added, "You too, Jimmy," over his shoulder as he made his way back to his seat.

"Rake Locker, huh?" Gina asked.

"Yeah," Jimmy said. "He's a pretty cool guy...if I remember correctly."

"I'm sure," Gina mumbled, looking at Aspen. "He sure remembered you."

"How could he not?" Aspen grumbled. "It's hardly been over twenty-four hours since I made a complete fool of myself." She rolled her eyes, shook her head, and felt sick to her stomach. "Arachnophobia girl?"

"At least you made an impression."

"All right! Bull riding is next," Brad said, pulling Gina and Aspen out of their private conversation.

"Arachnophobia girl?" Aspen muttered to herself. How horrifying! She glanced down to where the gorgeous Rake Locker sat laughing and talking with friends. Rake Locker? What kind of a name was Rake Locker? Just the coolest, most masculine name Aspen had ever heard—in her entire life!

❧

Late that night, after the rodeo—after Aspen had to literally struggle out of Brad Spencer's clutches—Aspen sat on her couch disappointed, tired, and confused.

First of all, she'd been entirely duped. Oh, sure, Brad had seemed like a nice enough guy. He'd treated her so politely, been so charming all evening—until he'd dropped off Gina and Jimmy at Jimmy's car at the park-and-ride. It was then that his true intentions were revealed and his true nature reared its ugly head. Oh, sure, Aspen had dealt with guys like Brad tons of times before. And that was the point—she was sick of it!

"I dropped thirty bucks on each of those rodeo tickets!" Brad had said. As Aspen struggled to get out of his car, he'd taken hold of her arm and growled at her, "And all I get is a 'good night, Brad' from you?"

Aspen reminded him that they hardly knew each other, but Brad didn't think it was a good enough excuse for not at least making out for an hour or two. In the end, Aspen had slapped him, plopped thirty dollars down on the seat of his car, and walked away.

"Just check another jerk off the list, Aspen, and move on," she said to herself as she sipped her cider. Gina had text messaged and said her experience with Jimmy was no better. Aspen shook her head, wholeheartedly disappointed with life in general at that moment.

And then there was the dashing Rake Locker—gorgeous, jogging, wild-cow-milking hunk of delicious masculinity!

"Arachnophobia girl?" she mumbled to herself. Gina had spent the rest of the rodeo assuring Aspen that Rake Locker calling her "arachnophobia girl" was a good thing. At least he'd remembered her, Gina had argued. But Aspen took no comfort in it. It was a lousy, rotten end to the evening—and very late.

Glancing up to the old key-wind chiming clock on the wall, Aspen frowned. Surely it was later than eleven. Yep—the pendulum of the old clock wasn't moving.

"Great," Aspen grumbled. She'd been having trouble with her uncle's old clock. She loved it more than almost anything, but it had been sticking of late, even making her late for work once the week before. She'd have to take it in for a cleaning. She hoped the business card her uncle had given her for the clock shop he preferred was still taped to the back of the clock.

Picking up the remote, Aspen turned on the TV. A *Magnum, P.I.* rerun was on. The satellite guide said it was midnight. She'd watch a few minutes of TV and then go to bed and try not to be sick over the fact that Rake Locker thought of her as "arachnophobia girl."

CHAPTER THREE

"No way!" Aspen argued. "After what happened last week…there's no way I'm going to the park for lunch."

"Come on, Aspen," Gina whined through the cell phone. "Now's your chance! Spider or no spider, he noticed you…and remembered you at the rodeo."

"Nope. Not going there. Maybe in a few weeks when he's forgotten all about the stupid spider thing."

"Um, Aspen," Gina began, "I really don't think he's gonna forget that…ever."

Aspen sighed as she pulled the key out of the ignition. "Thanks. I feel a lot better now."

"Seriously, you can't let this go," Gina said. "What if he's the one?"

"Tell you what. Meet me in Old Goldie tonight after work, bring a UPS man with you, and then maybe I'll have lunch in the park again."

Gina laughed, and Aspen couldn't help but smile.

"Anyway, I'm taking Uncle Guy's clock into the shop today. I'm there now…so I can't have lunch in the park," Aspen said as she stepped out of her car.

"So it's really gummed up, huh?"

"Yeah. It keeps sticking at one o'clock. I've had it for three years. Guess it's time to have it cleaned."

"Okay," Gina sighed. "But next week we're meeting at the park for lunch."

Aspen laughed. "You just bring that mystery UPS guy with you, and we'll see. I gotta go. I need both hands to carry this clock."

"Okay," Gina said. "See you in Old Goldie after work."

"Okay, 'bye."

"'Bye."

Aspen pressed end on her cell phone and dropped it into her purse. She pushed the trunk button on her key and lifted the old key-wind clock out of the trunk.

She loved the old wall clock her Great-Uncle Guy had given her before he'd passed away. The Westminster chimes at the quarter hours and strikes on the hour were deep and mellow—soothing like nothing else she knew. She'd missed the chimes and was determined to have them resounding through her apartment as soon as possible. She figured it would cost about a hundred bucks to have the clock fixed, based on what Uncle Guy had once told her. Pricey, but worth it. He'd also told her to take the clock to the Clock Shop down in Corrales to have it worked on. She was glad he'd taped a business card to the back of the clock. She pulled the business card off the back of the clock and studied it for a moment. It was an old business card, she could tell. Still, the Clock Shop was right where the card said it would be. She dropped the card into her purse and headed across the parking lot toward the little adobe building with the weathered sign out front.

The very moment she entered the shop, Aspen was entirely captivated. It was magnificent—like stepping through an enchanted mist and into a fairy tale! The room was dimly lit, the comforting aroma of thyme delicately woven through the air. Wistful, barely audible music—the type one would imagine being played in a castle centuries before—whispered through the room, adding to the sensation of having stepped into another world. Grandfather clocks stood like chivalrous, armor-clad knights, lining either side of a worn red carpet beneath Aspen's feet. Antique wall clocks of every variety adorned the walls, and weathered-looking shelves housed mantel clocks—all ticking a soft, soothing symphony.

"Wow!" Aspen breathed, awed by the calming atmosphere and sheer number of clocks in the small building. In truth, she'd never seen anything like the inner workings of the Clock Shop—not in her entire life!

"Good afternoon."

Aspen looked down the long red carpet to the counter at the other end of it. An older woman stood behind the counter looking very much as Aspen had always imagined Mrs. Santa Claus looking. Her hair was entirely white and swept up into a soft coifed bun at the top of her head. She wore a pair of delicate half-frame reading glasses, perched on her nose in such a fashion as to add to her Mrs. Claus appearance. Aspen couldn't help but smile at the vision of her. The Mrs. Claus—plump and gleeful-looking—wore a white blouse and red broom skirt. Aspen felt suddenly toasty warm inside.

"Can I help you with something, honey?" Mrs. Claus said.

"I think this clock needs to be cleaned," Aspen said.

The elderly woman smiled. "Well, bring it on over, and we'll see what we can do."

Aspen walked to the counter, saying, "It was my uncle's. He gave it to me before he passed away."

"I think I've seen this clock before!" the woman exclaimed. "Who was your uncle, honey?"

"Guy Falls?" Aspen answered.

"Oh, sure, I remember Guy! So he passed on, did he?"

"He did. About two years ago."

"Bless his little heart," the woman said. Aspen's smile broadened. For a moment, she was certain the little elderly woman was Mrs. Claus. "Now...are you just bringing it in for a regular cleaning or is something amiss?"

"It sticks at one o'clock," Aspen answered. "I was careful not to overwind it, so I don't think that's the problem. But it makes a big thunk sound and then sticks before it's able to strike the hour."

"I think you're right. Probably just needs a cleaning," Mrs. Claus said. "But we'll call you if it's anything else...before we do anything too costly."

"I'd appreciate that," Aspen said.

"Well, let's get a ticket filled out for you." Aspen watched as the women moistened the tip of an ancient-looking pencil with her tongue and asked, "What's your name?"

"Aspen Falls."

"Aspen Falls," the woman repeated as she wrote on a yellow claim check pad. "Phone number?"

"Eight nine one, one six nine eight."

"…one six…nine…eight," the woman repeated. "And we think we just need a good cleaning?"

"Yes, ma'am," Aspen said, trying not to giggle. She didn't know why she felt like giggling. It was just that some odd delight was skipping around in her chest.

"Now," Mrs. Claus began, tearing the claim ticket along the perforated line, "here's your ticket." She handed the small yellow claim ticket to Aspen and added, "We'll call you when it's ready…unless there's something else wrong, of course."

"Thank you," Aspen said.

"Oh, and you keep the key, honey," Mrs. Claus said. Aspen watched as the little lady carefully opened the door to the pendulum housing and removed the winding key. "Put that key some place safe and sound," she said, handing the key to Aspen.

"I will," Aspen giggled. She couldn't understand why she felt so giddy. It was the atmosphere, she was sure—and Mrs. Claus.

"Now, we're open six days a week," Mrs. Claus said, taping the other half of the claim ticket to the glass covering the clock face. "But the master watchmaker is only here Monday through Friday to work on clocks. But you can pick it up on a Saturday if you need to."

"Thank you, ma'am," Aspen said. The little lady peered over the top of her half-frames, smiled at Aspen, and then looked up when a tiny bell sounded at the front door.

"Well, speak of the devil," she said. "Here he is now. Did you have a good run, honey?" she said, looking past Aspen to whoever had entered the building.

"Yep," came a deep, masculine response from behind.

Mrs. Claus smiled, her eyes dancing with delight as she looked over her half-rims to Aspen. "That's my grandson. Gave up bull riding for watchmaking…thank the Lord. Though my husband would've been happy either way."

Aspen smiled, delighted with the woman's countenance.

"He goes out running every day during the lunch hour. Needs to move about a bit after working on clocks all morning, I suppose."

Aspen's smile faded a bit. She could hear the approach of Mrs. Claus's grandson behind her. For some reason, the hair on the back of her neck prickled a little—a good prickle.

"Hey, Gramma," a man's voice greeted. The man stepped up to the counter and stood beside Aspen. She felt strange—overly warm.

"You remember Guy Falls, don't you, Rake?" Mrs. Claus asked.

Aspen gasped and quickly looked to the man who had stepped up to the counter beside her.

"Yeah," Rake Locker answered his grandmother.

"Well, this is his niece…Aspen. She's brought his old French Westminster box in for a cleaning."

Aspen closed her gaping mouth as the gorgeous Rake Locker leaned one elbow on the counter and proceeded to study her.

An amused grin spread across his delicious-looking mouth as he said, "Hey there, arachnophobia girl."

"Hi," Aspen managed to respond. Her heart was pounding like a jackhammer was locked up in her chest. He was so close—so tall—so fabulous!

"You two know each other?" Mrs. Claus asked.

"Kind of…I guess," Aspen stammered when Rake Locker didn't answer—only continued to stare at her with an amused grin still complementing his handsome face.

"We've met twice before, Gramma," Rake explained. "Once in the park and then the other night at the rodeo."

"Well, I don't know where the arachnophobia comes in," Mrs. Claus began, "but this is my grandson, Rake Locker. Rake, this is Aspen Falls. She's Guy Falls's niece."

"It's nice to officially meet you, Miss Falls," Rake said, offering Aspen his hand.

Aspen mustered every ounce of self-control she could to keep her hand from trembling as she placed it in his. His hand was strong, callused, and warm. His touch sent a thrill racing down her spine.

"And you too, Mr. Locker," Aspen said.

Rake released her hand, and she watched as he studied the clock on the counter. "I remember this clock," he said. "My grampa used to work on it. A French Westminster box clock...walnut finish... approximately 1880 or 1881. It's got a deep, very mellow hour strike, if I remember correctly."

Aspen felt her lips part, her mouth gaping open just a bit with astonishment. This guy was a watchmaker? She couldn't believe it! Most drop-dead gorgeous guys she'd ever met—and she'd never met one as drop-dead gorgeous as this one—owned some sort of corporate career. That or a sports career of some kind. Furthermore, how could a clock guy know anything about wild cow milking? Her mind was spinning with puzzlement.

"What's wrong with it?" he asked.

Aspen closed her mouth and swallowed hard. "It sticks," she managed. "At one."

Rake Locker's handsome brow puckered into a slight frown. "Probably just needs to be cleaned," he said.

A stronger whiff of thyme scented the air suddenly, relaxing Aspen just a bit. So he was a watchmaker. He was still gorgeous—which meant, of course, that he was shallow and vain to some degree. All unusually handsome men were. Still, he didn't seem to be conceited. Then again, she'd heard him speak—what—three times?

"Did your uncle have you bring this in for him?" he asked. She watched as he carefully pivoted the clock on the counter and studied it further.

"No," Aspen answered. "He gave it to me...about a year before he passed away."

"I'm sorry to hear that," Rake said, a frown puckering his brow again. "Still, I'm glad to see the clock is in good hands. Most people don't appreciate clocks anymore." He looked at her and smiled, sending her heart into palpitations. "The fact you still have it and care enough to bring it in here says a lot for your character, in my opinion."

"Well, th-thank you," Aspen stammered. She gritted her teeth for a moment, mortified by the blush she felt rising to her cheeks. "But... it just needed to be fixed."

"Sadly, most people don't understand clocks these days," Rake's grandmother sighed. "They either let them fade away to nothing or value the money the timepiece or clock will bring...more than the clock itself."

"This one would probably go for as much as three grand," Rake said.

"You're kidding me," Aspen exclaimed. An odd sort of anxiety welled in her for a moment.

Rake chuckled, and she looked from the clock back to him.

"See there? Now I've scared you," he said. "Before you came in here, you loved this clock because it was a really nice clock...a clock a favorite uncle gave to you. Now you know what it's worth. Don't like knowing, do you?"

Aspen smiled at him. It seemed he'd read her very thoughts. "No...I don't," she admitted.

"Don't worry," he said, taking hold of his T-shirt sleeve and stretching it to wipe the residual perspiration from his temples. "In a moment or two, it'll sink in."

"What'll sink in?" she couldn't help but ask.

"The fact that this clock is over a hundred and twenty years old... that's it's struck the hour through more historic events than you and I could ever imagine...and that your uncle loved you enough, and trusted you enough, to entrust you with its care. He must've known you were sensitive enough to care for something that has traveled through time for over a century...and what it's worth to some antique dealer just doesn't matter to you."

Again Aspen felt her lips part, her mouth slightly agape with astonishment. How charming! She wondered if he really felt as sentimental about clocks the way he'd just so perfectly described her own feelings—or if his business sense simply told him to say what customers wanted to hear.

"Rake's grampa says there are two kinds of customers who come in here," Mrs. Claus—or rather, Rake's grandmother—said.

"That's right," Rake agreed.

"The first kind of customer sees the monetary value of an old clock," she began, "usually an antique dealer or someone who collects old clocks to resell." Rake nodded as his grandmother continued. "We prefer the second variety of customer—the customer who truly cherishes the treasure that is an old chiming clock. The person who recognizes chiming clocks are a thing of the past, something vanishing that needs to be protected and appreciated...respected."

Aspen smiled at the elderly lady. "I like to think I'm the second kind of customer."

"Oh, you are," Rake said, smiling at her. His dark brown eyes burned with approval. The fact made Aspen's heart swell. "Otherwise you wouldn't have brought the clock in here to be fixed."

"You would've just let it hang on the wall, silent and sad, until the day you decided to have a garage sale and some sneaky antique dealer stole it from you for twenty bucks," his grandmother added.

Aspen giggled with delight. "I can't think when I've had such kind and thorough—not to mention flattering—customer service."

Rake chuckled, and his grandmother laughed.

"Well," Rake began, glancing about the shop, "we ain't Wal-Mart." He looked back to Aspen and smiled. "It gives us more time to get to know our customers." He smiled—a rather mischievous smile—and added, "More intimately."

"You quit flirting and get back to work," Mrs. Claus scolded. She chuckled, however, and winked at Aspen.

Aspen was delighted! Oh, certainly she was irritated with herself for letting such a handsome man rattle her so. Handsome men weren't good for anything other than looking at and daydreaming about—pretending they really could be nice guys.

"Tell you what, Aspen," Rake began. Aspen tried to ignore the way her heart leapt at his speaking her name. "I'll fix your clock for you, no charge...if you'll go out with me this Friday night."

"M-me?" Aspen stammered. Surely he wasn't asking her out! Surely he was only teasing.

"I don't see any other girls named Aspen standing in this room, do you, Gramma?" Rake said to Mrs. Claus.

His grandmother chuckled, "Not a one!"

"You don't have to do that," Aspen said. She felt overly warm—blushing—downright giddy.

"You mean you'll pay me for fixing the clock *and* go out with me?" he asked. "Bonus!"

"I-I-I…couldn't possibly—" Aspen began.

But Rake interrupted. "I've been jogging past you, trying to get the nerve up to stop and introduce myself. And then the very day I do find the guts…a spider got to you first."

Was he kidding? Had he really noticed her? All the days she'd been sitting on the bench waiting for him to jog by—had he really noticed her sitting there?

"I'll vouch for him," Mrs. Claus interceded. "He's a good boy… fine manners, polite. My grandson knows how to keep his hands to himself."

"Gramma!" Rake scolded, chuckling and scowling at the same time.

"He's as fine a boy as was ever born…or my name ain't Charlotte Locker," Mrs. Claus—rather Charlotte Locker—added. "Run on back and rinse that sweat off you, Rake. Maybe then she'll consider on it more."

"Gramma!" Rake scolded once more. Shaking his head and grinning, he looked back to Aspen and asked, "What do you say? Friday night? I bet you've never been out with a wild cow milker before."

"Or a master watchmaker either," Charlotte added.

"Gramma…please," Rake chuckled. "You know women would rather go out with a wild cow milker than a master watchmaker. You're slitting my throat here."

Aspen giggled, amused by their banter—delighted by Rake Locker's mere presence.

"If you'll let me pay for the clock," Aspen began.

"Then?" Rake prodded.

"Then…I-I guess it wouldn't be a bad thing," Aspen stammered.

"Why ever would it be a bad thing, honey?" Charlotte asked.

Charlotte couldn't possibly know that Aspen never dated drop-dead gorgeous men—not since Mike Archuleta her senior year in high school.

"I promise," Rake began, "it won't be a bad thing."

Aspen looked at him—gazed into the dark brown of his mesmerizing eyes. How could one date with such an overall wildly attractive guy be a bad thing?

"Okay," she said. She bit her lip as he smiled at her.

"Great!" he said, taking a business card from the small business card box on the counter. He took the pencil from his grandmother's hand and offered it to Aspen. "Just put your phone number on the back of this, and I'll call you." He took another business card from the box and offered it to her. "And here's an extra one…so you won't forget who's fixing your clock."

Aspen giggled and took the pencil from him. She wrote her cell number on the back of the card and handed the pencil back to Charlotte.

"Okay then," Rake said, picking up the card and studying the number on the back. "But why don't you just tell me your address now and I'll pick you up at…what's good for you?"

"I'm off work at five on Friday," Aspen said.

"Where do you work?" he asked.

"The Book Nook…on Alameda and Coors."

"I adore that place!" Charlotte exclaimed. "I've been going there for over thirty years, since right after it opened."

"Yeah, I like working there," Aspen said.

"Here," Rake said, taking the pencil from his grandmother again and handing Aspen the business card already bearing her phone number. "Just write down your address, and I'll pick you up at your place at six on Friday. How's that?"

"Okay," Aspen giggled. She wrote her address down, wondering for a moment whether it was a wise thing to do. What if Rake Locker wasn't what he appeared to be? What if he was secretly some deranged serial killer or something? Still, his smile warmed her—thrilled her—and she forced her anxieties and overactive imagination to the far corners of her mind. "There you go," she said, handing the business card back to him.

"Thanks," he said, reading the back of the card.

Aspen blushed when she looked at Charlotte to see her smiling with delighted understanding. No doubt the elderly woman knew just how attractive her grandson was.

"Well, I-I need to be getting back," Aspen stammered. "Thank you, Mrs. Locker."

"Charlotte, honey," Charlotte said. "Just call me Charlotte."

"Okay," Aspen agreed.

"And you can call me anything you want," Rake flirted.

Aspen smiled with delight at his teasing manner.

"Friday at six. Okay?" Rake asked.

Aspen nodded. "Okay."

"You have a good day, honey!" Charlotte called as Aspen turned and followed the trail of red carpet through the grandfather clock centurions toward the exit.

"You too," Aspen called over her shoulder.

Pushing the door open, she stepped out of the enchanting atmosphere of the clock shop and into the bright New Mexico sunshine. It was only then she realized she was trembling a little. He'd completely undone her—and it was wonderful! Furthermore, he'd noticed her—noticed her sitting on the park bench as he jogged past every weekday for the past two weeks!

Giddy as a goofball, she hurried across the parking lot to her car. She had to call Gina! She looked at the clock on her control panel as she started the car. It would have to wait; Gina's lunch hour was over, and she'd be with a patient by now. Aspen drew the business card out of her purse.

"*Rake Locker, Master Watchmaker,*" she read aloud. In her wildest dreams, she'd never imagined the handsome real-man stranger jogging through the park would be a master watchmaker. She reached into her purse and dug around until she found the old business card for the

Clock Shop, the one her Uncle Guy had taped to the back of the clock. "*Ray Locker, Master Watchmaker,*" she read. "So your grandfather's name is Ray, huh?" she mumbled to herself. She frowned then, puzzled as something Mrs. Claus had said echoed through her mind.

My grandson...gave up bull riding for watchmaking...thank the Lord, she'd said.

"Bull riding?" Aspen asked aloud. Still, it would explain Rake Locker's knowing how to milk a wild cow—his presence at the rodeo.

Aspen smiled as she put both business cards back in her purse and checked to make sure the winding key was safe as well. She sighed and mumbled, "Rake Locker...the bull-riding master watchmaker. How wild is that?"

She plunged the key into the ignition and started the car. How would she ever settle down at work for the rest of the day? How would she settle down for the rest of the week? As she pulled out of the parking lot, gazing one last time at the Clock Shop, she began to worry. Handsome guys were trouble! They were always vain, conceited, self-centered, and usually way too confident in their overpowering effect on women. She thought of Brad Spencer—of his expectations that a ticket to the rodeo was worth some sort of physical give-in from his date.

Aspen shook her head and tried to dispel thoughts of lumping Rake Locker in with the rest of the men who had disappointed her. The fact that his name was Rake did little to reassure her. The constantly referencing thesaurus in her mind began to list off synonyms at breakneck speed.

"Rake," Aspen began aloud. "Synonyms are...rogue, rascal, rounder...seducer, Don Juan, playboy, womanizer, Casanova... blackguard, charlatan, knave, scoundrel, and, of course, rapscallion." She shook her head and mumbled, "Too many synonyms bouncing around in your head, Aspen. Let it go. Just let it go and have fun."

Later, as she entered the Book Nook, her gaze was instantly drawn to a new poster on the wall, near the little café in one corner. It was a poster advertising a new book.

"*Lambs to the Slaughter: Serial Killers Among Us,*" she read aloud.

"Oh, that's nice. Just great." Her anxieties over accepting a date with a man she didn't know began to return.

"Excuse me. Do you work here?"

Aspen turned to see a group of teenage girls standing behind her. There were five of them, and they all wore excited expressions of anticipation.

"Looking for the *Twilight* series?" Aspen asked. These girls were classic Stephenie Meyer fans. Being one herself, Aspen could spot them a mile away.

"We totally love Stephenie Meyer!" one of the girls exclaimed.

"Well then, she's—" Aspen began.

"But we've read them all already," another girl interrupted. "We're looking for that new book about the girl who goes out with this totally hot guy…only he turns out to be, like, totally a serial killer or something. Do you know which one we mean?"

Aspen couldn't keep from shaking her head and smiling at the irony. "Do you know the name of the author?"

Five inquisitive sets of brows puckered at her.

"No," the first girl said. "You work here. We thought you would know."

Aspen took a deep, calming breath. "I'm sure we can find it for you," she said.

As she walked to the computer, she glanced up at the clock on the wall. Four more hours and she'd be in Old Goldie with Gina. Four more hours. Four more days and she'd be on a date with the handsome Rake Locker—the bull-riding, watchmaking, potential serial killer.

❦

"That's because you read too many creepy mystery novels when you were in high school," Gina said.

Aspen watched as Gina dipped a crudely cut apple slice into the plastic container of caramel on her thigh. She smiled, amused by Gina's dragging a container of caramel and a pocket knife up into Old Goldie's branches.

"That is not true," Aspen argued. "Just watch the news or read the paper. Serial killers are a dime a dozen these days."

47

"Hottie jogger Rake Locker is not a serial killer…even if he is a clock guy."

"What does being a clock guy have to do with it?"

Gina shrugged and licked caramel off the back of her hand. "I read that creepy Edgar Allan Poe thing in school…the one with the ticking thing going on. It freaked me out. Why do they make kids read that kind of crap in school anyway? If you ask me, it does nothing to encourage literacy. Making kids read stuff they hate just makes them not want to read at all."

"First of all, it was a heart beating…not a clock ticking," Aspen explained. "Though I do think there's a clock striking it in."

"Yeah, that's it. 'The Tell-Tale Clock.'"

"'The Tell-Tale Heart'…and it is an awful story. I hated it too. And you're right. Why don't they choose good, uplifting stuff for kids to read?"

Gina nodded and, using the old pocket knife, sliced another piece off the apple in her hand. "Remember that awful one about the boys on the island or something? Stupid."

"But what if he's a nut job?" Aspen asked. She knew Gina was right—that there was really no reason to suspect Rake Locker of being some kind of deviant criminal. Yet he was just too good to be true—too handsome—too charming. There had to be something wrong with him.

"He's not a nut job, Aspen," Gina whined. "Just go out with him, and see what happens." Gina dunked the apple slice in the caramel bowl. She hadn't finished chewing yet when she said, "I mean…how can a guy whose grandma looks like Mrs. Santa be a nut job?"

"I'm sure even Jack the Ripper had a grandma, Gina," Aspen said.

"Not one that looked like Mrs. Santa."

Aspen laughed, and Gina smiled. Gina was so funny! Her dry sense of humor was so often just what Aspen needed to help her cast away her cares and worries.

"Let's worry about Mr. Rake Locker later," Aspen sighed. "How was work?"

"Oh my heck!" Gina began. "It was total drama today! You know the blond bimbo Kellie…new tech at the urgent care?"

"Yeah."

"So her boyfriend comes in, and he's all mad because I guess he saw her out with another guy Saturday night, right? So they get in this big argument—in front of all the patients and everything—and Kellie gets mad and slaps him, and it turns into this big thing, and Doctor Ortega walked by. You know Dr. Ortega? Anyway, Dr. Ortega had to call the cops, and, like, Kellie is freaking out, crying, screaming, and the boyfriend was, like, shouting and threatening. It was like one of those Spanish soap operas you see on late-night TV…only without the benefit of Erik Estrada." Gina frowned, puzzling. "How did Erik Estrada end up on those lame soap operas anyway?"

Aspen giggled, delighted by her friend's amusing narrative. "How do you even know who Erik Estrada is?"

"I watch the *CHiPs* reruns on the TV Land channel. How do you even know who he is?" Gina ate another bite of caramel-covered apple.

"My mom used to like him when she was a kid," Aspen said. She leaned back against Old Goldie's trunk and sighed. "I love these autumn evenings."

"Me too," Gina said. "The cottonwoods down by the river are starting to change a little. Did you notice?"

"Mmm hmm!" Aspen breathed, inhaling the warm autumn air and relishing the scent of the ripening fruit all around her. "They'll really be starting to turn by the time the balloons launch."

The Albuquerque International Balloon Festival was one of Aspen's favorite things in life. Every year, thousands of hot air balloons and their pilots arrived in Albuquerque for the event—two weeks of mass ascensions, Special Shapes Rodeos, balloon glows, and a myriad of other events involving hot air ballooning. It was fantastic, and Aspen loved it!

One of Aspen's favorite childhood memories, in fact, involved early October mornings, waking to the sound of a hot air balloon burner and then a shadow moving lazily across the early sun. With joy and delight bursting about in her bosom, Aspen would leap out of bed and dash to the window in time to see a low-flying balloon or two drift past her window. If she was quick enough, she could run outside—pajamas and all—to wave to the pilot and crew. They always waved back.

Aspen's parents' house was situated in a perfect location for viewing the balloons. Waves and waves—hundreds and hundreds—of colorful hot air balloons would drift over their house and yard, many of them quite low—low enough to wave and shout hello. It was magical, and the balloons had been the most exciting, beautiful things of Aspen's childhood. She still loved them, in fact. On the early October mornings when she was scheduled for the later shift, Aspen would get up early and drive to her parents' house. Her mom would always have hot chocolate and lawn chairs waiting. Aspen, her parents, and her younger brother would sit out in the yard, sipping hot chocolate and watching as the beautiful orbs of color and wonderment drifted lazily through the morning air.

"Did you ask for time off for the Special Shapes Rodeo?" Gina asked.

"I did!" Aspen assured her. Gina offered a high-five, and Aspen met it.

"I hope the buccaneer balloon is back this year. This will be our fourth year on the field, and we still haven't seen it again!" Gina noted.

"I know. And I did buy an extra memory card for my camera this time."

Gina nodded her approval and dunked another apple slice in her bowl of caramel.

"You're sure he's not a serial killer?" Aspen asked. For all their lighthearted talk of the past few minutes, Aspen was still nervous about her date with Rake Locker.

"Of course he's not!" Gina exclaimed, exasperated. "I mean," she began, shrugging her shoulders, "he might be a pervert...try to overpower you and—"

"Okay, shut up," Aspen interrupted. "I'll stop."

"What's the song playing in your head when you see him?" Gina asked.

Aspen smiled. Gina knew a song was always running through

Aspen's head. It had always been that way. Aspen called it her "life soundtrack." She found that the songs that would pop into her head during events in her life often matched the situation—or person.

"I mean," Gina continued, "is 'Kiss Me' by Sixpence None the Richer playing when you see him? Or is it some screamy, vocal-chord ripping, head-banger noise?"

Aspen smiled and giggled. "'Come Away with Me,'" she answered.

"Norah Jones?" Gina exclaimed, a delighted smile spreading across her face. "That's a total make-out song!"

"Well, it's calming, if nothing else," Aspen said. She agreed with Gina, however. It was a song to do some serious romantic kissing by.

"It's a good sign, Aspen," Gina sighed. "And he looks like he'll be a fabulous kisser!"

Aspen smiled. Gina was so funny. And it *was* a good sign—that "Come Away with Me" was the song playing in her mind whenever she saw Rake Locker. She was suddenly encouraged—relaxed about her upcoming date. Her anxieties suddenly washed away, and as Gina leaned back against Old Goldie's trunk too, there was nothing but the autumn breeze—the autumn breeze, the fragrance of harvest, and the comfort and company of a true friend.

CHAPTER FOUR

Aspen tried to calm herself—tried to stay seated on the couch—tried to keep her hands from wringing. She was so nervous! She stood and began to pace. Back and forth, back and forth in front of the couch—waiting. What if her hair didn't look right? What if the jeans and white blouse she wore weren't a nice enough outfit? What if he didn't show up? What if he'd changed his mind about taking her out?

Yet, in the next moment, the doorbell rang. Aspen stopped breathing for a moment; her heart was pounding so franticly within her chest that it hurt. It was him! She knew when she opened the door it would be to find Rake Locker waiting on the other side.

Swallowing the lump of pure nerves in her throat, Aspen inhaled a deep breath, plastered on a smile, and opened the door. She was instantly rendered breathless once more, however, for the sight of the handsome, gorgeous, delicious-looking Rake Locker momentarily paralyzed her.

"Hi," he said, flashing his movie-star smile.

"Hi," Aspen managed. He wore a pair of faded Levi's and a red button-up shirt and stood with his hands shoved casually in his front pockets.

"You ready to have the time of your life?" he asked.

Aspen smiled and felt a little calmer. He was so charming! And she was ready—ready to have the time of her life. Eye candy or not, shallow and conceited or not, Rake Locker would be nothing if not a good time, Aspen was sure.

"Sure," she said, stepping out of her apartment and closing the locked door behind her.

"You didn't eat yet, did you?" he asked.

"Nope," Aspen answered, distracted by the dark fire in his eyes.

"Good." Rake nodded in the direction of the parking lot. "It's the old white pickup over there." Aspen's smile broadened as she saw an old, pretty banged-up pickup parked near the walkway leading to her apartment. "I was thinking Sadie's for dinner." Rake added, motioning for her to precede him.

"I love Sadie's!" Aspen exclaimed. And she did. Sadie's was absolutely her favorite restaurant.

Nestled in an older part of the north valley, Sadie's Mexican Restaurant served up the best food in the entire world! Aspen's mouth began to water at the thought of Sadie's carne adovada enchiladas. At least she assumed it was the thought of carne adovada. Yet when she reached the pickup and Rake opened the door for her, she glanced at him and wasn't sure whether it was the anticipation of carne adovada or simply being in Rake Locker's presence that was making her salivate.

"And we'll probably have a long wait," he said.

"Sadie's is worth a long wait," Aspen assured him. Ooo—a long wait at her favorite restaurant with the likes of Rake Locker? Fabulous!

Aspen watched—couldn't keep from smiling as Rake stepped up into his pickup and turned the key in the ignition. The old engine smoothly roared to life, and Rake pulled out of the parking lot.

"So you like Sadie's, huh?" he asked as he turned onto the main street.

"I love it!" Aspen admitted. "I don't go there very often because...I don't know about you, but I tend to way overeat when I go there."

Rake chuckled and said, "Yeah. I'm usually pretty uncomfortable after the chips and salsa...not to mention the meal."

"I know!" Aspen exclaimed. "But...you can't stop! The salsa is so good, but if you stop..."

"You can't stop," he said, filling in the silence of her pause. "It's too good and too hot. If you stop..."

"It just totally burns too much," Aspen said, filling in the silence of his pause.

"You are a Sadie's girl," he chuckled.

"You have no idea!"

Rake changed lanes. "Do you mind going Alameda?"

"Not at all," Aspen said. "I'd rather go Alameda. Paseo is so congested anymore."

"So how was work?" he asked.

"Fine. Not much to tell," Aspen answered.

"Are you a reader? I mean…you do work at a bookstore."

Aspen shrugged. "I like to read, but I'm kind of picky. And I can't read a ton, ton, ton. How about you?" Aspen was amazed how comfortable she felt. Her nerves had settled so very quickly—it wasn't normal for her.

"I read some," he answered. "I read the paper, college football magazines, and stuff. I'm not much into…you know…books." Aspen giggled. "Though I do like biographies. Now that I think about it, I read a couple of those a year."

"Really?" Aspen asked. How intriguing! "Biographies about who?"

"Let's see," he began, his brow puckering a bit as he mused. "I read one on Ronald Reagan last Christmas, one on Johnny Unitas that my mom gave me for my birthday…um…a Clarence Thomas memoir, and…let's see…oh yeah! I really like the one someone gave me about Jimmy Stewart's bomber pilot experience."

"Impressive!" Aspen said.

Rake shook his head and added, "Not really. I still prefer college football magazines." He looked at her, his eyes narrowing. "I bet you're one of those Jane Austen fans. Am I right?"

Aspen's smiled. "Oh, I see. You must have sisters—at least one—and you must think every girl reads Jane Austen."

He smiled. "I do have a sister, yes…but it's the clock that makes me think you like that old Jane Austen stuff."

Aspen was curious. Why would the clock clue him into her delight in Jane Austen's works? "The clock?" she asked.

"Sure! That clock has been well cared for. I can tell it's been wound regularly, run constantly. The fact you brought it in, it shows you have an affinity for the things of the past. That's why I think you like that old stuff like Jane Austen." He smiled, chuckled, and added, "That and, I'll admit, the fact that my sister says all women love Jane Austen's books."

"Well, I do like Jane Austen," Aspen admitted. "But she's not my very favorite."

"Who's your very favorite?" The pickup's right blinker blinked rhythmically as Rake turned onto Fourth Street.

"Elizabeth Gaskell...though *Jane Eyre* by Charlotte Brontë is my favorite book."

Rake shook his head. "Like I said, I read the seasonal college football magazines and an occasional biography...and that's a stretch."

Aspen giggled. He was charming—so engaging when it came to conversation! Definitely too good to be true. She studied him for a moment, trying to discern any physical faults or odd expressions that would tip her off to his character flaws.

"Well, I can barely wind a clock...let alone fix one," she said. "And wild cow milking certainly isn't on my résumé."

"Got your attention with that, did I?" he asked.

"Yeah," she admitted. She wondered then—about what his grandma said about his giving up bull riding for watchmaking. "Your grandma said you used to ride bulls?"

Rake chuckled and shook his head. "Oh, no!" he breathed. "How long were you in the Clock Shop before I showed up the other day?"

"Five or ten minutes," Aspen answered. She could've sworn his cheeks were a little red, as if he were embarrassed. It was adorable!

"Gramma sure gives a lot of information in a short amount of time," he said.

"Well?" Aspen prodded.

He drew in a deep breath and began, "Well...it's true. My mom and dad were ranchers when I was younger. They ran a spread my grandpa owned between here and Santa Fe. I started out mutton busting when I was about four and was riding bulls as soon as my mom would let me. I've got a little nephew who mutton busts now. That's why I was at the rodeo the other night...to watch him. The wild cow milking thing just sorta happened because an old buddy of mine was short a team member."

Aspen was entirely intrigued! How did a boy who liked bull riding end up being a master watchmaker in a clock shop?

"I know what you're thinking," he said before she could open her mouth to ask the question.

"You do?"

"Sure," he said. "You're wondering how I ended up in the Clock Shop instead of in a rodeo arena."

"The thought was crossing my mind, yes," Aspen admitted.

"Well, I rode for a while…even rode as a professional for over two years," he said.

Aspen felt her mouth gape open in astonishment. He looked too big to be a bull rider. Still, Aspen had never really seen a professional bull rider up close. Maybe they just looked smaller because they were always so far way.

"You're kidding?" she couldn't help but ask.

Rake laughed and shook his head. "Nope. You can look me up on Professional Bull Riders. I'm listed as ineligible…but I'm really retired."

"Why did you quit?" Aspen asked. "I thought bull riders…you know…were obsessed most of the time."

Rake nodded. "Well, a couple of years into the pros, I came off a bull after a ride, and the bull caught me—gored my right hip and the back of my right thigh with a horn. Took a nice slice out of my calf before he was done with me too." He paused, shrugging his shoulders as Aspen looked at him, mouth agape in awe. "It wasn't a bad injury at all, and I wasn't scared of riding anymore or anything…but I just kept thinking of Lane Frost and decided I didn't love it enough to die for it."

"Lane Frost?" Aspen asked.

"Yeah. He was bull rider back in the '80s when my uncle was still riding. A bull got to him after a ride…broke one of his ribs. It severed an artery, and he died."

Aspen swallowed, entirely unsettled by the sudden realization of the dangers of bull riding.

"I loved riding…just not enough to die doing it."

Aspen swallowed the lump of awkward emotion in her throat. "Probably a wise career move...as far as safety goes."

"Yeah," he said. He smiled—a smile of mischief or amusement. His eyes narrowed as he looked at her and said, "I figured, if I'm going to die doing my job—drop in the harness, so to speak—what better way to go than cleaning antique clocks for pretty bookstore girls." He winked at her, and Aspen was overwhelmed by the sudden butterflies in her stomach. "My grandpa opened the Clock Shop over forty years ago, as a hobby at first," he continued. "But it turned out to be a really lucrative business, and when his eyesight started getting bad...well, I had always loved to work on clocks with him, so after my butt healed, I went out to St. Paul College and became a certified master watchmaker. I work on all the clocks now. Grampa can't see well enough anymore."

"Wow," Aspen breathed.

Rake chuckled. "Wow, what? Wow, you can't believe I was ever manly enough to be a bull rider? Or, wow, you can't believe anybody could actually find working on clocks interesting enough to do it as a career?"

"Wow, I can't believe how dull my life sounds next to yours," she answered. She did feel ridiculously plain and boring in those moments. How would he ever find anything of interest in her, with such an exciting past to his credit?

"Are you kidding?" he asked. "The stories you could probably tell about your adventurous encounters with spiders alone would completely trash anything I could come up with!"

Oddly enough, his teasing didn't bother her in the least. Rather it delighted her somehow. "That was so embarrassing," she said, blushing miserably at the memory.

"Naw," he said, turning left off of Fourth Street and toward the restaurant. "But I will admit...it gave me a whole new sympathy for the ladies in my life. I guess I'll never tease my mom again about putting mason jars over spiders when she finds one on the floor. She puts jars over them and waits for my dad to get home and 'take care of it'...as she puts it."

"Oh my heck!" Aspen exclaimed. "I do that too! Well, if they're not too big, and I can actually get up the nerve to get close enough." She sighed as he pulled into a parking spot and shifted into park. "Still, it was just about the most embarrassing incident of my entire life."

He chuckled as he took his key out of the ignition. "You oughta try having your jeans and underpants stripped off by the horns of a bull in front of a crowd of tens of thousands of spectators."

Aspen giggled. "So you were humiliated into retirement, huh?"

He grinned, mischief twinkling in his deep brown eyes.

"Oh, don't misunderstand. There ain't a bare behind in the world any nicer than mine," he began. "It was limping off all bloody and mangled that was humiliating." He winked at Aspen and added, "I'll come get your door."

Aspen watched him walk around the front of the pickup. His behind did fill out his Levi's to perfection. Still, it was the first hint of the conceit she'd grown to expect from perfect-looking men. The emotions in her were suddenly mingled—at odds. She didn't want him to be stuck-up and self-centered like most handsome men. She wanted him to be true, not too good to be true. And yet, she inwardly admitted she had baited him—teasing him about being embarrassed into retirement for losing his pants in front of a crowd. Natural self-defense dictated he had to try and one-up her.

"There are only about twenty people standing outside waiting," he said, taking her arm and helping her out of the pickup. "I don't think we'll have to wait long."

"Okay," she said. His hand gently gripping her arm had an astounding effect on the rest of her body. Goose bumps rippled over her legs; more butterflies erupted to flight in her stomach.

He closed the pickup door behind her and asked, "You ready?"

"For Sadie's? Always!" she answered.

Rake opened the restaurant doors for her, and Aspen stepped into Sadie's. She was immediately aware of the way every set of female eyes within viewing distance stuck to Rake Locker like flies to honey. Still, what right did she have to judge? Hadn't she spent her lunch hour in the park every day for two weeks, simply to get a look at the gorgeous real-man-stranger jogger guy? Her insides swelled with a sort of pride mingled with jealousy. Secretly, it was kind of pleasant and satisfying to have the women in the room ogle Rake and then look to Aspen with a "you lucky wench" expression. Yet it bothered her too. He was *her* date! They should all keep their eyes to themselves.

"How many, sir?" the girl at the hostess desk asked.

Aspen didn't miss the blush rising to the girl's cheeks as Rake smiled at her and said, "Two, please."

"And the name?" the girl asked.

"Rake," he answered.

"We're at an hour wait just now, sir. Is that all right?" the girl asked.

"Sure," he answered.

The girl handed him a square black restaurant buzzer.

"Thank you," he said.

"Oh, you're very welcome, sir," the girl answered, winking at Rake.

Rake turned to Aspen and asked, "Do you want to wait outside… or in here?"

Aspen smiled. He was completely unaffected by the girl's reaction to him and her flirting. It seemed he hadn't noticed at all.

"It's cool enough outside, don't you think?" she answered.

"Yeah. It's a great evening. Come on."

Rake took hold of her arm again, leading her toward the exit. Aspen couldn't help the impish thrill of delight welling in her as every set of female eyes followed their path as they left.

Once outside, Rake led Aspen to a bench, and they sat down.

"Ahhhh!" he sighed, stretching his legs and crossing them at the ankles. "It feels so good out here. I get tired of being cooped up in the shop sometimes."

"Me too," Aspen said.

The sun was setting, and its orange warmth felt good on Aspen's face.

"So…were you born here?" he asked.

"Born and raised," Aspen answered. She liked talking with him. He was a good conversationalist—very engaging. Again she noted how every woman who passed them on their way into the restaurant couldn't resist taking a second look at the handsome Rake Locker.

"Me too," he said. "Does your family live over here on the west side?"

"Nope. They're in the north valley, a little southwest of the balloon park," she answered.

"Man! I bet they have a good view of the balloons, huh?"

"Oh, yeah! We usually just set up a few lawn chairs in the backyard and have a great time."

"It's only a few weeks away," he said. "Man! I can't believe how fast this year went."

"I know."

Aspen sighed. She couldn't believe she was sitting next to the real-man stranger from the park—couldn't believe such a man had actually found her interesting enough to ask her out. She felt warm, filled with hope, delight, and giddiness. Oh, she had no doubt Rake Locker would show his true colors eventually. No doubt he would turn out to be exactly what all uncommonly handsome guys turned out to be—a real piece of work. Still, she decided she would enjoy his company, his seemingly good character, while she could.

The scent of green chili wafted through the air past her for a moment. This was what life was all about, she thought—the simple, wonderful moments like this. She'd enjoy the present—not worry about the future and whether Rake Locker were too good to be true.

༜

"I think I'm going to be sick," Rake said, leaning back in his chair. The remains of the gargantuan chicken burrito smothered in red and green chili on Rake's plate were few—far fewer than those of Aspen's carne adovada enchiladas. Still, she felt more uncomfortable than she had in months—more satisfied too, however.

"Why do I eat like this whenever I come here?" he asked.

Aspen giggled. He looked positively miserable for a moment.

"Because it's the best thing you could ever eat and you don't want to stop eating it," she answered.

"Here's your check, sir," the waiter said, placing the white slip of paper on the table. "More salsa or water?"

"Hell, no!" Rake said with a friendly chuckle. "But thank you, man."

"You're welcome," the waiter said. He turned, taking his pitcher of Sadie's salsa with him.

"Can't they tell when you're ready to detonate?" Rake asked.

"It's the only place I know where the waiters walk around with a pitcher of salsa in one hand and a pitcher of water in the other," Aspen said.

"I know. It's great, isn't it?"

Aspen giggled and reached for the tab receipt. As she picked it up, however, Rake's hand covered her own, pressing it to the tabletop.

"What're you doing, girl?" he asked.

Aspen shrugged. "Looking to see how much my tab is."

"It doesn't matter," he said. "I asked you out. It's my tab." The expression on his face was that of pure confusion.

"But I—" she began to argue.

"And if you would have asked me out…it would still be my tab," he interrupted. Rake reached under her hand and pulled the tab receipt out from under it. "There's something you should know about me, Aspen," he said.

Aspen's heart fluttered as the intensity of his smoldering brown eyes bore into her vulnerable green ones.

"What's that?" she asked.

"I'm the kind of man who thinks the guy should pay the restaurant tab, pump the gas, and change the flat tire. Okay?"

Aspen smiled, warmed by his modern chivalry. "Okay."

"Good," he said. He stood, pulling her chair away from the table as she stood. "Ready?" he asked, smiling at her.

"Yeah," she said, delighted as he motioned for her to precede him to the cashier's counter.

An elderly little Hispanic woman still sitting at the table next to theirs reached out, taking hold of Aspen's hand as they passed. "Where can I get one of those, mi hijita?" she asked with a wink.

Aspen smiled and shrugged. She patted the little lady's hand and returned her wink.

"What was that?" Rake asked.

"Couldn't quite understand," Aspen lied.

Rake paid the tab and then took an individually wrapped toothpick and two peppermints from the basket near the cash register. He handed one mint to Aspen as he said, "Let's go for a drive." It was a statement, not a question, and without waiting for her to respond, he added, "I'm running to the men's room first though. Okay?"

"Okay," Aspen said. She knew it was his delicate way of letting her know she might want to take the opportunity to visit the restroom herself. It seemed to Aspen most guys had bladders the size of swimming pools; men could wait for a week before needing to find some facilities! She was impressed he would be so considerate of her. It did cause her to wonder how long of a drive he meant to take her on, however. Still, she felt no warning signals flashing in her brain. Maybe Rake Locker wasn't a serial killer after all.

"I'll meet you back here. Okay?" he asked.

"Okay," Aspen answered.

⁓

The pickup's high beams lit the pavement of the freeway—the only light in the desert save the moon and stars. Aspen couldn't remember the last time she'd ridden with the windows rolled down. It was so invigorating—liberating somehow.

Warm New Mexico autumn nights were the stuff of dreams— perfect in temperature—soothing. The scent of desert sand, cactus, piñon, and sagebrush mingled with the night air. Aspen closed her eyes for a moment, inhaling the dusty perfume of the desert, relishing the feel of the cool breeze on her face.

She didn't know where Rake was heading, only that they were driving west. The city was far behind them, but she wasn't worried. She'd convinced herself that if Rake Locker were a serial killer, her instincts would've told her by now. Of course, he could be some predatory molester! The thought caused Aspen's eyes to widen. She glanced over at Rake. His right hand held the top of the steering wheel while his left arm rested in the open window.

"You've been quiet for a while. What are you thinking about?" he asked, grinning at her.

"I was wondering if maybe you're a serial killer."

His burst of amusement was wonderful! His broad smile and deeply intonated laughter caused Aspen's heart to swell inside her chest. Dang, he was gorgeous!

"A serial killer?" he laughed. "Gee...thanks." He shook his head, still smiling, residual chuckles of mirth echoing low in his throat.

"Well, you know how your mind...weirds out when you're getting to know new people," she explained.

He nodded, chuckled once more, and said, "I can honestly say... I've never once considered that *you* might be a serial killer."

Aspen rolled her eyes and shook her head at her own musings. "I guess I've just watched too many creepy movies."

He laughed again. "Maybe. But in truth, I should be flattered that you didn't ditch me after dinner," he said. He nodded, his eyebrows arching with self-approval. "I guess I didn't freak you out too badly, huh?"

"Not at all," Aspen said. "I'm just...just..."

"Paranoid?" he finished.

"Yeah."

"With a few trust issues thrown in too?"

Aspen's smile faded a bit. Trust issues? What did he mean?

"What do you mean?" she asked.

He shrugged, his smile fading to a grin. "I've had girlfriends, and I've got a sister too. Experience has taught me a lot. And I'm guessing the reason you were thinking you were going to pay for your own dinner is because you've gotten burned by that one before."

"By what one?"

"By a guy paying for a date and expecting you to...pitch in because he did?"

"Pitch in? To pay for the date, you mean?" she asked.

He shrugged and frowned a bit. "I guess 'put out' would be a better way to describe it...though it sounds a little vulgar when I say it to you."

Aspen didn't want to respond. Of course she'd had guys expect what Gina liked to call "favors of affection" after they'd taken her on a date. Still, she was uncomfortable talking to a guy about it. She breathed deeply of the night desert air as she gazed out the open window into the darkness.

"Am I right?" he asked. It was obvious he wasn't about to let her get away with not answering.

"Probably," she admitted.

"Well," he began, "if it eases your mind any…I always pay for my mom and my grandma if I'm out with them. My sister too. So don't worry." Aspen looked back to him. He glanced away from the road for a moment. "And I'm not a serial killer, a rapist, *or* a terrorist," he said. Aspen smiled when he added, "But I am a guy who knows how to show a girl a good time. Don't you think?"

Aspen nodded. "Yeah," she said. It was as if some shower of comfort had instantly rinsed away all her anxieties.

"And now it gets even better," he said. He bumped the turn signal, slowed down, and made an easy right turn.

They were on a dirt road now. Aspen couldn't see anything but the road and an occasional rabbit skittering across it.

"Where are we?" Aspen asked. What could possibly be way out in the middle of nowhere?

"This is where I bring all my victims," Rake said, both hands on the wheel, for the terrain was fairly rugged. His eyes widened, and he added, "This is where I bury them all."

"Now you're making fun of me," Aspen said, smiling at him. The pickup hit a bump, and she grabbed onto the door handle for extra support.

"Well, sure," he admitted. "You accused me of being a serial killer. You deserved it." He chuckled and braked to a stop. Taking the key out of the ignition, he said, "Come on."

Rake opened his pickup door and stepped out. Ducking his head back in the car for a moment—a dazzling smile on his handsome face—he said, "This is one of my favorite places in the world."

Aspen was nervous—torn between trepidation at being so isolated with him and delight for the same reason. Her nerves caused her to pause in getting out of the pickup, and before she knew it, Rake had hurried to her side and now held her door open.

"Come on," he said again. "We have to walk to the top of the hill to see it."

"To see what?" Aspen asked as she stepped down from his pickup.

"Are you kidding me?" he asked. He chuckled and said, "You weren't paying attention to where we were going, were you?"

"It's really dark out here," Aspen said. "We were talking and...I guess not."

"And you were too busy wondering if I was going to murder you," he chuckled.

"I'm sorry," she said. He seemed unaffected, however—seemed not to be too offended by her musings about him.

Rake took hold of Aspen's hand, turned, and began leading her up a fairly steep incline.

"Don't worry about rattlesnakes," he said over his shoulder. "It's too cool for them by now...I think."

"Oh, I'm so very comforted," Aspen nervously giggled as a shiver ran down her spine. Aspen's entire arm seemed to warm from the touch of his hand. He was so strong! She could feel the strength in his arm as he led her up the hill.

"There's nothing like it," Rake said as they reached the crest of the hill. Aspen gasped and smiled, instantly delighted as she stood atop the hill gazing out into the velvet night and the lights of Albuquerque below. "Is there?"

CHAPTER FIVE

Aspen was breathless—suddenly awash with awe and emotion! Oh, she'd always loved viewing the lights of Albuquerque from a distance. Many were the times her family had returned from one of her brother's basketball or football games, heading in from Gallup or some other city west of Albuquerque. Each time her mother would point out the soft glow on the horizon as they approached the city—the twinkling, glistening pool of sparkle in the desert. She'd always loved the lights. Still, never had she seen them from this particular point of view—from such a solitary place. They were magnificent! The sight of Albuquerque's countless jeweled lights along the Rio Grande valley below literally took her breath away.

"I-it's beautiful!" she breathed. "I've seen them so many times—you know, coming in from Gallup—but this is…it's amazing!"

She glanced to Rake. He stood grinning, gazing down into the valley with an expression as awestruck as her own.

"I know. I love it from up here," he said. "I could sit here all night." He looked to her quickly and added, "In fact…wait here."

"What?" Aspen asked as he turned and hurried down the hill toward the pickup. The night was black as pitch, and Aspen shivered, a bit unnerved without him near her. He returned in a few moments, however—carrying two fold-up armchairs under one arm, kindling and wood under the other.

"I come up here to think," he said as he dropped the wood at Aspen's feet. He pulled the protective sleeves off the two fold-up armchairs, unfolded them, and set them side by side. "It's so peaceful," he continued, "nobody to bother you...nobody to want you to do something. Nothing to do but watch the lights and relax."

Aspen smiled. He was too good to be true! A man who would rather sit up on a lonely hill at night and gaze at Albuquerque's diamond lights below, instead of doing the so many other things there were to do for entertainment? How romantic!

"I'll build a fire, and if you get cold, I have blankets behind the seat," he said. Aspen giggled as she watched Rake hurriedly pile the logs and kindling in a circle of rocks that had obviously been used before.

"You've done this a lot, I see," she said. How else could he have led her to just where a rock fire pit had been built, unless he'd built it himself?

"All the time," he said. "And the beauty of it is...my grandpa owns this land, so the state troopers don't bother me too much, even with a fire going." He hunkered down and began to light the fire, glancing up at her and flashing a bright, white, dazzling smile. Any girl with less resistance than Aspen would never be able to tell him no—about anything!

"Go ahead and sit down," he said as he struck a match on the side of his jeans and held it to the kindling. "I'll get you a blanket as soon as this catches." A moment later, the kindling caught fire. Orange and red flames began to lick up around the small logs.

Rake went to the pickup one more time, returning with two fleece blankets. He handed one to Aspen and draped the other over the back of his chair before sitting down.

"Ahhhh!" he sighed, stretching his arms out wide before tucking his hands behind his head. "It doesn't get any better than this."

Aspen sighed, snuggled into the warm cedar-scented fleece, and gazed out across the twinkling valley.

"They say you can see them for a hundred miles from certain angles," she said.

"Oh yeah!" he affirmed. "Though it's more of a glow in the night sky you see that far out. I prefer this...when it looks like some kindergartener knocked over a bottle of iridescent glitter."

Aspen studied him for a moment, delighted by his kindergartener and glitter analogy. Again she was struck by the pure attractiveness of him, and not just his physical magnetism. He had personality—loads and loads of it!

They were silent for long moments—not a sound but the breeze and the soothing coo of a mourning dove somewhere nearby. The lights in the valley below twinkled—winked and sparkled like a fairyland. Aspen shook her head and sighed, overwhelmed by the beauty of it.

"So," Rake began, leaning forward and poking at the fire with a stick, "I've never heard of anyone named Aspen before. Is there a story behind how you got your name?"

Aspen grimaced a little. She was always a little reluctant to tell the story of how she got her name. "Kind of," she admitted.

When she remained silent—didn't elaborate—Rake nodded at her and prodded, "Well?"

Aspen inhaled a deep breath and began, "After my mom got married, she found this poem…'The Time of Aspen Falls.'"

"About a place or something?"

"Kind of," she said. "I always thought there should be a comma or an ellipsis or something to help the title make more sense."

Rake chuckled. "Okay, comma I know, but ellipsis…you're over my head."

"You know…a pause," Aspen explained. "I mean, you thought it was about a place called Aspen Falls, right?"

"Yeah."

"If I say it this way instead—the time of aspen…falls…"

He nodded and said, "Oh, I get it. Like it's time for aspens to…happen."

"Exactly!" Aspen giggled, delighted by his understanding. "So my mom liked this poem—she'd always liked aspens; she grew up in Colorado. Anyway, one day she and my dad were driving up to the Crest, and they pulled over for a picnic. They hiked a ways and found this little grove of aspen, just thriving away on the east side of the mountain. My mom loved that spot. She still goes there a lot when she can. So, when she had me, she named me Aspen, mostly because of the poem she'd always liked…and the aspens themselves."

"Do you know the poem?" he asked.

"Yeah," she answered. She didn't want to tell him about it, however. It was very sentimental, and not everyone appreciated poetry at all—especially sentimental poetry.

Rake settled back in his chair and nodded at her. "Okay, I'm ready."

"For what?" she asked, though she already knew full well what he was ready for.

"To hear the poem you were named after," he said. "Recite away."

"I-I'm not very good at recitation." She was nervous. It was quite a romantic poem as well. "And anyway…it's pretty…sappy."

"Oh, don't be shy," he said. "Here, I'll go first." He cleared his throat and began, "There once was a boy name of Mutt…who sat on a railroad rut." He paused, grinning at Aspen as she giggled. "Do you want me to go on?"

"Of course," she said.

"Very well," he said, trying not to smile. "A big wooden splinter… did break off and enter…his soft little baby-smooth butt."

Aspen rolled her eyes. "I'm guessing you made that one up."

"I did," he chuckled. "Here's another. A nearsighted girl, name of Polly…she liked to eat popcorn, by golly…but sadly misjudged…for her glasses were smudged…and ate up her dear little collie."

Aspen frowned and exclaimed, "Ew!" though she couldn't help but giggle.

"It's a gift," Rake said, smiling. "I challenge you to beat my limericks with a recitation of 'The Time of Aspen Falls.'"

Aspen sighed as her insides began to quiver with nervousness. She hated reciting the poem! It was such a beautiful little collection of verse, and she never did it justice.

"Okay…let me take a breath," she said.

"Is it really that bad?" he chuckled.

"No…it just…here we go." She looked at him and asked, "Are you sure you're ready?"

"It can't be any worse than my limericks, can it?" The warmth of his smile comforted her.

"I hope not," she said. "Okay...here I go."

Aspen gazed out at the beauty of the glistening city below. She inhaled a deep breath of cooling autumn air and closed her eyes. Closing her eyes always helped whenever she was asked to recite the poem. First of all, it filled her mind with visions evoked by the poem—beautiful, romantic scenes that helped her relax. Second, it meant she couldn't see the listener—couldn't see whether they were grimacing or smiling. So, as visions of autumn-leafed trees and the peaceful flow of the river filled her mind's eye, she began.

Like a garland of glass, the river
Meanders on its way,
'Mid trees of scarlet and crimson
Through the valley yon holding sway.

Yet up on the mountain gypsy,
As sweet autumn finds her there,
Lush golden ribbons of aspen
Tie up her pine green hair.

And jewels of rubied leaves,
Of fiery orange and of plum,
Drip from the tips of her fingers
As she summons her lover, "Come!"

For the moon is the gypsy's lover,
And no sight makes the moon shine more
Than her golden ribbons of aspen
And the rubied jewels at her door.

Hark! Winter is coming...
And the time of aspen falls
Like a bridegroom's golden coverlet
As his gypsy lover calls.

"Come, lover!" cried the mountain,
"Oh moon of my autumn heart!
Come fall the aspen upon me…
Lest golden leaves depart.

"Weave me a golden bride's bed
To slumber 'neath 'til spring.
As the time of aspen befalls us,
Lay me on leafy wing."

So the moon spread wide his moonbeams,
As the breadth of her lover's arms,
And he bound her there within them
Safe from bleak winter's harms.

"Fear not, my gypsy lover,
For the time of aspen falls!
And as ribbons of gold clasp the pines
So my heart into yours enthralls."

Then the moon breathed a breath of autumn,
And the leaves of the aspen fell
And covered the mountain golden
From the peak to the low chaparral.

"Hold fast, my lover," said Moon.
"I'll keep you from winter's cold
In the time of aspen falling
'Neath a blanket of aspen gold."

Oh, Moon loves his gypsy mountain,
And the gypsy loves her moon.
As the aspen rained leaves upon them…
They bid autumn gone too soon.

Hence, the time of aspen befell them,
And winter's descending was near,
So the moon wove his fingers of moonbeams
Through the gold amidst mountain's hair.

Thus, ever the moon keeps his gypsy
As winter's white snow swathe sprawls,
And the moon and mountain blend kisses
As the Time of Aspen Falls.

As her mind's visions of the autumn lovers faded, Aspen sighed a deep, relieved breath. She'd finished! She'd made it through reciting the poem without one stammer. With great trepidation, she opened her eyes to see Rake staring at her, a slight frown puckering his brow. He'd hated it! She'd known he would. What man in the world could appreciate such a sappy poem?

"Wow!" he mumbled. His eyebrows arched, and a complimentary whistle escaped his lips. "Remind me not to recite any more of my stupid limericks to you."

She felt better, but only a little. "I warned you it was sappy."

"It was great!" he exclaimed, his face suddenly alight with a smile. "It made me want to…to, like…lick your face or something!"

"What?" Aspen asked with a delighted giggle. Sure, it was a very strange thing to say. Yet it thrilled her somehow all the same.

"You know what I mean," he continued. "It's like…I'm wanting to eat chocolate cake…or pumpkin pie or something. I can't explain it."

Aspen shook her head, confused by his reaction. "You don't think it's too sappy?"

"Sure, it's sappy!" he exclaimed. "It's poetry. Poetry is supposed to be sappy. Besides…it's about trees. What's a tree without a little sap?"

Aspen giggled. She knew he was only being nice—trying to lull her into being comfortable again after reciting such a syrupy poem.

"Do that one part again," he said. "That one part about his fingers. That part is so visual."

"You're mocking me," Aspen said, though she was not angry with him.

"No," he assured her. "I liked that part. Do it again."

"What's in it for me?" she asked. "Other than further humiliation?"

He chuckled and then seemed thoughtful for a moment. "I've got a Snickers bar in the jockey box of the pickup?"

Aspen smiled. He was too charming—too adorable!

"Are you really willing to make that serious of a sacrifice for it?" she teased.

"Yep!" he said. "But you have to do two stanzas...not just the one."

Aspen felt her eyebrows arch with approval. "Stanzas, huh?"

"Yep. Two of them."

"Okay," she said. She'd watch him this time—keep her eyes open and watch his reaction. "'Hence, the time of aspen befell them,'" she began, "'And winter's descending was near, so the moon wove his fingers of moonbeams through the gold amidst mountain's hair. Thus, ever the moon keeps his gypsy as winter's white snow swathe sprawls, and the moon and mountain blend kisses...as the time of aspen falls.'"

An approving, pleased grin spread across his handsome face, and he nodded. "I like it," he said. "I see why your mom named you Aspen. I'm guessing your mom's a diehard romantic."

"Yeah, she is."

"And I'm assuming, from your perfect recitation, that it runs in the family."

"Maybe," Aspen said, returning his smile.

"Do you want your Snickers now or later?"

"Later will be fine," Aspen told him. She didn't want him to leave— not even for the minute or two it would take him to run down to the pickup and get the candy bar out of the glove compartment.

"Okay," he said. She watched as his gaze fell to the city lights below once more.

"But now...I think it's my turn," she began. "Rake. That's an unusual name too. Does *your* name have a story behind it? Or did your mother have a premonition that it would come to describe you as you grew up?"

He chuckled. "It figures a poem-reciting, book-reading babe would think I was named after some rascal in a scandalous romance novel." He looked at her, smiling. "That's what you're thinking, isn't it? Rakish? Rogue? Scoundrel?"

Aspen giggled, remembering the day she'd met him in the clock shop—the way she'd come up with as many synonyms for his name as she could.

"Well?" she prodded. "Is that it?"

He shook his head, smiling and slightly rolling his eyes. "Actually, yes."

"Are you kidding me?" Aspen giggled.

"Nope. Though I usually don't admit it." His smile broadened, and she fancied his cheeks were a little redder than a moment before. "I usually tell people my mom tripped over a lawn rake when she was pregnant with me and was inspired by the incident to name me Rake."

Aspen laughed, feeling oddly free and happy. "Well…the real story is more romantic."

"You *would* think so," he said. "But when you're seven and your second-grade teacher gives you an assignment called 'How I Got My Name,' you pause in telling the truth of it. So my mom tripped over a rake, and that's how I got my name."

"Though in truth…you're secretly a dashing hero from some cliché romance novel," Aspen teased. How delicious! How delicious that he looked exactly the part. Aspen owned a secret of her own—though she was very selective, she loved romance novels! Not the smutty ones— not just Jane Austen either—but the others she deemed worthy of her time.

"That's right," he said. "Do you want me to prove it to you?"

He already looked like some fictional man—so handsome, well-built, and charming. Furthermore, his personality surpassed any fiction! So what exactly did he mean by asking her if she wanted him to prove it? She was wildly intrigued. "You can prove you're a romance novel hero?" she asked. Her insides were all atwitter!

"Yep," he said. "Do you want action or verbiage?"

"What?"

"Action or verbiage?" he repeated. "I can either act the part or speak the part. Which one do you want?"

Aspen felt a quiver of butterflies take flight in her stomach. Goose bumps broke over her arms, though she tried to rationalize it was the cooling breeze causing them. Every inch of her being—every shred of her flesh—wanted most for him to act the part. Yet it was their first date.

"Well, I did recite for you," she said. "So let's go with verbiage."

He said nothing—only continued to look at her. He seemed rather pensive for a moment. Then, as a grin of pure mischief spread across his gorgeous face, his eyes narrowed—smoldered as he looked at her.

"Old-fashioned romantic...or insinuative?" he asked.

Her first reaction was to respond old-fashioned. Yet some sort of flaw in her nature—an impish flaw—responded far too truthfully.

"Not old-fashioned. I just did that with my poem," she said.

"Okay then," he said.

Though Aspen thought it impossible, the mischievous, alluring expression on his face deepened. She shivered slightly as the smoldering look in his eyes turned to that of near seduction.

He leaned forward, taking her hand in his—caressing the soft, sensitive underside of her wrist with his thumb.

"Hey, Aspen?" he began. Her heart leapt as he bent and blew softly on the place his thumb had been caressing. "Now that you know my name..." She nearly melted as he blew on her wrist once more, lightly touching it with the tip of his tongue. "And now that I know yours..." His voice was low, alluring—seductive. Aspen was besieged by goose bumps. "I just thought I'd let you know...that I'd sure like to rake your leaves sometime."

"Oh my heck!" Aspen breathed. Her heart was near to fibrillation! Her mouth was watering, her insides trembling.

He released her hand, sat back in his chair, and said, "Stick that in your pipe and smoke it, poem girl."

"Oh, you're good. I'll give you that," Aspen said.

He shook his head, still smiling. "I'm just glad you picked insinuative instead of old-fashioned. I couldn't think of anything old-fashioned." His eyes narrowed, and his smile broadened. "But I've been thinking of that one since the minute I found out what your name is."

She was delighted! Elated! Ecstatic! Still, she couldn't let him know how ecstatic.

"Well, I suppose both our names lend themselves to teasing," she said.

"Who said I was teasing?"

"You're trouble," she said, smiling at him. Yep. He was the kind of guy she'd learned to avoid—handsome, charming, flirtatious, and dangerous because of it.

"Trouble?" he asked with a chuckle. "Why, Aspen…I take offense. I only meant I'd like to run my fingers through that soft brown hair of yours."

Aspen smiled. Oh, he was rascally!

"Rake Locker," she began, "the ex-bull-riding, wild-cow-milking watchmaker."

"Watchmaker. Hmm…it doesn't sound so bad when you say it like that," he said, returning his attention to the twinkling lights in the valley below them. "Aspen Falls—the book-selling, poem-reciting arachnophobe."

She knew he meant to tease her, but somehow she felt ridiculous. A quick vision of how stupid she must've looked—fainting right there in the park—popped into her head.

"Mine about you was way better," Aspen said.

"Of course it was," he said. "That's the secret I try to hide from the world."

"What is?"

"That I can come up with one flirtatious insinuation…but it empties my cleverness cup for the rest of the day."

Aspen giggled. "That's okay. The one clever line was a zinger."

"Well, I thought so," he said. He was quiet for a moment and inhaled a deep breath. "So tell me about your friend," he began, "the one from the park and the rodeo."

In truth, she'd just been thinking about Gina—imagining her

reaction when she repeated Rake's leaves raking line. She'd tumble right out of Old Goldie for sure!

"Her name is Gina," Aspen began. "We've been friends forever, she's hilarious…and she has this weird fixation with UPS guys."

He smiled. "Does she have one?"

"One what?"

"A UPS guy?"

"Not yet. Why?" Aspen's suspicion suddenly rose. Why was he so interested in Gina? Probably because she was so drop-dead gorgeous and a better physical match for the likes of Rake Locker. Still, she tried not to think along those lines. Perhaps he was just curious—getting to know Aspen better by finding out about her friends.

He shrugged. "I was just curious. I figured you guys were longtime friends…being she knew exactly what seeing that spider was going to do to you." Before Aspen could respond, he added, "Hey, check it out! I think you can see the midway on the fairgrounds from here. See?"

Aspen looked in the direction he pointed. It was true! The lights from the midway rides at the state fair were bright and colorful, standing out with obvious brilliance amid all the others.

"Oh, yeah," she said. "How cool!"

"I can't do the midway anymore," Rake sighed. "Used to love it. But about three years ago, I rode the Tilt-a-Whirl with my sister and totally launched the minute we got off. We all call it the 'Tilt-a-Hurl' now. Guess I'm getting old."

"But a bull ride doesn't bother you?" Aspen asked. He was so communicative! It was amazing.

"Nope," he answered. "But of course that's, like, eight to ten seconds…not three or four minutes."

"Good point," Aspen said.

"Man, I love it up here," he breathed.

Aspen studied him for a moment. What a nice guy! Or so it seemed. Surely he would show his true egotistical colors at some point. Still, for the moment, Aspen was determined to enjoy his company.

She looked out across the valley to the luminous string of pearls— the streetlights for Albuquerque's main thoroughfares. Crickets began chirping nearby, a rabbit skittered near the fire, and the scent of piñon and sagebrush enveloped the night like a soothing autumn cloak.

"Do you like piñons?" Rake asked.

"Of course!" Aspen answered. Aspen had never known anybody native to New Mexico who didn't crave the little brown seeds. Dropped by piñon trees, piñon nuts were a favorite treat to New Mexicans. Aspen had heard on the radio that a bumper crop of piñons was expected.

"We should go pick some," Rake said.

"Kind of hard in the dark," Aspen giggled.

"I mean in the daytime," he explained. "There are some good trees up here, but we could drive up between Santa Fe and Las Vegas where there are more. There are a ton up there, especially if you're willing to walk a ways away from the freeway."

Aspen smiled and felt a thrill of delight travel up her spine. He was asking her out again—sort of.

"We should," she said. "I love picking piñons."

"Me too," he said, smiling at her. "We'll go do it…soon."

Aspen sighed as Rake turned his gaze from her to the lights once more. What a night! Dinner had been wonderful—the drive west with him had been wonderful—the lights were wonderful—*he* was wonderful!

Aspen inhaled deeply the scent of burning cedar in the fire. As the lights of Albuquerque blinked and winked, she smiled, wrapped the fleece blanket more snuggly around her shoulders, and snuggled down into her chair. In that moment, she decided she could linger there forever, refreshed by the autumn air, poised above the beautiful city lights—with only the incredible Rake Locker for company.

She glanced at him when she heard him softly chuckle. "What?" she asked.

"You've got to admit it was pretty funny," he said. He chuckled again, his eyes smiling with the rest of his face as he said, "Aspen? Rake your leaves sometime?"

Aspen giggled. It was clever! And she adored the goose bumps rippling over her body at the memory of his tasting her wrist.

Yep! Gina would drop right out of that old tree—just like an overripe apple.

※

Rake opened the passenger's side door. Aspen was tired, yet she didn't want the evening—rather, morning—to end. Still, she stepped out of the pickup and into the first soft rays of a pink sunrise.

"What time do you have to be at work?" Rake asked as he walked with Aspen up the sidewalk toward her apartment.

"I'm off today. Just meeting my friend at noon," Aspen answered, fighting a yawn.

"Good," he said. "That gives you almost eight hours to recover so I won't feel too bad about keeping you out so late."

Aspen was tired. She couldn't remember the last time she'd been awake for twenty hours straight. Yet Rake Locker—he was so worth it!

"How about you?" she asked, fighting another yawn.

"I'm off too," he said. "I've got some things to do today…but they can wait. I'm not as young as I used to be, you know. I need a little more sleep than you pretty young things."

Aspen giggled. She couldn't believe she'd stayed out all night with him. She couldn't believe they'd spent almost nine hours sitting out in the middle of nowhere just talking.

As they reached the door to her apartment, Aspen said, "Thanks for dinner…and for taking me to see the lights."

"You're welcome," he said. A delicious grin of mischief spread across his handsome face. "Are you convinced now?"

"Convinced of what?" she asked. Convinced he was fabulous? Convinced he was too good to be true? Convinced she would be praying every night for him to ask her out again? Of course!

"Convinced that I'm not a serial killer."

"Well, considering that west of the city would be the perfect place to dump a body…and that I'm still here…I guess you're not one after all." She smiled as he chuckled.

"And are you convinced that I'm not going to expect favores especiales from you…just because I paid for dinner?" He winked at her, and part of her wished he would expect her to kiss him goodnight as compensation for paying for their dinner. She liked the way the Spanish phrase in the sentence rolled off his tongue, as if he hadn't even realized he'd blended two languages.

"Yes," she giggled, blushing.

"I mean, I even gave you my Snickers bar for breakfast...so I hope I've proven myself a gentleman."

"I think you have, Mr. Locker. And I thank you for that, as well as a wonderful time."

"Thank *you*, Miss Aspen Falls." He reached out, brushing a stray strand of hair from her forehead. Goose bumps, the likes Aspen had never experienced, raced over her arms and legs. She almost reached up and took his face between her hands—almost raised herself on her tiptoes—almost kissed him square on the mouth!

Disappointment washed over her as he said, "I'll see you later then."

"Okay," she said.

With one last dazzling smile, he turned and started to walk away.

Aspen felt her heart swell—felt fresh goose bumps ripple over her arms—as he turned back around and said, "Actually, Aspen...I never have been much of a gentleman."

Aspen gasped as he reached out and slipped both powerful hands around her neck, pulling her to him and pressing his lips to hers. It wasn't a long kiss, nor was it overly intimate, but it was the best kiss Aspen had ever experienced! Too brief it may have been, but it was confidently applied and absolutely thrilling. It left her breathless, tingling, with mouth agape.

"I'll see you soon," he said.

Aspen watched as he strode to his pickup, feeling as if she'd never be the same again.

CHAPTER SIX

"You recited the poem to him?" Gina asked.

"I did," Aspen said.

"And he sat still for it? Was he snoring by the time you finished? I mean, *I* love that poem…but a wild-cow-milking hottie like that?"

"An ex-bull-riding, wild-cow-milking, watchmaking hottie," Aspen corrected.

"Well, excuse me!" Gina exclaimed with a giggle.

"And you were right," Aspen began. "He didn't turn out to be a serial killer…yet."

"Yet? What the heck, Aspen? You seem determined to find a serious character flaw in this guy."

Aspen shrugged. "I know. It's just that…you know what they say. If something looks too good to be true, then it probably is."

"Probably is a lot different than definitely, Aspen," Gina said. "Take me for instance."

Aspen smiled. Any time Gina began a sentence with "take me for instance"—well, humor was sure to follow shortly—and usually unintended.

"I know that my Prince Charming will show up someday," she said. "I know he will."

"Dressed in warm chocolate-brown and holding a package," Aspen added.

"Exactly," Gina affirmed. "And when he does, I'm not gonna waste my time waiting for his flaws to show up! He'll have them, no doubt.

Everybody does. The trick is finding a person whose flaws don't drive you crazy—you know, someone whose flaws you can live with…someone who can stand your flaws too." Gina plucked an apple from Old Goldie's branches, rubbed it on the front of her shirt, and took a bite.

"You're right. I know you're right," Aspen sighed.

"I'm always right." Gina munched on her apple in verbal silence for a moment—but only for a moment. "I mean, let's analyze it. What were some things that *weren't* perfect about your date with him? Nothing's perfect…not in this whole world. Tell me what you would've deleted if last night were a movie and you could cut some parts out."

Aspen frowned. "I was really nervous for the first half an hour," she said.

"Good. Okay…nerves. Now what else?"

"He's eye candy…that's for sure. You should see the women stare at him." Aspen felt a wave of indignant jealousy well up in her at the memory of the many sets of female eyes that had lingered on Rake at the restaurant.

"Okay. Nosey she-skanks ogling your man. What else?"

"He kissed me…on the first date," Aspen ventured. "You know I don't go for that."

"Yeah…but you liked it, and it was a great kiss," Gina reminded. "He probably read your pheromones and knew it would be okay."

"Pheromones? Humans don't have pheromones," Aspen giggled.

"So he read your body language then." Gina smiled. "Or he read your mind and knew you were thinking, 'Kiss me, you gorgeous hunk of honey lusciousness!'"

Aspen laughed. "I swear, Gina, you're all talk when it comes to dating! I'm going to put an ad in the paper. Single woman obsessed with UPS men seeks—"

"No, no, no!" Gina interrupted. "It has to happen naturally. Someday, I'll open the door, and he'll be standing there. 'Sign here, ma'am,' he'll say…and I'll say, 'I do!'"

Both girls giggled—laughed until their backs ached. Still, as their laughter subsided, Aspen noticed a veiled shadow of heartache pass over Gina's eyes for a moment, and Aspen hated Nick Dalley all over again. Sure, it had been almost two years since he'd broken up with Gina, but Gina still endured horrible heartache over the loss. Aspen knew the whole UPS man thing—though based on Gina's lifelong infatuation with UPS men—was really just a way to keep everyone from pushing her into a normal dating life.

"You're a total hypocrite, you know," Aspen said.

"You mean because I'm telling you to go for it with this Rake guy while I'm sitting at home avoiding every man on earth?"

"Exactly," Aspen confirmed.

Gina nodded and took another bite of her apple. "I know. I really do know," she admitted. "But...but I just don't think I can go through that again."

"Maybe you won't have to. Maybe the next UPS guy to ask you out will be the one...and you'll marry him and live happily ever after."

"I was at my mom's house the other day," Gina began, "and the doorbell rang, and I answered it. The most gorgeous UPS guy you ever saw in your life was standing on the other side of the door. He wasn't wearing a wedding ring. The name on his shirt said Sean...and for one brief moment, I thought, 'I oughta take hold of this guy's collar and just kiss him right on the mouth.' You know, get it out of my system... kiss a UPS guy and finally kiss Nick good-bye for good at the same time."

"Why didn't you?"

Gina frowned. "Are you kidding? A total stranger? He might have had some gross lip disease or something."

"Now you sound like me—wondering if Rake would turn out to be a serial killer."

Gina wagged an index finger at Aspen and said, "Statistically, there's a bigger chance the UPS guy might have a lip fungus than there is of Rake's being a serial killer."

"Statistically?"

"Yeah. I think I read that somewhere," Gina said. Her eyes smiled with mischief.

"Well, usually a doctor can clear up a lip fungus...but he can't sew all your parts back together once you've been murdered and dismembered," Aspen said.

"True." Gina giggled, tossing her apple core to the ground. "Well... maybe next time I'm at my mom's and the UPS guy rings the doorbell... maybe I'll just bust out of my shell and lay one on him."

"You'd feel better," Aspen said. "I know you would. It would be, like, so liberating for you."

"Okay," Gina said—resolved. "I'll do it."

"Promise."

"Of course!"

Aspen knew Gina had no intention of following through with her plan to hit on the UPS man. It was just a deliberation to distract her from her broken heart. Aspen's own doubts returned then too.

"What if he doesn't ever ask me out again?" she asked. She'd been worrying all morning—all morning as she tried to sleep, tried to get some rest to make up for staying up all night. All morning she'd wondered if she'd been enough fun to be with—if she'd been interesting enough for Rake to consider asking out again. Still, he'd implied he would take her piñon picking. Surely he wouldn't have suggested it unless he liked her enough to spend the day searching through the wilderness for the small brown seeds with her.

"Oh, he will," Gina told her. "A guy doesn't take a girl on a twelve-hour, scandalous, all-night date and not ask her out again. Just be positive! Positive thinking—that's the whole key. Anyway...didn't he say he wanted to rake your leaves sometime?"

Aspen giggled. "He was teasing, Gina." Still, the memory of Rake's flirtatious comment caused her arms to prickle a bit with goose bumps.

"Are you so sure about that?" Gina asked, her brows arching in a daring expression.

"Yes," Aspen said. "But just for you...I'll keep myself thinking positive for the rest of the day."

Gina nodded and smiled. "Good. Oh! I almost forgot to tell you," Gina began, "I did take an early lunch on Monday...so I can help you with your event for sure."

"Oh, man!" Aspen whined. "I forgot all about that!"

Aspen dreaded certain kinds of book release events at the store. Some were fun, and some definitely weren't. The one scheduled for Monday—the *Willamina Dog in the Wobbly Wood* event—was definitely not on her fun list.

"How did you get stuck wearing the costume anyway?" Gina asked.

"I volunteered," Aspen grumbled. "Actually, I wanted the Fourth of July off. Remember? And in a moment of desperate insanity, I switched with Erlinda. She did the Fourth of July punch table, and I agreed to do the Willamina Dog event."

"Well, that'll teach you," Gina said, smiling.

"No kidding."

"What do you need me to do?"

"Just help me keep the kids settled down when I read the book to them," Aspen explained. "I can do the rest."

"Okay. I'll be there."

Aspen smiled at her friend. "Thanks," she said. Gina was a treasure. Aspen couldn't imagine her life without Gina—her confidant—her once-in-a-lifetime friend.

❧

Aspen yawned and pressed the off button on the remote. She glanced up at the wall, rolling her eyes when she remembered her Uncle Guy's clock was still at the Clock Shop. With a tired sigh, she leaned forward and picked her cell phone up off the coffee table.

"Only seven thirty?" she groaned. It felt so much later. Of course, she *had* been up the entire night before. It was no wonder she was so tired.

She and Gina had spent almost three hours in the branches of the old apple tree. Although Aspen enjoyed the time with her friend, combined with such sleep deprivation, it had worn her to a great fatigue.

"I can't believe I'm going to bed at seven thirty," she yawned. Struggling to her feet, Aspen went to the kitchen and turned off the stove. She removed the pan of boiling apples and cinnamon she'd been simmering to scent the apartment, inhaling one last delicious, aromatic whiff of the fragrant steam. Aspen checked the front door to make sure it was locked and then headed to her bedroom.

There, amid a décor comprising warm autumn colors—of muted gold sheets, a soft brown suede comforter, and throw pillows in a leaf motif—Aspen drifted off to sleep. Her dreams were of cool autumn nights, the beautiful lights of Albuquerque viewed from atop a mesa, and the dazzling smile of a handsome master watchmaker.

❧

"You look adorable!" Gina giggled.

Aspen sneered at her friend. Narrowing her eyes with annoyance, she said, "I look ridiculous, and you know it!"

"Not to these kids," Gina said. She nodded in the direction of the group of children starting to gather in the children's section of the store.

Aspen smiled and waved to a little girl sitting at one of the child-sized reading tables nearby.

"Hi, Willamina," the little girl giggled.

"Hi!" Aspen responded. She was a darling little dark-haired girl.

"Mommy! Willamina waved to me, Mommy! And she said hi! She said hi to me, Mommy! To me!" the little girl exclaimed to the woman sitting next to her.

Suddenly, Aspen didn't feel quite so ridiculous being dressed in a large pink dog costume.

Adjusting the paw mittens of the costume, Aspen turned to look at herself in the full-length mirror on the wall near the children's height chart.

"I guess it's not so bad," she said.

"It's cute!" Gina exclaimed. "Besides…what would you rather be? A giant pink dog with yellow spots and a big rear end, all happy and adorable…or an ugly old toad in a witch hat like last fall when *Mrs. Toad's Halloween Stew* hit the shelves?"

"Good point," Aspen said. She smiled, fluffed the long yellow ringlets boinging down from the costume's head, and inhaled a breath of resolve. "After all, you're right. It could be worse."

"And the kids love Willamina stories!" Gina giggled as she studied

Aspen for a moment. "Just be glad your honey sugar buns, Mr. Rake Locker, doesn't!"

"No kidding! The spider thing was bad enough," Aspen said. "He'd hightail it away from me as fast as he could if he got a load of me in this outfit!"

"Still," Gina began, "there is a certain voluptuousness about this look...especially on you."

"It just screams sophistication...doesn't it?" Aspen giggled. She looked at herself in the mirror once more and studied her new pink pear-shape, the long tail curling up from her outsized behind, and the big pink padded feet of the costume. It was hilarious!

She shook her head, feeling suddenly lighthearted and carefree. Children did love Willamina. She should be proud to wear the pink-and-yellow Willamina Dog costume—proud of the large floppy ears and yellow boinging ringlets framing her face.

"Boys and girls," Gina began, "are you ready for Willamina's new adventure?"

The cheers and clapping of the thirty or so small children sitting here and there in the children's section was almost deafening.

"Wonderful! Then let's give Willamina all our attention while she tells us about it. Okay?"

"Okay!" rose the shrill song of unified young voices.

Aspen skipped up to the little storytelling platform nearby. As the children clapped and called to her, she smiled, waving and blowing kisses to the tiny members of the audience.

"Good afternoon, girls and boys!" she called.

"Good afternoon, Willamina!" the children called in answer.

"Boy, oh, boy, did I have an adventure this week! I visited the Wobbly Wood!"

"Yay!" the children shouted.

"Shall I tell you all about it?" Aspen asked.

"Yay!" the children shouted again.

Gina winked at Aspen with encouragement as Aspen awkwardly sat down on the platform. She picked up the nearby copy of *Willamina Dog and the Wobbly Wood* and opened it.

89

"*Once upon a time,*" she began to read aloud, "*there was a pretty pink dog with lovely golden locks.*"

The children giggled, and their mothers tried to settle them down.

Aspen giggled, the delight of the children having spilled over onto her. She did love her job! Oh, maybe she didn't like wearing the uncomfortable and sometimes ridiculous costumes, but she did love working at the bookstore.

"*Her name was Willamina…and Willamina loved adventure,*" Aspen continued. She glanced up to see Gina grinning at her—entirely amused, entirely delighted, or maybe both. Either way, it buoyed her confidence, and she began to enjoy the read.

❦

Twenty minutes later, as the children flittered around among the books and tables in the children's section, Aspen breathed a sigh of relief as Gina approached her, applauding.

"You made it!" she said. "And it's a cute story too."

"Yeah. And at least I can take this costume off. I'm sweltering!" Aspen complained in a whisper.

"Aspen," Michael, the assistant store manager, said. He appeared suddenly, as if he'd just popped up out of nowhere. It was his habit, and it drove Aspen crazy. "The lighted village is out."

"Is it plugged in?" Aspen asked.

Michael was arrogant and lazy. He never lifted a finger—always delegated every task to someone else.

"I don't know," he said. "Why don't you crawl under the table and find out."

Aspen saw Gina open her mouth to speak but jabbed an elbow in her friend's ribs to silence her. No doubt Gina had a witty or cutting response to Michael's demands. But this was not the time.

"Okay, I will," Aspen said.

"And leave the dog suit on for a few more minutes. It'll help sales," he added. He turned on his effeminate heels and walked away.

"How can you stand that guy?" Gina asked. "He's such a jerk…not to mention he's more girlie than I am."

"I know," Aspen grumbled. "He drives me crazy. But he also

determines my schedule. I don't want to tick him off." She turned toward the display table. "Come on," she said to Gina. "I might need a little help."

"That guy needs a few shots of testosterone," Gina mumbled under her breath. "What I wouldn't give for one good Marlboro Man."

As Aspen approached the little village display table in the corner, it was indeed to see the buildings were not lit up. The train wasn't running around the track either.

"Somebody probably tripped on the cord and unplugged it," she said.

"It's so cute!" Gina exclaimed.

"It is, huh?" Aspen agreed.

The village always made her smile. Little porcelain houses lined the cobblestone streets on one end of the table, while small porcelain shops and stores lined the ones at the other end. Miniature autumn trees lined the streets as well, adding splashes of orange and yellow color to the backyards of the buildings. A little replica steam engine usually chugged about the perimeter, and a tiny sound effects speaker hidden beneath one of the buildings played soft, town-type noises—children playing, shop doors opening, footsteps on cobblestone. It was simply a magical little display.

"It's just like those Christmas villages you see in all the windows of those fancy stores at Christmastime!" Gina exclaimed.

"All these pieces are made by the same company that makes those. It's their autumn collection," Aspen said. She dropped to her knees and lifted the table skirt. Peering beneath the table, she said, "Yep! It's unplugged in the back here." She began to squirm beneath the table, but when the big pink tail of her Willamina costume got caught up on the table skirt, she paused. "Michael is such a jerk," she said. "This would've been so much easier for him to do. Will you hold up the table skirt for me, please, Gina?"

Gina nodded and lifted the skirt as Aspen, now on all fours, crawled under the table. Gina giggled, amused by the sight of Aspen's large pink doggy bum and curly doggy tail wagging this way and that as she struggled to illuminate the village.

"Have you got it?" she asked, trying not to giggle out loud.

"It's all tangled up," Aspen said. "Just a second. I'll get it."

Gina giggled just a little—resisted the urge to pat Aspen on the big pink bum. She glanced up, curious to see if any of the customers were privy to the same amusing view of her best friend as she was—gasping when she saw none other than the handsome Rake Locker striding toward them.

"Oh, no!" she breathed. The spider incident in the park would seem trivial compared with what would be unavoidable in the next split second. Gina knew Aspen would rather faint in Rake's arms because of a spider than have him see her in the Willamina Dog costume.

She looked down at Aspen's pink bum and tail. Maybe the table skirt was long enough to cover her. Yet if she tried to drop the table skirt over the costume's large bum and there wasn't enough fabric to allow for the give, then the village might come crashing down around them. Which was worse—wrecking the store's no doubt expensive porcelain building or letting Rake Locker find Aspen dressed up like a pink dog and scrounging around under a table?

Gina gulped as Rake walked up to her, a knowing smile spreading across his handsome face as he glanced down at the big pink doggy bum and tail sticking out from under the table.

"What's up?" he greeted. "Gina...right?"

"Yeah," Gina said. She felt her own cheeks turn crimson with an embarrassed blush—empathy for her best friend.

"I've just...about...just about...oh! It's so tangled up under here," Aspen complained from underneath the table.

Rake's smiled broadened. He pointed to the big pink doggy bum and tail. "Aspen?" he asked.

Gina bit her lip, winced, blushed a deeper shade of crimson, and nodded.

Rake wanted to laugh. He wanted to roar! What were the odds that he would be so lucky as to come upon Aspen in such an adorably ridiculous situation? He watched the pink rear end of the costume she was wearing wiggle back and forth as she struggled with whatever she was struggling with beneath the table. The big pink tail attached to the costume bobbed back and forth too.

Pointing to Aspen's rear end, he asked her friend, "Pig?"

"Big pink dog," the pretty girl named Gina answered.

"I can't get the cord to reach the outlet!" Aspen grumbled from beneath the table. "How did this happen? And it's hotter than heck under here!"

"Long day, huh?" Rake chuckled quietly.

"Oh, yeah," Gina answered, nodding.

He couldn't resist then—he had to do it. He had to! He couldn't restrain himself another moment. Reaching out, he took hold of the wagging pink tail. He tugged on it twice, chuckling when a pink paw reached back from under the table and pulled the tail out of his hand.

"Gina!" Aspen scolded. "This is hard enough without your teasing."

Rake took hold of Aspen's tail again, tugged a little harder, and said, "Um…excuse me…miss?"

He grimaced when he heard Aspen's head hit the underside of the table. The tail and big pink rear end stopped moving—cold-stone still for a moment. He laughed in his throat, completely amused as he watched Aspen slowly back out from under the table. As she turned to face him and rolled over to sit down on the big pink doggy bum, he struggled not to laugh. She was adorable! Dressed head to toe in a pink dog costume, complete with yellow hair and big floppy ears—well, he was glad the costume was the kind that had the ears and hair attached to a sort of face-fitting hood—for the expression on her pretty little face was priceless!

"Hello," Aspen said. Rake Locker? She wanted to curl up and die! How long had he been standing there? Why hadn't Gina warned her? She quickly glanced at Gina, who wore an expression of complete empathy. Gina shrugged her shoulders and shook her head. No doubt Gina had been as surprised as Aspen at seeing Rake—just not as humiliated.

"Hi," Rake greeted. The mirth and amusement in his eyes were obvious. His shoulders bounced for a moment as a low chuckle danced inside his broad chest.

He offered his hand to her, and she placed a pink paw mitten in it. He pulled her to her feet, and she brushed a yellow ringlet away from her cheek. His smile only broadened as he studied her from head to toe.

"It-it's the premier of *Willamina Dog and the Wobbly Wood* today," she explained.

"Oh, that's what I figured," he said, still smiling at her, his gorgeous eyes still alight with amusement.

Aspen brushed away another yellow ringlet, certain her face was at least the same color as her costume by now. The blush on her cheeks was almost painful!

She placed her hands at her waist, attempting to look as casual and sophisticated as possible. "What can I do for you?"

Rake seemed to be fighting to keep from laughing. And why shouldn't he? She looked ridiculous!

"I came to tell you your clock is ready," he answered.

"Oh," Aspen said. She nodded and added, "That's great."

"Yeah. You can pick it up anytime."

"Well…that's…that's…thank you," she stammered. "I'll pick it up as soon as I can."

"That's Willamina Dog you're talkin' to, mister."

Aspen looked down to see a little girl tugging on one leg of Rake's jeans. Her blush deepened. Yet she found herself smiling as she watched Rake hunker down and smile at the child.

"Is it?" he asked. "Well, do you think she's like other dogs? Do you think she likes to have her tummy rubbed?"

The little girl nodded, and Aspen was certain she would die—certain of it!

"And behind her ears too!" the little girl suggested. "It says so right in the book!"

"It does?" Rake asked as the little girl reached down and picked up a copy of *Willamina Dog and the Wobbly Wood* lying on the floor at her feet.

"Yes! See…it's right here," the little girl said. Aspen watched as the little girl opened the book and pointed to an illustration on one page. "Read it, mister." The little girl pointed to a section of text. "Right here…see? Read right here."

"Okay," Rake chuckled. "Let's see." He began reading aloud. "*For everyone in the whole Wobbly Wood…knew Willamina Dog just never could…resist a good, long scratchily scratch…behind her ears, on her tummy patch…or under her chin or over her nose…on the top of her head or between her toes.*"

"See there? I told you!" the little girl exclaimed.

"Rosa!" a woman exclaimed. Aspen sighed, relieved to see a woman rush over and take hold of the little girl's hand. "You scared me, mi hija! Don't run off like that!" The woman looked to Rake, her expression instantly changing to that of extreme approval. "I'm so sorry. She's just so excited about the new book."

"Oh, that's fine," Rake said, standing. "It looks like a really good one."

"You keep that one, mister," the little girl said. "I already got one."

"Thanks," Rake said.

"Again, I'm so sorry," the little girl's mother said, blushing as she looked at Rake.

"What are you—shredded wheat?" Gina whispered to Aspen. "You'd think you were invisible. She totally ignored you!"

"I told you," Aspen whispered back. "Eye candy for women…that's all he is."

"'Bye, Willamina!" the little girl called over her shoulder as her mother led her away.

"Bye-bye!" Aspen said, tossing a friendly paw-wave to the little angel.

"*Willamina Dog and the Wobbly Wood,*" Rake read as he looked at the front of the book. "And she likes to have her tummy rubbed."

"Apparently," Aspen said, reaching for the book.

Rake quickly moved it above his head and out of her reach, however. "I've got a niece who might like to read about Willamina," he said.

"It's a good book," Gina interjected. "Kids really seem to like it."

"I can see why," he said, studying Aspen from head to toe. His smile broadened again.

"You're still on the clock, Aspen," Michael said, appearing seemingly from nowhere again. "And that village still isn't lit up." He glared at Gina and quickly assessed Rake. "Talk to your friends on your own time."

"Oh, I'm not her friend," Rake said. "I'm just her boy toy."

Aspen's teeth nearly dropped out of her head.

"Oh," Michael said. He frowned, a look of astonished confusion on his puckered brow.

"H-he's here to fix the village," Gina stammered.

"Oh," Michael said again.

"Yeah. I'll get right on it," Rake said.

Aspen was sure she'd drop dead—or that her head would explode at the very least! Boy toy? Here to fix the village?

"Well, okay. Thanks…I guess," Michael said. He turned to leave but paused, looking back at Aspen. "And get out of that ridiculous costume. You look like an idiot." He took one last look at Rake and walked away toward the front of the store.

"You want me to lay that guy out for you?" Rake asked through clenched teeth. "I'm sure it wouldn't take much. I could probably just sneeze a little too hard and take him out."

"I-it's okay," Aspen said. She wanted to cry. How embarrassing! How frustrating! Rake Locker would have nothing further to do with her, she was certain.

"Well, let me get this little village display plugged back in for you, at least," he said, handing her the *Willamina Dog and the Wobbly Wood* book. "It looked like you were having a little trouble with it when I first came in."

"That's okay. You don't have to…" Aspen began. Still, before she knew it, Rake Locker had plopped down on his back and slid beneath the table. In a matter of a few seconds, the village sparked to life. Rake slid out from under the table, stood, and took the book from Aspen's hands—rather, her paws.

"So your clock is all finished," he said.

"Thanks again," Aspen said. She glanced to Gina, but her friend seemed distracted by something beyond them, toward the front of the store.

"And," Rake continued, "I mean…I know you're busy…but I wanted to know if you'd be willing to go to my grampa and gramma's harvest barn dance thing with me this Saturday."

"What?" Aspen asked, astonished.

"I'll be right back," Gina said.

Aspen watched for a moment as Gina headed for the front of the store. Was she about to have words with Michael? Still, Aspen didn't care if Michael messed with her schedule—or fired her, for that matter. Had Rake Locker just asked her out?

"My grandparents live down in Corrales, and they have this harvest barn thing every year," he explained. "It's a costume thing and…hey! You could wear that! It would be perfect. My gramma would love it."

"Oh, no!" Aspen sighed. "This was a one-time thing for me."

"But you look so cute…with your pink butt and all," he said. He reached out, scratching behind one of her ears.

Did he really think she looked cute? Aspen felt a smile finally spread across her face.

"It's this coming Saturday?" she asked.

"Why? Do you already have something going on?" He looked genuinely disappointed, and it caused Aspen's heart to flutter.

"Nope. Not at all." She smiled at him, and he nodded.

"Good! I'll pick you up at five. Gramma serves tons of food, so don't eat before."

"Okay," Aspen said.

"You can dress up however you want. There's no theme or nothing. And you really can wear this if you want."

Aspen giggled, delighted by his bad grammar. "I'm not wearing this," she said.

He chuckled. "Well, I don't see why not…but it's up to you. I'll see you at five then?"

"Yeah. That would be great."

"I'll even bring your clock for you. That way you don't have to come down to the shop." He was so handsome—owned such a good sense of humor. "I'll see you at five on Saturday…if not before. Okay?"

"Okay," Aspen said.

He turned to leave. "Oh, by the way," he began, turning back to her, "if you ever need your tummy scratched…just let me know." He winked and sauntered off toward the register.

Aspen's mouth dropped open in delighted astonishment. What a flirt! She loved it. She loved him! No, wait—she didn't love a man she barely knew. No. Of course not.

She watched Rake go to the register and pay for the book. He turned and lifted his chin in a "see you later" nod, and Aspen waved a large pink paw in return. She sighed once he'd exited the store and immediately began looking around for Gina. Aspen saw her, hiding at the back of the biographies bookcase. Her attention seemed to be arrested by something near the front of the store. Aspen followed Gina's gaze to see a very handsome UPS man, all swathed in warm brown, hand Michael a clipboard. Michael signed something quickly and handed the clipboard back to the handsome UPS man.

It's him! Gina mouthed to Aspen. *The hot one!*

As inconspicuously as possible, Aspen made her way to the biography section.

"He's the one from my mom's house…right here…right in your very own bookstore!" Gina exclaimed in a whisper.

"Well, have at him!" Aspen said.

Gina frowned and scolded, "He's a man…not a shish kebab!"

"He *is* handsome," Aspen whispered. And he was handsome. He was tall, owned wavy light brown hair, and was built almost as well as Rake Locker—but not quite.

"He's a dream!" Gina sighed.

Aspen watched with Gina as the attractive UPS man left the store. Gina sighed, her shoulders sagging.

"Did your bull-riding watchmaker ask you out?" Gina asked. It was obvious she didn't want to talk about her dreamy UPS man. Aspen wanted to offer support—encourage her friend to run out and talk to the guy. But she knew Gina too well, and she wasn't ready.

"He did, actually," Aspen said.

Gina's face immediately lit up, sincere joy apparent in her flashing blue-green eyes. "See? He likes you!" Gina exclaimed. "And I'm sure this costume was your ace in the hole."

"Oh, I'm sure!"

"No, I'm serious!" Gina assured her. "You should've seen his face when you had your big pink doggy fanny sticking out from under that table. I promise you…it was your ace."

"Well, he's taking me to a costume party at his grandparents' house, and I'm certainly not going as Willamina Dog," Aspen said.

"You should borrow my fairy costume!" Gina suggested.

"Are you kidding? I'd look like an idiot!" Aspen giggled.

"You'd look fabulous! And besides…you can't wear that dumb Snow White costume again. You'd be better off going in this." Gina took hold of the floppy pink ears on either side of Aspen's head. "And believe me, you may be cute in this…but it certainly won't inspire him take you in his arms and kiss your lips off."

"Aspen!" Michael scolded.

Aspen and Gina both startled at his sudden appearance.

"Dude!" Gina exclaimed. "You're like an evil little gnome or something."

"Get back to work, Aspen," Michael said, glaring at Gina. "Otherwise you can work all weekend."

"I'm going to change right now, Michael," Aspen said. She nodded to Gina and mouthed, *I'll see you later.*

As Aspen stepped out of the Willamina Dog costume, she smiled. Rake Locker had asked her out again! She tried not to get overly excited—tried to remember the way the little girl's mother had eyed Rake. He seemed nice, polite, and as charming as any fictional hero she'd ever read about. It would go badly—she knew it would. Yet something inside her resisted the truth—and couldn't resist him.

She thought of the way he'd freaked out Michael—shut him right up. A tingling thrill ran through her at the thought of his smile—the way he'd smiled at her when she first crawled out from under the table wearing the dog costume. Rake Locker would probably turn out to be the biggest jerk she'd ever known. Still, as she remembered the kiss he'd taken from her the morning after their first date, she knew she couldn't give him up—yet.

⁊⳯

"How was your lunch?" his grandmother asked as Rake entered the Clock Shop through the front door.

"Great," Rake told her, heading back toward the workshop.

"That's nice, dear," she said.

Rake paused at the front desk, leaned on it for a moment, and smiled at his grandmother. "I picked up a book for Elena." He plopped the *Willamina Dog and the Wobbly Wood* book down on the counter.

"Oh, she'll love it!" Charlotte Locker exclaimed. She turned the book toward herself and opened it up. As she leafed through it, she asked, "Have you decided who you're bringing to the party on Saturday?"

Rake nodded. "Yep. Do you remember the girl who brought in Guy Falls's old clock?" he asked.

"Oh, yes! She's lovely. Just lovely!" Rake watched as understanding washed over her. "Are you bringing her? What was her name again? Something rather unusual, wasn't it?"

"Aspen," Rake said.

"Oh, that's right. Well, I'm sure she'll be a wonderful companion for the evening."

"I'm sure she will," Rake said. He leaned forward, kissing his grandma on one soft, wrinkled cheek. "I'll be in the back."

"All right, sweetie," Charlotte said as she continued to leaf through the Willamina Dog book.

Rake grabbed a bottled water from the small fridge in the workshop. He sat down to work on the pocket watch he'd been working on before he'd left to run over to the Book Nook and ask Aspen to the barn party.

He had trouble getting back to work, however, for the vision of Aspen Falls dressed in that comical pink dog costume lingered in the forefront of his mind. Setting the bottled water on the floor next to him, he reached over and picked up the book he'd had his mother check out of the library for him.

Flipping to page 168, he read, *"Hence, the time of aspen befell them, and winter's descending was near, so the moon wove his fingers of moonbeams through the gold amidst mountain's hair."*

Rake smiled, shook his head, and put the book aside once more. After hearing Aspen recite it, he'd wanted to read the poem again, though there was really no point. He wasn't about to get serious with anybody—even a girl as sweet as Aspen Falls. Nope! Rake Locker understood women all too well. There wasn't anything redeeming about most of them. Still, Aspen was pretty—"lovely," as his grandmother had put it—and she was fun. There wasn't anything wrong with having a little fun. Was there?

Rake picked up the watchmaker's loupe he'd been using before lunch and fit it to his eye socket. He studied the winding wheel and click in Mr. Romero's antique pocket watch.

"Nope," he mumbled as he began to work. "Nothing wrong with just having a little fun. Nothing…what…so…ever." He worked for a moment and held his breath as he checked the hairspring. Exhaling, he muttered, "And the time of Aspen falls."

CHAPTER SEVEN

"Calm down, Aspen!" Gina demanded. "You're gonna get all upset and throw up, and then he won't ever want to *see* you again…let alone kiss you!"

Aspen inhaled a deep breath, slowly exhaling, trying to calm herself. She studied her reflection in the mirror. Her shoulders, arms, and cheeks shimmered with the gold sparkle dust she'd smoothed over her skin. Her hair hung in long, soft waves, woven with lengths of orange, olive, and gold ribbon. Gina had placed several small artificial tiger lilies throughout her hair too. The costume she'd borrowed from Gina was tailored from lengths and layers of orange, olive, and brown tulle, fitted over a gold satin corset-type bodice and skirt. Streamers of tulle, twisted together with ribbon of the same colors, hung from gold bracelets at her upper arm and above her elbow. Her wings were a glittery gold, orange, and green; Gina had picked up a new pair at the costume store since she'd ruined hers standing too near a fireplace the year before. The costume was gorgeous! Still, Aspen shook her head with disappointment.

"I look ridiculous!" she groaned. "This costume works way better on you! I should've stuck with my Snow White outfit."

"Are you kidding? That thing looks like it's ready for the ragbag, Aspen," Gina said. She primped Aspen's hair for a moment, standing behind Aspen and gazing in the mirror at her friend's reflection. "And your makeup is to die for! Even if I do say so myself."

Aspen smiled. Her favorite thing about the costume was Gina's makeup application. The iridescent green and orange eye shadow, perfectly accentuated by the dark brown eyeliner and black "eyelash" lines gliding up from the outer corner of her eye toward her brow, did give her a fantastically glamorous appearance. Aspen fancied her green eyes flashed emerald, skillfully embellished by the dark shades of the makeup. The tiny orange and green rhinestone clusters Aspen had used corn syrup to adhere to her temples gave Gina's original eye makeup job the faultless finishing touch. Brownish-orange blush, swept up from her cheekbones to her temples, gave the contours of her face a more angular appearance, and the metallic chocolate hue of her lipstick completed the look of a magical autumn fairy.

Aspen sighed. "The sad thing is," she began, "I actually look better than I have any other time in my entire life…and I still look ridiculous!"

"It's a costume party, you idiot," Gina said, primping Aspen's hair again. "Everyone there will look ridiculous. And besides, you look gorgeous…not ridiculous."

"I wonder what Rake will be wearing."

"If we're lucky…nothing but a loincloth and a smile," Gina answered.

Aspen laughed so hard her stomach hurt! Gina laughed too, entirely amused by her own wit, as usual.

"You are so bad," Aspen told her.

"Oh, like you weren't thinking the same thing," Gina scolded.

Aspen nodded. "That thought had occurred to me." Aspen's mood lightened; her nerves settled a bit.

"That's because you've always had a thing for Tarzan."

"Only Johnny Weissmuller's Tarzan," Aspen noted, raising one index finger. "He's the only Tarzan I ever liked."

"Until Rake Locker shows up tonight in a loincloth, that is."

"Exactly!"

"Wouldn't you just die?" Gina giggled.

"Probably so," Aspen admitted. She sighed and pasted on a smile. "How do I look?"

Gina began to giggle—the giggle turning into a laugh—the laugh turning into an uncontrolled belly-wrencher!

"What?" Aspen asked. She smiled and couldn't help but giggle. Gina's eyes were watering. She crossed her legs and doubled over—tried to keep from laughing—tried to catch her breath. "What? What is it? Share the joke, girl!"

Gina shook her head. She laughed for a few more moments and then inhaled a calming breath. Wiping the tears from her eyes, she sighed, "Ahhhhh," as her giggles finally subsided.

"What the heck?" Aspen asked. "Nothing is that funny."

"I'm sorry! I'm sorry!" Gina began. "It's just that I had a vision of Rake coming to the door with only a loincloth and you answering. I mean…leave off the wings and makeup, and you could pretty much pass for a fancy-schmancy jungle woman—you know, like Jane!"

"That is absolutely not true!" Aspen exclaimed, turning to look in the mirror once more. "I'm a fairy! I look nothing like a jungle woman."

"Quick! Let's pull the ribbons out of your hair," Gina began, "and wash your face and take off the wings. Then maybe wishful thinking will turn into premonition and Rake actually *will* come to the door in a loincloth!"

Aspen smiled, shaking her head. Gina was hysterical! Some of the things her mind concocted…

"Oh! What time is it?" Aspen asked. She glanced at the wall to where her Uncle Guy's clock should be.

Gina pulled her cell out of her pocket. "Almost five," she said.

"Oh my heck! He'll be here any minute!" Aspen suddenly felt frantic, all her nervous anxiety returning in one overwhelming instant.

"Okay, I'm gonna go. But I'm gonna sit in the car and watch until he gets here…just in case he does show up dressed like Tarzan," Gina said.

"He won't be dressed as Tarzan, Gina," Aspen giggled.

"You never know!" Gina picked up her purse and headed for the door. "Oh!" she exclaimed, pausing for a moment. "Did you want to borrow my camera? Just in case he is wearing a loincloth?"

"What am I supposed to say?" Aspen asked, shaking her head. "'You look great in a loincloth, Rake! Can I take your picture?'"

"Exactly!" Gina nodded, pulled her camera out of her purse, and offered it to Aspen.

"I've got mine in my purse," Aspen assured her.

"Okay, then," Gina said, dropping the camera back into her bag. "Have fun!"

"Thanks."

As Gina closed the door behind herself, Aspen looked in the mirror again. She shook her head. What had she been thinking? She couldn't pull off the gorgeous autumn fairy thing! At that moment, she actually wondered if she should've borrowed the Willamina Dog costume from work. It would've hidden her figure—hidden her altogether! Maybe she should've gone with ridiculous and cute rather than ridiculous and provocative.

Aspen twisted a piece of her hair with one of the ribbons Gina had tied in it. She tried not to be nervous—tried to tell herself it would be fun. She smiled, thinking of Gina's loincloth suggestion for Rake.

"She's such a kick in the pants," she giggled out loud.

The doorbell rang, startling Aspen so badly that she actually let out a little, involuntary yelp.

"It's him!" she whispered to her autumn fairy reflection. "Just relax. Be calm." She inhaled a calming breath and went to the door. A vision of Rake standing at the door dressed in nothing but a loincloth and a smile jumped into her mind so that when she opened the door, she was already smiling.

"Hi," Rake Locker greeted.

"H-hi," Aspen stammered. Forget the loincloth! Aspen was rendered breathless by the sight of him—breathless and speechless. For there before her—standing at her own threshold—was a vision of a man who had surely stepped directly out of a Charlotte Brontë novel.

Dressed in a perfectly tailored, early Victorian era costume, Rake Locker looked the vision of some gothic novel hero. His hair was rather tousled—roguishly tousled. He wore a white shirt, tall standing collar, white cravat, and a blue waistcoat beneath a dark blue tailcoat. Aspen tried to keep her mouth from gaping open in astonishment as her eyes traveled the length of him. Fitted, front-flap black breeches further pronounced his muscular form, and tall leather boots finished off the appearance of his having been conjured out of a Jane Austen–period film.

"You look fabulous!" he said, eyebrows arched, a grin of approval on his handsome face.

Aspen, however, still stood in utter, stunned astonishment. "R-really?" she managed to squeak.

"Oh, yeah!" he chuckled. "Like something that walked out of my dreams."

She recovered. Smiling at him, she asked, "*You* dream about fairies?"

"Not really," he admitted. His grin broadened but didn't quite stretch to a smile as he said, "But I think I will from now on."

Aspen giggled. "Oh, I see," she began. "You're a charmer this evening."

"Rochester Darcy at your service, madame," he said. He bowed and then straightened.

"Rochester Darcy?" Aspen giggled.

"Yep!" he said. He stooped and picked up a large wooden box that was sitting on the porch at his feet. "My sister says this costume will woo and win me any chick I want. Whatever woo means. I've got your clock. Can I come in?"

"Oh! Sure…sorry," Aspen stammered, stepping aside. As Mr. Rake Locker Rochester Darcy strode out of 1837 and into her apartment, an enchanted sort of thrill ran down her spine—beneath her fairy wings.

"So…did you come up with the name for your costume? Or did your sister?" Aspen asked. She refused to believe that a drop-dead gorgeous, ex-bull-riding watchmaker was familiar with the works of Charlotte Brontë or Jane Austen—let alone familiar enough to come up with a name derived of each author's most famous hero.

Rake chuckled, set the wooden box on the floor, and removed the lid. He removed some packing plastic from inside the box and then Aspen's Uncle Guy's clock.

"My sister's favorite Jane Austen book is *Pride and Prejudice*… and she did tell me the guy's name in that is Darcy," he admitted. "However," he began as he held up the clock, seeming to inspect it for a moment, "I told her your favorite book is *Jane Eyre*, and she says the guy in that is named Rochester. So we figured it out together. But there's even more."

"How could there be more?" Aspen giggled.

"Where do you want this?" he asked.

"Right there," Aspen said, pointing to the empty spot on the wall.

She watched as Mr. Rake Locker Rochester Darcy secured the clock to the wall via the large screw in the spot. He opened the face and pendulum housing. The clock was already set to five. Rake started the pendulum swinging, and Aspen smiled, immediately soothed by the familiar ticking of the old clock.

"There you go," he said.

"Thank you so much," Aspen said. "How much do I—"

"I told you it was on the house," he interrupted. "Consider it a gift from your man for the evening…the vampire Rochester Darcy."

"What?" Aspen exclaimed, a puzzled frown puckering her brow.

Rake chuckled and moved closer to her, until he stood directly before her, his dark eyes smoldering into hers.

"So…my sister thought the chicks would dig this costume, right?" he asked.

"Dig?" Aspen asked. She smiled. He was too handsome!

"Yeah," he affirmed. "So…I figured if the chicks dig guys out of books…right? Then why not take it a step further?"

He smiled then—a dazzling, brilliant, somewhat seductive smile—and Aspen gasped. How delicious! As his handsome smile revealed two no doubt artificial yet very authentic-looking fangs—one on each eyetooth—Aspen couldn't keep the delighted giggle from escaping her throat. They weren't huge and overdone—rather just enough of a pointed tip to make a person look twice.

"You're Rochester Darcy…and a vampire?" she breathed. She was totally mesmerized by his mouth, visions of kissing him dancing wildly in her brain.

"Yeah! Great idea, huh?" he said. "I mean…you work in a bookstore. You know how crazy the girls are about those vampire books that are out right now, right?"

"Right," Aspen breathed, still nearly hypnotized by his appearance—and the idea of a Victorian-era vampire hero standing in her apartment.

"So can you—as a woman who likes to read—can you think of a better costume for a guy than this?"

Aspen giggled, her arms rippling with goose bumps.

"Absolutely not," she admitted. He was divine. He was unearthly attractive! A sudden overpowering attraction to him rinsed over her, causing excess moisture to flood her mouth. "I'm sure all the chicks will totally dig you tonight." A twinge of jealousy pinched her heart, but what could she do? The chicks would dig him, and she would have to endure it as best she could.

Rake's smile broadened, and Aspen shook her head—awestruck by the sight of the striking vampire Rochester Darcy.

"Well," he began, lowering his voice to the sultry, alluring tone of a man trying to entice a woman into—something, "I really don't care if all the chicks dig it…just as long as one does. Just as long as you do."

Aspen smiled, elated by his flirting. She wondered if he were sincere—if he really meant he only cared whether she liked the costume—or if he were simply telling her what he thought she wanted to hear.

He reached out, loosely gripping her upper arms. Slowly, his hands slid down the length of her arms, leaving goose bumps in their caressive wake. His touch was completely exhilarating! She wanted him to caress her arms once more—her shoulders and neck—her legs!

Taking her hands in his, he said, "You, on the other hand…you are playing with fire."

"Me? What do you mean?" she said, feeling the heat of a blush in her cheeks. The way he was looking at her—it almost unnerved her! His eyes sizzled with approval and admiration. Aspen was suddenly very glad she'd borrowed the fairy costume. She knew her old Snow White getup wouldn't have provoked the pleased expression on his face.

"I mean, the blood coursing through your jugular would've been a lot harder to get to—a lot harder for a vampire to suck out—if you would've worn that big pink dog costume like I suggested," he said.

"Is that so?" Aspen asked, smiling with delight. She felt his grip on her hands tighten.

His eyes narrowed as he looked at her and said, "Yep. Your blood would've definitely been safer…not to mention your virtue."

Aspen gasped and tried to pull her hands from his, but he held fast. Here it came—she could sense it. In the next moment he would prove her right—prove that all devastatingly handsome men were jerks, self-centered, and interested in only one thing—and the one thing wasn't English literature.

"You can't say stuff like that!" she exclaimed.

"Stuff like what?" he asked.

"Stuff like…like…like virtue," she stammered.

"Do you mean the actual word…or the implication?" His eyes danced with a teasing spark.

"The implication," she told him, blushing clear to her toes. Still, she was all atingle inside, as if she'd never felt more vivacious in her life.

"But don't vampires always say stuff like that?" he chuckled.

"Well…well, yes," she admitted. "But Mr. Darcy never would."

He arched an inquisitive eyebrow. "Really? What about Rochester then?"

He had her there! Jane Eyre's Mr. Rochester would certainly have said something scandalous like that.

He didn't wait for her to answer—her pause obviously answering the question for her.

"Ahhh!" Rake breathed. "I see by your guilty reaction that Rochester would have."

"Yes, but he was a rake!"

The sentence was out of her mouth before she'd even had the chance to think better of it. He chuckled, and she felt her blush deepen.

"Was he?" he asked. "A *rake*, hmmm? And you like rakes…don't you? Rogues, scoundrels…and rakes?"

Aspen smiled. Perhaps he'd simply been flirting. Perhaps there was no serious undertone whatsoever in his enticing remarks.

"Yes," she admitted. "But only in literature," she added.

"Oh, sure," he chuckled.

He'd scared her. He'd seen the fear pass over her pretty fairy face like an ominous shadow. Still, Rake wasn't sure why his teasing had unnerved her so badly. She'd seemed completely delighted by his costume, his flirting—by him—totally charmed until he'd teasingly implied her virtue wasn't safe. Rake's mind thought quickly—concocted as many different possible scenarios for the sudden change in her as it could. Was she truly afraid he would press her and taint her virtue—on their second date? Had someone in her past pressed her to do so? The thought actually buoyed him up. If she were so sensitive about it, then chances were virtue was something she valued, even guarded. That would be admirable indeed—quite different from Rake's most recent experiences with women.

Still, he had to admit to himself—had to admit that his mouth had begun to water the minute she'd opened the door and he'd seen her standing there in her sexy fairy costume. Everything about her was tempting—everything! From her soft brown hair tumbling in ribboned waves over her shimmering bare shoulders to the bright green of her eyes. His attention had been affixed to her mouth for a long time. He'd had to bend down and pick up the clock box out on the front porch in order to force his gaze somewhere else for a moment. Every inch of his body—every instinct in him—wanted to reach out, pull her small, curvaceous form against his, and kiss her! His sudden and overwhelming attraction to her was freaking him out. This was the night of his grandparents' barn party. He didn't have time to be so distracted—so physically overcome by a pretty girl! A couple of lines from that stupid poem in the book sitting in his workshop kept playing in his mind.

So the moon wove his fingers of moonbeams
Through the gold amidst mountain's hair.

He wanted to do it! He wanted to take Aspen's face in his hands, pull her nearer to him, and weave his fingers through the ribbons in her hair. He was an idiot! What was the matter with him? Poetry? He'd never had poetry bouncing around in his head. Well—other than the stupid limericks he sometimes spouted off just to be funny.

Quickly, Rake pulled his thoughts back to the conversation. Somehow, he'd unnerved Aspen, and he didn't want her to be uncomfortable all night long.

"Okay, I'll make you a deal," Rake began.

"What's that?" Aspen asked. She was relaxing again. He'd only been teasing, and the truth of it was—if she were honest with herself—she did like it!

"I won't suck out all your blood or threaten your virtue any more tonight...*if* you admit that you like rakes, even outside of literature... and that you totally dig this costume."

Aspen giggled. She certainly didn't want him sucking out all her blood, but she was almost disappointed with his promise not to tease her about her virtue.

Still, she agreed, "Okay."

"Okay, what?" he asked.

"Okay...I admit that I like rakes."

He smiled, and Aspen was certain her knees were turning to liquid.

"And this costume? Do you dig it?" he asked. He dropped her hands and smoothed the lapels of his tailcoat as he smiled to show off his fangs.

"Yes. It's the best costume I've ever seen," she giggled.

"Then grab your jacket or whatever sexy fairies wear, and let's get going," he said.

"How cold is it?" Aspen asked. He'd referred to her as *sexy*, and it pleased her more than she wanted to admit.

He grinned. "Not cold at all. Just bring something light...in case."

"Okay."

Rake watched as Aspen walked over to a coat closet near the door to her apartment. He tried not to smile too much as his eyes traveled the length of her. She was hot! A tempting little bookstore clerk indeed. He smiled, recalling the vision of her dressed in that pink dog costume. He liked the fairy one better—much better! Oh, he'd promised not to drain her body of her life's blood, and that was obviously an easy enough promise to keep. Where the point of her virtue was concerned—well, there were times when his name was a bit too fitting. Still, as the devilish part of his nature began to rise in him, he decided that he would keep his other promise as well. He wouldn't threaten her virtue—too much.

❧

"It's kind of muddy right up here," Rake mumbled. His brow puckered into a frown as he studied the ground near the little bridge. "The rain last night must've been heavier down here."

Aspen didn't care about mud. She'd just spent ten minutes in a pickup with Rake Locker driving down to Corrales, still astonished at the perfection of his costume—rather the perfection of him *in* the costume.

She looked up into the evening sky—into the lattice of green and yellow cottonwood leaves overhead. The sun was making its lingering descent, casting warmth and shadow over the valley.

"I keep forgetting to bring some boards down here to put over this mud," Rake added. "Remind me when we leave to bring a couple with us. Nobody else will probably be coming this way…but you never know."

Aspen looked at the mud then. It was fairly sloppy. Still, even the mud did nothing to dampen Aspen's opinion of the beauty of the area. She could hear the river from where they were—the one mighty Rio Grande as it wound its way through the valley. The irrigation ditch in front of them was lined with green grass, and she smiled as a toad hopped from the bank and into the water.

"It's okay," she said, starting toward the bridge. "I can just—"

She gasped, however, when she found herself unexpectedly swooped up into powerful arms. Instinctively, Aspen placed one arm around Rake's broad shoulders, entirely captivated by being held by him—pleased by the sudden yet faint scent of his inviting cologne.

"Nope," Rake said. "You'll get your little fairy shoes all muddy if you try it." Cradling her in his strong arms, he stepped into the mud. "These boots will wipe off fine in the straw once we get to the barn."

113

He carried her through the mud and over the bridge. Letting her feet fall to the ground on the other side, he said, "The barn isn't far."

"Have your grandparents lived here long?" Aspen asked as she fell into step beside him.

"Fifty years," he said. "They moved here just a few years after they were married. They still own about fifty acres along the river here."

"Wow! That's probably a gold mine. Riverfront property in Corrales?" Aspen asked.

"Oh, yeah…but I hope they never sell it. I love it out here," he said. "I hope you have fun tonight," he added. "I'm kind of worried that you'll be bored and then never go out with me again."

Aspen smiled. "I'm more worried about being bor*ing*," she admitted.

"Impossible," he said. "Though…I kind of wish you would've worn that pink dog outfit…instead of being all soft and glittery."

"Really?" Aspen asked. He didn't like her costume? She'd thought he had! Back at the apartment, he'd said…

"Of course not!" he chuckled.

Aspen smiled and tried to ignore the heat rising to her cheeks.

As they stepped out of a grove of cottonwoods, she saw the barn. It was charming! It was an old barn—rustic-looking—nostalgic. The main doors were open, and warm light glowed invitingly within. Straw bales were stacked outside the barn on either side of the open doors, covered with lounging scarecrows and flickering jack-o'-lanterns. It was wonderful! Strings of tiny white lights lined the barn roof, windows, doors, and along the path leading from the grove of trees to the doors. Aspen could smell cider, pumpkin pie, and fresh-baked bread. Low laughter and voices danced on the air—the sounds of inviting merriment.

"Looks like the family is already there," Rake said.

"The family?" Aspen gasped, stopping dead in her tracks.

Rake looked at her and chuckled. "Sure! My mom and dad…my grampa and gramma…sister, brother-in-law, brother…a few cousins and aunts and uncles."

Aspen held her breath. His family? She hadn't even thought about meeting his family!

Rake smiled, revealing his dazzling white teeth and fangs. He reached out and took hold of her hand. "Don't worry," he said. "You already know my gramma."

Aspen nodded and forced a grin.

"But I probably should warn you," he began, appraising her from head to toe, "my grampa will love you in this!" He tugged on her hand. "Come on."

Aspen felt her feet move—followed him even though every instinct told her to turn and run.

Moments later she stepped into the warm-lighted barn. Instantly, every head in the building turned and looked at them—turned and looked at *her*. Aspen couldn't keep herself from moving closer to Rake.

"Mi hijito! You look so handsome!"

Aspen watched as the most beautiful Hispanic woman she had ever seen hurried toward them, arms outstretched and welcoming. She was dressed in a red-and-black flamenco dress, a high-standing black comb embellishing her piled ebony hair.

"Marissa said this would be perfect on you...and it is!" the woman said. Her thick local accent was comforting somehow. She threw her arms around Rake and kissed him on the cheek.

"Hi, Mom," Rake said, returning his mother's kiss.

Rake's beautiful mother then turned her attention to Aspen. She smiled—the same smile as Rake, only void of fangs. Placing her hands on Aspen's shoulders, she said, "And you must be Aspen. You're beautiful, mi hija!" She studied Aspen's costume for a moment and added, "A fairy tonight, huh?"

"Y-yes, ma'am," Aspen managed.

"Aspen, this is my mom...if you haven't already guessed," Rake said.

"I'm very pleased to meet you, Mrs. Locker," Aspen said. She reluctantly released Rake's hand to offer hers to his mom, but the woman either didn't see her hand or chose not to. Instead, she hugged Aspen tightly.

"You call me Valentina, mi hija," she said. She smiled and sighed—

115

an obviously pleased smile and sigh. "You're lovely. She's just lovely, Rake!"

"I know, Mom," Rake chuckled. "But quit gushing. You'll freak her out."

Valentina Locker made a long *s* sound with her tongue. "I'm not freaking her out, am I, mi hija?"

Aspen smiled and shook her head.

"Come on," Valentina said, placing an arm around Aspen's shoulders. "Come and meet everyone. You'll get bored if you have to spend the whole night talking to only Rake."

Aspen glanced at Rake anxiously. He winked at her, nodding his assurance she would be all right.

"Joe!" Valentina called toward a group of people standing near a long table laden with food. "Look what your son has managed to drag over here!"

A tall, handsome man, dressed in a pirate costume, turned and smiled as his eyes fell to Aspen. She could see it then, Rake's resemblance to both his parents—the beauty of his mother and the physique of his father.

"Hello!" the man greeted as he strode toward her. It was Rake's stride. Rake's father offered his hand, and Aspen placed hers in it. "We've heard a lot about you."

"All good, I hope," Aspen said, forcing a smile.

"Oh, there she is! She's here, Joseph! Guy Falls's niece!"

Aspen glanced over to see Mrs. Claus—rather, Charlotte Locker—dressed as Mrs. Claus, complete with a red dress trimmed in white fur and a sprig of holly tucked in her coifed hair. She rather quickly waddled toward Aspen, pausing for a moment. "Joseph!" she called over her shoulder. "You remember me, don't you, honey?" Charlotte asked, throwing her arms around Aspen in a warm embrace.

"Of course, Mrs. Locker," Aspen said.

"Charlotte...remember?" The older woman winked at Aspen.

"Yes," Aspen answered.

She gasped then. It was him—the very same elderly man she and Gina had often seen riding near the river or at Wagner's produce! He

116

wore worn-out Levi's, a nicely pressed, long-sleeved white shirt, and pristine straw Stetson. A large scar traveled down one side of his face, and his hands were leathery and gnarled. He was perfect—the perfect elderly man—the kind everyone wanted to have for a grandpa.

Aspen smiled and felt warm and giggly as the older man reached up and removed his hat. He nodded and said, "So you're Guy Falls's granddaughter?"

"His niece, dad," Rake's father said.

"Oh, yes! His niece," old Joseph Locker said. "I hear you've taken real good care of that old French Westminster of Guy's."

"I-I've tried to, sir," Aspen stammered. He was wonderful! They all were, of course, but the elder Mr. Locker was such a throwback to a different time. He was mesmerizing!

"And I'll say this for Rake," Joseph began, studying Aspen from head to toe. "If he's smart…he'll haul you on outta here and straight to the pickup for a little necking!"

Aspen felt a heated blush rise to her cheeks as Charlotte and Valentina simultaneously scolded, "Grampa!"

Rake's grandpa smiled and winked at her. "Well, if he's got any of his grandpa in him…he'll get around to it sometime tonight."

Relief washed over Aspen the moment she felt Rake's hands on her shoulders. He stood behind her, chuckling. "You guys will scare her off before I get the chance, Grampa."

"But everyone will want to meet her, hijito," Valentina began. "You must share when—"

"I'll share later, Mom," Rake said, taking Aspen's hand. "I've got to feed her…build up her strength before everyone else gets here to mob her."

"You'll be fine, sugar," Rake's father said. "We're not nearly as bad as all that."

"It-it's nice to meet you all," Aspen managed.

"It's nice to meet *you*, mi hijita," Valentina said. She glanced up to her son and frowned. "What's this?" she asked, reaching up and pushing Rake's upper lip back as if she were inspecting a horse. "Fangs? Why you got fangs on? I thought you were a gentleman tonight."

"I am," Rake said. "A vampire gentleman."

"Yep! He's planning on doing a little necking tonight," Joseph laughed. "That's my boy!"

Rake chuckled as he hugged his grandpa and then his father. He kissed his grandma on the cheek before taking Aspen by the shoulders and turning her toward the food table.

"I want Aspen to try Mom's tamales before they're all gone," he said.

"Try the green chili stew, Aspen," Valentina said. "I changed my recipe a little this time."

"Okay," Aspen said, smiling as Rake directed her closer to the table.

"They can be a little overwhelming when they're all together," he said as he picked up a plate and a napkin.

"All families are...aren't they?" Aspen said. Her knees were fairly knocking together with nerves.

Aspen watched as Rake used a pair of tongs to lift two delicious-looking tamales out of a warming tray. He put them on the plate in his hand, turned to her, and asked, "Two or three?"

"Only one!" Aspen exclaimed.

She watched as he removed the corn husks from each tamale, tossing them in the small plastic-bag-lined barrel at the side of the table. "Red or green chili on that?" he asked.

"Red," Aspen answered. "But I can do it."

"Naw," Rake said, smothering the tamales with a ladleful of red chili sauce from a nearby bowl. "I want to make sure you get enough to eat. Quieres frijoles?"

Aspen nodded and watched as Rake plopped an enormous spoonful of refried beans on the plate next to the tamale.

"How much do you think I can eat?" she giggled.

"Don't worry," he said. "I'll eat what you don't."

Aspen felt her eyebrows arch in astonishment. Surely he didn't mean to eat off her plate—food she didn't finish? They hardly knew each other!

"Here," he said, handing her the plate and picking up a bowl. "You will love my mom's green chili stew." Aspen smiled as she watched him ladle far too much green chili stew into the bowl. He picked up two napkins, two forks, and two spoons. "Let's go. We can come back for seconds."

"Rake!" Aspen's mother exclaimed as Aspen followed Rake to a little table sitting off to one side of the barn. "Algunos tienen modales, hijo! Ve por tu propia placa!"

Aspen giggled, understanding enough Spanish to know Rake's mother had just scolded him for having such bad manners—for not giving Aspen her own plate.

"This *is* her plate, Mom," Rake said, setting the bowl of green chili stew down on the little table. "We're sharing."

Aspen was delighted when Rake's mother rolled her eyes and exclaimed, "Híjole! You think you raise a boy right."

"You sit down, and I'll get some drinks," Rake said. Aspen smiled at the way he held her chair for her and pushed it in as she sat down. "Milk, cider, water, or pop?"

"I think milk," she answered.

"You're not a weenie, are you?" Rake chuckled.

"Not usually," Aspen said. "But I can smell your mom's chili and… well, it's better to be safe than sorry."

"Okay. But I'm sure you can handle it."

Aspen watched Rake walk to the food table—watched him talk to an older man who had just entered the barn. She glanced over to his grandfather, the weathered, old, bowlegged New Mexican cowboy. He was leaning up against one wall, his attention fixed on Aspen. He winked at her, and she smiled. His mother and grandmother were busily greeting more guests at the entrance to the barn, and his father was pouring fresh cider from a press barrel and into pitchers. It was too wonderful, all of it! Pumpkins were piled in every corner, and jack-o'-lanterns dotted the food table as centerpieces. Red chili ristras hung from strong beams overhead, some strung with white lights. Straw bales lined the room, obviously intended as places to sit, and the scent of green and red chili spiced the air. It was heavenly! Yet the most heavenly thing about it all was Rake.

Aspen smiled as he returned to their table, stepped over the back of his chair, and sat down.

"There you go, weenie girl," he teased, handing her a glass of milk. "Eat up!"

He handed her a spoon and pushed the bowl of green chili stew toward her.

Aspen dipped her spoon into the bowl. She held the spoonful of stew under her nose for a moment, inhaling the delicious, familiar scent of green chili. She blew on it a little. Her taste buds exploded with pure pleasure! The flavor of the chili was superb—the best she'd ever had.

"Oh my heck!" Aspen exclaimed.

"It's good, huh?" Rake chuckled.

"Yes!" Aspen said. As the familiar, magnificent burn of good green chili began in her mouth, Aspen took another bite. "Honestly…it's the best I've ever tasted."

"I know," Rake agreed. A strange thrill ran through Aspen as she watched Rake dunk his spoon into the bowl of stew. There was something a little too intimate about sharing a meal—on only the second date. Yet Aspen was pleased to know he liked her enough to do so—surprised that she liked him enough to do so.

"Try the tamales," he said. "They'll ruin you for life."

Aspen giggled and cut into red chili-drenched tamale. Again, her taste buds were under the illusion their owner had died and gone to heaven.

"Oh my heck, Rake!" Aspen couldn't help but exclaim.

"I know," he chuckled. "I love fall…and the holidays. My mom cooks a lot this time of year."

Aspen paused in taking another bite, momentarily distracted by the magnificent perfection of his costume. How did she get there, sitting with a vampire gentleman from another century—the most intriguing, gorgeous man she'd ever met?

As they ate they talked. Aspen was overwhelmed with delight at being in Rake's company. He was so very interesting, and again she was struck by how easily they conversed.

His mother had inquired as to how Aspen liked the green chili stew and was delighted by Aspen's sincere, gushing compliments. More and more people arrived, and Rake introduced her to his sister, Marissa—who was at least as beautiful as his mother—his brother, Mark—who looked the most like Rake's father of any of the siblings—and many other family and friends.

Everyone she met was friendly and welcoming and dressed in some of the most wonderful costumes she had ever seen. Aspen's nerves had quickly subsided, and now she sat on a straw bale next to Rake, watching the people at the barn party mingle, laugh, and eat.

"Your grandparents sure know how to throw a party," Aspen giggled as she watched Rake's grandpa dancing with a little girl of four or five.

"That's because they're real," he said. "They don't know how to *entertain*. They just know how to have fun."

Aspen nodded. He was exactly right. She'd been to the parties given by the partners at her father's firm. They were nothing like this! Stiff, serious, formal, and impersonal—that's what "entertaining" meant to Aspen too.

Abruptly, Aspen was distracted by applause, increased laughter, and a sudden mass exodus of the barn. Everyone was rushing out of the barn for some reason. She thought she heard music too.

"Come on!" Rake said, his face lighting up with excitement. He stood, took Aspen's hand, and fairly yanked her off the straw bale.

"What is it?" she asked.

"They're here!" he answered, smiling at her. His smile dazzled her as usual, and as he led her outside, she wondered if she were really walking—or walking on air!

As they exited the barn for the starlit night, the music grew louder—mariachi music!

Aspen felt goose bumps break over her arms as she saw a mariachi band approaching up the white lighted path. They stepped out of the grove of cottonwoods, wearing traditional black charro suits and performing "Cielito Lindo." Violins, trumpets, Mexican guitars—it was fantastic!

Aspen shook her head, unable to believe the perfection of that moment.

"I-I've never seen anything like this!" she breathed.

Rake chuckled. "They're my uncles…my mom's brothers."

Aspen giggled, overwhelmed with nostalgia and simply pure gladness.

"Next you'll be telling me your mother isn't just wearing a costume…that she really is a flamenco dancer," Aspen laughed.

Rake was silent, his silence causing her to look away from the approaching mariachis and to him. He shrugged his shoulders.

"You've got to be kidding me," she asked.

"Nope," Rake answered. "Does it make me more interesting? My mariachi uncles, my flamenco-dancing mother, my beat-up ex-bull-rider of a dad?"

Aspen sighed, her smile so broad it almost hurt. "Why am I not surprised about your dad riding bulls too?"

"Because I'm just like him…or he's just like me…however you want to look at it."

Aspen's eyes narrowed as she looked up at Rake. "But you *look* more like your mother," she said.

"Are you saying I'm girlie?" he teased.

"No! But you do look like her."

"I know. But once you get to know them better, you'll see I've got my dad's personality."

As the mariachis began another chorus of "Cielito Lindo," Aspen watched—awed as Rake's father took his mother in his arms and began to dance with her. She giggled when his bowlegged cowboy, ex-watchmaking grandfather did the same with Mrs. Claus.

"And maybe a little bit of your grandpa's?" she giggled as she watched the weathered old cowboy lumber through dancing with his wife.

"Oh, definitely!" Rake's eyes twinkled with admiration as he watched his grandpa dance with his grandma. "Only I'm a better dancer."

Aspen's heart leapt as he offered her his hand. She glanced around to see that nearly every couple in attendance was dancing now. Those without a partner kept time with the music with their hands or by bobbing their heads, joining in with each chorus repeat.

"I'm not very good," Aspen said.

"That's okay," Rake said, pulling her into waltz position. "Me neither."

He was liar—that was obvious! Aspen smiled. It would've been impossible for him not to have been a good dancer. She glanced over at his mother and father. Rake's beautiful mother held the hem of her dress to one hip with one hand as she danced with his father—swaying to and fro with an elegance Aspen had only seen in dance competitions.

"She's so beautiful," Aspen sighed.

"So are you," Rake said, pulling her body closer to his as they danced. His eyes smoldered with mischief as he gazed at her—led her in their dance.

"Oh, you're good," Aspen told him. She blushed, even though she knew he was only teasing.

"I'm only honest," he said.

The band repeated the chorus several more times before ending their song to be met with whistles and applause. Aspen was disappointed the song had ended, for Rake released her in order to applaud his uncles.

She watched as Rake's mother disappeared into the midst of charro costumes and instruments, hugging and kissing each brother.

"De Colores!" someone called out. One of the mariachis gave a high mariachi shout, and the band began to play.

Rake took Aspen's hand, whirling her under one arm several times and catching her in dance position.

"Come on, my delicious little fairy," he said. "Give me a chance to charm your wings right off!"

Aspen giggled as they joined the others in dancing. She wasn't sure she was awake. Surely it all had to be a dream! Rake flashed a dazzling, fang-embellished smile at her, and she sighed. If it *were* a dream, she hoped she would never wake up!

CHAPTER EIGHT

"Did you have fun?" Rake asked as they walked through the grove of cottonwoods toward the pickup.

"Did I have fun?" Aspen repeated with exaggerated sarcasm. "How could anyone not have had fun here?"

Rake laughed. "They're all pretty great, aren't they?"

"Everyone I met tonight was wonderful," she told him.

He hefted the two boards he was carrying over his shoulder.

"Well, I'm glad you liked it…and I'm glad that everyone managed to make a good impression." He looked down at her, smiling. "They liked you too, you know."

"Well, I hope so! I was on my best behavior," Aspen giggled.

"Do you have bad behavior?" he asked. "Maybe I'd like to see that…the bad-girl side to Aspen the arachnophobic autumn fairy."

"And does Mr. Rochester Darcy have a bad side?" she asked.

Rake stopped and frowned down at her. "I'm a vampire, ain't I?" he asked.

"I guess that does make you a little bit of a bad boy," Aspen said.

"Draining people dry of their blood…yeah, I'd say that's in the bad boy category." He smiled at her, his teeth seeming to glow in the moonlight. "I'm going to run these boards over to that muddy spot by the irrigation ditch bridge. Wanna wait here a minute?"

"Sure," Aspen agreed.

"I'll be right back."

Aspen watched Rake disappear into the darkness. The sudden

solitude unsettled her a little, but the warm, happy atmosphere of the evening was still sifting through her, and she was encouraged.

As she stood waiting for Rake to return, she tipped her head back, gazing up at the moon. It hung full and heavy against a velvet black sky. The stars winked and glittered against the same velvet black, just the way frost sparkles on new-fallen snow. The cool breeze lifted familiar autumn fragrances into the air—the scent of candles slowly cooking jack-o'-lanterns from the inside, straw and hay, and cattails. Crickets sang, soft and calming, and little wafts of wind swirled dried leaves in circles here and there amid the mist settling on the ground.

Aspen sighed, enchanted by the magical atmosphere of the warm autumn evening. Glancing around her, her gaze fell to a large, dark rock nearby. The rock had an interesting shape, sort of like a big black cooking pot. A deep, natural sort of hollow bowl shape rested in its center. Moisture from the rains the day before had puddled there, and several bright yellow cottonwood leaves floated in the water. Aspen fancied the dark rock with its worn bowl center resembled a cauldron simmering a lovely autumn brew of fallen leaves.

"I put the boards across the mud over there."

Aspen looked up when she heard Rake's voice—gasped when she saw him approaching. He appeared half-hidden in the evening mist, walking toward her through the swirling leaves, looking exactly like a handsome, roguish ghost! She bit her lip with delight, for had she not known better by now, she would've sworn he was only a spirit—a phantom from some past century. All night she'd seen him, gazed at him, danced with him, talked with him, and yet she was still awash with the feeling that the presence of some chivalrous hero had stepped directly from the pages of a Jane Austen novel.

Aspen's heart pounded, again frantic with delight at the sight of him. In those moments, she promised herself she would never forget the sight of Rake Locker advancing toward her through the autumn mist. She sighed as she studied him for the umpteenth millionth time—the tall boots and fitted front flap, black breeches accentuating his long, muscular legs, the blue waistcoat worn beneath the dark blue tailcoat pronouncing the broadness of his shoulders. He looked delicious—

simply delicious in the white shirt with a tall standing collar and white cravat. It was a dream. Surely it was! Surely *he* was a dream.

As she watched him progress toward her, she sighed when he removed his tailcoat, revealing the billowy white sleeves of the period shirt he wore. He smiled a dazzling smile just then—a dazzling, vampire-fanged smile—a smile meant only for her.

Rake felt the smile broadening across his face. Aspen Falls was adorable! Looking at her as she stood there in the gathering mist, he almost believed she *was* a fairy. He half expected her to take flight and leave a trail of sparkling pixie dust in her wake. He inwardly scolded himself, thinking his mom had let him watch *Peter Pan* just one too many times when he was a kid.

Moisture flooded his mouth as he continued toward her, and it unnerved him. What was it about this girl that made him literally salivate? She was fun, yes, and she was uniquely pretty. Still, Rake couldn't figure why he was so physically attracted to her. He was a guy, sure. But that alone wasn't it. There was something else—something drawing him to her—and it felt dangerous. He had it in his mind to walk to her, take her in his arms with brutal force, and kiss the taste right out of her mouth! It was a wicked, delicious feeling that filled him.

He thought back on the evening—the dancing and talking—the flirting and laughter. Aspen was a thoroughly fun person to be with. He thought how easily she'd fallen into conversation with the members of his family, how utterly accepting they were of her, and it freaked him out a little. Part of him had wanted his family to disapprove of Aspen—to see through a veil of cuteness and personality and find she was really a witch in sheep's clothing—to warn him against getting involved with her. But they didn't. They liked her, and now it was just as he'd feared—Aspen Falls was as good as she looked!

Fine, then! Maybe he'd just pull out a few of the stops—test the waters, so to speak. Rake knew, by the way Aspen had freaked over his teasing her—about threatening her virtue when he'd picked her up— that she was a good girl. Maybe he'd let a little more devil out—see if she were as attracted to him as he was to her. Surely she wouldn't be, but there was no harm in trying. Right? After all, she liked his costume, didn't she? Sure she did! He could tell by the way her pretty eyes had widened when she'd answered the door—by the delighted smile on her face at that very moment as she watched him walk toward her. Had he remembered to thank Marissa for helping him come up with the idea and for making the costume for him? He made a mental note to remember to thank her again.

He chuckled, remembering how mortified he'd been when he first put on the blousy shirt and tightfitting breeches. He was a Levi's guy through and through, and the period costume had been a stretch for his pride and confidence. Still, the boots were cool, and obviously Aspen thought the whole costume was cool. So he'd settled into accepting himself in the clothes—for one night, anyway.

Yep! He'd test her—see if the little fairy standing in the moonlight were as totally tripped out about him as he was about her. After all, it was all in fun. Right?

Aspen couldn't help but giggle. He was so handsome! In those moments—standing there in the dark, watching him approach through the mist—she didn't care if Rake turned out to be a jerk. He was gorgeous! Part of her figured he would've shown his true colors by now—surely! He couldn't have sailed through an all-night date on the West Mesa overlooking the city and a barn party at his grandparents' place without slipping up at least once. Could he have?

Maybe she'd just let go—kick all her inhibitions aside and just let whatever would be, be. Maybe—just for one night—maybe she'd let herself like him as much as she feared she already did. Maybe she'd just let the profound, supersensitive physical attraction he provoked in her linger; maybe she'd just let the reins slacken a bit. If he tried to kiss her good night, maybe she'd make sure it was a longer kiss than their first one had been.

He was almost to her, and she couldn't help but giggle. As the vampire Rochester Darcy descended on her at last, Aspen trembled a little—trembled with pure, delicious anticipatory delight.

"What?" he asked as he reached her.

"Nothing," she lied.

"Something made you smile," he said. "Is my fly down?" He glanced down, releasing a breath of relief as he saw nothing was amiss with his breeches. "You scared me," he said, chuckling as he looked back up to her. "Getting caught with your fly down is an entirely different thing than getting caught with this front flap thing down would be."

"I'm sure," Aspen giggled.

"Then what's so funny?" he asked.

Aspen was rendered breathless for a moment—simply by the sight of him and his proximity. He was magnificent! She let her gaze caress the angular line of his square jaw, the perfect shape of his nose and lips. She thought how soft and touchable his dark, dark hair looked—how his nearly black eyes smoldered with mischief. Yep—magnificent!

"It's just…just that you're so perfectly fitted to that costume," she answered. "Rake Locker…the ex-bull-riding, watchmaking, Austenian vampire."

He smiled and chuckled. "I told you chicks would dig this costume, didn't I?" He leaned forward—closer to her—and added, "You just thought you were gonna be immune…and you're not. Are you?"

Aspen held her breath once more, entirely mesmerized by the gorgeous, lethally attractive, ex-bull-riding, watchmaking, Austenian vampire before her.

"I guess not," she admitted. "I will admit…that it's just about the best costume I ever saw on anybody."

Rake smiled—a roguish, alluring smile. Aspen found her gaze affixed to it—to his smile, to his mouth, to the way his perfectly straight teeth seemed even more brilliantly white in the moonlight. She couldn't help but smile, for the two fangs he'd adhered to his top eyeteeth were so eerily attractive. *It's those vampire romances everybody's reading,* she thought. *They've got me as bewitched as they do everyone else.*

"You're staring at my mouth, you know," Rake said. His voice was low—tempting somehow. Aspen felt the heat of a deep blush warm her cheeks. He'd noticed her staring!

"Sorry," she mumbled. She averted her gaze for a moment, yet she could not keep from looking at his face—couldn't keep her mouth from watering as she again looked at his.

"It's—it's just..." she stammered.

"Just what?" he asked.

Aspen shook her head and silently begged the blush to fade from her cheeks. She shrugged. "It's just the moonlight...the fact we're out her alone...and your teeth."

"Oh. Then it's only that my fangs are freaking you out," he said, feigning disappointment. His smile faded for only a moment, almost instantly returning as a roguish grin. "I was hoping you wanted me to kiss you."

Aspen felt her own eyes widen; her heart's already frantic rhythm suddenly doubled. Of course she wanted him to kiss her! Was he kidding?

He sighed and shook his head. He stripped off his tailcoat, tossing it to a nearby tree stump. Stepping nearer to her, he said, "But I guess it's the whole vampire thing going on right now. Chicks don't want a guy to kiss them anymore." Aspen gasped as his strong hands suddenly encircled her throat. Sweeping her hair aside, he added, "They want you to bite them."

Rake forcefully, yet somehow entirely gently, wove his fingers into her hair at the back of her neck, grasping it loosely and softly tugging until she tipped her head to one side. Aspen felt her neck, arms, legs, back, and shoulders blanket in goose bumps as he caressed her throat, his fingers trailing teasingly over her skin. Aspen held her breath as he inclined his head—as it descended. She nearly fainted when she felt his mouth at her neck, his fangs gently pressing her flesh.

A wave of euphoria shuddered through her—traveled the length of her body—left her trembling. Oh, he didn't really bite her at all—just let the tips of his fangs press against her jugular vein a moment before softly kissing the place. Still, it was enough to keep her body covered in goose bumps—and he noticed.

"Goose bumps?" he asked, his voice low and no less than entirely seductive.

Suddenly shy and embarrassed by the powerful physical reaction he'd evoked in her, Aspen stepped back, out of his seductive grasp.

"M-my neck is very sensitive," she stammered, covering the place he'd kissed with one hand. Her cheeks were ablaze with blushing.

"Really?" he asked. Reaching out, he brushed her own hand aside, taking her neck between his powerful hands once more.

"Yeah," she breathed. His gaze was locked on her, his eyes smoldering with a sort of predatory determination.

"Hmm," he mumbled. "What about your mouth then?" he asked, drawing closer, his thumbs tracing the lines of her jaw and chin.

"M-my mouth?" she stammered in a whisper.

"Is it sensitive too?" he asked.

"I-I-I don't know what you—"

"Let's find out," he whispered.

The first touch of his lips to her own caused Aspen's lungs to draw a measured gasp. He kissed her slowly at first, drawing out each melding of their lips—as if savoring some rich, decadent dessert. His hands moved from her neck to her face as he coaxed her lips to part—the promise of deepening kisses between them.

Aspen was wonderfully warmed, as if something sweet and soothing were being drizzled over her, and as she accepted his deepening affections, she realized her trembling was borne not only of Rake's luscious, alluringly applied kisses but also of her own body's fighting to resist surrendering to him. Somehow, Aspen knew that if she would only release her inhibitions—let go of her anxieties concerning his good looks and her stereotypical judgment of him because of them— somehow she knew that melding mouths with Rake Locker would whisk her to bathing in a euphoria she never could've imagined!

"You don't trust me," he whispered against her mouth. "Either that or you're afraid of me," he added as he pulled his mouth further from hers.

He was going to stop kissing her! The thought caused an odd sort of panic to rise in her chest. Aspen's mouth watered—craving his kiss—and she swallowed the excess moisture. He couldn't stop kissing her! Not yet!

She stammered, "W-well, you are a-a vampire."

She heard a chuckle emanate in his throat, and it thrilled her. She focused her attention on his strong, rugged chin, trying not to look at his mouth. She swallowed the excess moisture in her own mouth—bit her lip to keep from taking his face in her hands and kissing him.

"We can just go home if you—" he began.

"No," Aspen breathed. Abandoning any common sense left in her, she reached out, grabbing hold of the lapels of his waistcoat. Pulling herself to the tips of her toes, she kissed him—astonished by the demanding manner in which she did so.

Rake's arms were around her instantly, gathering her against his strong body as he began to pilot their affections once more. Aspen surrendered and relaxed against him, her arms slipping around his waist. His kiss was heated, moist, easy, and teasing one moment, driven and demanding the next—and Aspen Falls was lost!

It seemed she couldn't get close enough to him—couldn't satisfy her thirst for the flavor of his kiss! His embrace lessened, though his kiss remained entirely intense. She felt the strength of his hands at her waist—moved her arms up to encircle his neck, losing her fingers in the dark softness of his hair.

She felt him shift his weight and firmly plant his feet apart. His powerful arms were steel bands around her as he pulled her against him—kissed her with such a demanding determination and ferocity as to take her breath away. She didn't even wince when she felt the sharp tip of one of his fangs catch her lip once.

He broke the seal of their lips, breathing, "Did I hurt you?"

"No," she whispered. She wouldn't have cared if his fang had cut her lip and made it bleed; she still wouldn't have wanted him to stop kissing her. What was wrong with her? She'd never let a man kiss her like this before. She'd never kissed a man back like this before! Her body felt weak and strong at the same time—hot and tingling.

His mouth hovered a breath from hers as he smiled.

"Man!" he exclaimed under his breath. "What broke down your defenses—the outfit or the fangs?"

Aspen giggled as she stared at his mouth and moistened her lips.

"I think…just you," she admitted, feeling a blush rise to her cheeks.

She cradled his strong chin in her hand a moment, letting her fingers feel the straight angle of his jaw—reveled in the sense of his five-o'clock shadow against her palm. She held her breath, overcome with physical attraction as she let her thumb brush over his lips. Rake's eyes narrowed as he looked at her, his handsome brow furrowing in a deep frown. She could feel the rhythm of his breathing increase.

Suddenly, he gripped her wrist in one powerful hand, and she heard him swear under his breath. Straightening her arm, he kissed the bend of it fiercely—kissed the tender, sensitive flesh there before letting his face caress the underside of her arm as it traveled up toward the gold bracelet of her bicep. He placed lingering, moist kisses to the underside of her arm, just below the bracelet, and the blissful sensation caused her to gasp—to tremble.

He took her wrists and quickly directed her arms to encircle his neck as he drew her to him. His fingers dug almost painfully into her ribs as his mouth devoured hers. Aspen had never experienced such a physical reaction—such explosive passion. She fancied she never wanted him to stop kissing her—never! The flesh around her mouth was beginning to hurt, her sensitive skin wondrously assaulted by the whiskers around his. Still, Aspen didn't care anything about any mild discomfort—she simply wanted to kiss Rake Locker forever!

"W-we better go," he breathed, breaking the melding of their mouths and placing one heated cheek against her own.

"Okay," she whispered with disappointment.

"Come on," he said. He took her hand, turned, and began leading her toward the bridge at the irrigation ditch.

Rake stopped short. He looked back at Aspen. His eyes narrowed, ablaze with residual passion. "We better go," he said again.

"Yeah," Aspen breathed, forcing an agreeing nod.

"We better go," he mumbled. Yet his hands went to her waist, and he forcefully pushed her back against the trunk of a nearby cottonwood. "Just one more minute," he breathed. She could feel the heat of his breath in her mouth as he spoke—almost taste it.

"Okay," she whispered.

Rake took possession of her mouth, drawing moist passion from her. Aspen's body had been alive with goose bumps from the moment she'd seen Rake walking toward her through the mist. She wondered if they would ever subside. Yet as he continued to kiss her—to weave a web of entrapment and feral fervor around her—Aspen realized she didn't care. Let him keep her in a state of bliss forever. She didn't care! All she wanted in those moments was what she had in those moments.

"We gotta go," he growled suddenly. Aspen gasped as he swooped her up in his arms and headed for the irrigation ditch bridge.

Rake hurried, nearly desperate to reach the pickup. The thoughts shooting around in his head were nothing if not inappropriate! *What the hell?* he thought. The girl had completely unraveled him. He could feel the perspiration on his forehead at his hairline—struggled to calm his breathing. He'd never gone after a girl on a second date the way he'd gone after Aspen Falls. Hell, he'd never gone after a girl that way at all! She'd done something to him, though he wasn't sure what. He wondered for a moment if maybe she *were* a fairy. Maybe she'd sprinkled fairy dust on him—some sort of magic passion powder.

"That damn Peter Pan," he growled.

"Wh-what?" Aspen asked as he stomped across the bridge.

He shook his head, afraid if he opened his mouth to answer her, it would just end up affixed to hers again. He had to get her to the pickup—had to get his hands on the steering wheel so they'd be too busy to go after Aspen again.

"Y-you forgot your coat," she stammered.

He knew she thought he was mad at her, but he needed a moment. Marissa had always told him, "Girls don't have a clue about guys. Good girls, anyway. They always think he's mad at them…when maybe he's just trying to get control of himself."

Rake didn't want Aspen to think he was mad at her—not even for a moment.

"Thanks," he said, stopping as they reached the bridge. "Marissa would kill me if I lost that."

Rake let Aspen's feet fall to the wooden planks of the bridge. Going back for his coat would give him a few moments of space between him and her. Maybe he could punch a tree trunk when she wasn't looking and release some of his frustration.

"Wait here," he told her. "I'll be right back."

Aspen watched Rake disappear into the mist and the darkness. The water in the irrigation ditch babbled on with a soothing rhythm, and it aided in relaxing her. She was feeling chilly now—now that Rake's arms were no longer around her—now that his mouth was no longer heating hers.

She buried her face in her hands for a moment.

"What are you doing?" she whispered to herself. "You don't even know him!" How could she be so entirely attracted to him? It was their second date. It was bad enough she'd let him kiss her after their first one, but this was scandalous! What would Gina think? Aspen shook her head. Gina would be standing on the sidelines, holding pompoms and cheering Aspen on—she knew that for sure. He seemed so angry. Yet Aspen's brother Adam had explained men to her long ago. Chances were Rake wasn't mad at her—just mad at himself for getting too involved too soon.

Aspen felt panic rising in her. What if he thought she was a hoochie? What if he thought she melted as easily in any man's arms as she had melted in his? Rake didn't seem the type to hanker after hoochie girls. Yet his profound good looks and physique—well, most guys like him did appear to be drawn to hoochies. Still, he didn't seem the type. His mother didn't seem the type who would've raised him to chase hoochies either. Aspen thought of the way she'd kissed him; when he'd first suggested they could go home, *she'd* been the one to keep it going. He must think she was a hoochie for sure! She felt sick to her stomach—nervous, worried, and entirely ill.

She looked up to see him striding through the mist toward her, still looking like a fantasy, still causing her heart to palpitate. He held his tailcoat clenched in one hand, and Aspen noticed his knuckles were bleeding.

"What happened?" she asked. What could've happened to his hand in the few moments it took him to retrieve his coat?

"Oh," he said, raising the hand and inspecting the bleeding knuckles as if he hadn't known they were there until she'd mentioned it. "I...uh...I ran into a tree."

"Oh, I'm sorry! Are you okay?"

Aspen's anxieties settled a bit as he smiled at her. He reached out and took her chin in one hand.

"I'm fine," he said. He leaned forward, kissing her softly on the lips. Aspen smiled as he placed the tailcoat around her shoulders. "But do you think I could taste you just one more time before we go?"

Aspen put her hands to her cheeks to cool her blush. Maybe he didn't think she was hoochie after all.

"You're a charmer," she said, stepping closer to him.

"Of course," he said, smiling. "Aren't all vampires charming? Isn't that how they lull you into thinking you're safe in their company?"

"I suppose," Aspen giggled. She loved the feel of his coat around her shoulders—loved the way he reached out, slipped a hand to the back of her neck, and pulled her toward him.

Their mouths met in a harmony of instant desire, and Aspen was sure her knees had turned to pudding. There in the velvet moonlight, Aspen let herself savor this last kiss of the evening. Rake Locker—what a dream! What a total, undeniably real man.

"Let's go," he said, kissing her cheek.

"Okay," Aspen whispered. He took her hand and led her over the wood planks he'd set over the mud on the other side of the bridge. His hand was warm and strong as he led her toward the pickup. Aspen sighed, bathing in the beauty of the perfect autumn night and the lingering sensation of having kissed the most astonishing man on the face of the earth.

Aspen sighed with an unfamiliar sensation resembling pure satisfaction. Rake winked at her a moment before he closed the pickup's passenger door. She smiled and tugged his tailcoat more snuggly around her shoulders. It smelled divine! Just like Rake—like masculine cologne and—and green chili! Aspen fastened her seat belt and watched Rake saunter around the front of the pickup to his own side. He climbed in and shoved a key in the ignition. The pickup roared to life.

Reaching over, Rake unexpectedly unbuckled Aspen's seat belt. Aspen was bewildered and felt her brow pucker.

"Do you honestly think after that little episode back there…that I'm going to let you sit so far away?" he asked. He took hold of her arm and tugged on it—a gesture she should slide closer to him.

Aspen giggled and moved to sit next to him. As she placed one leg on either side of the gearshift, she thought of how much she preferred older pickups to newer ones. Older ones required a middle-sitter to make allowances for the gearshift—and to snuggle closer to the driver. Goose bumps again raced over her arms when he proceeded to fasten her seat belt for her.

"Much better," Rake said as he revved the engine twice.

Aspen bit her lip, delighted as his hand suddenly came to rest on her knee. He caressed her knee with his fingers and palm for a moment. It was a wonderful sensation, and when she looked up to him, he smiled—the smile of a scoundrel.

"Oops! Sorry," he said, sliding his hand from her knee to the gearshift. "I was trying to shift into first."

Aspen giggled with delight. "You are so naughty!" she said. He was too adorable—so filled with mischievous wit!

He chuckled and shifted into first. The pickup eased forward, and he said, "Yeah, but you don't mind too much," he said, smiling. However, his smile quickly faded, and he looked to her, frowning, and asked, "Do you?"

"Of course I do," she lied, smiling and snuggling up against him.

His smile returned, and he shifted again, pulling onto the paved part of the road.

They were quiet as he drove—nothing but the hum of the engine and the low music on the radio. The night was still bright with stars—the lights of the west side decorating the darkness.

Once Rake had shifted into fourth, he let his right hand rest at her knee again, steering with his left. Aspen allowed her hands to rest on his forearm, inhaling the soothing scent of him.

She still could not believe how involved she'd let herself become—how involved in kissing him—and so soon after meeting him. It was entirely unlike her! Yet her anxiety was not so great as she expected it should be. She frowned for a moment, suddenly very aware of how good-looking Rake Locker was—how plain she must appear next to him. She glanced up at him to assure herself she wasn't just imagining his unique good looks. He glanced down at her, revealing a dazzling, fang-enhanced smile, and she giggled.

"You dig the vampire thing, don't you?" he asked. "Maybe I better not take off the fangs." He looked down at her again and added, "You might not ever let me kiss you again if I do."

"You can kiss me whenever you..." Aspen began. She blushed, mortified that she'd almost told him he could kiss her whenever he wanted—if he ever wanted.

"Whenever I what?" he teased. "Whenever I wear my fangs? Or just whenever?"

"Just whenever," she admitted. Her cheeks were so crimson they almost hurt. She couldn't believe her own honesty.

"Good," he chuckled. "I guess I'm not such a bad guy after all, huh?"

He looked down at her, expectant of a response.

"I guess not," she said. She frowned then, suddenly puzzled by what he'd asked. She looked up at him—studied his five-o'clock shadow and the perfect angle of his jaw. "Did you think I thought you were a bad guy?" she asked. Secretly, she knew she had suspected him of being a jerk—still slightly expected him to turncoat and be one of those eye-candy guys—all bulk, brawn, and ego.

He smiled. "Yep."

"Why?"

He shrugged. "Lots of reasons. I mean...I like to get all torn up at the rodeo...like to jog and lift weights. I work in an old clock shop instead of some big corporate office the way I probably should...so I figured you might think I'm not very ambitious...too much of an average Joe to take any real interest in. Not to mention I probably flirt and tease a little too much."

Aspen smiled. Everything, absolutely everything, he'd just listed—all the things he seemed to think made him a "bad" guy—were exactly the reasons she liked him.

"Those are all things I like about you," she admitted. She couldn't believe she was being so honest with him! She had a vision of herself sticking her neck out over a chopping block. It was, after all, the perfect analogy.

He smiled. "Ah, you can say what you want, arachnophobia girl. I know you just like the fangs."

Aspen giggled and admitted, "I do like the fangs."

"I knew it," he laughed. "Chicks dig the vampire thing…and guys just can't figure out why."

"It's a girl thing," she told him. "You're not supposed to be able to figure it out."

"I guess not," he said.

They rode in silence for a few moments, and then he asked, "What's your schedule like this week coming up?"

Aspen tried not to burst apart into a million pieces of pure rapture. Did he mean to ask her out again?

"I work Monday through Thursday. Then Gina and I are going to the Special Shapes Rodeo on Friday morning," she answered.

"Are you off Saturday?" he asked.

"Yeah." Aspen's heart was beating like crazy! She began to silently pray for him to ask her out.

"Well, if you want…we could watch the mass ascension from the river. There's this place right by my grandparents' house where the trees thin out—you know, where the pilots try to touch down on the sandbars."

Aspen's smile broadened. She loved watching the balloons with her family from her parents' backyard, but the thought of watching them with Rake was all the more wonderful.

"I would love that!" she exclaimed. "But I thought they didn't let people down by the river during the balloon fiesta."

"They don't….unless you live down there," he explained. "There's this great place down there. It's perfect. But we can't drive there. Are you okay riding?"

"Riding what?" she asked, too distracted with delight to think rationally.

He chuckled. "A horse."

"A horse?"

"Yeah," he answered. "We'll just take a couple of my grampa's horses down there. It's not far. Have you ridden before?"

"A couple of times," she admitted. She had ridden a couple of times in her life—on trail horses.

"Good," he said. "It'll be fun. You wanna go?"

"Of course," she answered, a little disappointed that he was already pulling into the parking lot in front of her apartment.

"Okay, then," he said, shifting into park and taking the key out of the ignition. "I'll pick you up at, like, six a.m., and that would put us down by the river by about seven." He smiled at her. "Dress warm."

"I will," Aspen said. His smile was delicious! She wanted to kiss him—never wanted to leave the pickup!

He opened the driver's side door, stepping out and taking hold of her hand. "Come on then," he said. "Let's get you inside. It's cooling off."

Aspen slid across the seat toward him—stepped down out of the pickup to stand before him. He smiled at her and pulled the lapels of his tailcoat together over her chest. He put a strong arm around her shoulders as they walked to her apartment.

"I really did have a lot of fun," she said. "Your family is wonderful!"

He shrugged. "They can be a little weird—a little overwhelming at times—but I like them too."

They were at the door. It was only at that moment that Aspen realized she'd entirely forgotten her purse! She'd left the apartment without it, having been so overcome with delight at Rake's arriving to pick her up. What an idiot!

"What's the matter?" he asked.

"I-I left my purse," she explained.

"At the barn?"

"No. In my apartment."

He grinned. "Guess I'll have to take you back to my place then, huh?" He winked flirtatiously at her. "I've got something you can borrow to sleep in."

Aspen blushed, thrilled, and giggled at his flirting.

"I've got a secret key hidden. Don't worry," she told him.

"I wasn't worried," he chuckled.

Aspen bent down and dug her fingers into the flowerpot to one side of the door. She knew how to avoid the thorns of the cactus in the pot and quickly found the key hidden in the soil. She pushed it into the key slot in the doorknob and twisted it, opening the door.

"Thank you, Rake," she said, turning to look at him once more.

"You're welcome," he mumbled, grinning at her.

Aspen heard the clock in her apartment strike midnight. "And thank you for fixing my clock."

"You're welcome," he said as his hands went to her waist.

Aspen felt her heart flutter and her stomach fill with butterflies as he pulled her body against his, slowly kissing her mouth. She let her hands go to his face, savoring his kiss and the feel of his jaw working to deepen it.

He sighed and broke the seal of their lips.

He wiped the moisture from his lips with his thumb and said, "I'll see you Saturday morning."

"Okay," Aspen said.

"Now…for your own safety…step away from the vampire, miss," he said.

Aspen giggled. Reluctantly she stepped into her apartment.

"'Bye," she said, turning to look at him once more.

"'Bye," he said. He smiled at her one last time and then turned and headed back to his pickup.

Aspen watched him walk away—watched the old white pickup pull out of the parking lot. Closing the door behind her, she exhaled a heavy sigh. She'd never get to sleep! Too many visions, emotions, and sensations were rattling through her mind and body.

"The vampire Rochester Darcy," she sighed. "How absolutely perfect!"

She locked her apartment door and walked toward her bedroom, pulling the ribbons and silk flowers from her hair. She wondered if she could somehow get a copy of the photo Rake's sister had taken of them together at the party—the one she'd asked them to pose for, saying she wanted to keep a photograph of Rake's costume for her portfolio. She was mad at herself for forgetting her purse. Gina would've loved to see the vampire Rochester Darcy!

CHAPTER NINE

"I cannot believe you forgot your camera!" Gina scolded. She sat next to Aspen on the couch, a bowl of freshly popped microwave kettle corn in her lap.

Uncle Guy's clock chimed the first four Westminster notes. Aspen glanced at the clock, wishing time would literally fly by. She couldn't wait until Saturday morning—couldn't wait to be with Rake again! She knew the upcoming week would seem to drag—drag on and on until Saturday, when Rake would finally arrive.

The evening before—Rake's grandparents' harvest party, the moments spent in his arms as the lucky recipient of his affections—had been the stuff of dreams! Aspen hadn't slept a wink during the night. Visions of Rake Locker—the vampire Rochester Darcy, the ex-bull-riding, wild-cow-milking, Austenian vampire watchmaker—had kept her awake with warm, delicious reminiscing. She couldn't wait to see him again. She couldn't wait! As Aspen continued to share the details of her magical evening with Gina, she felt as if Saturday morning were eons away.

"I can't believe I forgot it either," Aspen said. "But I was so distracted when he showed up looking like…you know…perfect!"

"I'm sure, but I still can't believe you forgot it," Gina said. "Although I'm totally glad you made out with him."

"I didn't make out with him," Aspen argued, a heated blush rising to her cheeks at the heavenly memory. Of course she'd made out with Rake—and it had been wonderful!

"Oh my heck! You *totally* made out with him," Gina argued. "But, of course, who wouldn't? *I'd* totally make out with him."

"No, you wouldn't! You always said the only guy you'd ever kiss without knowing first is—"

"I know, I know…Sean Connery," Gina interrupted.

"And he's, like, old enough to be your grandpa!" Aspen teased.

"I don't care. He's totally hot…especially the way he talks. You know, the way he says his *s*'s and stuff."

Aspen laughed. "You are so random!"

"I like Sean Connery…so sue me." Gina smiled and tossed a kernel of kettle corn into the air. She caught it in her mouth with ease and added, "It's that ruggedly mature look he has. Yummy!"

Both girls laughed, and Aspen reached into the bowl in Gina's lap, drawing out a handful of kettle corn.

"And anyway," Gina began, "I don't know what you're talking about. You've had that Sam Elliott infatuation for as long as I can remember!"

"That was before I met the vampire Rochester Darcy," Aspen said. She tossed a piece of popcorn into the air, catching it in her mouth as it tumbled back toward earth.

"Seriously, I know I've been teasing you…but I have to give him credit for being in tune with how to so entirely catch a girl's attention. Rochester Darcy…the vampire? Perfect!" Gina said. She giggled to herself. "In fact, I can only think of one thing that would have made his costume any better."

Aspen shook her head and smiled. "I already know. The vampire UPS man."

"Exactly!" Gina confirmed. She smiled and tossed a few pieces of popcorn into her mouth one right after the other. "You know what would make this popcorn better?"

"What?" Aspen asked.

"If you drizzled a little melted white chocolate over it."

❦

The sun wasn't yet breaking the horizon as Aspen put the car in park. The Balloon Fiesta Park parking lot was already filling up, and Aspen was glad she and Gina had left at five that morning instead of waiting until five thirty. It was six, and they'd managed to beat the worst of the traffic, allowing plenty of time to get down onto the field. The dawn patrol—the hot air balloons chosen to ascend while darkness still veiled the valley—were already aloft, their orange glowing shapes dotting the sky like giant fireflies.

"I hope I don't get too hot," Aspen said, pulling the extra University of New Mexico sweatshirt she'd brought along over her head.

"I know," Gina said, pulling on her "Go Lobos" sweatshirt as well. "I'm always cold when we first get here…and sweltering by the time we leave."

"Let's get hot chocolate first thing," Aspen suggested.

"Totally!" Gina agreed. "Do you have your camera?"

"Got it," she said. Aspen patted her front pocket. She could feel the thin, rectangular shape of her digital camera there. She felt her back pocket, double-checking to make sure her license, debit card, and cash were secure.

She closed the car door, pushed the lock button her on her key chain, shoved her keys into her other front pocket, and said, "Let's go!"

"I'm so excited!" Gina said as they began walking toward the entrance to the balloon field. "Can you even imagine not being able to see the balloons every year?"

Aspen shook her head. "No. And I can't believe so many local people take it for granted."

"Me neither. They better have fry bread this year…or at least funnel cake."

Aspen smiled. That was Gina, always worried about the food at an event—about food period.

The air was cool and crisp, fresh with October's beauty and brilliance. Aspen glanced off to her right—to the Sandia Mountain looming in the distance like an ancient southwest sentinel guarding the valley. The entire moment was simply invigorating, and Aspen felt her pulse increase with excitement. Oh, it certainly wasn't the same kind of pulse increase the thought of Rake Locker caused in her, but it was a wonderful feeling all the same.

Aspen looked down to the balloon field ahead, trying to keep her thoughts from wandering to Rake. This was her day with Gina—their annual Special Shapes Rodeo adventure. She smiled, thinking that it always did turn out to be an adventure somehow.

She thought of the year before. Now *that* had been an adventure! She and Gina were asked to ride with the chase crew of the special shapes unicorn balloon. What a blast they'd had! The unicorn crew was short a couple of chasers, and it turned out Gina knew the guy driving the lead chase crew vehicle. He was a pharmaceutical rep, and he invited Gina and Aspen to ride out on the balloon chase.

Having grown up around the hot air balloons and the fiesta, Aspen and Gina both understood that the balloons were slaves to the whims of the fickle winds. Chase crews followed their balloon, traveling across the landscape below and arriving at the landing site just before or as the balloon landed. Often the crew had to get permission from a land owner for the balloon to land on the owner's property. Crews were in constant radio contact with the balloon's pilot and ever available in case of emergency or for basic instructions. The chase crew also helped pack the balloon and equipment once the balloon had landed.

Aspen and Gina had been delighted and excited nearly to delirium at the prospect of riding with a chase crew. Every early October of their memories, they'd waved to chase crews as they raced down major or minor roads, American flags attached on either side of the pickups' tops and patriotically flapping in the wind. The sound of the chase crew flags was as familiar to Aspen as the soothing sound of the burner bursts used to heat the air inside the balloon envelope as it floated overhead. Thus, traveling with a chase crew had been like a lifelong dream come true for both girls. Oh, how they'd thrilled to be riding in the bed of the lead chase crew pickup, relishing the challenge of keeping the giant airborne unicorn in sight as it traveled through the beautiful New Mexico atmosphere. The excitement of watching the balloon land and helping to pack it away—envelope, basket, and burner—all before eight thirty in the morning had been wonderful.

Gina had offered her friend a gift certificate she had to Sadie's as recompense for letting her and Aspen chase. Yet he'd simply told them he was grateful for their help, thanked them, and given them free passes for the balloon glow scheduled for that night.

Aspen sighed.

"What?" Gina asked.

"How will we ever top being on the chase crew last year?" Aspen asked.

Gina shrugged. "Just take a ton of photos this year, I guess. There was hardly time last year, remember?"

"Yeah," Aspen said.

"I love to see the burners heating up when it's still dark," Gina sighed.

"Me too!"

Aspen smiled as she looked out over the field. She and Gina were still descending toward it, and their elevation provided a great view as the burners lit up the dark—randomly shooting flame into the air, speckling the field with flashes of firelight.

"Oh, let's hurry!" Aspen said, taking Gina's arm and quickening their step.

"Wait!" Gina said, stopping cold in her tracks and pulling her own camera out of her pocket. "Let me get a picture of you."

"Let's do one together," Aspen suggested.

The girls pressed their cool, rosy cheeks together, held their cameras out, and flashed several self-portraits. Giggling, they linked arms and hurried toward the entrance, where hot chocolate and adventure were waiting.

Once through the entrance to the park—after purchasing breakfast burritos and hot chocolate—Aspen and Gina hurried onto the field. Chase crews were busily spreading balloon envelopes over the dew-laced grass.

"There's the chili ristra!" Gina exclaimed. Aspen looked to see a crew working to spread the giant chili-ristra-shaped balloon envelope evenly over the ground. Aspen smiled. Just like every year she and Gina had come to the Special Shapes Rodeo, she felt her eyes mist with tears of pure delight and excitement. "Oh, the fish! I love the fish!" Gina giggled.

"Oh my heck! The witch on the broom," Aspen exclaimed as her eyes fell to the large green-faced witch balloon next to the fish.

"I *love* the witch on the broom!" Gina squealed.

"I hope the ship is here."

"The buccaneer?" Gina asked. "Me too. It's one of my favorites!"

The buccaneer was Aspen's favorite special shape balloon. Modeled after the cliché pirate ship, it was a marvel of hot air balloon ingenuity, from a distance looking more like a real ship than a balloon. The buccaneer had only been to the Fiesta once—several years before, when Aspen was still in high school. Still, she knew she would never forget the first time she'd ever seen it floating on the distant horizon. It had been awe-inspiring—like something from a dream! Aspen remembered telling her mother how much the moment reminded her of something from *Peter Pan*—as if Peter himself were steering a pixie-dusted pirate ship through the sky.

Tossing the remnants of their foil-wrapped breakfast burritos into a nearby trash barrel, the girls linked arms, wandering through a magical world of dawn-drenched balloon crews, burners, and photographers. Quick whiffs of propane from the burners wafted through the air, mingled with the delicious scents of green chili, donuts, and the fresh southwest air.

"Go Lobos!" someone called. Aspen saw Gina wave to a balloon crew, most of whom wore University of New Mexico sweatshirts themselves.

"Mmm!" Gina hummed. "That one guy is really cute!"

Aspen looked over to a handsome man waving at Gina.

"Maybe," Aspen said.

"You're just spoiled now, girlfriend," Gina giggled. "And who wouldn't be after something like Rake Locker?"

Aspen took a sip of her hot chocolate and nodded. It was true! She wondered if she'd ever think any other man was attractive again. Compared with Rake, it seemed unlikely. How could anyone compare to him in looks or personality? A small wave of anxiety washed over her. She was in danger already! Two dates and she was already in danger of having her heart broken—she knew it. The thought made her uneasy.

She took another sip of hot chocolate and forced her attention in the opposite direction—to the crew of the pumpkin special shape balloon to right. Yet the pumpkin balloon only caused her to think of all the pumpkins and jack-o'-lanterns piled in the corners and on the tables in Rake's grandparents' barn. She felt goose bumps prickling her arms— the effect of the sudden flashback of kissing Rake.

Aspen sipped her hot chocolate once more, and Gina giggled, "Go easy, Aspen! You don't want to have to use the pewey potties before you have to!"

"Ew, gross, I know!" Aspen agreed. Still, the hot chocolate helped a little—helped to keep her mouth from watering at the thought of Rake—and she took another sip.

Within the hour the balloons were inflated, fantastic shapes and characters of every kind hovering like fantasy creatures as the first rays of sun broke over the Sandia Mountain to the west. The battery in Aspen's digital camera was already down fifty percent, and she hoped it would make it through the rest of the morning. She'd have to be more selective in taking photos. She frowned as she looked at the battery strength indicator. She'd remembered to put the extra memory card in her pocket but had forgotten to bring the second battery.

"It's here!" she heard Gina exclaim.

"Where?" Aspen asked. She knew at once which balloon Gina was referring to—the buccaneer! After all, they'd both hoped it would be at the fiesta.

"Right over there…behind the Santa Claus balloon. See it?"

"Oh my heck!" Aspen squealed, snapping a quick photo as the bowsprit of the buccaneer appeared behind the Santa Claus balloon. Aspen hurried forward, wanting to see more of the ship.

"There it is!" Gina exclaimed.

And it was! Aspen gasped with delight as the sail-donned masts and hull of the balloon became visible. Aspen took several more photos and could hear Gina's camera shuttering away as well.

"It's beautiful!" she breathed. She shook her head, awed by the wonder of it. Enormous and expertly detailed, the buccaneer balloon was magnificent. She couldn't believe how detailed it was. It truly looked like a real pirate ship.

"Let's get closer," Gina urged, taking Aspen's hand and pulling her toward the balloon. As they approached, Aspen noted the lead chase vehicle and attached equipment trailer both had *The Buccaneer* blazoned on their sides. The pilot hit the burner, and the balloon slowly swayed to and fro, emulating the appearance of being tossed on gentle waves.

"I love it!" Aspen giggled, snapping more photos. "It's definitely my favorite special shape. How about you?"

When Gina—who was usually so verbose—did not respond, Aspen looked over to see her friend staring in the opposite direction, mouth agape in astonishment.

"What is it?" Aspen asked, following her friend's gaze. She knew at once why Gina's attention had been arrested from the buccaneer. She giggled when she saw the enormous brown UPS truck swaying to and fro, just as the buccaneer did.

"I can't believe it!" Gina exclaimed in a whisper. "It's a sign or something. It has to be!"

"A sign?" Aspen asked, giggling at her friend's awed expression.

"Seriously!" Gina assured her. "I mean…a UPS truck special shapes balloon? How can it not be a sign?"

"A sign of what?" Aspen asked, still giggling.

"I don't know! Just a sign. Come on!"

Aspen laughed as Gina took hold of her hand and began pulling her toward the UPS truck balloon.

"Oh my heck!" Aspen exclaimed as they neared the balloon. She couldn't believe her eyes. The entire UPS truck chase crew was dressed head to toe in UPS uniforms. "If this isn't your own dream come true, Gina…I don't know what is!"

"Look! A whole slew of them!" Gina breathed.

"Yep! Definitely your dream come true…a whole slew of UPS men!"

Aspen heard Gina gasp and looked over to see her put a hand over her heart.

"It's him!" she breathed.

"Who?" Aspen asked.

"Him! The UPS guy from my mom's house…a-and the bookstore that day you were dressed up like a big pink dog!" Gina whispered. Gina pointed to one of the men standing near the basket talking to the balloon pilot. Sure enough, it was him. The same wavy brown hair—the same handsome UPS guy!

"Nuh uh!" Aspen said, frowning. Surely she was imagining things. Surely they both were! There had to be millions of UPS guys working in and around Albuquerque. What were the odds of the same UPS guy who delivered to the bookstore on the west side being right there with them on the balloon field? Then again, what were the odds of the same guy having delivered to Gina's parents' house too? "Maybe it *is* a sign," Aspen breathed.

"It has to be a sign!" Gina exclaimed.

"Go talk to him then," Aspen urged, poking Gina in the ribs with one elbow.

"No way! I can't mess up the sign!" Gina said.

"Mess up the sign?" Aspen exclaimed. "Maybe that's the reason for the sign. Maybe you're supposed to walk right up to him and propose!"

"No," Gina said. "That can't be it."

Cheering erupted nearby, and Aspen turned around to see the Santa Claus balloon slowly lifting off. The fish balloon followed shortly.

"They're starting to go," Aspen said, turning to look at Gina. But her friend stood mesmerized, eyes wide and watching as the handsome UPS guy climbed into the basket of the UPS truck balloon.

"Oh my heck! He's going up," Gina exclaimed.

Sure enough, Aspen and Gina watched as two other UPS-uniform-clad men climbed into the basket. As the ground crew released the last tether, the UPS truck balloon began to ascend. Aspen giggled and heard Gina gasp as the handsome UPS man from the bookstore smiled and waved at them.

Aspen returned his wave, jabbing Gina in the ribs with one elbow to remind her to do so too.

"And there he goes," Gina breathed. "The man of my dreams!"

"We forgot to take a picture!" Aspen squealed, pointing her camera in the direction of the escaping balloon and keeping the shutter button depressed so it would snap a series of consecutive photographs.

Aspen stood silent, watching the giant UPS truck balloon ascend higher and higher. She glanced to Gina and saw the frown of disappointment puckering her brow.

"We could run to the car really quick and try to chase it if you want," Aspen said. "Maybe we could get close again when it lands."

Gina shook her head and exhaled a frustrated sigh. "No. It's okay. I'm just being stupid."

Aspen knew Gina was thinking of Nick—the jerk. Nick had done such a number on Gina. Aspen loathed him for breaking her best friend's heart. For a moment, anxiety washed over her once more as she thought of Rake. Would he break her heart too? Aspen had watched Gina struggle and battle depression, low self-esteem, and everything else negative because of Nick's cruelty. She suddenly had a vision of herself struggling the same way—a vision of Rake dumping her flat the way Nick had dumped Gina. Still, in truth, Gina had had a narrow escape. Nick Dalley was a jerk, and Aspen knew it was good Gina had found out what a total jerk he was before they'd gotten married. All the worse it would've been had Gina married Nick, only then to find out the truth.

Gina sighed, shook her head, and forced a smile. "Well, if it's meant to be...then it won't be the last time I see him, right?"

"Exactly," Aspen confirmed. Her own anxieties were still rising, however, and she inhaled a deep breath of calm. Less than twenty-four hours remained until she would see Rake again. Less than twenty-four hours and she'd be with him—able to try and read him again. Part of her still maintained he would turn out to be an egotistical jerk, but that was only the defensive part of her—the part warning her of impending heartache. Surely Rake was of a better character than Nick Dalley! She shook her head, dispelling all doubtful thoughts. Of course he was better. Through simply the way he'd treated her thus far, he'd proven he was better.

"Oh, the buccaneer is ready to launch!" Gina exclaimed. She took hold of Aspen's arm and began pulling her back toward the enormous pirate ship balloon.

Aspen laughed, delighted by her friend's returning enthusiasm.

"I'm glad the Santa already launched," Aspen said. "Now we can get some really good pictures of the ship."

"There it goes!" Gina giggled.

Aspen sighed as she watched a crew member release the last tether. The buccaneer slowly lifted. Looking like an enchanted phantom ship, the balloon ascended—a vision of wonderment against the blue of morning's sky.

"It's beautiful!" Aspen sighed, taking several more photographs.

In that moment—as she watched the giant ship-shaped balloon rise farther into the atmosphere—Aspen thought of Rake. Was he still in bed? Or was he somewhere on the west side, watching the special shapes take to the air? She wondered if a person could see the balloons drifting over the river from the parking lot of the Clock Shop.

Her heart leapt, trillions of butterflies taking flight in her stomach as she thought of meeting him in the morning—of riding out on horseback to the riverbank to watch the mass ascension. Her mouth watered at the memory of his kiss, and she again wondered if Rake could now see the beautiful buccaneer ship adrift in a sky bluer than any sea.

Rake raised a hand, shading his eyes from the brilliance of the morning sun. Yep, the special shapes were in the air, and he couldn't help but smile. Ever since he was a kid, he'd loved the balloons—been glad the balloon fiesta was held in Albuquerque every year. Of course, as a child, the special shapes had always been his favorite. He preferred the regular shapes now—or the regular shapes mixed in with a few of the special shapes. The regular shapes were more soothing somehow—or so *he* thought.

He wondered if Aspen were having fun with her friend at the Special Shapes Rodeo. It had taken every ounce of self-control not to crash their party—not to show up at the balloon field just to see Aspen, even for a few moments. But this was her time with her friend, and he knew girls needed their space, just like guys.

His mouth watered as he thought of kissing her—as he remembered the feel of holding her in his arms, the scent of her skin. Oh, yeah! He knew he was in trouble, but he'd calmed down a bit since his grandparents' barn party—gotten his head screwed back on straight. Sure, he liked Aspen—a whole lot more than he wanted to consciously admit—but he wouldn't be caught in any traps this time. Still, his heart did a somersault in his chest cavity when he thought of the prospect of seeing her in less than twenty-four hours.

"Cowboy up, Rake," he chuckled, shaking his head. "Get a grip. She's just fun…that's all."

He chuckled, however, when he saw a new special shape balloon drift over—a brown UPS truck balloon. Aspen had mentioned her friend had a thing for UPS guys, and he wondered if the two of them had seen the new special shapes balloon. The UPS balloon was traveling low, probably trying to hit a sandbar nearby.

The balloon was low enough Rake could easily see the passengers in the basket.

"Good morning!" he called.

"Good morning!" the pilot called.

"Hey, Rake!" one of the passengers shouted. "Is that you, man?"

Rake moved his hand, more adeptly shading the sun from his view. He smiled, recognizing the man at once.

"Sean! No way, man!" he hollered. "You didn't tell me anything about this!"

"It was a last-minute thing, man!" his friend Sean called. "I'll give you details later. We're gonna try and hit the sandbar."

"Good luck, man! I've seen three miss it already this morning."

"Thanks, man!" Sean called, waving.

Rake watched as the giant UPS truck headed toward the clearing in the middle of the river. He knew special shapes had an even harder time than other balloons trying to land or basket-bump the sandbar in the middle of the river. For one thing, they were so much bigger. He laughed as he watched the balloon descend—held his breath as he saw the basket full of passengers near the sandbar.

"Oops!" he chuckled as he saw the basket miss the sandbar and touch down in the river. The pilot was good, however, hit the burner, and sent the balloon ascending once more. They barely cleared the trees. As Sean shrugged then waved, Rake raised his arm and waved again.

"They almost had it," he said to himself. He chuckled again as he hunkered down and rearranged the tinder and logs in the small fire pit. He didn't know why he was going to so much trouble to make sure everything was ready down by the river for his date with Aspen the next morning. He could tell she was the kind of girl who didn't expect all the bells and whistles about anything. Still, he wanted to make sure everything he could do ahead of time was done.

He heard the slow blast of a burner and glanced up.

"Nice!" he breathed as he saw the buccaneer balloon appear overhead. He stood up and shaded his eyes once more. "Awesome!"

Rake had only seen this particular special shapes balloon once, years before, but the same thrill rose up in him at the sight of it—the same youthful excitement he'd felt when first he'd seen it.

Sails and hull inflated, the buccaneer drifted across the sky in a perfect vision of fantasy. He heard the burner again—watched, mesmerized, as the balloon floated over the river toward the west.

He chuckled, thinking that if he were still a kid, he would've been convinced it was Captain Hook himself steering across the early October atmosphere.

He rubbed his left arm, remembering how badly his skin had itched inside the cast when he'd broken it at age four—when he'd thought of a happy thought and jumped off the roof, certain he could fly like Peter Pan.

Thoughts of Peter Pan kicked his mind back to the pretty, pixie-dusted fairy he'd kissed almost a week before. He wondered if Aspen had seen the buccaneer balloon launch from the balloon field. His mouth began to water at the thought of her, and he shoved his left foot in the stirrup and mounted Jerry, his grandpa's old buckskin gelding.

Rake clicked his tongue and sent Jerry off at a quick trot. He shook his head as he rode, realizing that every time he thought of Aspen, he felt like a stupid teenager—all excited and wound up with anticipation. He had less than twenty-four hours to kick himself back into the mindset of a watchmaker in his midtwenties—twenty-four hours before he'd be tempted by cute little Aspen Falls. Besides, he told himself, she'd be dressed for cool weather—a sweatshirt and jeans rather than a pretty little fairy costume that showed off her figure and smooth, fragrant skin. Furthermore, it would be early morning. Surely he'd have more self-control then, when a cool morning was chafing his cheeks—more self-control than he'd obviously had on a warm romantic midnight.

As he rode, he noticed the way the cottonwood leaves had seemed to change overnight. Where there was still a majority of green leaves the week before, now there was nearly all gold. He glanced at the river—smooth and serene as glass. He shook his head, amused by the lines of Aspen's poem popping into his head. He thought of the references to gold ribbons being woven through the mountain's hair—which led him to thinking of the soft ribbons that had been woven through Aspen's hair the night of his grandparents' party.

As he rode beneath the ribbon of gold along the river he mumbled, "'So the moon wove his fingers of moonbeams through the gold amidst mountain's hair.'" He mused that if he could have a favorite line from a poem—and that thought alone disturbed him—it would be that one. That one—or the very last lines. He frowned, trying to remember the exact phrase at the end of the poem, but it escaped him. He looked back at the buccaneer balloon. It was fast disappearing behind the cottonwoods.

"'And the moon and mountain blend kisses as the time of aspen falls.' That's it," he mumbled, suddenly having remembered the poem's conclusion.

He clicked his tongue again, urging Jerry on at a quicker pace. It was time to distract himself from the idea of blending kisses with Aspen. What the hell was she doing to him? Poetry bouncing around in his head—where there should be nothing but a focus on work and moving that load of rock for his grandpa when he got back to the house.

"Aspen Falls," he breathed, frowning. "I think you're getting too far under my skin." He exhaled and gritted his teeth. "Come on, Jerry," he growled, nudging the horse with his heels. He needed a gallop, needed to get back to the house and move that rock for his grandpa, needed to get his mind off Aspen and her pretty smile—her pretty mouth!

CHAPTER TEN

"Oh, I remember when I was young," Charlotte Locker sighed. "Young enough to enjoy getting up in the dead of night to ride down to the river."

"You're still young, Gramma," Rake said, bending down to kiss his grandmother on one cheek.

"They'll be launching the balloons in about an hour, Rake," Joseph Locker said. "You better get your girl on out there before your grandma makes you miss 'em." Joseph grinned at Aspen, and she blushed when he whispered, "You see, I'm on your side. Wanna make sure you two have plenty of time left for some serious necking." He winked, and Aspen thought she might explode from embarrassment.

"Do you have everything you need, honey?" Charlotte asked Rake.

"Yep. I already packed the saddlebags, and I left everything else out there yesterday," Rake answered. He finished the last bite of one of his grandmother's breakfast burritos, rinsed his plate, and stacked it in the sink.

"I thought we were just riding out to watch the ascension," Aspen asked. "What did you need to pack?"

Rake smiled. "You can't sit by the river and watch the balloons without hot chocolate. How would you stay warm?"

"Keeping warm…that's what the necking is for," Joseph chuckled, winking at Aspen again. This time she put a hand to one of her crimson cheeks. What a tease Rake's grandpa was! It grew more and more obvious from whom Rake inherited his teasing sense of humor.

"Joseph! Now you stop that," Charlotte scolded, putting a comforting arm around Aspen's shoulders. "You'll scare her off completely!"

"Oh, she won't scare off too easy," Joseph said. Aspen did not miss the familiar twinkle of mischief in his eyes—so exactly like Rake's. "I figure if Rake's as good at necking as I was in my day…" he began, nuzzling his wife's neck with his chin.

"Now you stop that, Joseph Locker!" Charlotte giggled. "Stop that right this minute!"

"Come on, Aspen," Rake said, taking hold of her arm. "Let's leave Gramma and Grampa to their necking." He laughed and said, "We'll see you two later," as he pulled her toward the front door.

"Thank you for breakfast, Mrs. Locker," Aspen said over her shoulder.

"You're welcome, honey. You kids have fun now!" Charlotte called. Aspen smiled as she heard the elderly woman giggle and tell her husband to behave himself in front of the children.

"We will, Gramma," Rake chuckled.

Aspen smiled as they left the house. It was still dark—a cool and crisp October morning.

"Did you spend a lot of time with your grandpa when you were growing up?" she asked.

"Yeah. Why?" Rake answered.

Aspen shrugged. "Just wondering." Aspen had noticed how much Rake was like his grandfather, even down to the way he walked—a sort of rhythmic saunter.

"I'm gonna have you ride Jerry," he said as he led her toward the two horses tied to a nearby tree. "He's really gentle and knows the riverbank."

"Thanks," Aspen said. She smiled as she watched Rake untie the buckskin horse's reins.

"Come on, Jerry," he said, leading the horse to Aspen. "You'll like Aspen. She smells good."

Aspen couldn't help but smile as she studied Rake. She figured her smile hadn't faded for a moment—not from the first instant she saw

160

Rake that morning. He wore a worn-out pair of Levi's, a really banged-up pair of black ropers, a blue-and-white flannel shirt, and a tattered blue Nike baseball cap. He was perfect—absolutely perfect—from the way he wore his shirt untucked to the small holes at each top corner of his back pockets, visible whenever he lifted his arms over his head, causing his shirttail to raise enough to see them. She raised an eyebrow as she watched him—as her attention fell to the holes at his pockets as he lifted his arms to test the saddle. She bit her lip with delight. It was obvious his underwear were white.

"Here you go," he said, taking hold of the reins and saddle horn with one hand, steadying the stirrup with the other.

Aspen was a little nervous. It had been years since she'd been on a horse. She wasn't sure she could mount with any sort of grace or coordination. Still, reaching up and taking hold of the saddle horn, she shoved her foot in the stirrup, smiling when she realized she'd made a pretty smooth mount. Rake handed her the reins and then went to the tree to retrieve his own horse—a big black horse that Aspen was glad she didn't have to ride. Rake's horse looked younger—wilder than Jerry—and Aspen patted Jerry's neck, silently thanking him for being old and gentle.

"You ready?" Rake asked, flashing a dazzling, fangless smile.

"Yep," Aspen answered. She wondered what he'd used to glue those fake fangs to his teeth the weekend before—if they were easily removed or took some effort.

"Then let's go," he said. He clicked his tongue, and both his horse and Jerry lurched forward. "We've got plenty of time to take it slow," he began. "It's not very far."

"Okay," Aspen said.

"Did you have fun with your friend yesterday?" he asked as they rode side by side through the cool darkness. "I saw that new UPS balloon and thought of you guys."

Aspen started to feel disappointed—upset that it would take Gina's UPS man fixation to make Rake think of her. Still, perhaps he was just making conversation. Perhaps there wasn't an underlying interest other than he truly wanted to know if they had fun.

"We did," she answered. "And Gina loved the UPS balloon. There was some guy in it that she's seen around town. I swear, she almost dropped dead when she saw him get into the balloon."

"How funny," he chuckled. "Yeah, I saw it yesterday. It was drifting pretty low, trying to hit the sandbar." He was quiet for a moment, and then he asked, "Did you see the ship?"

"I did!" Aspen exclaimed. "I love it! I saw it a few years ago when it was here and have always wished it would come back."

"Yeah, I think it's from Spain or somewhere. It probably costs a lot to bring it over here just for this."

"Well…wherever it's from, I'm glad they made the trip. It was beautiful!"

They rode in silence for a moment, nothing but the sound of the river and the coo of a mourning dove somewhere near.

Aspen slowly inhaled, relishing the scents of nature all around her—the water, the cottonwood trees, the sandy soil of the riverbank. She was a little chilled and wondered if maybe she should've worn a light coat instead of just a sweatshirt. Still, she didn't care. Cold or not, it was a glorious morning.

"The leaves changed really fast this year," he said. "When the sun's up, you'll see what I mean. It seems there was a lot more green even just last week."

"I know," Aspen said. "It's always kind of…you know…like you're so happy it's autumn because the hot heat of summer is over and everything seems to settle down. But then…then you know winter is just around the corner, and everything is dead and brown…colder. I don't like winter. I always feel sort of…sort of insecure or something."

"Probably another reason you like that poem so much…the one your mom named you after," he offered.

"Probably," she said, smiling.

"Tell it to me again," he said. "What's that part about winter coming?"

"There are a couple of parts about winter," she said. Aspen felt her cheeks heat with a blush. She didn't like reciting the poem; it always made her so nervous. Sure, she'd recited it to him before, but she was

162

shy. Still, if he wanted her to—Aspen's heart swelled as she realized she'd do just about anything Rake Locker asked of her.

"Just recite the whole thing," he said.

"Right now?" she asked.

He chuckled. "You sound bashful about it," he said.

"I am," she admitted. "It's...it makes me nervous."

"Then I'll give you a break...for the moment. As long as you promise to recite it for me later."

"Okay, I promise," she said. Odds were he'd forget about it. She was off the hook.

In a short time, Rake had led them to a clearing on the riverbank and dismounted. Dropping the reins to his own horse, Aspen was thrilled with he reached up and put his hands at her waist, lifting her down from hers.

"Let's get the fire going," he began, "get you some hot chocolate made, and warm you up."

"Okay," Aspen said. He paused, smiling down at her. Even in the dark, his eyes seemed to smolder, and she felt goose bumps ripple over her arms—simply from looking at him.

She followed him over to an undersized fire pit. He pulled a small box of matches from his pocket and hunkered down. Taking a match out of the box and striking it on the seam of his well-worn Levi's, he touched it to the kindling in several places. Aspen smiled as flames nearly instantly began to lick up around the logs. He retrieved a small grate that had been leaning up against a nearby rock, placing it over the fire.

"I'll be right back," he said, and she watched him saunter away from the bank to a small thicket of bushes. He reached in to the brush, drawing out an old metal teapot and a plastic thermos.

Aspen held her hands out over the fire as Rake filled the teapot with water and set it on the grate. He went to his horse and opened a saddlebag, rummaging around and finally withdrawing two tin cups and several packages of hot chocolate mix. She giggled when she saw him pull out a spoon and shove it in his back pocket.

The fire crackled, flaming the mellow scent of dry wood. Aspen watched as Rake stuck his finger in the water inside the kettle. She giggled at his ease, surprised at her own lack of concern that he was sticking his finger into water she would be drinking soon. Somehow, it didn't bother her—the idea of drinking water he'd tested that way. Had anybody else done it, it would've ruined her appetite.

"Still too cold," he said. He stood and took off his cap. Running his fingers through his hair, he sighed as he gazed up at the sky. The sun was just breaking over the mountains. He smiled and plopped the cap onto its rightful place on his handsome head.

"Do you come out here often?" she asked. His actions seemed almost routine.

"Yeah, I do," he admitted. "Especially during the fiesta." He was facing east, and Aspen turned to gaze in the same direction. Brilliant pinks of every hue reached across the sky. "The sun's almost up," he said. "The balloons should be launching any minute." He smiled, biting his lip and rubbing his hands together with excited anticipation. "Maybe we'll get lucky and someone will try for the sandbar."

"When the old Alameda bridge was still up, I used to love to drive down under it and park…watch them try to splash and dash," Aspen told him. "I saw one guy way underestimate it once. I bet the basket was three feet down in the water."

"Happens all the time," he said. "I'd say only about ten percent of the ones that try for the sandbars actually hit them. Most of those bounce once or twice and end up in the water anyway."

He hunkered down and stuck his finger in the water again. "Ouch!" He breathed the exclamation and shook his hand to cool the burn. "You want some?" he asked, smiling at her.

"Of course!" she giggled.

She watched as he unfastened the first few snaps at the bottom of his shirt, using the fabric of his shirt to protect his hand as he lifted the teakettle off the grate and set it in the sand next to the fire. He plopped the two metal cups down in the sand and poured steaming water into each one. Aspen bit her lip, delighted as she watched him rather fumble around with the hot chocolate packets. It amazed her that a man whose very profession required precision and dexterity—a man who worked with the tiny gears and parts involved in clock- and watchmaking—should struggle so with hot chocolate packets. He emptied one packet into each cup, pulling the spoon from his back pocket and alternately stirring each mixture.

At last he grinned up at her. "Ready?"

"For hot chocolate? Always!" Aspen giggled. She gasped when Rake tore a strip of fabric from the bottom of his shirt, two or three inches wide and about a foot long. "What are you doing?" she asked. She watched as he wrapped the strip of fabric around the handle of the tin cup.

"I forgot to bring something to hold it with. It'll burn your hand," he explained, standing and handing the cup to her.

"But you just ruined your shirt," she said, accepting the cup.

He shrugged. "It's an old shirt. And anyway…your hand is more important." She shook her head as he tore another length of fabric from his shirt, using it to hold his own cup.

It seemed an awful lot of work and garment destruction to go to for a couple of cups of hot chocolate. Aspen smiled, delighted with his willingness to go to such lengths.

"You're really cute in your little University of New Mexico sweatshirt," he said, smiling at her. He sipped some hot chocolate from his cup, never taking his eyes off her.

Aspen felt herself blush. She wasn't very good at accepting compliments—even from people who weren't insanely good looking!

"Thanks," she managed. "But I'm sure nothing beats that big pink dog costume." A quick thanks followed by a humorous remark to distract, that was her way—the only way she could usually manage it.

He chuckled. "That dog costume *was* pretty sexy."

Aspen giggled and took a sip of her hot chocolate—the hot chocolate Rake Locker had made for her with his little packets of mix and the spoon from his back pocket. He was so fabulous! A rough-around-the-edges, wholly masculine real man—equipped with the extra and magnificent bonus of having a fabulous personality! In truth, Rake Locker was everything Aspen had ever dreamed of in a man. Everything! At least so it seemed—so far.

Her heart pinched a moment—ached with sudden fear and anxiety. Yet somehow fear and anxiety mingled with attraction, hope, and pleasure.

"Hold on," he said, striding back to the horse. He opened the opposing saddlebag and pulled out an old serape. It was well-worn, yet the variegated colors of the traditional Mexican blanket still rang rich and bright. Rake chugged the rest of his hot chocolate, setting the empty cup in the sand by the fire. He spread the serape on the ground near the fire. "We'll be more comfortable sitting down."

Rake stretched out on the blanket, crossing his feet at his ankles and propping himself on one elbow. Aspen sat down beside him, making a pretzel with her own legs and taking another sip of her own hot chocolate.

"The sun's up," she said. "It shouldn't be long now."

Rake grinned. "You really don't mind this?"

"Mind what?" she asked. What could she possibly mind? Being with the most attractive man in the universe? Sitting on the banks of the Rio Grande in autumn, drinking hot chocolate, and waiting for the beautiful hot air balloons to drift over? What was there to mind?

"All this," he said, shrugging. "Getting up at the crack of dawn, riding through the cold and dark, just to sit in the dirt and watch balloons go over?"

Aspen giggled. "Of course not! I can't imagine anything more wonderful…more peaceful and relaxing. *You* don't mind, do you?" She wondered suddenly if the entire thing were too boring for him. Maybe he'd done all this purely for her sake. Of course, she couldn't think of a nicer sacrifice, but she wanted him to enjoy it all the same.

"No way! I love this," he assured her. "It gets me out of the shop… and I love it out here."

Aspen smiled. She finished her hot chocolate and set the cup aside, next to Rake's.

"Do I have you all day?" he asked.

"What do you mean?" Aspen giggled.

"Do I have you all day…or did you plan something else after this?"

Aspen shrugged. "I-I didn't plan anything. I wasn't sure how long this would take or anything."

"Then do you want to drive up north of Santa Fe and pick piñons after the balloons are down?"

Aspen felt her stomach fill with butterflies. He wanted to spend the entire day with her? She couldn't believe it! As she sat staring at the most beautiful man she'd ever seen—as she tried to convince herself she was truly worthy of having his attention—she sighed.

"I would love it!" she told him.

"Good! Then after...hold on." He paused, listening. "I hear them!"

Aspen was on her feet even more quickly than Rake rose to his. The familiar sound of a balloon burner was barely discernable. She followed his gaze, east toward the mountain. She could hear it—the familiar whoosh of a burner heating the air in a balloon envelope. She smiled as the noise grew louder, and then, just above the tree line, she saw it—a rainbow-colored hot air balloon lazily drifting toward them. The balloon's base color was a beautiful royal blue. Hot pink, lavender, and bright, sunshiny yellow squares rippled diagonally over the blue. It was a lovely balloon!

"He's low," Rake said. "He's gonna go for a splash."

Aspen watched and waved a friendly greeting as the balloon carried the basket directly overhead.

"Good morning!" a friendly woman called from the basket.

"Good morning!" Rake and Aspen responded.

"Let's see how they do," Rake said, smiling.

Aspen was so dazzled by Rake's handsome smile she almost forgot to watch the balloon.

"You're up early," another woman in the basket called, drawing Aspen's attention back to the balloon.

"You can't enjoy this any other way," Rake said.

Aspen watched as the balloon ever so slowly approached the river. Drifting, drifting—slowly lower and lower until the bottom of the basket slid along the surface of the water for a moment before the pilot laid on the burner to send the rainbow globe gaining altitude once again. It was a slow process but wonderfully exciting.

Rake clapped and shouted, "Nice one!"

"Have a great day!" the pilot called as the colorful balloon drifted over the opposing tree line.

Rake chuckled. He looked at Aspen, his dark eyes bright with pleasure.

"Fun, huh?" he asked. "Usually ten or twelve of them try it… almost every morning I've been out here."

"It's great!" Aspen said. A moment later, two more colorful balloons lazily drifted overhead. It was obvious they weren't going to try for the sandbar or the water, and Aspen simply enjoyed the sight of them wandering across the canvas of blue overhead.

Rake sighed and stretched out on the blanket once more.

"Ahhh!" he exhaled. "Now *this* is living. Don't you think?"

Aspen giggled. "Definitely!"

She sat down beside him, placed her hands behind her, and leaned back, gazing up at the balloons slowly drifting over them.

"Okay…so I'm ready," he said. He stretched out on his back, tucking his hands under his head and looking up at the sky—at the balloons beginning to speckle it in the higher altitudes.

"For what?" Aspen asked. It was hard—resisting the urge to lean over and kiss him right on the mouth.

"For the recitation," he said. "I want to hear that poem again."

"You do not," she laughed.

"I do! I really do," he told her. His eyes narrowed, and he asked, "Do you think I'm a weenie because I want to hear it again? Maybe you don't like guys who want to hear a poem recited. But keep in mind, it's the only poem I've ever listened to…other than in high school when they make you listen to all that crap in English."

Aspen felt her eyes narrow. "Why do you want to hear it again?" she asked. She couldn't fathom why a guy like Rake Locker would want to hear her recite "The Time of Aspen Falls." Hadn't he already had to suffer through it once?

He shrugged where he lay on the blanket. "I don't know. It intrigues me for some reason. I guess because it inspired your name."

"You know I hate reciting it," she reminded him.

He smiled. "Come on, Willamina Dog. If you can run around in a pink dog costume all day, in front of hundreds of customers, then you can surely find the guts to recite that poem to me one more time."

"Maybe," she admitted.

"Come on, Aspen. Don't make me beg."

"Hmm. What an interesting idea," she said. "You mean there's the possibility you'd beg me to recite it?"

"How about if you don't recite it, I'll pick you up and drop you on your seat in the river…help you out with a little splash and dash of your own," he chuckled.

"You wouldn't," she challenged. But when he started to sit up, she said, "Okay! Okay!" She was sure he wouldn't have dropped her in the river, but the idea of being picked up by him again was tempting. "I'll do it," she agreed. "But you can't laugh."

"Did I laugh last time?" he asked.

"No," she admitted. "And I thank you for not laughing."

"Okay…I'm ready," he said.

Aspen inhaled a deep breath. She still couldn't understand why he wanted her to recite that stupid poem, but he did—and she would. Again she was awash with the feeling that Rake Locker could talk her into doing just about anything simply by asking.

"Fine," she breathed.

A triumphant grin spread over Rake's handsome face, and Aspen began.

Like a garland of glass, the river
Meanders on its way,
'Mid trees of scarlet and crimson
Through the valley yon holding sway.

She paused, intrigued with the idea of reciting the poem while sitting next to a river. She glanced up to the ageless Sandia to the east and continued.

Yet up on the mountain gypsy,

169

As sweet autumn finds her there,
Lush golden ribbons of aspen
Tie up her pine green hair.

And jewels of rubied leaves,
Of fiery orange and of plum,
Drip from the tips of her fingers

She glanced at Rake and couldn't help but smile as she added,

As she summons her lover, "Come!"

She thought how wonderful it would be to be the mountain—to count Rake as the moon—the mountain's lover.

For the moon is the gypsy's lover,
And no sight makes the moon shine more
Than her golden ribbons of aspen
And the rubied jewels at her door.

Hark! Winter is coming…
And the time of aspen falls
Like a bridegroom's golden coverlet
As his gypsy lover calls.

"Come, lover!" cried the mountain,
"Oh moon of my autumn heart!
Come fall the aspen upon me…
Lest golden leaves depart.

"Weave me a golden bride's bed
To slumber 'neath 'til spring.
As the time of aspen befalls us,
Lay me on leafy wing."

She paused again, gazing up into the clear October sky—to the now hundreds of colorful hot air balloons lazily drifting overhead.

So the moon spread wide his moonbeams,
As the breadth of her lover's arms,
And he bound her there within them
Safe from bleak winter's harms.

"Fear not, my gypsy lover,
For the time of aspen falls!
And as ribbons of gold clasp the pines
So my heart into yours enthralls."

Then the moon breathed a breath of autumn,
And the leaves of the aspen fell
And covered the mountain golden
From the peak to the low chaparral.

"Hold fast, my lover," said Moon.
"I'll keep you from winter's cold
In the time of aspen falling
'Neath a blanket of aspen gold."

Oh, Moon loves his gypsy mountain
And the gypsy loves her moon.
As the aspen rained leaves upon them…
They bid autumn gone too soon.

Hence, the time of aspen befell them,
And winter's descending was near,
So the moon wove his fingers of moonbeams
Through the gold amidst mountain's hair.

Thus, ever the moon keeps his gypsy
As winter's white snow swathe sprawls,

171

And the moon and mountain blend kisses
As the Time of Aspen Falls.

Aspen finished the poem, and Rake swallowed—tried to dispel the thirst rising in him—the thirst for her kiss. He shouldn't have had her recite the poem. He should've known the enchanting sound of her voice—the romantic lilt of the poem—he should've known they would rattle him!

Yet he chose to ignore the warning rising in his chest and mind.

"Do that last part again," he rather ordered. He felt his eyes narrow as he looked at her—gritted his teeth to maintain his self-control.

"'Thus, ever the moon keeps his gypsy as winter's white snow swathe sprawls'—" she began.

"And the moon and mountain blend kisses…as the time of aspen falls," he finished.

"That's right!" she exclaimed. He could see by the smile on her face, the bright twinkle in her eye, that she was impressed he'd remember the end. Little did she know he nearly had the thing memorized. Sitting in his workshop with the poetry book from the library so close at hand, he must've read it a hundred times.

"Yep…I guess it's true," he sighed.

"What's true?" she asked. She twisted, laying down on her stomach and propping herself on her elbows.

"I like that poem…so I guess I really am a weenie," he explained, smiling at her. Uh oh! He could feel the devil rising in him as he let his attention linger on her lips; he could feel the mischief pumping through his veins. She was distracted for a moment—looked skyward as several more balloons appeared low over the tree line, heading for the water. He smiled, remembering the warm taste of her mouth—the smooth silk of her skin beneath his palms the night of his grandparents' barn party. He swallowed hard, trying to draw on his resolve to act appropriately. He'd brought her out here to watch the balloons, not to start making out with her before the day had even begun. Still, as she looked back to him, her eyes were warm—inviting. There was mischief in her expression too—or something akin to it—and his resolve was lost.

"Go ahead," he said, smiling at her.

It was the increasingly familiar smolder of his dark eyes that caused the butterflies to go off in Aspen's stomach. His grin implied pure misbehavior, and her mouth flooded with moisture. He'd read her thoughts! She was sure he had. She'd been lying there looking at him, considering how fabulous it would feel to kiss him. And somehow—somehow he knew! She felt her cheeks pink up a bit.

"Go ahead what?" she asked. She'd play dumb. Then maybe he'd change the subject.

"Go ahead and do what you're thinking of doing," he said. He remained just as he had been—stretched out on his back, legs crossed at his ankles, hands tucked back behind his head. Yet the smolder in his eyes told her he was thinking the same thing she was.

"I-I'm just—just watching the balloons," she lied. She sat up, leaning on one hand and gazing off into the sky. He sat up too. And as she sat facing east toward the mountains, he sat facing east toward the river.

"You should've done it," he said, smiling at her. "I would've let you. You know that, right?"

"Done what?" she asked, attempting innocence of knowledge.

"Done exactly what you were thinking of doing," he chuckled.

"And…and just what do you think I was thinking of doing?" she asked. She couldn't confess—couldn't admit she'd nearly leaned over and kissed him! She couldn't.

"This," he said, reaching out and slipping a hand beneath her hair to the back of her neck as he pulled her toward him.

Aspen trembled at the first touch of Rake's lips to hers. He kissed her softly just once—once softly before his mouth captured hers in a heated, moist, and teasingly driven kiss. She accepted him at once—didn't pause in returning the passionate nature of it. She felt flushed with fever, awash with desire and the need for his attention to continue at her mouth. Though her eyes were closed, a vision of Rake in his worn Levi's, Nike cap, and now-tattered flannel shirt flashed in her mind. He was so handsome—so rugged and naturally attractive! He pulled her into his arms, drinking deeply of her kisses, as if trying to quench some insatiable thirst. She let one arm go around his waist, the other hand sliding up his muscular arm, over one broad shoulder, around to the back of his neck.

His manner of kissing was so masterful, so perfect—as if he'd somehow been trained to execute the perfect blending of mouths. Aspen suddenly wondered if that was indeed it. Had Rake Locker done so much kissing with other women that he was considered a pro? The thought slightly interrupted her bliss, and she pulled back from him, breaking the seal of their lips.

"What's the matter?" he asked, frowning.

She glanced up into the smoldering brown of his eyes. He was gorgeous! Of course he'd kissed other girls. He'd probably had his pick of girls when he was a teenager—and women as a man. The thought made Aspen suddenly shy—shy and jealous!

"I-I probably shouldn't be doing this," she stammered.

"Probably not," he chuckled, brushing a strand of hair from her cheek.

"W-we really haven't known each other very long," she began to explain. She was distracted by his mouth, however—by wanting him to kiss her again.

"Not really," he agreed, letting his lips hover a breath above her own. "Do you want me to stop?" he asked. "I'll stop if you want me to."

Aspen was breathless, overcome by his nearness—by the desire to have his mouth pressed to hers again. She couldn't stop herself, and she moved to meet his lips with her own.

"I'll take that as a 'don't stop,'" he breathed a moment before he kissed her again—kissed her hard—a demanding kiss, drenched with desire.

CHAPTER ELEVEN

Aspen was entirely delirious, her mind void of any reason or rationality. As Rake kissed her, quick sparks of warning, of an urgency to run from him, flashed in her mind. He was too wonderful—absolutely too wonderful! No one was as perfect as they seemed, especially someone as attractive as Rake Locker. Yet she couldn't push herself out of his arms—couldn't find the willpower to stop kissing him. He would be the death of her, she knew it! The death of her—or at least of her heart. Still, she couldn't pull herself out of his arms—only longed for their kissing to continue—forever!

He broke from her, suddenly—frowning.

"Hold on," he mumbled. A deepening frown furrowed his brow, and he turned his head as if listening. Releasing her, he nearly leapt to his feet, turning around and shading his eyes from the sun to the east.

Aspen heard it then—the quick, short burst of a balloon burner. She scrambled to her feet in time to see a large red balloon appear just barely above the tree line.

"He's descending way too fast," Rake mumbled, more to himself than to Aspen. She knew he was right. The balloon barely cleared the tree line and was headed for the river, descending at an alarming rate. The basket wouldn't just bounce on the sandbar or skim the water—it would hit with brutal force.

"Oh, no!" she gasped, her hands covering her mouth.

Rake swore under his breath and, turning toward the horses,

shouted, "Stay here!" Aspen watched as he ran to his horse, turning his cap and putting the bill at the back of his head.

Fairly leaping into the saddle, Rake slapped the horse's flank with the reins, sending the horse galloping toward the river. Aspen's heart hammered with anxiety as she watched Rake ride through the shallow river toward the sandbar just as the basket hit with devastating force. She screamed when it tipped, spilling several people into the water as the hot air in the envelope tried to lift the balloon into the air again. But it came down again, the basket dragging in the water. Aspen watched, helpless, as a woman fell out of the basket—went under the water's surface as the still sky-bound balloon dragged the basket over her.

Yet Rake was there in the next instant—leaping off his horse into the water, pulling the woman to the surface. He picked her up in his arms and struggled through the waist-deep water to the sandbar. He laid her down and said something to the other three people who had fallen from the basket and were now standing in the middle of the Rio Grande River, stunned and no doubt very banged up.

"I'll call 911!" the pilot of the balloon shouted to Aspen as he hit the burner, sending the balloon rising and narrowly missing the tree line.

"Okay," Aspen squeaked out, nowhere near loud enough to be heard. She waved at the pilot of the balloon as he and one other man remaining in the basket floated up and toward the west. She knew there was nothing the pilot and the other man could do. Ballooning was a dangerous hobby, and unfortunately accidents did happen. Calling 911 was the smartest and best response to what had happened. Aspen knew the pilot would radio his chase crew as well, and they probably had some emergency medical supplies on hand.

She looked back to the sandbar, relieved to see that the woman who had fallen into the water appeared to be conscious and was sitting up. Rake's horse had followed him to the sandbar, and Aspen watched as Rake pulled another serape from a saddlebag, wrapping it around the wet woman's shoulders.

He stood then, conversing with the three other passengers who had fallen out of the basket—two men and another woman. Each of the two men shook his hand, and the woman hugged him. Aspen was frustrated with being so useless. She couldn't do anything but stand on the riverbank and wait.

Rake picked up the woman in the blanket again and nodded to the others. Carefully, he waded through the river; the others followed, as did his horse. Aspen began to run down the riverbank, toward the place they were headed. He was smart to get them to the bank. They were in a remote area as it was, and the emergency vehicles would no doubt have enough trouble getting to them without having to wade out into the river.

"Oh my heck!" Aspen exclaimed as the others came ashore. "Is she badly hurt?"

It was the woman herself—the one Rake was carrying—who answered.

"I-I think I broke my ankle," she said. She was a young woman, perhaps Aspen's age—very pretty, even drowned-rat wet.

"The pilot said he'd call 911," Aspen told Rake as he set the woman down on the ground.

"Good," he said. "They'll probably come down off Alameda. I'll ride over and find them." He mounted and turned his horse south. "Will you stay here until I get back, Aspen?" he asked.

"Of course," she said. It seemed a silly question. What else did he think she was going to do?

"Thanks," he said. "I'll be right back," he said to the stunned balloon passengers. He was off then, riding at a gallop south, toward the old Alameda bridge.

Aspen looked back to the three standing strangers—glanced down at the woman with the injured ankle.

"What a morning, huh?" she asked, shaking her head and smiling. It worked. All four people chuckled and nodded.

Rake almost reined in—almost turned his horse around and went back. What was he thinking, leaving Aspen alone with four complete strangers? He didn't like the way the younger of the two men had looked at her. What if he'd left her in an unsafe situation? Still, there

177

were women there and another man. Surely three of the four startled balloonists would be decent people.

He rode hard, cussing under his breath at the way his morning had been interrupted by disaster. He could still taste Aspen's kiss in his mouth, and it caused a thirst to rise in him the like he'd never known before. She was the sweetest thing he'd ever tasted—the prettiest thing he'd ever set eyes on—the most tempting woman to ever cross his path—ever.

Rake was so preoccupied by his thoughts of Aspen that he almost rode right under the old Alameda bridge instead of heading up the bank to the street. He could hear the flags flapping in the wind and reached the street bridge in time to see a chase crew slowing down, a woman in the back of the truck using a pair of binoculars to look down the riverbed. He put his fingers to his mouth and whistled, pointing in the direction they should go when the woman looked over to him. As the truck and trailer rig started down onto the sandy road along the river, Rake heard sirens. He'd stay until he'd made sure they knew where to go; then he'd head back. A horse could move faster over the sandy riverbank than the chase crew or EMT vehicles could, and he had to get back—just in case he'd been stupid enough to leave Aspen in the hands of a serial killer.

Rake smiled, shook his head, and chuckled a little. A serial killer? He couldn't decide whether his concerns were legitimate or whether Aspen had totally infiltrated his mind—right down to her irrational fear of meeting up with a serial killer.

❧

"So, we're just sitting there—you know…just innocently making out," Rake explained, drying his hair with a fresh towel.

"Yeah?" his sister, Marissa, prodded—her eyes wide with anticipation, as if it were the most natural thing in the world that her brother and Aspen were sitting on the banks of the Rio Grande making out at seven thirty in the morning.

"And this balloon comes over the trees…way too low. I could tell he wasn't going to make it," Rake explained.

Aspen swallowed hard and tried not to blush—tried to avert her attention from Rake's bare torso before her. She couldn't believe how uninhibited he was! After the EMTs had left the river to take the ballooning passengers to the hospital, Rake and Aspen had ridden back to his grandparents' house. Wet and cold from his time in the river, Rake had asked Aspen if she minded waiting while he showered—then they could head up to Santa Fe to pick piñons. She'd gladly agreed, excited about spending more time with him. Still, as she'd been sitting in his grandmother's kitchen waiting for him to finish showering, not only had his sister walked in but also her husband. Only minutes later, his brother, Mark, had arrived and his mother. Now they all sat in the kitchen, listening to Rake tell about the ballooning accident she and Rake had witnessed. Furthermore, not only was he standing in the kitchen relating the story while wearing nothing but a smile and towel wrapped around him at his waist, he'd just announced to the entire assembly that he and Aspen had been "making out" just before the balloon crashed.

"The basket hit the sandbar and dumped out three passengers," he continued, "but this other girl got dumped out in the water, and the balloon dragged the basket right over her."

"Eeee!" Valentina Locker exclaimed. "Was she okay?"

Rake shrugged. "I guess…but I think she broke her ankle. She couldn't walk or nothing."

Aspen grinned, delighted by the way Rake spontaneously slipped up with colloquialized bad grammar every once in a while.

"Eee! Were you freaking out, Aspen?" Marissa asked, sounding so much like her mother it was uncanny.

"It was just frustrating…not being able to help," she said. "I just had to stand there and watch." She was somewhat relieved, for although she had been mortified Rake had mentioned the fact they were kissing when the accident happened, none of the members of his captive audience seemed to have noticed.

"That's why I always get nervous when I see the balloons down by the river," Valentina sighed. "There are so many things that can go wrong down there."

"Oh, they're all okay, Mom," Rake said, running his hands through his wet hair to comb it. "Nobody got killed or anything."

"Well, thank goodness," Valentina said. "I love to see the balloons, but it's so dangerous. You'd have to really like it to take such risks."

"You'd have to love it enough to die for it," Rake said. "Remember that accident last year when that lady fell? It killed her." He shook his head. "It's amazing…but it ain't worth dying for."

"Not very many things are worth dying for, mi hijo," Valentina said. "Still, they're beautiful to watch."

Aspen smiled. She gazed at Rake, consciously realizing in that moment he may have actually saved a woman's life. He was such the perfect package of a real man that it hadn't seemed strange to her at all—watching him ride out on a horse into the middle of a river to save a stranger. She couldn't help but let her eyes travel the length of him where he stood in the kitchen, not a stitch of clothing on him—just the fluffy white towel wrapped around his waist. She decided then and there that Gina would drop dead at the perfection of his build—the strong definition of the muscles in his arms, shoulders, back, and chest. Rake just kept getting better!

"A mouse!"

Aspen looked over as Charlotte entered the kitchen shaking her head, her eyes wide and startled looking.

"What's the matter, Gramma?" Mark asked.

"There's another mouse in the basement!" Charlotte exclaimed. "I've told your grandpa if he doesn't get some traps set, I'm going to wring his neck."

"A mouse? Cool!" Aspen heard Marissa's husband exclaim.

Aspen had never officially met Marissa's husband. He hadn't been at the barn party, and no one had thought to introduce him to her now. She had gathered his name was Clinton, and he was very tall—easily six foot four—handsome, with blond hair and blue, blue eyes. Aspen smiled, noting the perfect contrast between Marissa's ebony-haired, dark-eyed beauty and average height and Clinton's fairer hair, light eyes, and towering frame.

"Get the guns while I find some pants!" Rake ordered with excitement.

"Get the guns?" Aspen asked.

Valentina shook her head, and Marissa rolled her beautiful black eyes.

"Of course," Rake answered, smiling down at her. "What else would you expect us to do?" To her great surprise, Rake leaned forward, kissing her cheek before he turned and hurried out of the room. She felt her cheeks go crimson as she turned to see Valentina and Marissa both smiling at her.

"Guns?" she managed to stammer, looking to the women as the other men in the room dashed away.

"Yep," Marissa answered. "Guns…for a mouse."

"Real guns?" Aspen asked. She couldn't imagine anyone being a good enough shot to shoot a mouse—and in the house? They had to be joking.

"You can blame my husband for this family tradition," Valentina said.

"Or mine," Charlotte sighed.

Aspen shook her head, still unable to believe the Locker family used guns to get rid of a mouse—and in the house to boot.

"BB guns, Aspen," Marissa explained. "Every time Gramma finds a mouse downstairs, my brothers—and now my husband—think they're at a carnival shooting metal ducks or something."

"Oh!" Aspen said as realization hit her. Yet in the next moment, she laughed. BB guns or not, it was still a very strange practice.

Aspen watched as a bowlegged Joseph Locker hurried through the kitchen toward the basement stairs, BB gun in hand.

"He's mine!" the older man shouted as Clinton and Mark trailed behind him.

"Whoever nails him has to buy dinner!" Mark laughed.

Rake raced out of a nearby bedroom in nothing but a pair of Levi's—zipped but still unbuttoned at the waist.

"Wait, wait, wait!" he laughed. "No one shoots until we're all in position!" He cocked the BB gun he carried and headed downstairs after the others.

"Whatever happened to just setting a trap?" Charlotte sighed.

Aspen laughed, entirely delighted. She smiled when Valentina winked at her. The beautiful woman shook her head as shouting and laughter erupted from the basement.

"So," Marissa asked, smiling at Aspen and tucking a strand of long ebony hair behind one ear, "you're not planning on breaking my brother's heart, are you?"

Aspen was so stunned by the question, she couldn't immediately answer. She knew her mouth was gaping open in surprise, but she couldn't think of anything to say at first.

"Marissa!" Valentina exclaimed. "Don't be rude, mi hija!"

"I'm not being rude," Marissa said, winking at Aspen. "I just figured I'd ask...since I've been wondering." She smiled, and Aspen could sense she didn't mean to be cruel or accusing—just curious.

"Marissa is very protective of Rake, Aspen," Valentina explained. "Especially since—"

"Well?" Charlotte interrupted. "*Are* you...going to break Rake's heart?"

Aspen blushed, entirely uncomfortable.

"I-I don't think there's the slightest possibility of that happening," she managed. "I-I mean...I haven't really known him that long. And anyway, if someone's heart was going to be broken here...I'm sure it wouldn't be his."

"He likes you," Marissa said, smiling. "I can tell."

More shouting erupted from the basement, and Aspen saw her chance—her chance to change the subject.

"Won't they ruin the basement?" she asked. "BB guns? And if they can really hit a mouse...won't the blood and stuff spray all over?"

The women giggled, shaking their heads, amused by the antics of the men downstairs as laughter erupted in the basement.

Charlotte explained, "There are some rules...and I enforce them militarily!" She held up a thumb and said, "Number one: no shooting at the walls. They can only shoot at the mouse if it's somewhere on the carpet." She held up an index finger in addition to the thumb. "Number two: I can never see the poor little thing...ever. They have to dispose of it...in a sanitary fashion."

"But what about the mess?" Aspen asked.

Charlotte shrugged. "With the BB guns, for some reason they don't make a big mess. I've never seen any evidence at all."

Aspen shivered. "Ooo! I hate mice," she mumbled.

"Me too! That's why I let the men take care of them. However they do it, I don't care! I just don't want them in my house spreading disease." Charlotte sighed and waved a hand in a gesture of letting the men downstairs continue to act like boys.

There was a burst of cheering, followed by low, masculine conversation.

"I guess they got it," Valentina sighed.

In the next moment, Rake bounded up the stairs and into the kitchen.

"It's all taken care of, Gramma," he said, smiling and propping the BB gun on one shoulder. "I got him for you."

"Thank you, sweetie…but who's cleaning it up?" Charlotte asked.

"Clinton," Rake said. "He was talking trash, so he gets to clean it up. Besides," he added, putting an arm around Aspen's shoulders, "we're going up to Santa Fe to pick piñons."

"Oh, is that what they're calling it these days?" Rake's grandpa said, appearing at the top of the basement stairs.

"Yep!" Rake said. "That's what they're calling it these days, Grampa."

Aspen wondered if she'd ever quit blushing. She wished Rake would simply cover up his well-sculpted torso so they could be on their way.

As if he read her thoughts, he said, "I'll grab a shirt, and we can go."

He sauntered off toward one of the back rooms, leaving Aspen at the mercy of his family yet again.

"Did you find any time for some necking down there by the river?" Joseph teased.

"Joseph!" Charlotte scolded. "She's had enough of the Locker family for one day."

Valentina put an arm around Aspen's shoulders and said, "You just ignore the men, mi hija. You and Rake have fun picking piñons."

"You just be sure to remind Rake to stop alongside the road and buy some piñons from a vendor so his mama will think that's what you kids were really doing," Joseph teased.

"Dad!" Valentina exclaimed. "Silencio! She won't want to come here anymore."

Joseph winked at Aspen. "Make sure he buys raw piñons. If they're already roasted, it'll only prove you were out there necking!"

"Híjole!" Valentina and Marissa exclaimed in unison.

Aspen smiled at last. He was such a tease, just like his grandson. "Okay, Mr. Locker," she said. "I'll make sure he buys raw piñons."

Everyone laughed, and Marissa nodded her approval. "You're learning fast, Aspen," she said.

"Let's go, arachnophobia girl," Rake said, entering the room as he plopped his Nike cap back on his head. He wore another flannel shirt—red and black.

Aspen smiled as he took her hand and hurried toward the front door.

"Thank you for everything, Mrs. Locker," Aspen called, waving to everyone as they nodded.

"You come back anytime, honey!" Charlotte called, tossing a wave in return.

Everyone offered their individual good-byes, and Aspen smiled as Rake closed the door behind them.

"Sorry about all that," he said once they were in the pickup.

"That's okay," she said. And it was.

⅔

Picking piñons was fun! More than fun—it was wonderful. And not just the actual piñon hunting. Oh sure, Aspen loved hunting through the leaf, needle, and pinecone litter on the high desert floor to find the small brown piñon seeds, but it was the time spent with Rake that was so wonderful. They talked, about everything it seemed. He'd wanted to know more about her family, her job—her! She answered his questions without pause too, feeling unusually comfortable and at ease. At one point, he'd even gathered her in his arms, kissing her mouth with a delicious, ravenous thirst, nearly melting her spine altogether. He'd said they'd never gotten to finish what they'd started that morning by the riverbank, having been interrupted by the balloon accident. So he kissed her! Kissed her and kissed her and kissed her some more—driven, moist, heated kisses, administered under the beautiful blue of October's sky, amid the quiet grove of piñon trees. Her mouth still watered at the thought and want of his kiss!

It had been one of the best days of Aspen's life. And now—nestled beside him in his pickup—she was astounded at how the simplest activities could be the most dramatic of a person's life if they were experienced with the right and wonderful someone.

They'd stopped off for some dinner at Blake's Lotaburger on their way back into town, and Aspen sipped the last bit of her chocolate shake through the straw in her cup.

"You don't mind, do you?" Rake asked. "Grampa just wants me to pick up an old invoice for him."

"Of course not," Aspen answered. Why would she possibly mind spending more time with Rake? His grandpa had called on Rake's cell, asking Rake to pick up an old invoice from the Clock Shop. Since the shop was on the way to Aspen's apartment, Rake had asked her if it was okay if he stopped on their way.

"It'll only take a minute," he said, pulling the pickup into an empty parking space behind the shop. He took the key out of the ignition and said, "Do you wanna come in with me?"

"Sure!" Aspen said, smiling. She knew they were entering through the back of the shop—that she probably wouldn't get to see all the beautiful clocks in the showroom this time—but she didn't care. She just wanted to be with Rake.

She tossed her empty Blake's Lotaburger cup into a garbage can at the back entrance of the shop as Rake shoved a key into the lock and turned the knob.

"Not many people have seen the workshop," he said as he stood aside, gesturing she should precede him. "We have to keep our secrets closely guarded."

Aspen smiled and stepped into the workshop of the Clock Shop. The familiar scent of thyme filled her nostrils, instantly soothing to her senses.

"Ooo!" Aspen breathed as she looked around the cluttered room. "I can't believe you're allowing me a glimpse of your lair."

Rake smiled and chuckled. "Yeah…it's pretty exciting," he said with sarcasm. "I mean, there ain't too many things that'll grab a girl's attention more than a work table littered with tiny gears and stuff."

Aspen giggled as she studied the old table strewn with tiny tools and magnifying glasses, the old rolltop desk in one corner, piled high with aging paper. It was delightful!

Two walls of the work area were lined with clocks—every type of hanging wall clock imaginable. One wall was covered with photos, newspaper articles, and other paraphernalia relating to Rake's career as a bull rider. The fourth wall was plastered ceiling to floor with purple and blue ribbons. The only thing breaking up the wallpaper of ribbons was a bookshelf stuffed full of trophies and belt buckles—more evidence of Rake's bull-riding past.

"Wow!" Aspen breathed, going over to more closely inspect the trophy shelves. "You won all this?"

Rake shrugged and began rummaging around through a pile of papers littering the top of a nearby desk. "That's part of it—all the stuff I won when I was really young…before I turned pro. Grampa keeps all the early stuff here and the pro stuff in his office at the house."

Aspen glanced back at Rake. He was frowning, still shuffling through loose papers. She returned her attention then to a framed photo sitting on one of the trophy shelves. A mean-looking bull was in the air, caught mid-twist. The rider on his back was wearing a white hat and arching his own back—right arm extended high over his head, the legs of his chaps flying horizontally out from his knees. It was an almost frightening still photograph—an illustration of the danger of the event—and Aspen glanced back at Rake again, suddenly very thankful he'd given it up.

"So this is where you fixed my clock," she sighed. She looked around the room again, adoring it somehow. It was such a delightful atmosphere—cluttered, unorganized. She smiled.

"Yep," he said. She watched as he unearthed a particular sheet of paper, nodding with relief. He folded the paper, shoving it in his back pocket. "Yep," he repeated, looking around the room. "This is where I work. I'm certain you're very impressed." Again his comments were laced with sarcasm.

"I am!" Aspen exclaimed. "Honestly, it's like…the most interesting room I've ever been in."

"Really?" he asked, smiling. He glanced around for a moment. "I suppose it's just about as different from a bookstore as you can get. You're probably used to things being really organized…but I'm too much like my grampa."

Aspen studied one of the walls covered with clocks. "Are these special ones…or just ones waiting to be fixed?" she asked.

"They're all part of my grampa's personal collection," he explained. "Most of them are very rare, very old…or both. I keep telling him they're not safe here, but he insists no one would realize their monetary value…not the average person anyway. He says most people would think they were just a bunch of broken junk."

"They're beautiful!" Aspen sighed. "I love it in here."

"Really?" he asked, eyebrows arched with doubt.

"Yes!" Aspen giggled. "It's amazing."

"Well…if you're this impressed with my lair, as you put it," he began, "wait until you see this!"

Aspen watched as he picked up a pair of glasses. The glasses had some sort of magnifying lens attached to them.

"What are those?" she asked.

"These glasses have a loupe attached to one lens…so I can see the really small stuff," he explained as he put the glasses on. "I call these my sexy specs. Chicks can't resist them."

Aspen giggled, delighted by his teasing. He sauntered over to her, taking her waist between his hands.

"I dare you to try and resist me now, Miss Aspen Falls," he said, smiling down at her. "With my sexy specs on…you're putty in my hands."

Aspen giggled again—further enchanted by his flirting—by his hands at her waist. "Is that so?" she asked.

"Yep!" he chuckled. "My sexy specs…well, they're like a magical superpower or something." He gathered her into his arms, all the while gazing down at her through the lenses of the glasses. "You won't be able to resist me as long as I'm wearing them."

Secretly she wished he would just take the silly glasses off so she could better see the smolder of his dark eyes, but his flirting and teasing her about them were entertaining too.

Gazing up into his handsome face, she breathed, "Okay."

He grinned. "Okay," he said as his head descended toward hers.

Aspen Falls determined she could spend her entire life kissing Rake Locker. His mouth crushed to hers, sending goose bumps rippling over her body. Her toes literally tingled as he coaxed her mouth to join his in a mingling of warm, moist savoring of affection.

Seriously, she thought. *I seriously could kiss him forever!*

How did she get here? How was it that she was standing in a clock shop, locked in the powerful arms of the most attractive man she'd ever known? How could he possibly have found something in her, something interesting enough to spend time with—interesting enough to kiss?

Aspen gasped, drawing a deep breath as he broke the seal of their lips. Taking hold of her waist, he effortlessly lifted her, setting her on the top of his work bench. Rake smiled—a truly roguish smile—and stripped the sexy specs from his face, tossing them aside. He took her face between his powerful hands, gazing into her eyes. She could've sworn she saw the flicker of tiny flames leaping in the deep brown of his eyes as he studied her face for a moment. She let her hands cling to his forearms, trying to hold on—to hold onto her self-control. She stared at his mouth—swallowed when the thought of his kiss caused hers to flood with excess moisture.

Rake tipped Aspen's head back—lowered his mouth toward the soft curve of her throat. Inhaling deeply the fragrant scent of her skin, he allowed his lips to trail over the flesh of her neck, pausing to kiss her now and then. He felt her tremble and smiled—pleased he was able to effect such a reaction from her. Maybe his sexy specs really did hold some bewitching power! He released her face, letting his arms go around her, pulling her body against his as his lips lingered at her neck just below her ear. No doubt Aspen assumed he was teasing her—kissing her neck and cheek in order to increase her desire that he pay more attention to her mouth—but it wasn't true. He needed a moment—a reprieve—in order to settle himself, to rein in his self-control. His thoughts and desires toward Aspen Falls surprised even him, and he had to retrench—fortify his willpower. He felt his own hands trembling as he held her—wondered if his heart might burst from his chest if it didn't settle its hammering rhythm soon. He was considering—considering he might take a chance on Aspen Falls—might endeavor to trust her with his affections—even his heart. He paused in his contemplation to do so and drew back from her, studying her face for a moment. Should he leap? Should he just go for it—throw caution and all his previous experience to the wind?

She placed a soft palm against his whiskery cheek—let her thumb trace his lips—and Rake made a decision. He'd take a chance on her! Not just because she heated his blood—not just because she stoked a fever in him that started in his chest and fanned out through his whole body. He liked the way she smiled—the way he kept wishing their conversations would never have to end. He liked her voice—liked to hear it reciting that sappy poem her mother named her after. He liked that she was fun—made him feel more alive. Rake realized in those moments just how much he liked Aspen Falls. Yep, he liked her enough to take a chance.

"You're right about those glasses," she whispered, smiling at him.

"Am I?" he asked, grinning with triumph.

"Yeah," she breathed.

Rake heard the Westminster clock on the wall chime the half hour. *Fifteen minutes*, he decided. He'd limit their kissing to fifteen minutes—until he heard the next chime. Surely he could stay in control for fifteen more minutes—long enough to really drink of the passion growing between them but short enough to keep himself in check. Rake grinned at Aspen. He knew he couldn't keep his mouth from hers any longer. So—he didn't.

❦

As Aspen sat in the pickup nestled against Rake's strong form, she sighed with pure contentment. She couldn't believe how tired she was—how entirely satisfied she felt. What a day it had been! Balloons at sunrise, picking piñons at noon, dinner at dusk, and kissing Rake intermittently through it all. Could he really like her as much as it appeared he did?

She glanced up at him, studying his unearthly attractiveness. Surely he didn't like her as much as she liked him. Yet she wondered if maybe he did. It wasn't just the kissing or even the activities they'd enjoyed together over the past couple of weeks. It was everything, including the way he treated her in front of his family—as if it were the most natural thing in the world for her to be with them.

Aspen could feel her heart literally adhering to Rake—dreaming of being with him forever—and it was dangerous. She knew it was. Still, she knew she couldn't tear herself away from him. In the beginning she'd wondered if maybe she should heed the warnings in her brain—the silent murmurs telling her he would turn out to be a jerk. But now—now she had slipped beyond rational thought. He was wonderful, and she was secretly considering surrendering—surrendering to the idea of letting things play out—wondering if it was worth the risk of total emotional annihilation.

"What are you thinking about?" he asked.

Aspen giggled. "Just thinking how glad I am that you didn't turn out to be a serial killer."

He smiled, shook his head, and said, "Well, as glad as I am for the acquittal…I was kind of hoping you were considering whether or not I'm worth the risk."

"Worth what risk?" she asked—although his ability to follow the same line of thought she did was uncanny!

He hit the brakes, pulling to the side of the road in a cloud of dust.

"The risk," he said, looking at her. "Let's face it. There's always a certain amount of risk involved…when you start going out with somebody—a risk of disappointment, betrayal, heartache. Do you think I'm worth the risk?"

190

She couldn't respond—only sat staring at him, astonished at his forthrightness.

"At least I'm a good kisser," he said, grinning at her, attempting to soften the question perhaps. When she didn't immediately answer, he frowned and asked, "Aren't I?"

Aspen blushed scarlet, clear to her toes. Of course he was a good kisser. Fabulous! Magnificent! A true master! Was he kidding?

"How can I possibly answer that without incriminating myself?" she asked.

He chuckled. "You're a good kisser…and I ain't afraid to say it," he said.

"That's because you're a boy," Aspen said, smiling at him. "Boys can say stuff like that and not get in trouble."

"A boy?" he asked, quirking an eyebrow.

Aspen giggled, delighted with his offense. "A man, then."

"A man worth taking a risk with?"

Aspen paused and smiled at him. At last she breathed, "Yeah."

Rake smiled, leaned over, and kissed her softly on the lips.

He shifted into first and said, "Good. Then hang on, baby! I'm gonna take you on the ride of your life."

As he peeled out, sending dust and gravel kicking up behind the truck, Aspen drew a deep breath—a breath of courage. The ride of her life? With Rake Locker at the wheel, she had no doubt it would be exactly that.

CHAPTER TWELVE

October waned, and November settled in crisp and cool. As Aspen sat at a booth in Blake's Lotaburger waiting for Gina to return from the bathroom, she sighed. In that moment of waiting—lingering with nothing to do—she let her mind wander over the events of the past couple of months. It all seemed like a dream—meeting Rake, their first date, their many, many, many days and evenings together since. In those quiet moments, the kind she rested in now, she still couldn't believe he'd chosen her—couldn't believe she was Rake Locker's girlfriend! Even just thinking of him caused goose bumps to prickle her arms.

She thought of Thanksgiving, the week before—how delighted her family had been to meet him, how friendly and personable and how comfortable he'd appeared to be. It seemed as if he belonged there—right there—at their family table. Her family had adored him, naturally. Who couldn't? She smiled when she thought of the look on her mother's face when Rake had offered to help with the dishes after dinner.

"You slaved over cooking the meal, Mrs. Falls," he'd told her. "You shouldn't have to clean it up too."

Aspen had wondered if Rake were just trying to score some big-time brownie points with her mom. Yet when she heard him explaining to her mother that his own dad always made sure his mom didn't have to clean up after working so hard over a meal, well, she realized it was just another positive notch in Rake's already uniquely good character. He'd spent some time watching football with her dad and brothers that evening—even played with their dog for a few minutes. Yep—he'd won over her family without any effort at all.

Over the past weeks, Aspen had also gotten over the waiting—waiting for Rake to turn into some egotistical jerk. She'd prejudged him just because he was gorgeous. He was just as humble, kind, and wonderful as he appeared to be. The truth of what he actually was in contrast to what she had expected him to be had taught Aspen a valuable lesson: be careful in judging.

The one thing that had turned out to be a little difficult for Aspen to deal with was the reaction of other women to Rake. She'd been absolutely mortified at the brazen attitudes of some of the women who had crossed their path when she and Rake were together. One waitress had the audacity to proposition Rake while Aspen was sitting right there!

They'd just finished their meal, and the waitress, a striking brunette about Aspen's age, had handed Rake the check and a napkin with her phone number on it.

"Call me anytime," she'd said. The waitress had winked at Rake and smiled, totally ignoring the fact that Aspen sat right across from him.

She'd winked at Rake again and walked away, hips swinging like a pendulum. At first, Aspen thought Rake was unaffected—so used to having women hand him their phone numbers that the incident hadn't even rattled him at all. Still, when he'd left cash for the ticket amount, completely stiffing the waitress of any tip, Aspen knew he had been affected—silently perhaps, but affected all the same. Rake was a great tipper, and Aspen knew the waitress had ticked him off.

The waitress had been one in a very long line of forward women—women hitting on Rake with brazen abandon. Then there were the "Ogling Olgas," as Gina had dubbed them. The Ogling Olgas weren't as forward and pushy, but they could disturb Aspen all the same. The Ogling Olgas unashamedly stared at Rake—entirely unguarded and casting propriety to the wind, as if he were a big ice cream sundae smothered in hot fudge. What unnerved Aspen about the Ogling Olgas was the fact she knew darn well they were all thinking the same thing: *What's that gorgeous guy doing with* that *girl? How did a girl like that snag a guy who looks like him?* Yep—that's what they were all thinking. Aspen knew they were thinking it because she would've been thinking the same thing. Still, the Ogling Olgas were easier to deal with in a way. They were basically harmless for one thing. And for another—well, in her secret-most self, Aspen could admit she liked the fact Rake sent the hearts of women to hammering. It made her feel okay about being so incredibly attracted to him.

Aspen bit her lip as she thought of hers and Rake's wild attraction to one another. At that very moment, her mouth flooded with moisture at the thought of kissing him. They'd kissed so much—almost every day for the past month—and still she felt thirsty for his mouth to mingle with her own. Sometimes her physical desires toward Rake frightened her. They were so strong—so overwhelming! Yet she'd set her standards long ago, and apparently so had he, for they each knew when enough had to be enough—for the moment.

In an attempt to satisfy her hunger for Rake's kiss at that moment, Aspen snitched one of Gina's remaining seasoned fries. It did little to gratify her, however, and she glanced to the restroom door, wondering where the heck Gina was.

Snitching another one of Gina's fries, Aspen smiled. Everything seemed brighter, more wonderful, more hopeful, and simply fabulous. She was Rake Locker's girlfriend! She still couldn't believe it, but it was true—and she loved him! Aspen loved Rake deeper and more obsessively than she could ever have imagined loving anyone before meeting him. She often daydreamed about marrying him. Of course, nobody knew about that except Gina, and Gina was sure it would happen. Without any hint of owning doubt, Gina was Aspen's biggest advocate for the future being perfect—for the future forever including Rake.

Aspen shook her head and snuck another seasoned fry. What would she do without Gina? What a loyal, loving friend she was. Aspen wished the right UPS man would come along and sweep Gina off her feet. And maybe he would. Maybe the mystery UPS guy—the one Gina had seen at her mother's house and at the bookstore—the one Aspen and Gina had seen at the Special Shapes Rodeo, riding in the new UPS balloon—maybe he'd show up one day and just whisk Gina away.

Oddly, both Aspen and Gina had begun to wonder if the handsome, wavy-haired UPS man were truly meant to be in their lives somehow, for Gina had seen him multiple times since the Special Shapes Rodeo—and in the strangest places. There was the park-and-ride incident. When Gina had stopped to pick up her brother, the handsome UPS guy had been there picking up someone himself, still wearing his uniform but lacking his signature UPS truck. Then there had been the time Gina had seen him dropping something off at the gift shop next to the urgent care where she worked. All in all, Gina had seen the same guy almost weekly since the Special Shapes Rodeo. Still, Gina's broken heart feared meeting him.

"What if he turns out to be a total jerk like Nick?" Gina had asked only the day before.

"I used to think that about Rake," Aspen had told her.

Still, Gina had insisted Rake was different—the only exception to the rule that all handsome men were cruel jerks.

"Sorry," Gina said, sliding into the red vinyl seat across from Aspen.

Interrupted from her musings, Aspen shook her head. "Are you okay? You were gone a long time," she said.

"I got an eyelash in my eye," Gina explained, picking up one of her seasoned fries and popping it in her mouth. "It got all the way up under my eyelid, and I couldn't get it. It was killing me!"

"Ew! I hate when that happens," Aspen said.

"What were you thinking about just now?" Gina asked.

Aspen shrugged. "Just stuff."

"Just stuff, meaning sexy man Rake Locker, no doubt." Gina giggled, smiling at her ability to read Aspen's thoughts.

"Maybe," Aspen said.

"Oh, go on! It's all you think about anymore...and I don't blame you one bit." Gina sighed and ate another fry. "If he was mine...I wouldn't want to think about anything else. Why bother?"

"I-I just still have trouble believing he likes me," Aspen admitted.

Gina sighed, exasperated. She rolled her eyes dramatically.

"You've got to be kidding," she exclaimed. "I mean…his lip prints are permanently adhered to yours! I mean…if the cops were going to try and solve a case using lip prints, they wouldn't be able to tell whose lips were yours and whose lips were his! You guys spend so much time kissing, you're starting to look more like Angelina Jolie than Aspen Falls."

Aspen laughed. Gina was so random! "Cops? Using lip prints to solve a case? Angelina Jolie?" She picked up her cup and straw-slurped the last few drops of her chocolate shake.

"Yeah! You know how her lips always look swollen…like she's a sucker fish or something."

Aspen laughed so hard she snuffed chocolate shake into her sinuses.

"I mean, seriously…you guys make out that much," Gina said, apparently unaffected by Aspen's near drowning in chocolate shake.

Aspen coughed and wrinkled her nose at the burning inside it.

"We do not," she giggled.

"You do too!" Gina countered. "And I'd think there was something wrong with you if you weren't kissing him every chance you got! He's absolutely one of the hottest—"

Aspen coughed again and frowned when Gina's sentence trailed off into silence, her eyes wide as saucers as she looked past Aspen to the restaurant door. The color had literally drained from her face, and she held a seasoned fry midair between the table and her mouth.

"No stinking way," she breathed.

"What?" Aspen asked in a whisper.

"It's him! It's the hottie-with-the-naughty-body UPS guy!" Gina said.

"Here?" Aspen asked.

"Right behind you. He's walking up to the counter as we speak!"

"He must be on lunch!"

"He's ordering," Gina whispered. "A Lota Combo…with double green chili *and* bacon! No way!"

"How do you know he ordered that?" Aspen asked.

"I can see the order monitor from here."

"That's exactly what you order."

"I know!"

Aspen shook her head. "Go talk to him, Gina! This can't all be coincidental."

Aspen chanced a glance—turned in her seat and looked back toward the order counter. Sure enough, he was there—the same UPS guy from the bookstore and the Special Shapes Rodeo.

"Do it, Gina!" Aspen ordered in a whisper.

But Gina shook her head. "No. Let's just go."

"B-but..." Aspen began to argue.

Gina stood, hurriedly gathering up the remains of their lunch trash and piling it onto a red plastic tray.

"Let's go before he sees us," Gina said. She reached over, dumping the trash on the tray into the nearby garbage can and stacking the tray on the counter next to it. "Hurry up."

"Wait!" Aspen began, but Gina was in escape mode. There would be no stopping her.

Yet as they turned toward the door, they heard his voice—heard the handsome UPS guy say, "Hold on, man. I left my wallet in my truck."

Aspen and Gina both watched as the handsome UPS guy strode toward the door, easily reaching it before they did.

Gina blushed as the man held the door open, flashing a brilliant smile and saying, "There you go, ladies. Have a nice day."

"Thanks," Aspen said as they walked out the door.

"You're welcome," he said, still smiling.

As they walked to the car, Aspen jabbed Gina in the ribs with one elbow.

"What's the matter with you?" she asked. "You didn't even thank him."

"Because I thought I was going to die!" Gina grumbled. Aspen started to scold Gina, but Gina interrupted, "And don't go nagging me! Who was it that didn't have the guts to talk to the hot guy jogging through the park a couple of months ago?"

It was true. Aspen couldn't argue that point. If it hadn't been for that stupid spider, she might never have met Rake.

"Okay," Aspen relented. "But promise me. Promise me that the next time you see him, you'll say something. Maybe go wild and say, like, hi or something brazen like that."

"I'll think about it," Gina said. She sighed, obviously discouraged. "Come on. I'll be late getting back to work."

Aspen wouldn't press Gina any further. She had no right to. Still, it upset her that her normally outgoing, confident friend should look so defeated in those moments. She'd talk to Rake about it—later that day, after work. She was supposed to meet him at the shop so they could run to the mall and pick up some new jeans for him. Maybe Rake could give her some comfort, some encouragement where her worries over Gina were concerned. She was sure he could. Rake always made her feel better—about absolutely everything.

۞

"Hey, baby," Rake greeted, smiling at Aspen as she entered his workshop. He didn't pause—simply gathered Aspen into his arms, pulling her body flush with his as he kissed her. As always, Aspen felt her knees turn to jelly, goose bumps racing over her arms and legs—a blissful wave of pure pleasure! His kisses were teasing at first—playful and restrained. His kiss grew more demanding—drinking pleasure from her lips—drowning her in euphoria!

The taste of his kiss, the scent of his skin, the wonderful feel of his whiskers against the tender flesh around her mouth—all of it was familiar now—marvelously familiar!

"We don't have time for this," Aspen breathed as his mouth toyed with her neck a moment.

"Time?" he chuckled. "You belong to a watchmaker, mi hija." Aspen smiled as she watched him reach over to his workbench and stop the pendulum of the mantel clock he'd been working on—cease its rhythmic timekeeping tick-tock. "See? I can stop time. Now we have plenty…plenty of time to bathe in kissing…the dangerous kind of kissing."

Aspen's heart—already entirely aflutter—leapt in her chest.

"The dangerous kind?" she asked.

"You know what I mean," he mumbled, his mouth only a breath

199

from her own. "The kind that would get us in trouble…if we ever let it."

He started to kiss her again but paused, smiling.

"What?" she asked, reaching up to run her fingers through the softness of his hair.

"It just hit me," he began. "The time of Aspen Falls."

"What do you mean?" Aspen asked.

"I'm a watchmaker," he explained. "Actually, I control time, right? I mean, you've just seen it—my power over time."

"Yeah," she giggled, playing along.

"Well, don't you see? I control the *time* of Aspen Falls. Not only that…maybe I *am* time itself…the time of Aspen Falls. Cool! I'm in the poem now," he said.

Aspen smiled at him and traced his rugged jaw with the back of her fingers.

"You were already in the poem, Rake Locker," she whispered.

"How?" he asked.

Aspen smiled, no longer shy about reciting the poem to him.

"'For the moon is the gypsy's lover,'" she began, tracing his lips with one finger, "'And no sight makes the moon shine more'—"

"'Than her golden ribbons of Aspen,'" he said, brushing a strand of hair from her face. He cupped her chin, caressed her lips with his thumb, and added, "And the rubied jewels at her door." He smiled. "So I'm the moon, huh? And you're the mountain gypsy?"

"Yes," Aspen giggled.

"Ooo," he breathed. "'For the moon is the gypsy's lover.' I like that…especially the *lover* part." Aspen giggled, desperate for his kiss. "'And the rubied jewels at her door,'" he repeated. He kissed her lightly. "I get it now. Your lips are the rubied jewels, and your mouth…" He kissed her again. "Your mouth is all I can think about sometimes— actually, most of the time. And there's that *time* thing again."

His mouth captured hers in a deep, driven, demanding kiss at last. She loved him! It's all she could think of. As he kissed her, held her in the power of his arms, all other thoughts were gone from her mind.

All Aspen could fathom in those moments was how entirely she loved Rake Locker.

"Hello? Rake? Are you still here?"

Rake sighed as he broke the seal of their mouths. Aspen smiled at him and wiped the excess moisture from her lips with her fingers. It was a man's voice that had interrupted them—probably a customer.

"It sounds like Sean," Rake said, smiling at Aspen and brushing another strand of hair from her face. "Looks like you were saved by the UPS guy."

"What?" Aspen asked.

"It's my friend Sean," he explained. "He works for UPS. Gina would probably totally dig him."

Aspen felt the hair on the back of her neck stand on end as Rake called, "I'm comin', man! I'll be right there."

"Y-you have a friend who's a UPS guy?" Aspen asked.

"Yeah," Rake said. "You'll like him. He was on the crew for that new special shapes UPS balloon this year." He took her hand and began pulling her toward the showroom. "Come on. I want you to meet him."

Aspen gulped—literally quit breathing—when she entered the Clock Shop showroom to see Gina's handsome, wavy-haired UPS man standing at the counter.

"Hey, man," Rake greeted. He dropped Aspen's hand, shaking the offered hand of the UPS guy. The two men bumped opposing shoulders and patted each other once on the back. "What's going on?"

"Looks like you've got some new parts, man," the UPS guy said to Rake, although his eyes were fixed to Aspen. "I saw you today at Blake's," he said. "And the Special Shapes Rodeo too, I think."

"Y-yeah," Aspen stammered. How could it be? How could it be that Rake was friends with Gina's dream man?

"You know my woman, dude?" Rake asked, looking from Aspen to the man and back.

"I've seen her a couple of times," the man said. "But we've never actually met."

"Well…Aspen…this is Sean. Sean, this is Aspen. And don't get any ideas. I saw her first."

"Nice to meet you, Aspen," Sean said, smiling and offering a hand.

"Nice to meet you," Aspen said, accepting his handshake.

"You gonna play this year?" Sean asked, handing a scanner and a stylus to Rake.

"I don't know," Rake said, shaking his head. "I guess I'm in…if Aspen's willing to waste her time coming to some basketball games."

"He's a mad roundballer, Aspen," Sean said. "Our team won't win one game if you don't let him play."

"Let him play? Wh-what do I have to do with whether or not he plays basketball?" Aspen asked.

Rake and Sean looked at each other, an expression of amused mutual understanding passing between them.

Rake used the stylus to sign on the scanner. Handing the scanner and stylus back to Sean, he said, "Sean knows that if it comes down between time spent with my woman and playing basketball with a bunch of sweaty men…."

He shrugged as Sean said, "Us sweaty men will lose by a mile."

"When's the first game?" Aspen asked. She had an idea. She not only wanted Rake to play basketball—wanted to watch him play, knowing it would be fabulous—but maybe she could coax Gina into coming to one of Rake's games and meeting Sean!

"Next week," Sean said.

"You should play," Aspen said, taking hold of Rake's arm. He smiled but frowned a little too, curious about her anxious reaction.

"Okay," he said, his smoldering eyes narrowing with suspicion.

"Cool!" Sean said, nodding toward a box on the counter. "Meet me at the gym on Thursday, and we'll hoop it up."

"Okay, man," Rake said, still looking at Aspen.

"Nice to meet you, Aspen," Sean said. "I can see why Rake's been off the grid for so long."

"'Bye," Aspen said. She tossed a wave at Sean as he left the shop.

"Okay, baby," Rake said. "What's going on? You sure took to Sean like a kitten takes to tuna."

Aspen smiled. "It's him! Rake…it's him!"

"Who?" he asked. Aspen thought he looked a little worried—jealous maybe.

"Gina's UPS man!" she explained. She wanted him to understand—understand it was Gina who was interested in his friend, not her.

His frown deepened. "The one that's always showing up wherever she is?" he asked. Aspen had mentioned Gina's mystery UPS man to Rake on occasion. She was delighted he remembered. "You're kidding me."

"No! We saw him today at Lotaburger. It was weird! He ordered the same exact thing Gina gets," she explained.

"My friend Sean," he said, pointing to the door. "He's the UPS guy Gina has been bumping into all over town?"

"Yes!" Aspen giggled. "I can't believe you didn't tell me you knew him!"

"I didn't know I did…know the mystery UPS dream man, I mean." He smiled, his eyes suddenly lighting up with mischief. "He's single, you know."

"Really?"

"Yep!"

"Girlfriend?"

"Nope. Not for a while now."

"Gina keeps seeing him, Rake," Aspen explained. "It's like they're meant to be." She wondered if he would doubt her—think she was silly for believing Gina was seeing Sean everywhere for a reason.

He grinned, gathered her into his arms, and said, "It might be. Kind of like the way my mouth and your mouth fit together so perfectly… as if they were two pieces to a puzzle."

"Exactly," Aspen said.

She recognized the fiery smolder in his eyes, but he didn't kiss her.

"Let's go…before I lock that door, stop every clock in this place, and have my way with you, Aspen Falls," he said.

"What if I want you to—" she began.

"Don't tease me about that today, Aspen," Rake interrupted.

Aspen frowned. He always teased her about having his way with her, and she always reciprocated. It had become a running joke between them.

"But we always—"

"Today's different," he said.

"Why?"

He smiled, tracing her lips with his thumb as he laid a palm against her cheek.

"Because today…I'm not teasing."

"Oh," she breathed, an impish delight rising in her. "Okay then," she said, taking his hand. "Let's go get you some new jeans. It's getting to where the whole world knows what color of underwear you're wearing." It was true too. Aspen couldn't remember the last time she'd seen Rake in a pair of jeans that didn't have some progression of holes at the corners of the back pockets.

Rake watched Aspen as she piled three new pairs of Levi's on the register counter. She was too adorable! His mouth watered; every inch of his flesh seemed on fire.

"Do you need anything else while we're here?" she asked. "I get the feeling you're not into shopping. So if you need anything else…maybe you should get it now."

Rake looked down at the front of the blue-and-white flannel shirt he wore—the same one he'd been wearing the day the hot air balloon bumped the sandbar and dumped some passengers out of the basket. He'd torn the shirt—ripped a couple of strips off the tail.

"Maybe a shirt," he said, smiling at her. He glanced around and saw a display of flannel shirts stacked on a nearby shelf. He reached out, pulling an extra-large, red-and-white shirt from the pile. "Here," he said, tossing it onto the counter on top of the stack of jeans.

Aspen giggled. Shaking her pretty head, she looked at the cashier and said, "That's it, I guess."

The cashier glanced at Rake and then to Aspen. Rake watched the cashier blush, smile, and say, "With a man like that…I'm guessing the fewer clothes the better."

Rake quickly looked to Aspen. Would she be mad? He'd expected her to lose her cool so many times at the way women flirted with him, but she never had—not yet—at least not that he could tell. She seemed to have accepted it and had an easier time than he had accepting it when he caught other men checking her out. He watched her face for some sign of blame—of blaming him for the woman's insinuative remark.

Aspen smiled, however, nodded at the cashier, and said, "Oh, you have no idea!"

Touché! He couldn't help but grin at Aspen being so quick on her feet.

"I'm sure," the cashier mumbled as she scanned the items Aspen had placed on the counter. "That'll be a hundred and thirty-two ninety-seven. Will that be debit or credit?"

"Debit," Rake answered, taking his wallet out of his back right pocket. Instead of taking his debit card out of his wallet, however, he handed the wallet to Aspen. "Use the gold one," he said, winking at her. He leaned forward, whispering the pin number to her. He could tell by the smile on her face that she was delighted. There was something about trusting a woman with your debit card that made her feel trusted and important.

Aspen opened his wallet, removed his gold Visa debit card, and started to slide it through the cashier's card machine.

"Oh! Are you sure you don't want to try this shirt on first?" she asked.

Rake glanced around the store. He counted at least five women staring at him and Aspen. He didn't understand it—why women always stared at him the way they did. He knew he was better looking than a lot of men but nothing to deserve the kind of staring he'd always had to endure. His temper was a little tweaked in that moment. Fine! They wanted a show, then he'd give them one.

"Maybe you're right," he said.

Aspen felt her mouth gape open as Rake put his hands to his chest. The quick snips of snaps unsnapping echoed through the room as Rake pulled his old flannel shirt open, stripping it from his body and handing it to Aspen. He opened the bag the cashier had put his purchased items in and removed the shirt. Breaking the white plastic tag fixture, he tossed the cost tag to the counter and put the shirt on. He nodded at Aspen as he buttoned the buttons up the front of the shirt.

"It's fine," he said.

Aspen—mouth still gaping—slid Rake's debit card through the card reader. She glanced around a moment before entering his pin number. Every woman in the store was staring, smiles plastered on their faces, eyes bright with delight.

"H-here's your receipt," the cashier said, blushing as she continued to stare at Rake.

"Thank you," Aspen said. She wrapped the receipt around Rake's debit card, put the card back in his wallet, and handed his wallet to him.

"Thanks," Rake said. He shoved his wallet into his back pocket and grabbed the bag off the counter. "You ready to go?"

"Yeah," Aspen said. She shoved his discarded shirt in to the bag she was still carrying from another store and nodded.

She smiled when Rake put one strong arm around her shoulders. He kissed her mouth rather ravenously as they left the store.

"You are a naughty boy," Aspen giggled once they'd cleared the store's entrance and were walking in the mall once more.

He shrugged. "Sometimes you just gotta…you know…do stuff."

Aspen giggled, and Rake smiled.

"I guess so," she said.

He chuckled, warmed by the sound of her giggle. He wanted to make her giggle again—wanted to be the cause of all her smiles.

"I've got an idea," he said. And he did. He'd been working something out in his mind ever since they'd left the shop.

"What's that?" she asked. "Do you wanna run into Old Navy and do some stripping now?"

Rake felt his cheeks warm up. She'd actually made him blush.

"No," he mumbled. "I want you to bring Gina by the shop tomorrow about five thirty."

"Okay. Why?"

He liked the way she agreed before she even knew why he wanted her to do it.

"I've got an order coming in—via UPS—and Sean usually shows up about five thirty, like he did tonight. The tracking number for the package says it will be here tomorrow."

Aspen stopped and turned to face him. "Then what?" she asked.

"Then we let nature take its course," he said, smiling at her.

"You're gonna play matchmaker?" she giggled. The light in her eyes—the pure joy and excitement—was worth anything.

"*We're* gonna play matchmaker," he chuckled.

Aspen squealed and threw her arms around his neck. He inhaled deeply, relishing her sweet, fresh fragrance as he rested his chin on the top of her head. He had her in his arms—he did—and he would never let her go!

❧

Aspen lifted her arm to her face, breathing in the lingering scent of Rake's cologne. When he'd dropped her off at the Clock Shop parking lot to get her car, she'd asked him if he wanted to take his old torn-up flannel shirt home.

"Naw," he'd said. "You keep it. Wear it to bed, and maybe we can make out in your dreams."

So, when she'd gotten home and stripped off her clothes, she'd put on Rake's old flannel shirt instead of her pajamas. At the first touch of the soft flannel to her skin, Aspen knew she would definitely see Rake in her dreams that night. His scent enveloped her—fresh, rich, masculine. She felt more secure somehow. She loved wearing his shirt—knowing that something that had once rested against his skin now caressed hers.

She stared up at the ceiling of her bedroom, secretly wishing she were lying in her bed wrapped in Rake's arms instead of just his shirt. She tried to imagine how it would feel—how it would feel to really own him, to be married to him, to sleep in the strength of his arms every night. She sighed, wishing he were there at that moment—knowing she should wish it. She breathed in the scent of his shirt once more—

Rake's shirt against her skin instead of his arms. His shirt would have to do—for now.

CHAPTER THIRTEEN

"It's cold today," Gina said, shivering as she walked with Aspen toward the Clock Shop. "I guess December is really here."

"Feels like it," Aspen said.

"Are you sure Rake wants me along with you guys tonight?" Gina asked. "It's always weird…when there's just the three of us."

"It's not weird," Aspen assured her. "But if you want to bring a date next time, you can."

"A date? Like who?"

"Like that cute tech you were with right before we left." Aspen smiled. The giddiness rising in her was almost unbearable! She wondered what would happen when Rake's friend Sean walked into the shop. She hoped he and Gina would instantly hit it off—feel undeniably drawn to each other. Of course, Gina was already drawn to him—or at least to his UPS uniform. Still, Aspen hoped something would spark in her friend—something to pull her out of the depths of brokenhearted fear Nick Dalley had thrown her into.

"You mean Eric?" Gina asked. "No way! He's too soft for me. He goes in about every ten days for a manicure. It wigs me out."

Aspen laughed. "Sorry," she said. "He's just cute, and I thought—"

"Don't worry, Asp. Someday my own Mr. Right will show up…just like Rake did for you."

"How do you know Rake is my Mr. Right?" Aspen asked.

"Are you kidding?" Gina giggled. "You guys are perfect for each other. I can't wait 'til the wedding! I get to be your maid of honor, right?"

"Wedding?" Aspen asked, feigning ignorance—even though her arms rippled with goose bumps at the thought of marrying Rake.

"Oh, don't play dumb with me, Aspen Falls," Gina said. "If he dropped to his knees and asked you to marry him the minute we walk into the Clock Shop…you wouldn't hesitate! You'd marry him tomorrow if he asked."

Aspen shrugged as an odd sort of nervous feeling rose in her chest. "I would," she admitted. "I admit it…but there's no chance that's going to happen."

"He loves you," Gina said. "It's so obvious. Every time he looks at you, his expression turns into this starving panther look. I swear, sometimes he looks like he's just going to take hold of you and…well, you know…have you."

Aspen shook her head and smiled. "You're so dramatic. He does not look at me like that," she said.

"Oh my heck, he does too! The other day, we were at his house helping paint the spare bedroom. I swear…that's what he was thinking. I can totally read men."

"Oh really?" Aspen challenged. They'd reached the shop, and Aspen opened the front door. "You think so?"

"Totally!" Gina said. "Other than Nick…name one guy we've ever known that I haven't read like a book."

Aspen smiled. Gina was a pretty good judge of character. It's why Nick had destroyed her so completely. He'd been the only guy who had managed to pull a snow job on Gina Wicksoth. Aspen still didn't know how he'd managed to do it, but he had—tricked her into really believing he was everything he claimed and appeared to be.

All at once Aspen's excitement—her anticipatory anxiety—was almost overwhelming. What if Sean walked in and there was nothing more? What if Gina didn't like him up close as much as she did from a distance? What if it was only the idea of liking him that kept Gina so wound up whenever she happened across him? Worse yet, what if Sean didn't like Gina? Rejection would be a harsh blow to her cherished friend—Aspen knew it. Suddenly, she wasn't as certain as she had been before—wasn't as confident in a happy outcome. Still, Rake had assured her it would work out. He knew Sean—had known him for quite a while—and Rake felt positive Sean and Gina would hit it off.

Aspen swallowed and tried to buoy her courage. There had to be a reason Sean and Gina were always crossing each other's paths. There had to be!

"Well, hello, girls!" Charlotte greeted as Gina and Aspen entered the shop. "What are you up to this evening?"

"Just meeting Rake for dinner, Mrs. Locker," Aspen said. Charlotte hurried between the rows of grandfather clocks toward the girls. She hugged Aspen and then Gina. Aspen smiled, warmed by her grandmotherly attention.

"He's in the back," she said. "Rake! The girls are here," she called. "He's almost finished, I think."

"Thanks," Aspen said.

"I'm off to my quilters' club, honey," Charlotte told Aspen. "You kids have a good night."

"We will," Aspen said.

"You too," Gina added as Charlotte headed to the front door.

Charlotte nodded and smiled, closing the door behind her.

"I love this shop," Gina said, glancing around the room. "Every time I come in here…well…it just makes me want to buy clocks!"

"I think that's the idea," Aspen said.

Gina nodded, arching two lovely eyebrows. "Oh, yeah…I guess so." She frowned. "There's something else too…something that makes me want to go home and read Charles Dickens…or watch medieval-themed movies."

Aspen giggled. "I know, me too. I think it's the thyme. Rake's grandma keeps it simmering in a slow-cooker behind the counter. She leaves little bundles of it here and there too."

"Well, whatever she does…I always want to go home and eat spaghetti after I've been here," Gina said.

"Hey, ladies!" Rake greeted as he entered from the back room.

At the sight of him, Aspen's heart began to race. She knew she would never get used to the way she felt when he first entered a room—to the breathless, awed sensation that always washed over her. He smiled, leaning over to place a lingering kiss on her lips.

"And what have you girls been up to today?" he asked. Aspen smiled when Rake hugged Gina in a friendly greeting before gathering Aspen into his arms and kissing her again.

"Not much. We just hung out at the humane society and played with some stray puppies, auditioned to be Victoria Secret models, did a little skydiving...the usual stuff," Gina said.

Rake chuckled, as ever amused by Gina's sarcasm. "Sounds like a very fulfilling day."

"It was," Gina said, smiling at him.

Aspen smiled too. She loved the fact Gina and Rake got along so well. It was important to her that they did.

"How was work, baby?" he asked Aspen.

Aspen sighed, shaking her head. "Good...other than Michael was a nightmare...as usual. A little boy had an accident in the children's section too, and I got to clean it up. But it was good otherwise."

Rake smiled. "Same here."

"A little boy had an accident in your shop?" Gina teased.

Rake chuckled. "No...but I did—"

"Hey, Rake," Sean greeted as he stepped through the front door of the shop. "Man...I guess you're popular this week."

Aspen smiled with delight—bit her lip as she saw the color drain from Gina's face.

"Oh my heck!" she heard Gina exclaim in a whisper.

What made the moment even better was the expression on Sean's face. His face seemed to drain of a little of its color too, and his handsome brow puckered in a slight frown.

"Gina," Rake began, "this is my friend Sean. Sean...this is Gina."

"Sean?" Gina exclaimed. "As in Sean Connery?"

"Well, more like Sean Kelley," Sean explained, "but I guess it's close."

Gina looked to Aspen, then back to Sean. At first Aspen was afraid the damage done to Gina by Nick was still too deep—too scarring to allow her friend to take a leap of faith. She wondered if Gina would simply bolt and run—not even give herself a chance to get to know Sean. Yet in the next moment, Aspen smiled and felt her own heart soar as she saw an all-too-familiar expression wash over Gina's face—an expression of pure mischief entirely void of any apprehension.

"I've seen you around," Gina said, walking toward Sean. Aspen watched as Sean set the package he'd been carrying down on the floor and began sauntering toward Gina.

"And I've seen you," Sean said.

"You delivered a package to my mom once," Gina said.

"You were at the Special Shapes Rodeo," Sean countered.

Gina giggled, and Aspen's heart soared. The mutual attraction between Sean and Gina was like an electric current running through the room.

"I think I should take you to dinner," Sean said. His smile was warm and inviting—entirely alluring—and Gina moved closer to him.

"I think you should too," Gina said.

Aspen glanced up to Rake. He was smiling and winked at her, obviously as entertained by the exchange between Gina and Sean as she was. Her heart swelled as she studied his face for a moment. Oh, how she loved him—everything about him! She loved the way he smiled, the way he walked, the sound of his voice. She loved the fact that he used to ride bulls, was a watchmaker, and had the guts to wear the vampire Rochester Darcy costume his sister had made. And now—now she loved the fact he would involve himself in a little matchmaking between Gina and Sean. He was too wonderful, and she knew she would love him forever.

Aspen's attention was drawn back to Gina and Sean when she heard Gina say, "I think you're very handsome," as she brazenly appraised Sean from head to toe. Aspen grinned. Gina was back in the saddle! She'd seen Gina operate before. There wasn't a man on earth who could resist Gina Wicksoth when she was on top of her game.

"I think you're very beautiful," Sean said. Aspen bit her lip, delighted by the flirtatious, predatory expression on Sean's face.

"I think there's a reason I've been seeing you everywhere I go," Gina said. She reached out, running an index finger over the name patch on the front of Sean's shirt.

"Me too…and I think we've wasted enough time," Sean said.

Aspen gasped as Sean gathered Gina into his arms and kissed her. Gina didn't hesitate—simply let her arms go around Sean's neck, meeting his affectionate advances with the same lack of inhibition with which he offered them.

"Oh my heck!" Aspen whispered, looking up to see Rake smiling with amused approval. "Rake?" she asked, suddenly worried for Gina—for the safety of her heart as well as her person.

Rake smiled. "Don't worry, baby," he whispered. "I wouldn't have hooked them up if I didn't totally trust him. He's a good guy. And anyway…don't worry about Gina. You know she can take care of herself."

He was right. Gina *could* take care of herself. Furthermore, Gina Wicksoth would never kiss a stranger unless her soul had prompted her to do so—to trust him—to take a chance with him.

"Let's go," Rake said. "I know Sean. He'll totally sweep her off her feet."

Rake put a strong arm across Aspen's shoulders and directed her toward the front door. He paused as they reached the couple.

"You guys go ahead," Gina said, her face crimson with delight. "I-I'll catch up with you later."

"She won't be catching up with you later," Sean said, winking at Aspen. "You two have fun. I'll take good care of your friend Gina here."

Rake smiled and reached into his pocket, dropping a key on the red carpet near Sean's feet.

"Lock it up when you leave, man," Rake chuckled. "And Merry Christmas!"

"Merry Christmas indeed," Sean chuckled, returning his attention to Gina.

Rake smiled as he walked toward the pickup with Aspen. He glanced down at her, noting how good it felt to have his arm around her—to have her arm around his waist. Sean would make Gina happy, and that would make Aspen happy. And when Aspen was happy, Rake was content. He shoved his left hand into his front pocket—let his fingers clasp the little trinket he'd been carrying around for over two weeks. Maybe the time had come at last. With Gina on her way to a wonderful relationship of her own—and Rake knew she was—maybe he could finally take his relationship with Aspen to the next level. Maybe.

Still, he paused—not because he was uncertain about where he wanted his relationship with Aspen to go next but because of his past. He had to tell her; he knew he did. Mark and Clinton said he didn't need to tell her—that the past was the past and it didn't matter. Yet Marissa had urged him to talk to Aspen about it—to make sure there were no secrets between them. The matter ate at him a great deal more than he would've liked, and that in itself was a sign he should talk to Aspen about it. Still, he was afraid. What if she didn't understand? What if she didn't believe his side of the story? Well, he had proof—proof to support his claims. But he hoped Aspen would take his word for it—that he wouldn't have to show proof of his integrity to the woman he loved. He did love Aspen—more thoroughly than he'd ever imagined! His love for her kindled a frantic sort of desperation in him—the need to own her, have her, entirely and in every respect imaginable.

"What are you thinking about?" Aspen asked, jolting him from his thoughts.

Rake shrugged and let go of the trinket in his pocket. "A lot of stuff," he said. It was an honest answer—honest without being too revealing. He shook his head and forced an amused-sounding chuckle. "I guess Sean isn't one to mince words."

Aspen giggled. "I guess not," she said. "I've never known Gina to act anything like that before! I mean, she's her own woman—does whatever she wants and everything—but she always said she would never kiss a guy she didn't already know really, really well first."

"Would you have kissed me without knowing me really, really well?" he teased. He stopped their advance toward the pickup and turned her to face him.

"I did kiss you before I knew you really, really well," she told him. He liked the way her cheeks pinked up at the confession.

"If we'd never gone out—if we'd just seen each other here and there, never spoken before—if I had just walked up to you one day in the park and asked, 'Hey, baby…can I kiss you?'…would you have let me?"

He watched her blush deepen to a pretty scarlet. He loved to rattle her this way—to send goose bumps rippling over her arms, the way she sent them racing over his.

"Yes," she admitted, shyly glancing away.

"Why?" he asked, slipping a hand around to the back of her neck.

"Because you're so…so…attractive," she said.

He chuckled. "You would've let me kiss you just because you think I'm cute?"

"Cute?" she giggled. "Rake, I don't want to offend you…but you're far from being just cute. And besides, it's more than that. It's you…all of you…the whole package. Everything about you is attractive."

He smiled, knowing it was a hard admission for her to make—thrilled that the wonderful girl standing before him thought he was worth bothering with.

"I wanted to kiss you the very first time I saw you sitting on that park bench," he confessed. He wanted her to know—know he was instantly drawn to her, from the very first moment.

"Really?" she asked, her eyes bright with being pleased.

"Really," he said. "Kind of like right now." She bit her lip with delighted anticipation. "Actually, right now I want to haul you off to my house, carry you into my bedroom, throw you on the bed, and—" He chuckled when her hand covered his mouth, stopping his scandalous confession. He adored Aspen's habit of covering his mouth to silence him whenever he was about to say something outrageous. It was part of the reason he said some of the things he did.

"You can't say things like that!" she scolded, a smile of pure delight brightening her face.

Rake pushed her hand away and said, "Well, I think them…so I might as well say them." She blushed and giggled, and he gathered her into his arms, inhaling the sweet fragrance of her hair.

Rake loved Aspen, more than he could ever have imagined loving someone, and it was time—time to step up to the plate and tell her what he needed to so their relationship could advance to the next level. Yep! Tomorrow—he'd tell her tomorrow. And if she forgave him his transgressions the way he prayed she would, then he'd take the next step—hoped she'd take it with him.

As Rake's mouth captured hers in a heated and driven kiss, Aspen sighed. He was delicious. Rake Locker was wonderful—her every dream come true! As she wrapped her arms around his neck, returning his kiss with her own demanding ardor, Aspen thought nothing could strip her of the pure euphoria expanding inside her—nothing! Rake loved her—she knew he did. He'd told her he loved her many, many times, and she believed him. She trusted him—trusted him to continue loving her, trusted him not to break her heart—and it was a magnificent sensation. For her part, she never imagined she could love someone so entirely—so desperately—but she did! Rake had become everything to her—her happiness, her reason for getting up in the morning, her life. At times she couldn't believe the handsome real man who had once been a stranger had chosen her—plain little Aspen Falls—to be the one he loved. But he had. He had, and it was wonderful!

Aspen giggled as Rake suddenly swooped her up in his arms, carrying her toward the pickup.

"Brrr!" he exclaimed, shivering as he carried her. "Let's go to my house for dinner. I've got a couple of chicken pot pies in the freezer, not to mention some barbecue potato chips…the wavy kind."

"Ooo! The wavy kind?" Aspen giggled.

Rake let her feet drop to the ground as he dug in his pocket for the keys to the pickup. He kissed her cheek as he opened the driver's side door. Aspen crawled into the pickup, snuggling up against Rake as the engine roared to life.

"It's freezing!" Rake said, shivering again as he turned the heater knob to high.

"That's because you never bring a coat," Aspen scolded.

"I don't need a coat," Rake said, smiling at her. He shifted into reverse and said, "I have you to keep me warm."

Aspen giggled with delight. She sighed as Rake pulled the pickup out onto Corrales Road and headed toward his house. Everything was perfect—especially Rake Locker.

※

Aspen was tired—tired and resentful. She hadn't wanted to work the midnight release event, but she'd ticked off Michael the week before, and he'd scheduled her to work it anyway. She'd gotten in so late, having stayed way too long at Rake's house after dinner—just talking and kissing and being lost in the bliss of his company. Then when she'd returned home at one a.m., it was to her cell ringing—to Gina's report on her evening with Sean. And what a report it was! Sean had taken Gina to Sadie's for dinner and then to a movie. Afterward, they'd sat in his car for four hours just talking and getting to know each other.

"I swear, Aspen," Gina had said over the cell, "it's like I've known him my whole life. Actually, like I knew him before my whole life!"

Aspen and Gina had talked for over an hour—about Sean and the miracle of his knowing Rake, about how it all just seemed meant to be. Aspen was elated—ecstatic over hearing the joy and hope in Gina's voice. Nick was finally beaten, Gina was revitalized, and Sean was meant to revitalize her.

Now—now Aspen was at the store, working the midnight release event, and she was tired. It was nearly one a.m. The store would be closing in a few minutes, and Aspen couldn't wait to get home and fall into bed.

"Excuse me," a woman said, smiling at Aspen.

"May I help you find something?" Aspen asked.

"Well, if you're Aspen…then I think I've found it," the woman said. She smiled, and Aspen thought her smile held something not quite kind—something that made the hair on the back of Aspen's neck prick.

"Excuse me?" Aspen asked. The woman was very beautiful—dark-haired, dark-eyed, with a supermodel figure. She looked to be a bit older than Aspen but not by much.

"Are you Aspen?" the woman asked.

"Yes. Did the front desk refer you? I do work in the children's section if you're looking for—"

"I'm looking for you," the woman said. "I'm Serena."

"I-I'm Aspen," Aspen stammered. Quickly she searched the archives of her memory trying to put some sort of recognition to the woman's face or name. Did she know her? From high school or something?

"Do you mean to tell me you don't know who I am?" the woman named Serena asked.

Aspen bit her lip, frowned an apologetic grimace, and said, "I'm sorry. I just don't remember where we've met. I—"

"We haven't met," Serena said, "but you should know who I am."

"I-I just can't seem to—"

"I'm Rake Locker's ex," the woman said.

So many thoughts and feelings began racing around in Aspen's mind, she felt sure she would faint. Rake's ex? His ex what? Ex-girlfriend, his ex—his ex-wife? Instantly Aspen's mind fought the concepts—each of them—all of them. Rake would've told her if he'd been married before. She knew he would've! And as far as ex-girlfriends, he'd mentioned a couple, but Aspen couldn't remember any of them having been named Serena.

"His ex?" Aspen managed.

"That's right," Serena said. "Serena Sanchez. Rake and I dated for two years. Surely he's mentioned me. I mean…we do have a son together. You'd think he would've at least mentioned his son." The women smiled, her eyes narrowing with the triumph of owning a knowledge Aspen didn't. "I mean, I know all about *you*…so I just assumed Rake had told you about us."

Aspen swallowed hard—tried to keep the contents of her stomach from spilling out onto the floor by way of her mouth. It couldn't be true! He would've told her! She knew Rake would've told her if he'd had a child. Rake was different than other profoundly good-looking men—she was certain he was. He wasn't a liar and a jerk—he wasn't! And yet, as a little dark-haired boy of about three ran up to the woman, wrapping his arms around her leg, Aspen stopped breathing.

"This is Manuel…our son," Serena said. "I can't believe Rake hasn't told you about Manuel. Of course, I guess it is kind of a big revelation to make to a new girlfriend."

"I-it's a little late for him to be out...isn't it?" Aspen stammered. She couldn't think of anything else to say. Rake's son? He had a son? She was sure she felt her heart begin to ache—ache at the thought of Rake's having been intimate with the woman standing before her—ache with the knowledge he had a child and never told her about it.

"Manuel loves the Boggy Froggy books," Serena explained. "I let him take a longer nap so we could be here for the midnight release of the new Boggy Froggy book tonight."

Aspen nodded. When Serena had announced she was Rake's ex—when she'd produced Rake's son—Aspen had totally forgotten the reason she was even at the store. Earlier in the day, she'd simply been glad she hadn't been the one to have to wear the giant green Boggy Froggy costume coinciding with the new Boggy Froggy book release. Now she was having trouble remembering she had a job at all. All she could think of was that this woman—Serena—had been Rake's girlfriend, that he'd been intimate with her, that the little boy gazing up at her with deep, dark eyes was Rake's son.

"So, you're Aspen," Serena said. She studied Aspen from head to toe, smiling. "You're very different from any of the other girls Rake has dated since we broke up. He usually only goes out with really beautiful women."

"Can I help you find a copy of the new Boggy Froggy book or something?" Aspen asked. She could feel the tears welling in her eyes and frantically fought to contain them. "It is why you came in, isn't it?"

"Oh, we've got our copy," Serena said. "I just wanted to get a look at Rake's next victim."

"Well, you've seen me," Aspen said.

"Don't let him fool you the way he did me, Aspen," Serena said. She reached down and tousled her son's hair. "He puts on a really good act—a real gentleman, kind, considerate...and so in control. But, in the end, he's just out for one thing. And once he gets it...you'll be old news."

"Thank you for your concern," Aspen said. "I'm sure it's well-meant and totally sincere."

"Totally," Serena said.

"Good night," Aspen said. "You enjoy your new book, Manuel," she said to the toddler a moment before she headed for the front of the store.

Grabbing her coat from the coat rack, Aspen was glad she'd left her purse in the car. She reached into her pocket and found her keys.

"Where do you think you're going?" Michael asked as Aspen pushed the front doors open.

"I'm sick," she told him. "And unless you want my dinner all over the front of your shirt…you won't give me a hard time, Michael."

Aspen couldn't even enjoy the look of forfeit on Michael's face. She hurried to her car, barely holding down the remains of her dinner. Her stomach heaved and lurched with overwhelming anxiety and heartbreak. She slid into the driver's seat—watched as her own hand struggled to push the key into the ignition. Tears were streaming down her face, and she covered her mouth to keep from throwing up.

She shouldn't be driving; she knew she was in no condition to drive. As heartache, anger, and fear wracked her body, Aspen reached behind the seat and retrieved her purse. Frantically digging through it, she sobbed when she found her cell. Gina! She'd call Gina. Gina would calm her down—help her to think rationally. But as she pressed her speed dial, she shook her head. No. Rake hadn't been truthful with her. That or the beautiful vixen in the bookstore was lying. She hoped the second were true, yet doubt gripped her like a vise. Still, Gina couldn't solve anything. Rake could. Either solve it or confirm it, and she had to know.

Peeling out of the bookstore parking lot, Aspen angrily brushed at the tears on her cheeks. He would've told her—he would've! Aspen knew Rake could not be the creep this Serena chick had made him out to be. Yet what about the little boy? She couldn't have been lying. It was too easy to disprove.

Aspen gasped, realizing how frantic she was as she ran a red light. She'd seen the intersection camera blink; she'd be getting her ticket in the mail soon enough, so she'd worry about that later. All she could think about was Rake—how desperately she loved him! He would've told her if he'd had a son. She was sure he would've!

Rake growled as he opened his eyes.

"Who the hell would be banging on the door at this hour?" he grumbled as he tossed his blankets aside. Almost instantly, full consciousness washed over him, however. Aspen! That idiot Michael had scheduled her to work the midnight release event. What if something were wrong? A weird sort of fear rose in his chest as he fairly leapt out of bed and headed for the front door.

Fumbling with the deadbolt, he opened the door, relieved to see Aspen standing before him safe and sound. He frowned in the next moment, however—for her face was red, tears streaming from her eyes.

"What's the matter?" he said, reaching out, taking her by the shoulders, and pulling her into the house. "Are you okay, baby? What's wrong?"

Aspen tried to ignore the titillated thrill running through her at the sight of Rake standing there in nothing but a black pair of boxer briefs. His tousled hair, muscular torso, and legs only accentuated his already magnetic good looks, and she couldn't afford to weaken toward him— at least, not until she knew the truth.

"I just met Serena," she said. It was all she needed to say. The expression on his face was all she needed to see. His broad shoulders slumped forward, and he exhaled a heavy breath.

"Where?" he asked.

CHAPTER FOURTEEN

Aspen knew then. It was true! She felt sick and tried to swallow the burning in her throat as she burst into tears.

"It's true? It's true and you never told me about it?" she cried.

"I meant to," he began, running his hand through his hair. "I started to tell you…so many times…"

"She had Manuel with her," she sobbed. "How could you not tell me about him?"

"Manuel? You mean Manny?" he asked. "Her little boy?"

"Rake…I-I thought I knew you. I-I wanted to believe you were everything you seem to be. I-I really thought you…I can't believe this!" Aspen buried her face in her hands, bitterly sobbing, certain she would die. The pain in her heart was overwhelming, suffocating, and destructive. She couldn't endure it. She couldn't!

"What did she tell you?" he growled. He took her shoulders again, glaring into her face. "What did she tell you? Why are you so upset? You do know me, Aspen. So please…don't tell me you would believe something a stranger told you if it contradicts what you know about me."

Aspen covered her mouth—willed the contents of her stomach to stay where they were. She studied his face for a moment. Anger and pain mingled in his expression—some sort of fear too. He was right. Somehow a rational thought penetrated the heartache and pain overtaking Aspen's body and mind.

"Did you really date her…for two years?" Aspen asked.

"Yes," Rake said.

"Is the little boy yours? She says he's yours. Is he?"

She saw Rake's jaw clench. "No," he growled.

"Are you sure?" Aspen asked, still irrational with heartache.

Rake's eyes narrowed, his jaw still clenched. He leaned forward, glaring down at her. "It would be pretty miraculous if he were mine... considering I never slept with her, don't you think?"

Aspen tried to breathe, tried to calm herself down. She gazed into the dark flames in his eyes—and she believed him.

"Sh-she came into the store just now," she whispered. "She knew who I was...and she told me she was your ex and that..."

"And what? That I had a son?" Rake growled.

"Sh-she had him with her...and she said...she said..."

"I know what she said, Aspen!" Rake shouted. "She's been saying it since the day she found out she was pregnant!" He swore and turned away from her, his shoulders rising and falling with his labored, angry breathing. He shook his head and swore several more times. It was obvious he was infuriated.

Aspen felt a wave of nausea wash over her, but it was different this time—for its source was different. He was right to be angry with her. After all their time together—months together—she'd believed a stranger's accusations over what she knew his character to be. Her faith in him had been tested—and failed. She'd proven herself weak and disloyal, and she knew Rake was strong and fiercely loyal. She'd lose him over this, and it was exactly what Serena had wanted. In those moments, Aspen realized it had been Serena's plan all along—to drive Rake away from Aspen, not to drive Aspen away from Rake.

"I-I'm sorry, Rake," Aspen stammered. "I-I...it was just such a shock. I-I just couldn't imagine anyone would lie about something like that. I-I know you would never—"

"No, you don't!" he growled, turning to face her. Tears burst from Aspen's eyes as she saw the moisture welling in his. "Obviously you don't know that I would never...now do you?"

"It just caught me so off guard," she began. "I-I'm just tired, and...

and I have such a hard time believing someone like you could really care for me and—"

"Stop!" he growled, raising a hand in a gesture she should stop trying to explain. "Just stop, Aspen." He put his hands on his hips, clenched his jaw once more, and nodded. "I should've told you about this. I knew I should've." His eyes narrowed as he looked at her. "But I didn't want to. I was afraid of how you'd react."

Aspen brushed tears from her cheeks and swallowed the hard lump of guilt in her throat.

"I-I'm sorry, Rake," she began, "Please don't—"

"Come on," he growled, taking hold of her arm and pulling her toward the bedroom.

"Rake...really...I'm so sorry," she stammered. He didn't say a word—simply pulled her into his bedroom and pushed her to sit down on his bed.

"I can't believe her," he mumbled as he picked up a pair of jeans that had been tossed onto a nearby chair. Aspen watched as he stepped into the jeans and rather violently zipped the fly. He strode to a chest of drawers on one wall, pulled open a drawer, withdrew a pair of socks, and then slammed the drawer shut. Sitting down on the chair where his jeans had lain, he pulled on the socks, all the while shaking his head. "I don't know what I ever saw in her," he mumbled as he pulled on one beaten-up roper boot.

"She's beautiful," Aspen whispered.

Rake paused in pulling on the other boot, glaring at her a moment.

"Yeah...she is," he grumbled. He pulled on the other boot and grabbed a black leather jacket hanging on a hook nearby. "Come on," he said, taking hold of Aspen's hand and pulling her to her feet. "We're going for a drive."

It was a command, not a request.

"Y-you need a shirt," she stammered as he led her toward the front door.

"I don't need nothing," he growled, hefting her onto his shoulder and opening the front door. Carrying her over the threshold and out into the cold winter night, Rake slammed the door behind them.

Aspen's stomach bounced against his shoulder as he carried her toward his pickup. She didn't understand why he felt the need to haul her away like she were a sack of flour. She was perfectly capable of walking, even if she was blinded by the tears still streaming from her eyes.

Her tears only increased in profusion as he deposited her in the passenger's seat of his pickup, rather than sliding her in from the driver's seat as he normally did. He angrily buckled her seat belt for her, slammed the door, and stormed around to the driver's side. Aspen sat shivering against the cold vinyl of the seat—shivering with fear and hurt and heartbreak.

The engine roared to life, and Rake peeled out of his driveway. He didn't say a word until they were through the first stoplight and traveling west.

"I knew Serena in high school," he said. "She was the hottest girl in the school, and she was totally freaked out over me, for some reason… pursued me like you can't even imagine."

Aspen swallowed and brushed tears from her cheeks. She was trembling—uncontrollably trembling—even though she wasn't cold.

"We started going out after we graduated," he continued. "I don't know where my head was. I guess I was just a guy…you know… flattered because the hot chick liked me. Plus, I didn't know where I was going. I was riding rodeo and just sort of…you know…sailing… and Serena was along for the ride." He paused, breathing a heavy sigh, seeming to calm down somewhat. "My family couldn't stand her… and she was smothering me…completely smothering me. She was so possessive and demanding. But she was familiar, you know. And besides, she'd freak out every time I'd try to cool it down or break it off with her. She'd tell me she was gonna kill herself…go off on these screaming rage tantrums. She was a psycho."

Aspen brushed the tears from her cheeks—tried not to gasp as she cried. Rake reached over, opened the glove compartment, and handed her a box of tissues.

"So one day…I'd had it," he continued. "I woke up and realized what a total idiot I'd been…what a stupid coward I was. So I met her at a restaurant for dinner after work one night…told her I wanted to break up with her. I gave her this whole bunch of bull about how she was too good for me…how I couldn't take being her boyfriend because of all the other guys who wanted her and crap like that. But she didn't buy it. She ran out of the restaurant cussing and crying." He sighed and shook his head—rubbed his forehead the way Aspen had seen him do on occasion when he had a headache.

"Well, I followed her out to her car…because she had me conditioned, thinking she was going to kill herself every time I mentioned breaking up…right? So I walk out into the parking lot to find her—to make sure she's okay—and she hit me with her car."

"What?" Aspen gasped, shocked from silence.

"She plowed right into me," he said. "Broke my right leg doing it."

"You're kidding me," Aspen asked.

Rake shook his head. "Nope. She backed up and tried to get me again…but I was able to get out of her way in time." He breathed a sigh and shook his head. "I guess we're all allowed to be the fool once in our life…right?" He looked to Aspen, and she nodded.

"So then, like, two months later, she stops by my dad and mom's house and tells them she's pregnant…that it's my baby and I better marry her and make it legitimate."

Aspen gazed out the window, watching the headlights illuminating the black pavement as they drove.

"I told my parents she was lying, but she wouldn't quit," he said. "She kept telling everybody the baby was mine. She dragged my name through the mud. But it bit her in the butt when she tried to take it too far. She actually tried to get child support, and the court ordered a test."

"A paternity test?" Aspen asked.

Rake nodded. He looked at her, his eyes narrow with indignation. "In case you're still wondering, it proved I wasn't the father."

Aspen winced and looked away from him, ashamed to have doubted him in the first place—devastated her doubt had stripped her from his heart.

"The paternity test proved she was lying, and I thought it was over…until she showed up at my girlfriend's house a couple of years ago with the same song and dance she just spun on you."

"D-did your girlfriend believe it?" Aspen asked—afraid of his answer—already knowing what his answer would be.

"Oh, she bought it all right…hook, line, and sinker," he affirmed. He ran a hand through his hair, a saddened smile spreading across his face. "It's funny how people are so willing to believe the worst about you…even when they should know better." He looked at her, glaring through narrowed eyes. "Isn't it funny the way that always works?"

"If-if I'd really believed her…I wouldn't have shown up at your house at one in the morning," Aspen said.

"Maybe," he said, pulling the truck to a stop. "And I should've told you about it before she had the chance to plant any doubt in your mind." He chuckled and rubbed his forehead again. "But the funny thing is…girls always assume that I'm…you know…that I sleep around. I'll date a girl…never touch her, never try to take her to bed… and she'll still operate on the assumption that I'm…you know…"

"Promiscuous," Aspen finished for him.

"I see you know exactly what I mean," he growled. He was angry, lumping her in with every other girl he'd ever known.

"I-I just thought you were a serial killer," she reminded.

His expression softened a bit; a slight chuckle even escaped his throat. "Yeah…I'm just raking in the character references tonight."

"I-I am sorry, Rake," Aspen began. "It's just that…I was tired. And…and I admit it. I'm always afraid something will happen to take you away from me. So I guess…I guess I just thought a little boy who tied you to another woman would be it."

Rake sighed, frowning. He gazed out the windshield to the lights of the city below. He hated Serena—hated her for what she'd put him through—hated her for planting doubt in Aspen's mind. He closed his eyes for a moment, remembering the expression on Aspen's face when he'd opened the door not fifteen minutes before—the undeniable expression of utter heartbreak. He tried to imagine how she'd felt— being at work at one a.m., a strange and admittedly beautiful woman walking in and claiming a little boy belonged to him. He grimaced, knowing it was his fault—none but his. He should've told Aspen about the mess with Serena a long time ago. But the fact was, he'd been afraid—afraid she'd bolt and run. He glanced at her, his heart aching as she brushed more tears from her pretty cheeks. Aspen hadn't bolted, however. She'd come to him. She'd come to him to hear the truth.

"You know," she began, "I've got her number."

"What?" he asked.

"Your friend Serena," she explained. "She didn't tell me all that to get me to break up with you. She told me because she knew that when you thought I didn't trust you anymore…" She looked at him, her beautiful eyes filled with tears and pain. "She knew you'd break up with me. You broke up with that other girlfriend, didn't you, Rake? The one who bought Serena's story hook, line, and sinker…as you put it. You cut her loose, didn't you?"

"I cut her loose, as *you* put it, because she didn't mean that much to me," he grumbled. "Among other reasons."

Aspen nodded. "It's her unexpected MO…to destroy your trust in a person," she began, glancing over at him, "not to destroy another person's trust in you. And it looks to me like it works just the way she wants it to."

She was right. It was only in that moment he realized that Serena had always done just that. He'd quit dating several girls after Serena had pulled her strings. Yet he knew it was only that Serena's junk offered him the exit—the exit he'd already been looking for in his other relationships. Rake didn't want an exit from Aspen. That was the big difference. Rake wanted to keep Aspen—always.

Yet his heart was hammering so hard he was sure it would bust right out of his chest. Did she still love him? Knowing he'd kept such an important part of his past from her—letting her go along so completely unprepared to face Serena—could she forgive him for it?

He wanted to hold her, to reach out and pull her into his arms, to kiss her mouth raw! He couldn't lose her—not Aspen. She was so very different from anyone else he'd ever known—so much a part of his soul—he couldn't lose her. Yet he was rattled—humiliated by the fact he'd ever even been involved with someone like Serena, that he'd kept the truth of it from Aspen. How would he sew up this mess—earn her trust again?

Aspen glanced out through the windshield. The lights of Albuquerque glistened below in the valley, mirroring the stars twinkling overhead. She tried to appear calm outwardly, but inwardly she was in a state of panic. She was about to lose the only man she had ever loved—the only man she could ever love! He'd cut her loose, just like he had the other girlfriend who'd doubted him. One moment of doubt and she'd lost everything; her world was shattering.

She considered begging—dropping to her knees and begging his forgiveness. It wouldn't work, of that she was certain, but she thought about doing it anyway. She closed her eyes, remembering their first date—the way they'd lingered together above the lights, talked for hours upon hours. Aspen's heart hurt. She pressed a hand to her chest, trying to ease the pain there.

"I'm sorry I didn't tell you about it, Aspen."

His voice startled her, almost as much as his unexpected apology.

"What?" she asked.

"I-I should've told you about it…before she had the chance to try and cause a problem between us."

Try? Had he said she'd *tried* to cause a problem? Did that mean she hadn't? Aspen's heart began to race with hope.

"You're not mad at me anymore?" she asked.

"Why would I be mad at you, Aspen?" he asked. Aspen was breathless—awed by the sudden and very familiar smolder in his dark eyes. Yet still—she feared to hope.

"Y-you're not gonna cut me loose?" she squeaked.

He grinned, pure mischief playing across his face. He reached under the seat, producing a large sheathed knife. He pulled the knife from its sheath and leaned toward her, smiling.

"Of course I'm going to cut you loose," he said. Aspen gasped as Rake carefully slipped the blade of the knife between her abdomen and the seat belt, cutting the seat belt and freeing her from its restraints.

He tossed the knife to the floor, took hold of her coat at the chest, and pulled her across the seat into his arms. "Because I don't like you sitting so far away…and now you never can again."

His mouth was warm and inviting—delicious and familiar—and Aspen didn't care if he tasted her tears moistening their lips. Her hands pressed against the bareness of his sculpted chest, the sense of his skin against her palms sending butterflies soaring in her stomach. His arms were powerful, securing her against him as he kissed her, and she never wanted him to ease his embrace. She wanted him to hold her forever—never stop kissing her! He put one hand to the back of her head, pressing her mouth more firmly against his own as he tried to quench some passionate thirst. Thirst—that was exactly what his kiss evoked in Aspen—what his touch evoked—a thirst that seemed impossible to satisfy!

Rake broke the seal of their lips for a moment, gazing down into her eyes as he held her face between his hands. She was so beautiful, in every way he could ever have imagined a woman being beautiful. He was lost—lost in desire and love for Aspen Falls!

Her eyes were bright, sparkling with emotion, and he could see his reflection in their depths. She loved him! He knew she did. She trusted him too; otherwise she would never have come to him so quickly about Serena. He'd found her, the only woman he would ever love—Aspen Falls.

"Do you like to kiss me as much as I like to—" he began. But his words were silenced—replaced by a pleased chuckle as Aspen took hold of the front of his leather jacket, pushing him back against the seat as she kissed him hard on the mouth. He kissed her brutally for some time, drinking in the flavor of her mouth, the feel of holding her in his arms.

Then, once again, he paused, holding her face in his hands, smiling as the words began to bounce around in his head.

"What?" Aspen asked as Rake gazed at her. His eyes smoldered with barely restrained passion, and she loved it!

"Just thinking," he said.

"Just thinking what?" she asked, smiling.

"'Come fall the aspen upon me,'" Rake quoted, smiling at her. He buried a hand in her hair, causing goose bumps to break over her neck and shoulders. "I like that line in the poem. Actually...I like the idea of Aspen falling upon me. Tell me that whole part."

Aspen giggled and caressed his cheek with her palm.

"'Come, lover!' cried the mountain," Aspen began, "'Oh moon of my autumn heart! Come fall the aspen upon me...Lest golden—'"

She giggled as Rake's mouth captured hers in a long, moist, lingering kiss.

"Call me lover again, Aspen Falls," he mumbled, "and the next paternity test I'm involved in might prove that I *am* the father of—"

Aspen gasped and clamped a hand over his mouth.

"You cannot say naughty things like that, Rake Locker!" she exclaimed, blushing clear to her toes with delight.

Rake chuckled and pushed her hand away. "Then you better find a way to shut me up."

Aspen smiled—brushed her fingers over his lips.

"I love you," she whispered, her heart swelling to near bursting in her chest.

"I love you more," he said, caressing her cheek with the back of his hand.

Rake kissed her then—soft and tender—and pulled her against him, softly whispering, "I love you," trailing tender kisses against her neck.

❦

As he pumped unleaded into the tank of his pickup, Rake glanced up into the convenience store. Aspen stood at the counter, smiling as she paid for a water and the small bottle of Advil she'd insisted Rake needed for his mounting headache. Rake ran a hand through his hair, wishing he hadn't let his gas tank get so close to empty. He didn't like getting gas at the station way up on the mesa, especially late at night. Still, he'd been afraid he and Aspen wouldn't make it home if he didn't stop, and he couldn't risk any more time alone in the car with her. His self-control was fading fast.

The throbbing in his head increased suddenly, and he clicked the pump lock to keep the gas pumping while he rubbed the back of his neck. He thought of Serena then, his resentment of her complete in that moment. He figured the sudden thought of Serena was what had caused his headache to increase so abruptly. He wondered how close he'd actually come to losing Aspen because of Serena's lies. Rake pressed a fist to his chest as the pain of the thought of losing Aspen gripped him. He could never lose her; he felt sure he'd die if he did.

Rake continued to massage the back of his neck with one hand as he watched Aspen through the convenience store windows for a moment—watched her friendly manner with the clerk, the way she kept smiling. She must be worn out! She'd worked so late, and now it was nearly four a.m. He wondered how she could be so friendly to a stranger when she must feel like doing nothing more than falling into bed and sleeping for a week. He chuckled, thinking he'd like to fall in bed with her for a week.

Rake's gaze was drawn to the kid standing near the drink section. He was big kid—six foot, at least—and bulky too. He frowned, noting the big, baggy coat the teenager was wearing. As the hair on the back of his neck prickled—as his heart increased its rhythm—Rake felt his feet begin to propel him forward. He broke into a dead run, however, when he saw the kid reach into his coat—saw the kid walk toward the counter where Aspen stood. Every fiber of his being screamed, burned with anxiety and panic, as he reached the door to the store in time to see the kid pull a handgun out of his coat and point it at the clerk.

"Give it up, man!"

Aspen turned—gasped when she saw a young man standing behind her holding a gun in his hand.

"Don't close that register! Give me the money, man!" the young man shouted.

"I don't keep much cash in here," the man at the register said.

"Just give me what's in there, man!" the young man shouted, gripping the gun with both hands to steady his aim.

Aspen couldn't breathe. She took a step sideways, away from the cashier, but the gunman pointed the gun at her, and she stopped.

"Don't move, chica," he said. "Just chill, and it'll be over in a minute."

An electronic bell chimed, signaling the front entrance had opened, and Aspen glanced over to see Rake step into the store.

She shook her head at him—whispered, "Rake...no." But the kid robbing the store was already nervous, and he leveled the gun at Rake.

"It's cool, man," Rake said, raising his hands out to his sides. "Just don't hurt the girl. I ain't gonna try and stop you. Take the money, man. Just let me take the girl out of here so she doesn't accidentally get hurt."

"You move and I'll kill you, man! You hear me?" the robber shouted.

"It's cool, man," Rake said. "I won't try to stop you. Just keep the gun pointed at me, okay?" Rake looked to the cashier, frowned, and growled, "What're you waiting for? Give him the cash."

Aspen swallowed hard—glanced away from the gunman long enough to see if the cashier was doing as he was told. The cashier's hands were trembling so violently he could hardly get the money out of the register.

"Hurry up, man!" the gunman shouted.

Aspen looked back to Rake—terrified! The kid's hands were shaking, but he was too close to Rake to miss if he decided to pull the trigger. Everything, every moment spent with Rake, began flashing through her mind—the day they'd met, their first kiss, the moments they'd spent in each other's arms only a short time before. How could this be happening? How could it be that a man was now pointing a gun at Rake, threatening his life?

"This is all there is," the cashier said, shoving cash into a plastic grocery bag.

"Give it to me!" the kid shouted. "Now!"

The cashier tossed the bag to the floor at the kid's feet. Keeping the gun leveled at Rake, the gunman reached down and picked up the bag.

"See…it's all good, man," Rake said.

"Give me your wallet, man," the kid said, nodding at Rake.

"No problem," Rake said, starting to reach around to his back pocket.

"No way! No way!" the gunman shouted. "She can get it." He looked at Aspen and said, "Get his wallet for me."

Aspen nodded and moved toward Rake, glad to be nearer to him. She reached into his back pocket and removed his wallet.

"Put it in my hand, and get behind me," Rake told Aspen, though his attention never left the gunman.

"But—" she began to argue.

"Aspen…just put it in my hand," he growled.

Aspen handed the wallet to Rake.

"Get behind me," Rake said. Aspen stepped behind Rake, trembling with terror—trying to comprehend what was happening.

Rake slowly stretched out his hand, offering his wallet to the kid with the gun.

"Take it, man," Rake said. "Just take it and be done with this."

The gunman reached out, snatching the wallet and shoving it in his own back pocket. Arrogant with his own success, the kid chuckled, waving the gun at Rake.

"You some kind of hero or what, man?" the kid asked. "Look at you…all standing in front of your girlfriend like you could keep her safe." He seemed to study Rake from head to toe—chuckled again.

"Man, you got your money," Rake said. "Just take off."

"Don't be telling me what to do, man!" the kid shouted. "I'll go when I feel like going!"

"That's cool," Rake said. "That's cool. Take your time. But I'm guessing there's a silent alarm by the register…so take your stuff and get out before the cops get here."

The kid looked to the cashier, then back to Rake.

As if simply by the power of suggestion, Aspen saw an unmarked police car pull up to one of the gas pumps. Unfortunately the kid saw it too. He swore as panic engulfed him. He leveled the gun at the cashier and fired once. The cashier ducked behind the counter, and Aspen screamed as she felt Rake throw her to the floor a split second before two more shots rang out!

In a whirlwind of confusion, two police officers suddenly broke through the door, shouting at the gunman to drop his weapon.

"You okay, baby?" Rake asked as he raised himself to a sitting position.

"I'm fine," Aspen sobbed, throwing herself into his arms. She clung to him, trembling and sobbing, frightened beyond any description by what had just happened. It wasn't until she felt the warmth of it—the silky warmth of Rake's blood on her hand at his back—that she realized exactly what had happened.

Pulling away from him, she screamed as she saw the blood draining from his body from the two bullets holes in him. One was at his shoulder, blood trickling down over his torso. The other wound, however, was worse, right below his left pectoral muscle—and bleeding with profusion.

"Rake!" Aspen screamed. She took his face in her hands as he coughed, spitting blood over his chin.

One of the police officers hunkered down next to Rake as he sat back hard on the floor. He pulled the radio from the shoulder of his vest and called for an ambulance.

Aspen looked at her hands, now soaked in Rake's blood.

"Rake!" she breathed as the police officer inspected the wounds.

"He's hit twice," the officer said. "Looks like it got his lung." He pulled his radio from his vest again and gave further instructions to the dispatcher.

Aspen didn't hear what he said, however. Rake was bleeding—coughing up more blood—his face suddenly as pale as death.

"Rake?" she cried. "Oh, no! Please…please don't…"

"I-in my l-left pocket," Rake choked. Aspen couldn't breathe—felt her heart hammering so hard she was sure she would die!

"S-shhh," she soothed, stroking his hair as he coughed. He turned his head, spitting blood from his mouth, struggling to put his left hand in the front pocket of his jeans.

"Aspen!" he coughed. "D-don't argue with me right now." He

choked—spit more blood from his mouth. "In m-my left pocket. R-reach in there. Do it now."

Aspen shook her head. "Rake, I-I..." she began. She couldn't think—could hardly breathe! She felt unconsciousness threatening—clouding her thoughts—making her dizzy.

"J-just reach in there," he moaned. He grimaced again, and she knew he was enduring incredible pain.

"Just take shallow breaths, sir," the policeman said to Rake. The police officer looked to Aspen. "The EMTs are on their way...but we have to keep him calm...keep him breathing."

Aspen gasped as Rake's trembling, bloody hand reached up, taking hold of her chin.

"Listen to me," he breathed. His dark eyes seemed empty—void of the smoldering fire that so often burned in them when he looked at her. "Here," he said. He struggled to slip his left hand into his left front pocket. He released her chin and took hold of one of her hands, drawing it away from his face. She looked down, nearly paralyzed by the sight of the blood trailing down his chest, soaking his pants at the waist. She felt him slip something into her hand.

"I finally found something worth dying for, Aspen Falls," he whispered. Aspen opened her hand—now soaked in the crimson of Rake's blood. She couldn't breathe! As she looked at the diamond solitaire engagement ring bathed in a pool of Rake's blood puddled in the palm of her hand, Rake Locker closed his eyes and breathed, "You."

EPILOGUE

Aspen forced one eye open to a narrow slit. The red digital numbers on the alarm clock said four fifty-five. She sighed, wondering why she always managed to wake up five minutes before the alarm was set to go off. Reaching over, she slid the alarm button to off and snuggled deeper beneath the covers.

She'd been dreaming—a remembering sort of dream—dreaming of the night Rake Locker had been shot. She hated the memory and certainly hated when she dreamt about it. Almost a year later, the shooting still haunted her dreams.

Rolling over, Aspen let her hand softly travel over the firm contours of her husband's stomach and chest. She snuggled against the warm security of his strong body.

"It's almost five," Aspen whispered, nuzzling his shoulder with her cheek.

"You've gotta be kidding," Rake grumbled. He inhaled a deep breath, stretching for a moment before gathering Aspen into his arms and kissing the top of her head.

Aspen smiled, blissful in the loving protection of Rake's arms. Oh, how she loved him! Most mornings she still couldn't fathom how it all happened—meeting Rake, falling in love with him, him falling in love with her. She couldn't believe it had been almost a year since the shooting—that they'd been married almost nine months! Yet there he was—holding her in his arms as they lay in the comfort of their bed— toying with a strand of her hair as he endeavored to wake up.

"Let's just stay here," he said. "I can be as interesting as the special shapes balloons…I promise." Aspen giggled, tilting her head to look up at him. He was grinning, though his eyes were still closed.

"I know that," she said, raising herself on one elbow. He opened his dark eyes and looked at her. "But we promised. And anyway…at least we didn't have to get up in time to be out at the field."

"But it's so warm in here," Rake said. "I'll be cold if I get out of bed." He raised himself up on one elbow, smiling as he lounged next to her.

"That's because you never wear pajamas," Aspen said. "If you'd wear something besides your underwear…"

"Look who's talking," he chuckled, toying with the collar of his old flannel shirt Aspen had taken to wearing as a nightgown.

"It's flannel. It's warm," Aspen said. She loved Rake's old shirt—the one he'd been wearing the day he'd taken her out to the river to watch the balloons a year before. Sure, it was missing part of one of the front tails. Rake had torn it into strips to hold tin mugs of hot chocolate. Still, Aspen knew it was one reason she liked the shirt so much. It held significant value—not to mention she loved wearing Rake's shirts. Wearing his shirts always made her feel like he was right next to her— and that she cherished!

"It's a rag," he said. Smiling, he added, "But I'll admit it's my favorite thing you wear to bed."

"Well, it's why I'm warmer in the mornings," she giggled.

"Fine," he said. He kissed her squarely on the mouth. "Then I guess it's just like ripping off a Band-Aid, right?" Aspen squealed as he pulled the covers off the bed, sending a blast of cold air breathing over them both. "Up and at 'em, arachnophobia girl! The balloons will be launching in a couple of hours…and we still need to saddle the ponies." Aspen giggled as Rake stood and walked across the room to the bathroom. She frowned for a moment, however, as her attention fell to the scar on his back—the scar left by the bullet that had pierced his lung and exited his body there. Again she was reminded of how close she'd come to losing him that night at the convenience store. She shook her head, forcing the memory to retreat to the darkest corners of her mind. It was over. Rake had survived, and he didn't like her to dwell on it.

"Let's see if they're on schedule," Rake said, flipping the switch on the wall that turned on the radio.

"Good morning, Albuquerque!" the DJ was saying. "It's a beautiful day for ballooning, and the Special Shapes Rodeo is right on schedule!"

Aspen sighed. Life was good! Crawling out of bed, she hurried over to the counter and double sinks of the bathroom area. Hopping up on the counter between the two sinks, she watched as her lethally handsome husband brushed his teeth.

"What?" he asked, spitting toothpaste into the sink. He rinsed his mouth a couple times, washed off his toothbrush, and put it back in the cabinet.

"Nothing," Aspen said, smiling at him. "I just love you."

He smiled. "Well, I love you too," he said, moving to stand between her knees and taking her face in his hands. "But if you want to get down to the river in time to see the balloons go over…then you need to quit distracting me."

Aspen placed the back of her hand against his whiskery cheek. He was so handsome—even more handsome than the very first time she'd seen him, jogging through the park last fall. She studied his dark eyes, straight nose, delicious lips, and square jaw. Perfection!

"Okay," she said. "You hurry and shower, and I'll get everything together."

"Yes, ma'am," he said. As Rake Locker placed a moist, lingering kiss to Aspen Locker's mouth, she sighed. She was reminded exactly what heaven was—it was Rake's kiss!

❦

"Here they come!" Rake chuckled.

Aspen turned to follow Rake's gaze. Sure enough, just over the tree line to the east, the giant brown UPS truck special shapes balloon was drifting toward them. Aspen raised her hand to shade her eyes from the sun. As the balloon drifted closer, she smiled.

She waved as Rake called, "Good morning, kids!"

"Good morning!" Gina called from her place in the basket.

Aspen pulled her camera out of her pocket and began snapping photos of Gina and Sean aloft in the basket of the balloon.

"I didn't think you guys would drag yourselves out of bed long enough to come out here!" Sean hollered as the balloon descended a little. "We barely made it ourselves!"

"It was a sacrifice," Rake laughed. "But we love you guys enough to do it!"

"Aspen!" Gina called. "Take one of us kissing!"

Aspen giggled as she watched Gina take hold of the lapels of Sean's brown UPS jacket and kiss him. Holding the shutter button down, she let the camera continually snap for a few moments as Sean wrapped Gina in his arms as they kissed.

"Hold on!" the man piloting the balloon shouted.

Rake stepped up behind Aspen, wrapping his arms around her waist and pulling her back against him as they watched the bottom of the basket smoothly skim across the water. As the balloon began to ascend again, the passengers in the basket clapped with delight.

"Meet us at Weck's for breakfast!" Sean called.

"You got it, man!" Rake shouted as the pilot laid on the burner and the balloon rose up and up—higher and higher.

Aspen sighed as the UPS truck balloon disappeared into the west. Several other balloons hovered overhead—peaceful, serene in their drifting. She inhaled deeply, relishing the crisp October air—the scent of the cottonwoods, of Rake's cologne. The river meandered on its way, glistening like a ribbon of glass in the morning sun.

Suddenly, Aspen turned in Rake's arms, pressing her body against his as his strong embrace enveloped her.

"What a perfect morning! It's one of the most perfect mornings I've ever known," she sighed. She looked up at him, and he smiled, his dark eyes smoldering with love and affection—adoration and happiness.

"Why's that?" he asked, brushing a strand of hair from her face.

"Because I woke up with you," Aspen whispered.

Rake caressed her lips with his thumb and said, "But you wake up with me every morning."

"I know," Aspen said. "That's why every morning is so perfect now."

He laughed for a moment and slipped a hand around to the back of her neck.

"Wanna make out before we head over to Weck's for breakfast?" he asked.

Aspen giggled. "Of course!"

She watched as his brow puckered into a frown. "Do you think your stomach can handle breakfast yet? It's kind of early."

"The morning sickness hasn't been so bad these past couple of days. I'll just eat light," Aspen said. "Now shut up and kiss me, you big ex-bull-riding, watchmaking, vampire daddy-to-be."

"Whatever you say, arachnophobia girl," Rake breathed as his head descended toward hers. He kissed her lightly at first—teasing her with the promise of a deeper, more passionate exchange. His kiss consumed her next—raining bliss over her body—sending a surge of euphoric ecstasy through her veins.

Rake paused, the smoldering fire of his eyes mirroring her reflection as he whispered, "'And the moon and mountain blend kisses...as the time of aspen falls.'"

AUTHOR'S NOTE

In reality, there are more true-to-life moments, personal affinities, and incidents in *The Time of Aspen Falls* than in any other book I've written—at least, since *An Old-Fashioned Romance*. Those closest to me know how desperately I have missed my beloved Albuquerque, New Mexico, from the moment I left almost twelve years ago. Likewise, anyone who knows me even a little and reads *The Time of Aspen Falls* can't possible miss the obvious affection I hold for the city of my birth.

Nestled in the Rio Grande Valley—the Sandia Mountain to the east and the Mesa to the west—Albuquerque has a way of sifting into a person's soul and never leaving. I've talked to so many people along the life's road, so many who have lived in Albuquerque and had to leave, yet eternally long to return. Albuquerque settles in your heart the way no other place does.

Just as *An Old-Fashioned Romance* incorporated many aspects of my personal life—Breck's four best friends and my love of pumpkins, for instance—*The Time of Aspen Falls* is almost a mini travel log of a few of the things I love about Albuquerque. A couple of friends who once lived in Albuquerque read this book as I was writing it. They expressed to me the profound sense of homesickness it initially rinsed over them, but the humor and romance soon distracted them into wholeheartedly enjoying it—thank goodness!

Just for fun:

The restaurant Sadie's, where Rake takes Aspen on their first date, is real! It's located in Albuquerque's North Valley, close to where I grew up. Waiters and waitresses at Sadie's walk around with a pitcher of water in one hand and a pitcher of the best salsa you ever tasted in the other. Sadie's is absolutely my favorite New Mexican restaurant! How could I resist incorporating Sadie's fabulous food into this book? Hello? Delicious! Though you can order their salsa online, it does taste different, being that it's canned instead of fresh from the pitcher. So order online if you like, but it's best to just pop on down to 6230 4th Street and have a few bowls of the fresh stuff.

Nestled across the river to the west of Albuquerque is the tiny town of Corrales, New Mexico. In the book, this is where Rake's clock shop is located, where Gina saw Rake's grandpa when she was at Wagner's Farm buying green chili, where Rake's grandparents live, and where it is implied that Rake himself lives. Wagner's Farm is where I used to buy my apples for canning and dehydrating, where my children used to adventure on autumn field trips to buy pumpkins, and where green-chili-roasting in the big chili roasters smells the best!

Of course, trying to describe the Albuquerque International Balloon Fiesta was an impossible feat! The most photographed event in the world, the Albuquerque International Balloon Fiesta is one of the things I miss most. It's inexplicable—the awesome emotions washing over you when you see eight hundred hot air balloons drifting through the beautiful blue New Mexico sky. Whether you're standing at a bus stop as a kid or driving to work as an adult, it's overwhelming! Go to http://www.balloonfiesta.com and visit the Photo Gallery—Flying, Special Shapes, and Ascension links. But I promise they don't begin to do it justice. As I said, it's something you have to experience—because it truly is beyond description!

My tender feelings for Albuquerque aside, we come to Aspen's friend Gina. Gina Wicksoth is based on the uniqueness of one of my most cherished friends! Her name—Gina! (I hope she doesn't sue me for defamation of character.) The real Gina's wit, wisdom, and often sarcastic sense of humor inspired Aspen's best friend in the book. Loyal, encouraging, and always a blast to be around, the real Gina's personality epitomizes Gina's character—a dark-haired, blue-green-eyed, autumn-loving jewel!

In the end, I can't even begin to tell you how very "me" *The Time of Aspen Falls* truly is—how writing it lifted me on restful wings of contentment. Creating *The Time of Aspen Falls* was an escape for me—a reprieve—and I hope reading it was a literary getaway for you. My one wish: that your experience in reading *The Time of Aspen Falls* is simply this—I hope it made you smile! I hope *The Time of Aspen Falls* was able to lighten your heart a little, help you to rise above the stressful times we're all enduring right now, even if it was only for a little while. We need more humor, hope, romance, and sweet, simple delights in our lives. I hope *The Time of Aspen Falls* helped you to find a few of those much-needed, worry-free escape moments that carry us through.

So download a copy of the song "The Lights of Albuquerque," sit back with some chips and salsa, and just daydream for a while. We all need more of that—more time to breathe—more time to daydream!

~Marcia Lynn McClure

My everlasting admiration, gratitude and love…
To my husband, Kevin…
My inspiration…
My heart's desire…
The man of my every dream!

ABOUT THE AUTHOR

Marcia Lynn McClure's intoxicating succession of novels, novellas, and e-books—including *The Visions of Ransom Lake*, *A Crimson Frost*, *The Rogue Knight*, and most recently *The Pirate Ruse*—has established her as one of the most favored and engaging authors of true romance. Her unprecedented forte in weaving captivating stories of western, medieval, regency, and contemporary amour void of brusque intimacy has earned her the title "The Queen of Kissing."

Marcia, who was born in Albuquerque, New Mexico, has spent her life intrigued with people, history, love, and romance. A wife, mother, grandmother, family historian, poet, and author, Marcia Lynn McClure spins her tales of splendor for the sake of offering respite through the beauty, mirth, and delight of a worthwhile and wonderful story.

BIBLIOGRAPHY

A Better Reason to Fall in Love
A Crimson Frost
An Old-Fashioned Romance
Beneath the Honeysuckle Vine
Born for Thorton's Sake
Daydreams
Desert Fire
Divine Deception
Dusty Britches
Kiss in the Dark
Kissing Cousins
Love Me
Saphyre Snow
Shackles of Honor
Sudden Storms
Sweet Cherry Ray
Take a Walk With Me
The Anthology of Premiere Novellas Romantic Vignettes
The Fragrance of her Name
The Heavenly Surrender
The Heavenly Surrender 10th Anniversary Special Edition
The Heavenly Surrender Hardcover Edition
The Highwayman of Tanglewood
The Highwayman of Tanglewood Hardcover Edition
The Light of the Lovers' Moon
The Pirate Ruse
The Prairie Prince
The Rogue Knight
The Tide of the Mermaid Tears
The Time of Aspen Falls
The Touch of Sage
The Trove of the Passion Room
The Visions of Ransom Lake

The Whispered Kiss
The Windswept Flame
To Echo the Past
Weathered Too Young

A Better Reason to Fall in Love
Contemporary Romance

"Boom chicka wow wow!" Emmy whispered.

"Absolutely!" Tabby breathed as she watched Jagger Brodie saunter past.

She envied Jocelyn for a moment, knowing he was most likely on his way to drop something off on Jocelyn's desk—or to speak with her. Jocelyn got to talk with Jagger almost every day, whereas Tabby was lucky if he dropped graphics changes off to her once a week.

"Ba boom chicka wow wow!" Emmy whispered again. "He's sporting a red tie today! Ooo! The power tie! He must be feeling confident."

Tabby smiled, amused and yet simultaneously amazed at Emmy's observation. She'd noticed the red tie, too. "There's a big marketing meeting this afternoon," she told Emmy. "I heard he's presenting some hard-nose material."

"Then that explains it," Emmy said, smiling. "Mr. Brodie's about to rock the company's world!"

"He already rocks mine…every time he walks by," Tabby whispered.

A Crimson Frost
Historical Romance

Beloved of her father, King Dacian, and adored by her people, the Scarlet Princess Monet endeavored to serve her kingdom well— for the people of the Kingdom of Karvana were good and worthy of service. Long Monet had known that even her marriage would serve her people. Her husband would be chosen for her—for this was the way of royal existence.

Still, as any woman does—peasant or princess—Monet dreamt of owning true love—of owning choice in love. Thus, each time the raven-haired, sapphire-eyed, Crimson Knight of Karvana rode near, Monet knew regret—for in secret, she loved him—and she could not choose him.

As an arrogant king from another kingdom began to wage war against Karvana, Karvana's king, knights, and soldiers answered the challenge. The Princess Monet would also know battle. As the Crimson Knight battled with armor and blade—so the Scarlet Princess would battle in sacrifice and with secrets held. Thus, when the charge was given to preserve the heart of Karvana—Monet endeavored to serve her kingdom and forget her secreted love. Yet love is not so easily forgotten...

An Old-Fashioned Romance
Contemporary Romance

Life went along simply, if not rather monotonously, for Breck McCall. Her job was satisfying, she had true friends. But she felt empty—as if party of her soul was detached and lost to her. She longed for something—something which seemed to be missing.

Yet, there were moments when Breck felt she might almost touch something wonderful. And most of those moments came while in the presence of her handsome, yet seemingly haunted boss—Reese Thatcher.

Beneath the Honeysuckle Vine
Historical Romance

Civil War—no one could flee from the nightmare of battle and the countless lives it devoured. Everyone had sacrificed—suffered profound misery and unimaginable loss. Vivianna Bartholomew was no exception. The war had torn her from her home—orphaned her. The merciless war seemed to take everything—even the man she loved. Still, Vivianna yet knew gratitude—for a kind friend had taken her in upon the death of her parents. Thus, she was cared for—even loved.

Yet as General Lee surrendered, signaling the war's imminent end—as Vivianna remained with the remnants of the Turner family—her soul clung to the letters written by her lost soldier—to his memory written in her heart. Could a woman ever heal from the loss of such a love? Could a woman's heart forget that it may find another? Vivianna Bartholomew thought not.

Still, it is often in the world that miracles occur—that love endures even after hope has been abandoned. Thus, one balmy Alabama morning—as two ragged soldiers wound the road toward the Turner house—Vivianna began to know—to know that miracles do exist—that love is never truly lost.

Born for Thorton's Sake
Historical Romance

Maria Castillo Holt…the only daughter of a valiant Lord and his Spanish beauty. Following the tragic deaths of her parents, Maria would find herself spirited away by conniving kindred in an endurance of neglect and misery.

However, rescued at the age of thirteen by Brockton Thorton, the son of her father's devoted friend Lord Richard Thorton, Maria would at last find blessed reprieve. Further Brockton Thorton became, from that day forth, ever the absolute center of Maria's very existence. And as the blessed day of her sixteenth birthday dawned, Maria's dreams of owning her heart's desire seemed to become a blissful reality.

Yet a fiendish plotting intruded, and Maria's hopes of realized dreams were locked away within dark, impenetrable walls. Would Maria's dreams of life with the handsome and coveted Brockton Thorton die at the hands of a demon strength?

Daydreams
Contemporary Romance

Sayler Christy knew chances were slim to none that any of her silly little daydreams would ever actually come true—especially any daydreams involving Mr. Booker, the new patient—the handsome, older patient convalescing in her grandfather's rehabilitation center.

Yet, working as a candy striper at Rawlings Rehab, Sayler couldn't help but dream of belonging to Mr. Booker—and Mr. Booker stole her heart—perhaps unintentionally—but with very little effort. Gorgeous, older, and entirely unobtainable—Sayler knew Mr. Booker would unknowingly enslave her heart for many years to come—for daydreams were nothing more than a cruel joke inflicted by life. All dreams—daydreams or otherwise—never came true. Did they?

Desert Fire
Historical Romance

She opened her eyes and beheld, for the first time, the face of Jackson McCall. Ruggedly handsome and her noble rescuer, he would, she knew in that moment, forever hold captive her heart as he then held her life in his protective arms.

Yet she was a nameless beauty, haunted by wisps of visions of the past. How could she ever hope he would return the passionate, devotional love she secreted for him when her very existence was a riddle?

Would Jackson McCall (handsome, fascinating, brooding) ever see her as anything more than a foundling—a burden to himself and his family? And with no memory of her own identity, how then could she release him from his apparent affliction of being her protector?

Divine Deception
Historical Romance

Life experience had harshly turned its cruel countenance on the young Fallon Ashby. Her father deceased and her mother suffering with a fatal disease, Fallon was given over to her uncle, Charles Ashby, until she would reach the age of independence.

Abused, neglected, and disheartened, Fallon found herself suddenly blessed with unexpected liberation at the hand of the mysterious Trader Donavon. A wealthy landowner and respected denizen of the town, Trader Donavon concealed his feature of face within the shadows of a black cowl.

When Fallon's secretive deliverer offered two choices of true escape from her uncle, her captive heart chose its own path. Thus, Fallon married the enormous structure of mortal man—without having seen the horrid secret he hid beneath an ominous hood.

But the malicious Charles Ashby, intent on avenging his own losses at Trader Donavon's hand, set out to destroy the husband that Fallon herself held secrets concerning. Would her wicked uncle succeed and perhaps annihilate the man that his niece secretly loved above all else?

Dusty Britches

Historical Romance

Angelina Hunter was seriously minded, and it was a good thing. Her father's ranch needed a woman who could endure the strenuous work of ranch life. Since her mother's death, Angelina had been that woman. She had no time for frivolity—no time for a less severe side of life. Not when there was so much to be done—hired hands to feed, a widower father to care for, and an often ridiculously light-hearted younger sister to worry about. No. Angelina Hunter had no time for the things most young women her age enjoyed.

And yet, Angelina had not always been so hardened. There had been a time when she boasted a fun, flirtatious nature even more delightful than her sister Becca's—a time when her imagination soared with adventurous, romantic dreams. But that all ended years before at the hand of one man. Her heart turned to stone...safely becoming void of any emotion save impatience and indifference.

Until the day her dreams returned, the day the very maker of her broken heart rode back into her life. As the dust settled from the cattle drive which brought him back, would Angelina's heart be softened? Would she learn to hope again? Would her long-lost dreams become a blessed reality?

Kiss in the Dark

Contemporary Romance

"Boston," he mumbled.

"I mean...Logan...he's like the man of my dreams! Why would I blow it? What if..." Boston continued to babble.

"Boston," he said. The commanding sound of his voice caused Boston to cease in her prattling and look to him.

"What?" she asked, somewhat grateful he'd interrupted her panic attack.

He frowned and shook his head.

"Shut up," he said. "You're all worked up about nothing." He reached out, slipping one hand beneath her hair to the back of her neck.

Boston was so startled by his touch, she couldn't speak—she could only stare up into his mesmerizing green eyes. His hand was strong and warm, powerful and reassuring.

"If it freaks you out so much…just kiss in the dark," he said.

Boston watched as Vance put the heel of his free hand to the light switch. In an instant the room went black.

Kissing Cousins
Contemporary Romance

Poppy Amore loved her job waitressing at Good Ol' Days Family Restaurant. No one could ask for a better working environment. After all, her best friend Whitney worked there, and her boss, restaurant owner Mr. Dexter, was a kind, understanding, grandfatherly sort of man. Furthermore, the job allowed Poppy to linger in the company of Mr. Dexter's grandson Swaggart Moretti—the handsome and charismatic head cook at Good Ol' Days.

Secretly, Swaggart was far more to Poppy than just a man who was easy to look at. In truth, she had harbored a secret crush on him for years—since her freshman year in high school, in fact. And although the memory of her feelings—even the lingering truth of them—haunted Poppy the way a veiled, unrequited love always haunts a heart, she had learned to simply find joy in possessing a hidden, anonymous delight in merely being associated with Swaggart. Still, Poppy had begun to wonder if her heart would ever let go of Swaggart Moretti—if any other man in the world could ever turn her head.

When the dazzling, uber-fashionable Mark Lawson appeared one night at Good Ol' Days, however, Poppy began to believe that perhaps her attention and her heart would be distracted from Swaggart at last. Mark Lawson was every girl's fantasy—tall, uniquely handsome, financially well-off, and as charming as any prince ever to appear in fairy tales. He was kind, considerate, and, Poppy would find, a true, old-fashioned champion. Thus, Poppy Amore willingly allowed her heart and mind to follow Mark Lawson—to attempt to abandon the past and an unrequited love and begin to move on.

But all the world knows that real love is not so easily put off, and

Poppy began to wonder if even a man so wonderful as Mark Lawson could truly drive Swaggart Moretti from her heart. Would Poppy Amore miss her one chance at happiness, all for the sake of an unfulfilled adolescent's dream?

Love Me
Contemporary Romance

Jacey Whittaker couldn't remember a time when she hadn't loved Scott Pendleton—the boy next door. She couldn't remember a time when Scott hadn't been in her life—in her heart. Yet Scott was every other girl's dream too. How could Jacey possibly hope to win such a prize—the attention, the affections, the very heart of such a sought-after young man? Yet win him she did! He became the bliss of her youthful heart—at least for a time.

Still, some dreams live fulfilled—and some are lost. Loss changes the very soul of a being. Jacey wondered if her soul would ever rebound. Certainly, she went on—lived a happy life—if not so full and perfectly happy a life as she once lived. Yet she feared she would never recover—never get over Scott Pendleton—her first love.

Until the day a man walked into her apartment—into her apartment and into her heart. Would this man be the one to heal her broken heart? Would this man be her one true love?

Saphyre Snow
Historical Romance

Descended of a legendary line of strength and beauty, Saphyre Snow had once known happiness as princess of the Kingdom of Graces. Once a valiant king had ruled in wisdom—once a loving mother had spoken soft words of truth to her daughter. Yet a strange madness had poisoned great minds—a strange fever inviting Lord Death to linger. Soon it was even Lord Death sought to claim Saphyre Snow for his own—and all Saphyre loved seemed lost.

Thus, Saphyre fled—forced to leave all familiars for necessity of preserving her life. Alone, and without provision, Saphyre knew Lord

Death might yet claim her—for how could a princess hope to best the Reaper himself?

Still, fate often provides rescue by extraordinary venues, and Saphyre was not delivered into the hands of Death—but into the hands of those hiding dark secrets in the depths of bruised and bloodied souls. Saphyre knew a measure of hope and asylum in the company of these battered vagabonds. Even she knew love—a secreted love—a forbidden love. Yet it was love itself—even held secret—that would again summon Lord Death to hunt the princess, Saphyre Snow.

Shackles of Honor
Historical Romance

Cassidy Shea's life was nothing if not serene. Loving parents and a doting brother provided happiness and innocent hope in dreaming as life's experience. Yes, life was blissful at her beloved home of Terrill.

Still, for all its beauty and tranquility…ever there was something intangible and evasive lurking in the shadows. And though Cassidy wasted little worry on it…still she sensed its existence, looming as a menacing fate bent on ruin.

And when one day a dark stranger appeared, Cassidy could no longer ignore the ominous whispers of the secrets surrounding her. Mason Carlisle, an angry, unpredictable man materialized…and seemingly with Cassidy's black fate at his heels.

Instantly Cassidy found herself thrust into a world completely unknown to her, wandering in a labyrinth of mystery and concealments. Serenity was vanquished…and with it, her dreams.

Or were all the secrets so guardedly kept from Cassidy…were they indeed the cloth, the very flax from which her dreams were spun? From which eternal bliss would be woven?

Sudden Storms
Historical Romance

Rivers Brighton was a wanderer—having nothing and belonging to no one. Still, by chance, Rivers found herself harboring for a time beneath the roof of the kind-hearted Jolee Gray and her remarkably attractive yet ever-grumbling brother, Paxton. Jolee had taken Rivers in, and Rivers had stayed.

Helplessly drawn to Paxton's alluring presence and unable to escape his astonishing hold over her, however, Rivers knew she was in danger of enduring great heartbreak and pain. Paxton appeared to find Rivers no more interesting than a brief cloudburst. Yet the man's spirit seemed to tether some great and devastating storm—a powerful tempest bridled within, waiting for the moment when it could rage full and free, perhaps destroying everything and everyone in its wake—particularly Rivers.

Could Rivers capture Paxton's attention long enough to make his heart her own? Or would the storm brewing within him destroy her hopes and dreams of belonging to the only man she had ever loved?

Sweet Cherry Ray
Historical Romance

Cherry glanced at her pa, who frowned and slightly shook his head. Still, she couldn't help herself, and she leaned over and looked down the road.

She could see the rider and his horse—a large buckskin stallion. As he rode nearer, she studied his white shirt, black flat-brimmed hat, and double-breasted vest. Ever nearer he rode, and she fancied his pants were almost the same color as his horse, with silver buttons running down the outer leg. Cherry had seen a similar manner of dress before—on the Mexican vaqueros that often worked for her pa in the fall.

"Cherry," her pa scolded in a whisper as the stranger neared them.

She straightened and blushed, embarrassed by being as impolite in her staring as the other town folk were in theirs. It seemed everyone had stopped whatever they had been doing to walk out to the street and watch the stranger ride in.

No one spoke—the only sound was that of the breeze, a falcon's cry overhead and the rhythm of the rider's horse as it slowed to a trot.

Take a Walk with Me
Contemporary Romance

"Grandma?" Cozy called as she closed the front door behind her. She inhaled a deep breath—bathing in the warm, inviting scent of banana nut bread baking in the oven. "Grandma? Are you in here?"

"Cozy!" her grandma called in a loud whisper. "I'm in the kitchen. Hurry!"

Cozy frowned—her heart leapt as worry consumed her for a moment. Yet, as she hurried to the kitchen to find her grandma kneeling at the window that faced the new neighbors yard, and peering out with a pair of binoculars, she exhaled a sigh of relief.

"Grandma! You're still spying on him?" she giggled.

"Get down! They'll see us! Get down!" Dottie ordered in a whisper, waving one hand in a gesture that Cozy should duck.

Giggling with amusement at her grandma's latest antics, Cozy dropped to her hands and knees and crawled toward the window.

"Who'll see us?" she asked.

"Here," Dottie whispered, pausing only long enough to reach for a second set of binoculars sitting on the nearby counter. "These are for you." She smiled at Cozy—winked as a grin of mischief spread over her face. "And now…may I present the entertainment for this evening…Mr. Buckly hunk of burning love Bryant…and company."

Romantic Vignettes—The Anthology of Premiere Novellas
Historical Romance
Includes Three Novellas:
The Unobtainable One

Annette Jordan had accepted the unavoidable reality that she must toil as a governess to provide for herself. Thankfully, her charge was a joy—a vision of youthful beauty, owning a spirit of delight.

But it was Annette's employer, Lord Gareth Barrett, who proved to be the trial—for she soon found herself living in the all-too-cliché governess's dream of having fallen desperately in love with the man who provided her wages.

The child loved her—but could she endure watching hopelessly as the beautiful woman from a neighboring property won Lord Barrett's affections?

The General's Ambition

Seemingly overnight, Renee Millings found herself orphaned and married to the indescribably handsome, but ever frowning, Roque Montan. His father, The General, was obsessively determined that his lineage would continue posthaste—with or without consent of his son's new bride.

But when Roque reveals the existence of a sworn oath that will obstruct his father's ambition, will the villainous General conspire to ensure the future of his coveted progeny to be born by Renee himself? Will Renee find the only means of escape from the odious General to be that of his late wife—death? Or will the son find no tolerance for his father's diabolic plotting concerning the woman Roque legally terms his wife?

Indebted Deliverance

Chalyce LaSalle had been grateful to the handsome recluse, Race Trevelian, when he had delivered her from certain tragedy one frigid winter day. He was addictively attractive, powerful, and intriguing—and there was something else about him—an air of secreted internal torture. Yet, as the brutal character of her emancipator began to manifest, Chalyce commenced in wondering whether the fate she now faced would be any less insufferable than the one from which he had delivered her.

Still, his very essence beckoned hers. She was drawn to him and her soul whispered that his mind needed deliverance as desperately as she had needed rescue that cold winter's noon.

The Fragrance of Her Name
Historical Romance

Love—the miraculous, eternal bond that binds two souls together. Lauryn Kennsington knew the depth of it. Since the day of her eighth birthday, she had lived the power of true love—witnessed it with her own heart. She had talked with it—learned not even time or death can vanquish it. The Captain taught her these truths—and she loved him all the more for it.

Yet now—as a grown woman—Lauryn's dear Captain's torment became her own. After ten years, Lauryn had not been able to help him find peace—the peace his lonely spirit so desperately needed—the peace he'd sought every moment since his death over fifty years before.

Still, what of her own peace? The time had come. Lauryn's heart longed to do the unthinkable—selfishly abandon her Captain for another—a mortal man who had stolen her heart—become her only desire.

Would Lauryn be able to put tormented spirits to rest and still be true to her own soul? Or, would she have to make a choice—a choice forcing her to sacrifice one true love for another?

The Heavenly Surrender
Historical Romance

Genieva Bankmans had willfully agreed to the arrangement. She had given her word, and she would not dishonor it. But when she saw, for the first time, the man whose advertisement she had answered…she was desperately intimidated. The handsome and commanding Brevan McLean was not what she had expected. He was not the sort of man she had reconciled herself to marrying.

This man, this stranger whose name Genieva now bore, was strong-willed, quick-tempered, and expectant of much from his new wife. Brevan McLean did not deny he had married her for very practical reasons only. He merely wanted any woman whose hard work would provide him assistance with the brutal demands of farm life.

But Genieva would learn there were far darker things, grave secrets held unspoken by Brevan McLean concerning his family and his land. Genieva Bankmans McLean was to find herself in the midst of treachery, violence, and villainy with her estranged husband deeply entangled in it.

The Highwayman of Tanglewood
Historical Romance

A chambermaid in the house of Tremeshton, Faris Shayhan well knew torment, despair, and trepidation. To Faris it seemed the future stretched long and desolate before her—bleak and as dark as a lonesome midnight path. Still, the moon oft casts hopeful luminosity to light one's way. So it was that Lady Maranda Rockrimmon cast hope upon Faris—set Faris upon a different path—a path of happiness, serenity, and love.

Thus, Faris abandoned the tainted air of Tremeshton in favor of the amethyst sunsets of Loch Loland Castle and her new mistress, Lady Rockrimmon. Further, it was on the very night of her emancipation that Faris first met the man of her dreams—the man of every woman's dreams—the rogue Highwayman of Tanglewood.

Dressed in black and astride his mighty steed, the brave, heroic, and dashing rogue Highwayman of Tanglewood stole Faris's heart as easily as he stole her kiss. Yet the Highwayman of Tanglewood was encircled in mystery—mystery as thick and as secretive as time itself. Could Faris truly own the heart of a man so entirely enveloped in twilight shadows and dangerous secrets?

The Light of the Lovers' Moon
Historical Romance

Violet Fynne was haunted—haunted by memory. It had been nearly ten years since her father had moved the family from the tiny town of Rattler Rock to the city of Albany, New York. Yet the pain and guilt in Violet's heart were as fresh and as haunting as ever they had been.

It was true Violet had been only a child when her family moved. Still—though she had been unwillingly pulled away from Rattler Rock—pulled away from him she held most dear—her heart had never left—and her mind had never forgotten the promise she had made—a promise to a boy—to a boy she had loved—a boy she had vowed to return to.

Yet the world changes—and people move beyond pain and regret.

Thus, when Violet Fynne returned to Rattler Rock, it was to find that death had touched those she had known before—that the world had indeed changed—that unfamiliar faces now intruded on beloved memories.

Had she returned too late? Had Violet Fynne lost her chance for peace—and happiness? Would she be forever haunted by the memory of the boy she had loved nearly ten years before?

The Pirate Ruse
Historical Romance

Abducted! Forcibly taken from her home in New Orleans, Cristabel Albay found herself a prisoner aboard an enemy ship—and soon thereafter, transferred into the vile hands of blood-thirsty pirates! War waged between the newly liberated United States and King George. Still, Cristabel would soon discover that British sailors were the very least of her worries—for the pirate captain, Bully Booth, owned no loyalty—no sympathy for those he captured.

Yet hope was not entirely lost—for where there was found one crew of pirates—there was ever found another. Though Cristabel Albay would never have dreamed that she may find fortune in being captured by one pirate captain only to be taken by another—she did! Bully Booth took no man alive—let no woman live long. But the pirate Navarrone was known for his clemency. Thus, Cristabel's hope in knowing her life's continuance was restored.

Nonetheless, as Cristabel's heart began to yearn for the affections of her handsome, beguiling captor—she wondered if Captain Navarrone had only saved her life to execute her poor heart!

The Prairie Prince
Historical Romance

For Katie Matthews, life held no promise of true happiness. Life on the prairie was filled with hard labor, a brutal father, and the knowledge she would need to marry a man incapable of truly loving a woman. Men didn't have time to dote on women—so Katie's father told her. To Katie, it seemed life would forever remain mundane and disappointing—until the day Stover Steele bought her father's south acreage.

Handsome, rugged, and fiercely protective of four orphaned sisters, Stover Steele seemed to have stepped from the pages of some romantic novel. Yet his heroic character and alluring charm only served to remind Katie of what she would never have—true love and happiness the likes found only in fairytales. Furthermore, evil seemed to lurk in the shadows, threatening Katie's brightness, hope, and even her life!

Would Katie Matthews fall prey to disappointment, heartache, and harm? Or could she win the attentions of the handsome Stover Steele long enough to be rescued?

The Rogue Knight
Historical Romance

An aristocratic birthright and the luxurious comforts of profound wealth did nothing to comfort Fontaine Pratina following the death of her beloved parents. After two years in the guardianship of her mother's arrogant and selfish sister, Carileena Wetherton, Fontaine's only moments of joy and peace were found in the company of the loyal servants of Pratina Manor. Only in the kitchens and servants' quarters of her grand domicile did Fontaine find friendship, laughter, and affection.

Always, the life of a wealthy orphan destined to inherit loomed before her—a dark cloud of hopeless, shallow, snobbish people…a life of aristocracy, void of simple joys—and of love. Still, it was her lot—her birthright, and she saw no way of escaping it.

One brutal, cold winter's night a battered stranger appeared at the kitchen servants' entrance, however, seeking shelter and help. He gave only his first name, Knight…and suddenly, Fontaine found herself experiencing fleeting moments of joy in life. For Knight was handsome, powerful…the very stuff of the legends of days of old. Though a servant's class was his, he was proud and strong, and even his name seemed to portray his persona absolutely. He distracted Fontaine from her dull, hopeless existence.

Yet there were devilish secrets—strategies cached by her greedy aunt, and not even the handsome and powerful Knight could save her from them. Or could he? And if he did—would the truth force Fontaine to forfeit her Knight, her heart's desire…the man she loved—in order to survive?

The Tide of the Mermaid Tears
Historical Romance

Ember Taffee had always lived with her mother and sister in the little cottage by the sea. Her father had once lived there too, but the deep had claimed his life long ago. Still, her existence was a happy one, and Ember found joy, imagination, and respite in the sea and the trinkets it would leave for her on the sand.

Each morning Ember would wander the shore searching for treasures left by the tides. Though she cherished each pretty shell she found, her favorite gifts from Neptune were the rare mermaid tears—bits of tinted glass worn smooth and lovely by the ocean. To Ember, in all the world there were no jewels lovelier than mermaid tears.

Yet one morning, Ember was to discover that Neptune would present her with a gift more rare than any other—something she would value far more than the shells and sea glass she collected. One morning Ember Taffee would find a living, breathing man washed up on the sand—a man who would own claim to her heart as full as Neptune himself owned claim to the seas.

The Touch of Sage
Historical Romance

After the death of her parents, Sage Willows had lovingly nurtured her younger sisters through childhood, seeing each one married and never resenting not finding herself a good man to settle down with. Yet, regret is different than resentment.

Still, Sage found as much joy as a lonely young woman could find, as proprietress of Willows's Boarding House—finding some fulfillment in the companionship of the four beloved widow women boarding with her. But when the devilishly handsome Rebel Lee Mitchell appeared on the boarding house step, Sage's contentment was lost forever.

Dark, mysterious and secretly wounded, Reb Mitchell instantly captured Sage's lonely heart. But the attractive cowboy, admired and coveted by every young unmarried female in his path, seemed unobtainable to Sage Willows. How could a weathered, boarding house proprietress resigned to spinsterhood ever hope to capture the attention of such a man? And without him, would Sage Willows simply sink deeper into bleak loneliness—tormented by the knowledge that the man of every woman's dreams could never be hers?

The Trove of The Passion Room
Contemporary Romance

Sharlamagne Dickens cherished her family, was intrigued by the past, adored antiques, and enjoyed working at the antique store owned by her parents. Her life, like most, had been touched by tragedy and loss, yet she was happy. Though her life was not void of romance, it was void of a certain emotional passion. Still, she was young and assumed that one day some man might manage to sweep her off her feet. Sharlamagne did not expect to be entirely bowled over, however. And the day she first set eyes on Maxim Tanner, she was!

Elisaveta Tanner's grandson, Maxim, was the dreamiest, most attractive archetypal male Sharlamagne and her sister, Gwen, had ever seen! Tall, dark, and illegally handsome, Maxim Tanner possessed not only fabulous looks, money, and the sweetest grandmother in the world but also a fair amount of local fame. He was gorgeous, clever, and pathetically out of reach for any average girl.

And so Sharlamagne went about her life happy and satisfied—for she had no idea what sort of emotional intensity the right man could inflame in her. She had no conception of how an age-old mystery and one man could converge to unleash a passion so powerful that it would be either the greatest gift she had ever known—or her final undoing.

The Visions of Ransom Lake
Historical Romance

Youthful beauty, naïve innocence, a romantic imagination thirsting for adventure…an apt description of Vaden Valmont, who would soon

find the adventure and mystery she had always longed to experience…
in the form of a man.

A somber recluse, Ransom Lake descended from his solitary
concealment in the mountains, wholly uninterested in people and
their trivial affairs. And somehow, young Vaden managed to be ever
in his way…either by accident or because of her own unique ability to
stumble into a quandary.

Yet the enigmatic Ransom Lake would involuntarily become
Vaden's unwitting tutor. Through him, she would experience joy and
passion the like even Vaden had never imagined. Yes, Vaden Valmont
stepped innocently, yet irrevocably, into love with the secretive,
seemingly callous man.

But there were other life's lessons Ransom Lake would inadvertently
bring to her as well. The darker side of life—despair, guilt, heartache.
Would Ransom Lake be the means of Vaden's dreams come true? Or
the cause of her complete desolation?

The Whispered Kiss
Historical Romance

With the sea at its side, the beautiful township of Bostchelan was
home to many—including the lovely Coquette de Bellamont, her three
sisters, and beloved father. In Bostchelan, Coquette knew happiness
and as much contentment as a young woman whose heart had been
broken years before could know. Thus, Coquette dwelt in gladness
until the day her father returned from his travels with an astonishing
tale to tell.

Antoine de Bellamont returned from his travels by way of Roanan
bearing a tale of such great adventure to hardly be believed. Further, at
the center of Antoine's story loomed a man—the dark Lord of Roanan.
Known for his cruel nature, heartlessness, and tendency to violence,
the Lord of Roanan had accused Antoine de Bellamont of wrongdoing
and demanded recompense. Antoine had promised recompense would
be paid—with the hand of his youngest daughter in marriage.

Thus, Coquette found herself lost—thrust onto a dark journey of
her own. This journey would find her carried away to Roanan Manor—

delivered into the hands of the dark and mysterious Lord of Roanan who dominated it.

The Windswept Flame
Historical Romance

Broken—irreparably broken. The violent deaths of her father and the young man she'd been engaged to marry had irrevocably broken Cedar Dale's heart. Her mother's heart had been broken as well—shattered by the loss of her own true love. Thus, pain and anguish—fear and despair—found Cedar Dale and her mother, Flora, returned to the small western town where life had once been happy and filled with hope. Perhaps there Cedar and her mother would find some resemblance of truly living life—instead of merely existing. And then, a chance meeting with a dream from her past caused a flicker of wonder to ignite in her bosom.

As a child, Cedar Dale had adored the handsome rancher's son, Tom Evans. And when chance brought her face-to-face with the object of her childhood fascination once more, Cedar Dale began to believe that perhaps her fragmented heart could be healed.

Yet could Cedar truly hope to win the regard of such a man above men as was Tom Evans? A man kept occupied with hard work and ambition—a man so desperately sought after by seemingly every woman?

To Echo the Past
Historical Romance

As her family abandoned the excitement of the city for the uneventful lifestyle of a small, western town, Brynn Clarkston's worst fears were realized. Stripped of her heart's hopes and dreams, Brynn knew true loneliness.

Until an ordinary day revealed a heavenly oasis in the desert... Michael McCall. Handsome and irresistibly charming, Michael McCall (the son of legendary horse breeder Jackson McCall) seemed to offer wild distraction and sincere friendship to Brynn. But could Brynn be content with mere friendship when her dreams of Michael involved so much more?

Weathered Too Young
Historical Romance

Lark Lawrence was alone. In all the world there was no one who cared for her. Still, there were worse things than independence—and Lark had grown quite capable of providing for herself. Nevertheless, as winter loomed, she suddenly found herself with no means by which to afford food and shelter—destitute.

Yet Tom Evans was a kind and compassionate man. When Lark Lawrence appeared on his porch, without pause he hired her to keep house and cook for himself and his cantankerous elder brother, Slater. And although Tom had befriend Lark first, it would be Slater Evans—handsome, brooding, and twelve years Lark's senior—who would unknowingly abduct her heart.

Still, Lark's true age (which she concealed at first meeting the Evans brothers) was not the only truth she had kept from Slater and Tom Evans. Darker secrets lay imprisoned deep within her heart—and her past. However, it is that secrets are made to be found out—and Lark's secrets revealed would soon couple with the arrival of a woman from Slater's past to forever shatter her dreams of winning his love—or so it seemed. Would truth and passion mingle to capture Lark the love she'd never dared to hope for?